A SHARED DESIRE

With infinite patience, Ryan eased Brianna forward, allowing himself space to unhook the tiny fasteners that held the bodice of her gown closed.

There was no protest when his hands caressed the silken wall of her back. His fingers splayed outward, gliding across the surface until the bodice slipped free, exposing her bare shoulders.

The garment continued easing downward under his gentle guidance until it reached her waist. He pulled her backward, breathing deeply as her bare flesh pressed to his.

Ryan's hungry mouth caught Brianna's, tentatively exploring, then boldly possessing as his passion grew. She rubbed her cheek across the ruffled silk of his partially opened shirt, anxious to touch the rough texture of his flesh. Not a word was spoken.

Then Ryan rose, lifting Brianna in the circle of his arms, and carried her toward his bed . . .

BARBARA McINTOSH

MISSISSIPPI KISS

ZEBRA BOOKS
KENSINGTON PUBLISHING CORP.

ZEBRA BOOKS are published by

Kensington Publishing Corp.
850 Third Avenue
New York, NY 10022

First Printing: December, 1994

Printed in the United States of America

*To Shera Dee, for starting me on this journey into the future, and
to Carol J., for seeing that I took all the right roads.
Thanks.*

Chapter 1

Brianna Calhoun stared at the attorney, unable to give credence to his words. It was impossible. For years her father had taught her to think for herself, gain knowledge, and make decisions.

It had been a heady experience for one so young to be treated as an equal, but she had learned. She deserved better than this. "How could he? Are you certain there isn't some mistake, *M'sieur* Westman?"

"Quite certain, my dear. Your father's instructions were most specific. Until you reach the age of twenty-five or find a suitable husband, he has decreed that the Earl of Tyrone be your legal guardian and conservator of your estate. I dispatched a missive to Lord Tyrone at your father's urgent request."

Brianna squared her small shoulders, tilting her head a fraction higher so she could look him in the eye. "You sent for this . . . this . . . stranger? Before my father even passed on? How could you?"

"I told you, my dear. It was at his request. He was a practical man, and no doubt, he knew the end was near. I'm sure he felt it best to have Lord Tyrone here as soon as possible to attend the many duties of the plantation."

"M'sieur Westman, as you well know, Papa was ill for a goodly span of time. Who do you think attended the duties of Lagniappe during his confinement? And since his death?" Contempt hung heavy with each word. It had been nearly eight months and Lawyer Westman was only now coming to Lagniappe with the will.

"Why, I haven't given it much thought, but I'm certain the neighboring gentlemen did what they could to assist. With a competent foreman, things could continue indefinitely, I suppose."

"You suppose?" Brianna's voice rose, her anger bringing a flush to her face. "The neighbors were far too concerned with their frivolous pursuits to give thought to Lagniappe. As for the foreman, he was a slovenly, ill-mannered lout with nothing to recommend him. I was forced to dismiss him some six months past."

"Oh, dear. Then who has been managing everything? Your father's estate is quite sizable and needs a strong hand and a keen mind, else it shall fall to ruination."

"I have managed quite nicely . . . without the assistance of any man. Papa knew and fully approved my decisions."

"It behooves me to contradict a lady, but if Richard Calhoun was as approving as you say, it would be unlikely he would have taken such pains to secure other arrangements in the event of his death."

Brianna gave a soft gasp, rendered speechless by the cruel bluntness of his statements. She could not refute his words. She had seen the papers, recognized the handwriting.

She whirled about, her skirts rustling softly as she ran from the room. She had to get away. She had to think.

Her shoes tapped lightly over the gleaming wooden floors as she hurried toward the front door.

Tugging, frantic to leave the horrid gloating lawyer who had toppled her world, Brianna wrenched the heavy door open and ran outside.

She bolted toward the mount tied at the metal post. It was the hated attorney's horse. It would serve him right to be forced to remain at Lagniappe until she chose to return.

Lifting her skirts, Brianna struggled to mount. Unaccustomed to a man's saddle, it was a difficult task but her rising anger gave her the strength needed to achieve her goal.

Aloft, she took control and urged the horse across the drive. Crushed oyster shells ground loudly beneath the hooves of the galloping bay. She reined hard to the left, plunging horse and rider through the fallow south fields. Onward she rode toward the gulf waters.

"Oh, Papa! How could you?" Her plaintive cry was swallowed by the salt-laced wind that parted with a roar before her charge.

Pewter skies reflected the gloom within her heart. The air was damp, heavy with brine. A storm hovered but Brianna paid it no heed. Surely it could not match the raging fury building within her.

All his talk of women being as capable as men was just that . . . talk! He had used her. Her own father had fostered a dream within her soul and then dashed it with nary a thought. "A guardian, indeed!" she cried. "We'll see about that!"

She pushed on through the canebrake, slackening her stride until she burst into the open spaces of sandy beach.

The gulf waters greeted her, foam-tipped waves rising

as though in sympathy with her suffering. The bay
slowed, his hooves sinking into the loose shifting sand.
She made her way to the gulf's edge. Here the sand was
darker, firmly packed by the water's never-ceasing touch.
"Run, boy, we're free! No one will say nay to Brianna
Calhoun!" The horse obeyed, his legs stretching as he
resumed a full gallop.

The wind caught her hair, pulling the neatly arranged
chignon free from its restraints. Mahogany tresses billowed behind her; her spirit soared with a sense of exalted
freedom. Blindly, she rode, giving no thought to destination or reason. Brianna only knew she had to vent her
rage.

The bay snorted, pulling back with a suddenness that
caught the rider off guard. She barely held her seat.
Thunder rumbled in the distance; a flash of lightning lit
the sky. An eerie shade of green spilled across the heavens; a vile poison oozing from a body wracked with pain.
Her mount reared in protest when she tried to prod him
onward. A light rain began to fall, distorting her vision.
"Whoa! Steady, boy. Steady," she commanded.

She hauled back on the reins, gradually bringing the
nervous animal under control. Without success, she tried
to coax him forward.

Wiping the rain from her eyes, Brianna peered at the
shoreline. A long object lay directly in her path. "It's
only a log, boy," she said, stroking the animal's neck.
"You aren't afraid of an old log, are you?"

The horse whinnied, the pawing motions resumed, his
hooves digging deep furrows in the wet sand. "I guess
you are," she murmured in exasperation. She tightened
her grip on the reins, then coaxed the animal around the

inert mass. "You're like your owner," she scolded. "A bit of coward in you."

She glanced toward the object, scorn pulling her mouth into a tight line as she compared beast to master. Her contempt withered, replaced by fear as the log was transformed before her eyes. "Oh! Oh, no! Whoa!" she cried, yelling to be heard above the rising wind.

"God in heaven, forgive me," she said as she hastily dismounted. Not daring to trust the animal, who was now fully aroused, Brianna shed her short fitted jacket and used it to hobble the horse in place. "Please give me strength," she prayed aloud as she made her way toward the still body of a man.

Pausing only to give the sign of the cross, she dropped to her knees before the limp body. Then she studied his still form, trying to determine how to remove him from the water's edge.

He was stretched prone, flat on his stomach, and she could see he was a big man. Being scarce more than five feet herself, Brianna doubted her ability to drag him away. She glanced back toward the cane.

Lawyer Westman was the only one at the house except for the servants, and she had no faith that he would pursue her. She was alone and time was growing more precious with each passing moment. Already the waves licked at the man's boots. Even though he was past saving, she couldn't let the sea claim his body again.

Just then she heard a low groan, causing her to stare at the body. No, she decided. It was the wind or the movement of the riotous waves. It only sounded human. She stood, determined to move him farther from the sea.

Gripping the man under his arms, she strained to pull him away from the edge of the water. The low moan was repeated, this time more forcefully. *"M'sieur?"* she queried.

A broad hand moved, the fingers clawing weakly at the wet sand. "Alive. *Mon Dieu.* My God. He's alive." She had to get him from harm's way. *But how?* It was raining steadily now, and the downpour was becoming stronger.

Pushing the heavy mass of long wet hair away from her face, she scanned the area in search of something . . . anything that would aid her.

"Of course," she said. "Why didn't I think of that before?" Without hesitation, she returned to the bay. Taking firm hold of the reins, she bent to remove her sodden jacket from his fetlocks. "Like it or not, boy, you're elected to play pack mule."

She guided the animal toward the unconscious man, all the while talking in soothing tones. "We're going to make everything all right, aren't we, boy?" The horse wickered nervously. She looped one end of the reins about her wrist. She couldn't afford to take the risk that the skittish horse would bolt. She needed him too much.

Despite every effort, it proved impossible to lift the stranger onto the horse. In his state, she couldn't even turn him over by herself. She angrily brushed away the tears of frustration. Two defeats in one day would not be tolerated. There had to be a way. "No more," she said, her voice strong with defiance. "This time Death will lose."

Water inched toward his knees. If only . . . "Yes, it might work," she said aloud.

Ignoring the chilled numbness of her fingers, she began lengthening the stirrups, letting them hang as close to the ground as possible. Once more, she took the precaution to shackle the recalcitrant horse. Satisfied, she turned her attentions to the man whose fate rested in her ability to rescue him from certain death.

"M'sieur? M'sieur? You must arouse yourself."

At the touch of her cool hand against one cheek, heavy lidded eyes opened, forming narrow slits. She pressed closer, her mouth coming nearer to his ear as she sought to encourage him to further alertness. "Please help me, *m'sieur.* We must move or the sea will claim you. I cannot move you alone."

Brianna sat back on her heels. Did her words have any effect? Long lashes fluttered upward, revealing eyes of deepest gray.

"You . . . jest . . . lovely. The sea . . ." he hesitated ". . . already claimed . . . this soul." He was groggy, his words badly slurred, but there was hope.

"No, no. You are better." She pulled at him, urging him to his knees. "Come. We must leave. I know an abandoned cabin nearby. We will rest there 'til the storm passes."

He faltered, his muscular torso wavering as darkness threatened to reclaim him. "Not now. Not now," she pleaded, bracing her slight body against his massive chest to prevent his falling. He couldn't die. She wouldn't let him. The blood of one death on her hands was enough. This time would be different, she promised herself.

Desperate, Brianna reverted to her original plan. She reached for the stirrup while she held him upright with her body. Not wasting a moment, she plunged one of his limp arms through the stirrup.

There was no time to consider modesty. Using her body as a brace for the nearly unconscious man, she wiggled out of her blouse. Shivers chased over her exposed flesh in the chill of the pouring rain.

Using her blouse as a rope, she bound first his wrist, then looped it under the stirrup and tied it off at his biceps. She offered a silent prayer that her efforts would not be in vain.

She rose and allowed his limp form to lower until the makeshift rope held. His face was barely off the gritty sand.

"Come on, boy. Easy now. We must go slowly." She guided the horse across the sand, keeping close watch to insure the man suffered no further injuries from the hooves of her unwilling assistant.

His hijack boots dug deep grooves in the sand, but her plan was working. His arm remained secure within the confines of the boot strap, and despite his long frame, he was steadily being distanced from the angry waves that encroached further inland.

Time seemed to drag as laboriously as her burden, but Brianna would not, could not afford to stop. She held fast to the horse, brushing the rain from her eyes as it continued to threaten her watch on her patient.

"We've made it," she gasped aloud, relieved as the dilapidated cabin came into view. "Just a little way now," she said, stroking the glistening neck of the horse.

Brianna strained harder, using the last of her reserves to reach the door. Her back and arms ached as never before, but she felt an intoxicating flow of victory as her hands touched the solid wood.

The stranger groaned, his pain aggravated by the unusual mode of travel he had endured. "Nooo," he whispered.

Brianna stooped to offer comfort. She brushed wet

strands of ebony hair from his face. "You will be comfortable soon."

Thick lashes raised, revealing his fevered gaze. "Comfort? In death, my sweet mermaid?" he mumbled.

She pursed her lips in consternation. No doubt he is hallucinating, she decided. But lucid or not, she still needed his help. The door was too narrow to admit both horse and man, and she couldn't manage alone.

"Don't give up, *m'sieur.*" Once more, she wedged her slight frame between him and the muddy ground. She pushed, her strength holding as she managed to raise him to his knees. "We must get you inside," she said. Untying his bonds, she bore the weight of his body against her back.

"Inside . . . belly of . . . whale," he murmured, his breath warm and caressing against the nape of her neck.

"If it's whales you wish, *m'sieur,* no doubt you would pass as a small beached whale, but you can't swim. Please try to stand."

She pushed her body to his, twisting so she might help him rise. "Up. Up," she commanded, her voice husky with exhaustion.

Obediently, he rose, grabbing the saddle for support. Her face, shining with rain, seemed to beckon him forward. His legs moved like heavy weights across the threshold. His arms left the security of the saddle as he reached for the vision before him.

"Wonderful, *m'sieur,*" she said. "Only a few more feet and you can rest." Brianna guided him forward, scarcely daring to breathe until she had maneuvered him into the dry safety of their temporary haven.

The exertion was too much. He felt the room begin to spin. His legs were like rubber, unable to support his weight any longer. With a sigh, he collapsed to the dusty floor.

"Confound it!" she groused. Kneeling, she gave him a cursory examination.

The gash near his left temple was bleeding again, and beneath his tan, he appeared ashen. "You cannot die now. I won't let you!" she screamed in frustration.

Hurriedly, she set about binding his head wound. She tore a remnant from her petticoats and wound it tightly about his head, then slipped one small hand inside his shirt to press it close to his heart. The beat was somewhat faint, but she took satisfaction in the steady throb.

Encouraged, she set about making the room more habitable. The previous tenants had left a supply of wood, and to her relief, she found the means of lighting a fire near at hand.

In her eagerness, Brianna forgot the horse she had appropriated. A flash of lightning with the accompanying roar of thunder reminded her of her slight. "Oh, no," she cried, racing for the doorway.

She stood there, helpless to do more than watch the animal gallop in wild flight across the barren fields. Why hadn't she tied him? she silently berated herself. Now she was stranded . . . and with a complete stranger.

With caution, she turned her attention back to him. He was still lying where he had fallen, oblivious to all her efforts in his behalf. "A lot of help you are," she said. "And *M'sieur* Westman claims *I* need a guardian."

The thought of Westman rekindled her anger, and Brianna fumed inwardly as she set about making herself comfortable. It was growing dark and she hastened to search for a lamp.

Her search proved fruitless and she resigned herself to

the bleak prospect of no light beyond the faint glimmer of the fire burning brightly.

Pausing, Brianna realized she was becoming chilled in her wet clothes. Sparing only a glance at her newly acquired charge, she slipped out of her petticoats and skirt, leaving only her chemise to protect her modesty.

Moving to the fire, she used the tattered remains of an old cotton cloth to cover her flesh as she skimmed away the last of her clothing and laid it out to dry.

Her attention turned again to the man sprawled upon the bare floor. No doubt he was far more chilled than she, Brianna reasoned. But what should she do? She moved toward him, studying him for the first time. Viewing men was a new experience. She'd had no time, no need to concern herself with men in the past. Brianna felt unsettled, wishing she had turned inland. Then she wouldn't have known. She shook her head, dispelling the notion. He would have died.

He slept on, unaware of her intense perusal of him. The face was strong, with high prominent cheekbones and a firm slightly squared jawline. She knelt beside him, unable to still her hand as her fingers brushed lightly across the full sensuality of his lips.

He stirred, fitful as he gave a deep sigh. Her hand jerked away as though burned and Brianna felt her face grow warm.

She untied the sleeve of her blouse from his wrist, moving quietly so as not to disturb him. Then, taking a deep breath, she unlaced the thong that held his silken shirt closed.

Not once did he stir, not even when she removed his cumbersome boots and slid his breeches free from his muscular form.

Sitting back, she stared in amazement at the unclothed man before her. Never had she seen any male so displayed. *Surely not all men are so . . .* Brianna swallowed, leaving the thought unfinished.

As though possessing a will of their own, her hands slid slowly up his powerfully shaped chest, her fingers rising and falling across the hard planes. He smelled of sea and fresh rain, his skin slick and smooth with water.

Mesmerized, she traced the hills and valleys formed by the sinewy muscles of his bare arms. Her breath came in shallow gasps, leaving a peculiar ache that seemed to originate within the pit of her stomach. He stirred, his lips parting slightly.

Jerking away, Brianna felt the fevered rush of blood coursing to her face. Not waiting for him to waken, she gathered the sodden apparel and headed for the fire.

Deliberately refusing to acknowledge his presence, she busied herself laying the garments before the fire, wishing she had not been so bold as to remove all her own clothing. She felt so vulnerable. She cleared her throat, striving to regain some of her earlier confidence. "Ridiculous," she muttered lowly. "He's only a man, nothing more."

"Look out!" he yelled. She jumped, whirling quickly toward the shouted warning. He was thrashing wildly upon the floor, seemingly reliving some devastating horror.

Hurrying to his side, Brianna tried to restrain him, but even in his weakened condition, she was no match for his strength. He grabbed her, pulling her atop him, his eyes staring into hers with a look of disbelief.

She felt the steely tenseness within him begin to dissolve. He relinquished his grip, offering her a slow smile.

"Ah, sweet mermaid. Have you come to spirit me away to the coral castles of the denizens of the deep?"

His voice was deep and sonorous, the strangeness of his words sending shivers through her slender frame.

"I am no mermaid, sir," she whispered.

" 'Tis for the best, for I've no intent to relinquish control of my destiny just yet. I've promises to keep," he sighed. His voice grew faint and she leaned closer to hear his words. "Duty calls and alas, honor requires I answer." He drifted off, his breathing slightly labored from his meager exertions.

His naked body trembled and he pressed her closer. Brianna could feel the clammy chill of his flesh, and she gave a tiny cry of dismay.

"How could I be so unthinking?" Taking care not to disturb him, she eased away. Her fingers sought the knot she had tied to secure the cotton blanket about herself. Releasing it, she lay beside him, offering her body heat to assuage his chill. She pulled the blanket over them, gently tucking one corner about his far shoulder and resting her head atop the other.

Her hands soothed the icy flesh, kneading and stroking to restore the circulation. Her own muscles ached but she ignored her minor pains, seeking only to provide some measure of comfort to this man who intrigued her with his beautiful and mysterious words.

Her hands slowed, her eyelids growing heavy as the fire's heat reached their makeshift bed upon the floor. With a whisper of a sigh, she joined him in blissful, healing sleep.

* * *

Even as the morning sun beckoned, dreams swirled through her head as Brianna languidly stretched beneath her thin covering. Gradually, wakefulness nagged her to a more alert state. Her hand pressed to warm bare flesh.

She opened her eyes, disoriented and confused, her bewildered gaze meeting twin pools of gray.

A smile of amusement teased the corners of his full mouth as his eyes drank their fill of her upturned face. "I know not what brought you to my bed, my lovely lady, but I am grateful beyond measure."

"Oh." She pushed away, the palms of her hands tingling from the sudden contact with his chest. "Oh," she repeated, grasping the threadbare material as it slid downward to reveal her firm upturned breasts to his view. "I . . . it's . . . I mean . . ." she stammered. "*M'sieur.* Do not look at me like that."

"Like what?" he asked.

"You know! I am a lady."

"Have I said otherwise?" he countered, reaching to slip one arm around her diminutive waist.

Angrily, she slapped at his hand. "You do not have to speak, sir. I see the words plainly etched on your face. You take much for granted for one whose life I have so recently saved."

A puzzled frown furrowed his brow. His thoughts turned backward in time. "My ship . . ." He remembered now. Tully climbed the ropes to cut the canopy but had fallen. He had given the helm to his first mate and taken the dangerous task for himself.

His fingers moved upward, skimming lightly over the bandage that covered his temple. "I fell. Hit a beam. Must have blacked out," he said.

Forgotten was her initial anger. She responded to the

pain that darkened his face. "You're safe now." Laying one hand upon his shoulder, she continued. "Your ship must have been nearby and you were washed ashore."

"You found me?"

She nodded, her face filled with concern. "At first, I thought it was a log cast ashore. It was raining and I didn't realize the truth until I passed you."

He glanced about the empty room. "Where are we now?" he asked.

"It's an old deserted cabin at the south edge of my plantation."

"Plantation?"

"You are on Lagniappe," she informed him, pride lacing her words.

"Lagniappe," he repeated. "That's French."

"Yes. My maman was French. When she and Papa were married, this plantation was his wedding gift to her. She named it Lagniappe. It means 'something extra' in French."

His smile returned as he renewed his slow perusal of her. "Yes, I know. Does Lagniappe always promise something extra to wayfarers?"

Brianna sought to distance herself from him, but her efforts only added to the confusion. Her awkward position brought a flush of heat to her face.

The thin barrier of cloth slid across his chest, offering her a tantalizing view of his bronzed torso. Her body was besieged by exquisite tremors of desire, even as she chafed at his own apparent disregard of his magnificent nakedness.

"*M'sieur,* you are too bold." She glared at him in indignation, lifting her head in her haughtiest manner.

"Now, if you'll be so kind as to close your eyes, I should like to make myself more presentable."

"And if I don't?"

"Then you are no gentleman!"

"I don't recall making such a claim," he said, his tone husky with barely leashed passion.

"Very well. If you are not a gentleman, then you shall have to settle for being cold." Before he could gather her intent, Brianna rose, hastily gathering the blanket about her and leaving him devoid of cover.

"Hey! Where are my clothes?" he shouted in protest.

"The same place as mine," she retorted, careful to avert her gaze. "By the fire."

His surprise was replaced by low seductive laughter as he boldly followed her movements, his eyes twinkling with appreciation. "Perhaps my memory shall take pity and provide me with the details of how such a delightful situation came to pass," he teased.

"There is no situation, sir. And since you were unconscious, there are really no details of importance."

Keeping the cover draped over her back, Brianna struggled to don her smallclothes. Under her breath, she roundly castigated this brash man who taunted her without mercy.

At long last, she achieved a degree of respectability and tossed the no-longer-needed blanket in his direction.

With her back rigidly straight, she focused her attention on the glowing embers of the fire. How could so small a glow leave her as weak as though she had suffered extreme exposure to some searing heat? Her thoughts troubled her, but she refused to dwell on them. "If you will be so kind as to tell me when you are no longer exposed, sir, I shall wait outside while you make yourself decent."

"If that is what you truly wish, then you may absent yourself whenever you desire, my sweet."

She whirled to face him, her face burning with anger. "It is what I wish, and . . . I am not your sweet. My name is Brianna Calhoun, and I'll thank you to avoid any further familiarity."

"Calhoun?"

"Precisely, *m'sieur*. I am not only your rescuer, but your reluctant hostess. I own Lagniappe Plantation."

Before he had a chance to answer, she hurriedly made her exit.

He stared after her retreating form in silence, breaking it only when the door slammed closed. "Damn!"

It was hardly the way he would wish things to be. In consternation, Ryan Fleming ran his fingers though his unruly hair, grumbling aloud. "And I thought my ward to be some young chit I should have to pack off to boarding school."

He reflected on her enticing beauty. The sweet fragrance of her lingered on his flesh. "So soft," he murmured. There were many places he would have her, but away from himself was not on the list.

Chapter 2

Brianna sat on a nearby stump, worrying her bottom lip with even teeth. This man from the sea was obviously a common sailor, far beneath her own lofty station. Why, then, did she feel so peculiar in his presence?

"Perhaps Papa was right," she mused. "Maybe I do need a guardian to protect me from myself."

The thought, once spoken, was quickly rejected. She needed no one to run her plantation or decide her future. Hadn't she been managing well so far? "Oh, Papa," she whispered, her anger yielding to despair, "why did you betray me so?"

"Did you say something?" She recognized his voice instantly. How could it be possible? She had known him such a short time, and for most of that time, he had been unconscious.

"I was thinking aloud. That is all," she answered.

"It must be very serious to bring such a frown to so lovely a face."

"It is."

"Is there anything I can do to help?"

"Why?"

He shrugged, nonchalant as he lowered himself to the ground beside her. "As you pointed out, you did save my life. I would like to repay the favor, if possible."

She shook her head, sighing softly. "Thank you, but I'm afraid there is nothing anyone can do."

"That sounds pretty ominous."

"It is. My father recently died.

"My sympathy," he said. "Your family must miss him."

"There is no one but myself now. Maman died when I was a small girl. Since then, it has been Papa and me. Now there is only myself and . . ." Her voice trailed off.

"And?" he prodded.

"The Earl of Tyrone." She spoke the words with a vehemence that couldn't be denied.

"You say it as though the earl is some sort of monster," he said, moving with caution.

"He is, though I have never met him personally."

"Wait a minute. If you've never met him, how can you be sure he is so terrible? You might find him to be charming and a very likable sort of fellow if you give him a chance."

"Well, I have no intention of giving him a chance. He is coming here to be my guardian. Of all things!"

A smile teased the corners of his lips. "And of course, you have no need of a guardian," he prompted.

"Indeed I do not. Papa was ill for quite some time and I managed the entire plantation by myself. Why should I allow some stranger to come in and take over . . . tell me what to do?"

"Come now, Bri . . ." he paused, looking at her solemnly. "May I call you Brianna?" he asked.

She felt her face grow warm. Considering the night just

spent, it did seem foolish to demand formality. She nodded. "And what should I call you?" she asked.

"I'm the . . . I'm Ryan Fleming. Ryan to my friends," he answered with a smile.

"Ryan Fleming," she repeated. "Is that Irish?"

"Yes, it is."

"My father was Irish. He used to say I inherited my green eyes and a touch of red in my hair from my grandmother."

"She must have been a beautiful woman."

Brianna lowered her eyes, unable to meet his gaze. Why did he affect her so strongly? she wondered. What kind of man was Ryan Fleming to hold such easy sway over her emotions?

The silence between them lengthened. She felt her heart beating faster. She could still smell the scent of fresh rain about him, could feel his disconcerting closeness. "I . . . I'm afraid we will have to walk back to the plantation," she said.

"How far would that be?"

"About six miles, if we go straight across the fields."

"Six miles! You walked six miles to the beach? With a storm in the offing?"

"Not really. When I started, I was on horseback. I was so busy trying to get you inside the cabin, I forgot to tie my mount. I'm afraid he was spooked by the lightning and thunder and ran off before I could stop him."

"Why is it no one has come searching for you?"

"There's no one at the house except Papa's attorney and the slaves. No doubt, he would consider it a blessing if I never return."

A scowl darkened Ryan's face. "Now, there is a man who fits the mold of monster. To allow a lady to remain out in the elements without lifting a finger to locate her is unthinkable."

Her lips parted, laughter spilling forth with a musical quality. "It would have been a bit difficult, considering I chose his mount for my journey."

"Are there no other animals on this plantation?"

"Oh, yes. Papa raised horses. I fear they are far too high-spirited for *M'sieur* Westman, though. He is a somewhat timid person."

He chuckled, envisioning the portrait she painted of the erstwhile attorney. "Very well. I shall reserve final judgment until I meet your *M'sieur* Westman."

Brianna tilted her head to one side, eyes twinkling as she watched him briefly before speaking. "Reserve judgment, is it? And pray tell, what do you intend if you find yourself in disagreement with my opinion?"

"Perhaps I shall decide to have him drawn and quartered," Ryan suggested. "A gentleman would never let a slight so grave go unpunished."

"Earlier you said you did not claim the title of gentleman. Have you had a change of heart?" she countered.

"You don't miss much, do you?"

"Not usually." She stared at him with open curiosity. "How is it you came to be upon a storm-ravaged beach in Mississippi?" Brianna asked, changing the subject with aplomb.

"The storm caught us unawares, and when we tried to strike the mast, the halyard became entangled in the rigging. I climbed up to correct matters."

Again his hand lifted to touch his wounded temple. "Guess the crossbeam must have swung around. I don't even remember falling." A smile touched his lips. "The next thing I knew, I was looking at the loveliest sea siren imaginable."

"You called me a mermaid," she primly reminded him.

"I stand corrected. Siren is more suitable. A mermaid lures men with her beauty, and when the man of her choice arrives, she places a magic cap upon his head and they can live together beneath the sea. You, my lady, are far different."

"And if my recollection serves me, *m'sieur,* the sirens of the sea lured men to their shores also."

"Ah, yes, but there is a vast difference. Men were lured by the haunting beauty of their song so completely as to totally forget all else; family, friends, all were abandoned for the lovely sirens."

She smiled, amused by his play with words. "You forget. I did mention I have some knowledge of mythology, Ryan. You call the sirens lovely, yet none could claim such things, for there were none who returned once meeting with the sirens."

"True," he acknowledged, his eyes sparkling with mischief. "But what could possess a man to allow himself to be lured to his death besides incredible beauty such as yours?"

"Are you suggesting I would be party to a man's death?" She spoke with care, her manner remote.

He chuckled, choosing to ignore her aroused suspicions. "I suggest only that you are a most complicated lady. In the short time of our acquaintance, I find you have stolen a horse, saved my own personally valuable life, and I have learned you are also capable of running a plantation. None of these things are common to the average lady." He leaned forward, drawing so close, she could see her reflection in the depth of his eyes. "I can but wonder what other talents you possess."

She flushed under his bold appraisal; her pink tongue licked delicately at suddenly-dry lips. He would kiss her. She could feel it in the very depths of her soul.

Oh, how she yearned to feel the touch of his lips to hers, to taste the essence of this man who evoked such a turmoil of sensation within her heart.

"Miss Brianna! Miss Brianna!" The faraway call pierced the air. She bit back a fierce retort.

"Sounds as though someone has been concerned for your welfare after all," he commented, his voice a silky purr.

Ignoring him, she climbed atop the stump that had been her perch. It seemed impossible he could remain so calm, so unaffected. Brianna fumed at the untimely intrusion. "Over here," she yelled, waving her arms back and forth. "I'm here."

She could hear her rescuers thrashing through the cane, cutting the stalks as they made new pathways to her.

"Lawdy, Miss Bri. We'se been half crazy with worry about you." A black face appeared through the cane, its ebony hue glistening with joy and relief. Brianna feigned an enthusiasm she didn't feel.

"Oh, Toby. It's so good to see you," she cried, flinging herself into the arms of the aged black butler.

"Easy now, Miss Bri. I ain't no young sprout. I'se a plumb tuckered old man. Don't go a-straining this old worn-out body like that."

She pulled back, grinning with pleasure. "I don't care how old you are, Toby. You're still the most wonderful

sight I've seen. If you hadn't come along, we would have
been forced to walk back."

Toby scratched his nappy white head. "Well, that
might be how youse gets back anyhow. That fuzzy-
headed Willy was done 'posed to meets up with us with
the wagon, but Lawdy if I don't think he's up and gots
hisself lost."

Her laughter filled the air. "That's hardly likely. There
is only one road down to the water."

"Yes'm, but that road goes both ways, and I ain't so
sure what he done turned right when he shoulda' turned
left."

"Excuse me, but could that be the conveyance under
discussion?" Ryan asked, interrupting the affectionate
reunion. As one, Toby and Brianna turned their attention westward.

"Shore enough," Toby said. Turning to the men hovering behind him, Toby issued quick commands. "Go
gets that fool 'fore he ends hisself up in New Orleans."

Obediently, two men started off across the beach at a
brisk trot, calling after the driver as they ran.

"Miss Bri, youse best sits yourself down and rest. You
look like youse done had a tough time of it, and I expects
it's going to take a spell 'fore they gets back."

"I'm fine, Toby."

The black man eyed her with suspicion. "Can't prove
it by looks. Sudie shore going to be upset when she sees
you."

Brianna gave a wry smile in return.

"Who's Sudie?" Ryan wanted to know.

"Sudie's a little difficult to explain," Brianna answered. "You'll understand when you meet her."

Ryan smiled, saying nothing. At least he knew he now

had a definite invitation to join her at the main house. There was still time. Somehow, he would find the right words to convince her he wasn't the monster she imagined, even if he was an Irish lord.

Brianna sat in back of the wagon, showing no concern over the substantial jostling as the vehicle bumped and rocked along the pitted pathway.

Ryan was less fortunate, for the jarring motion set his head to pounding. Every muscle within his body screamed in tortured rebellion.

By the time their destination was reached, he was none too sure the lovely siren of the sea would not be the cause of his death.

"Toby, get a couple of men to help *M'sieur* Fleming up to the Blue Room in the east wing," she ordered, her face filled with concern for his well-being.

"The east wing? That's a mite close to yore quarters, ain't it?"

"If I'm going to nurse him back to health, I would prefer not walking myself to death in the process. Now do as I say."

"Yes'm, but Sudie ain't going to like it. Naw suh, she ain't going to like it at all."

Toby selected two husky field hands and led the way into the house, moving aside as Sudie came hurrying down the stairway as fast as her bulk would allow.

"My baby. Oh, Lawd, it's my baby. I done 'bout give you up for dead, chile." Sudie wrapped her arms about Brianna in a smothering embrace.

"I'm just fine, Aunt Sudie. You should know I can take care of myself."

"I know, but it don't stop de worrying none. Let me look at you." Sudie held her at arm's length, her black eyes inventorying every inch of the young woman before her. "Lawd, but you is a mess, a plumb awful mess."

Brianna followed her gaze, surprised by the complete dishabille she presented. Her bombazine black jacket was missing, leaving the muddy and wrinkled blouse uncovered. Large globs of mud soiled the matching black skirt and pale stains were vivid reminders of the trials she had endured in the wet sand. A torn edge of petticoat peeped from beneath the hem.

Her hands went to her hair. Feeling the windswept tangles, she surmised her coiffure fared no better than her wardrobe. Ryan came to mind. No wonder he labeled her a siren, she thought, chafing at the comparison.

"You best come with Aunt Sudie. A good hot bath and shampoo will does you a world o' good, and whilst we's at it, you can tell me 'bout that man those men done brung in this house."

"Yes, Aunt Sudie," Brianna answered with unaccustomed docility.

She followed the older woman up the stairs, listening idly as Sudie filled her in on the happenings during her absence.

"That Massa Westman done gone. He jest up and left as soon as that horse o' his come galloping in. Toby and me tried to tell him he ought to go hunting you, but he says he would jest leaves that to us." Sudie stopped at the front door, shaking her head to and fro.

"It's all right, Sudie. I'm glad he didn't come looking for me. *M'sieur* Westman is the last person I want to see." She thought of the earl. "Well . . . almost."

"Yes'm. Anyhow," Sudie paused, sucking in deep

gulps of air, "it being so dark and all, Toby said we would have to wait till sunup if we was going to find you. That's what we done, too. Soon as that old sun peeped through de trees, Toby gots some men and went a-lookin'. I shore is glad they found you in one piece. I shore is."

"Me too, Aunt Sudie." Giving in to impulse, Brianna hugged the woman, grateful that at least some things in her life never changed.

Together, they climbed the stairs and headed for the east wing. Brianna paused only briefly by the closed door of her visitor. She wanted to go in, to see how he was doing, but she knew Sudie would only scold her. And she did want to be more presentable when she saw him. A bath was just what she needed.

Brianna slid deeper into the water, enjoying the feel of the silky warmth spreading across her aching muscles. She hadn't realized how uncomfortable sleeping on the floor could be. Her lips parted slightly as she recalled the presence of her companion throughout the night. It seemed impossible she could have rested even a moment under the circumstances in which she had been unwittingly placed. Yet, somehow, it seemed right.

"Hold still, chile. Lawd, but yore hair is a sight. I never seen such a twisted tangle."

"Owh," Brianna complained as the brush was pulled vigorously through the thick mass. "Take it easy, Aunt Sudie, or I'll have no hair to clean."

"It ain't my fault. I is not de one done this. How'd it get this way, anyhow?"

"I was riding. I guess my pins slipped loose. What with

the wind, the rain, and . . ." she paused, leaving the remainder of her words unspoken. How could she tell Aunt Sudie she'd spent the entire night lying in the arms of a man, a complete stranger at that?

"That don't account none for all de dirt in this hair. If I'se didn't knows better, I'd swear you'd been down a-rolling in de dirt."

Brianna felt her face grow warm. "Aunt Sudie," she gasped.

"Now, don't gets yore feathers all ruffled. I has done said I knows better. My baby is a lady and she acts one, too; at least she does most o' the time."

"What do you mean by that?"

"You still ain't told me 'bout that common man you has done brought in this here house. Who is he and what's he doing with you?"

"I found him on the beach. He was injured, unconscious. At the time, the tide was pushing inland. I had to help him."

"Humph. You didn't have to help him all the way to Lagniappe, missy."

"And what would you have me do? Leave him stranded on the shore, alone and injured? You saw him, Aunt Sudie. He barely had the strength to stand when we arrived."

"From what I seen, he looked like he's well used to taking care o' hisself. Don't reckon he needed you none."

"Well, he's here now, so there's no use arguing about it. Once he's well, I'm sure he'll be on his way." A frown turned her full lips downward. *Why does the thought of his leaving bother me?* But he would have to leave. He couldn't remain at Lagniappe forever. What would people say? And Lord Tyrone!

The thought of the stuffy Irish earl finding a common sailor being entertained by the lady of the manor amused her. That ought to set him back on his aristocratic heel, she thought.

"You going to answer me, chile?" Sudie's voice penetrated her reverie.

"I'm sorry, Aunt Sudie. My mind was wandering. What did you say?"

Sudie tilted Brianna's head back, sluicing the warm water through the thick tresses. "I asked if you has any idea how he come to be on yore beach."

"Oh. He said he was on a passing ship that got caught in the storm. He got knocked overboard by some kind of beam, if I recall correctly."

"Why, he's a sailor. Nothing but white trash. It's best you keep yore distance from him, chile. Old Sudie will takes care o' his needs, and as soon as he's able, I'll send him on his way."

"No," Brianna cried, sitting up so fast water spilled over the rim of the tub, soaking the carpeting.

"Lawdy, chile. Look what you done now. I declare, but you is a heap o' trouble."

Brianna ignored her protest. "I plan to tend Ry . . . *M'sieur* Fleming myself."

"You'll do nothing o' the kind! You is a lady, and there ain't no lady what goes attending a strange man's needs. It ain't proper. You hear me?"

"I hear. There's no call to raise your voice," Brianna answered, her own tone one of firmness. "I don't care what you say. I'm going to take care of him, and I don't want to hear another word."

"Whats you want and whats you gets ain't always de same thing, missy! You best heed old Sudie. That man spells trouble. I feels it in my bones, and I ain't going to stand by whilst you get yourself in a mess o' trouble. No suh, I ain't going to do it." She massaged Brianna's head with vigor, attacking the grime with determination.

"I'm not going to get in trouble. I can assure you, I'm quite capable of taking care of myself," Brianna said. "Ouch!" Sudie ignored her cry of pain.

"That's what you keep saying alright, but you ain't never had no dealings with anyone like him. I gots me a good look at him, missy. You may think he's all helpless now, but waits 'til he gets cleaned up some and some food in his belly. I tells you he's going to be trouble . . . big trouble!"

Sudie punctuated her feelings with another pitcher of water over Brianna's soap-filled hair. The young woman sputtered as the water poured over her face. "Sudie!"

Ignoring the outcry, Sudie continued, mumbling gruffly under her breath as she removed the remaining soap and began toweling the luxuriant mane. "Shore enough trouble."

Brianna rose, wrapping toweling about her slender figure, refreshed despite the rough treatment.

With graceful movements, she padded across the room, suddenly eager for the comfort of the large poster bed. She did need rest. Toby would see to her guest for the moment. He would be fine. Brianna's thoughts once more turned toward the enigma who had entered her quiet little world. She allowed Sudie to help her into her nightgown. She was tired, so very tired. She slid between the covers, her eyes closing even as her head touched the pillow. Forgotten was the dreaded arrival of the Earl of Tyrone. Her last thoughts centered on eyes of soft gray, aswirl with silver mists that lent a mysterious element to his inquiring gaze.

Shivering slightly, Brianna pulled the coverlet more closely about her, her memory teasing her with recollections of strong muscular arms heavy upon her bared flesh. "Trouble," she murmured softly, surrendering to the tantalizing dreams that skirted the edge of her mind.

"That shore is a nasty cut you got, mister," Toby said. Ryan remained still, unflinching as the man cleaned his wound. In truth, he scarcely noticed the butler's presence. His thoughts were focused on the woman who had spent the night by his side.

So this was Brianna Calhoun, he thought, a smile caressing his mouth. Hardly what he had expected from the missive he had received. The letter! "My waist pouch. Where is my pouch?" he asked.

"It's right here, mister. Ain't nobody going to takes it." Toby indicated a nearby chair. The oilskin pouch lay draped across the armrest, soiled but seemingly in one piece. Ryan relaxed, relieved to know the letter was safe.

He would need it to present himself to the attorney for Richard Calhoun. A scowl marred his strong countenance. The attorney. What was his name? Westman. Yes, that was it. What sort of man would leave a young woman, one who had just recently lost her father, to the cruel fates of a fickle Mother Nature? He had never met the man, but despite Brianna's assertions, Ryan felt an intense dislike for him welling within his chest.

Toby tied off the bandage, stepping back to admire his handiwork. "Looks like you is going to live after all, mister."

Ryan smiled. "That's a relief," he said with a friendly

drawl, his casual manner bringing a smile to the face of the elderly Negro.

"Would you likes some food, suh?"

"Not now, Toby. If you don't mind, I think I would prefer rest. I'm feeling rather fatigued at the moment."

"Yes suh. I shore can understand that. You is mighty banged up. From de bruises, it looks like that old sea done tossed you about like a piece o' driftwood." He gave a low chuckle at his own analogy. "Reckon you is going to be mighty stiff for a couple of days or so."

"You're probably right, but being stiff is a lot better than being drowned."

"That's a fact," Toby said, laughing in amusement. "Well, suh, if there is nothing more you needs, I'll jest be on my way."

"Ah . . ." Ryan paused for a moment. "Where is your mistress?"

"Miss Bri? Why I s'pects she's retired by now. She looked most near done in herself."

Ryan thought of the small, delicate-looking woman and the strenuous efforts she had put forth in saving his life. Yes, he decided. She would be in a complete state of exhaustion. It would wait. He would speak with her, tell her who he was, after he talked with Westman. "Thank you, Toby."

Toby quietly left the room, leaving Ryan to consider the peculiar situation in which he found himself.

Long moments passed as Ryan thought of his reasons for being in this new land. At last, he roused himself, sitting on the side of the tester bed and staring at the pouch. So near, yet so far away in his weakened condition.

Determination forced him to his feet. Slowly, he made his way to the chair, ignoring the pain within his head and his bruised ribs. He would rest easier once the document was in his possession.

He thought of Brianna, of her proud assertion of independence. No doubt, it would not be beyond her to search his belongings at the first available opportunity. He didn't want her to prematurely learn the true reason for his presence.

Grasping the pouch within firm hands, Ryan unlaced the bindings, pulling forth the wrapped paper he sought. He made his way back to the bed, gingerly settling in before turning his attentions to the missive that had arrived so unexpectedly.

I take pen in hand to inform your Lordship of a matter requiring your most urgent attention.
My client, Richard Calhoun, Earl of Kenney, now lies upon his deathbed.
His most grievous thoughts are for the future of his only heir, Brianna Calhoun.
It is his most fervent desire that you be and are hereby appointed the sole and legal guardian of his only child until such time as she becomes of proper age or weds.

"Of course," he muttered lowly. Westman made no mention of her being a youth. He merely stated that Calhoun did not consider Brianna to be of proper age to assume control of his estate. He continued reading.

Born to plantation life, the girl has no knowledge that her holdings extend far beyond the boundaries of the lands known as Lagniappe.
It is for this reason, my client wishes you to assume

absolute control of all his estate to insure the proper handling of his only heir's vast fortunes.

At his request, I beseech you to come quickly to his aid and assume the rightful duties of your appointed station.

> I remain your obedient servant,
> Oliver Odell Westman

Ryan folded the parchment, sliding it back into its protective casement. Once finished, he wedged the pouch and its contents under the mattress. Reassured of its safety, he allowed his thoughts to drift to the haunting beauty of his newly acquired charge.

No doubt she would vigorously protest his usurping what she deemed to be her rights, but there was really no option.

Upon receiving the communication, he had taken the time to consult with his own barristers and had discovered it was a great risk to leave property to a young woman. They had so few rights. It was an easy matter for them to fall prey to unscrupulous speculators. Obviously, Calhoun had had no choice but to secure a proper male conservator.

He grinned, wondering how the old gentleman would have felt about his decision had he known the Earl of Tyrone was no longer Jason Fleming, but rather his son, Ryan.

The memory of his late father washed away his amusement, leaving him in somber thought.

He closed his eyes, resting his throbbing head upon the soft down pillow. The Earl of Kenney. Often he had heard his father speak of his old friend. He had told of how he had sailed to the new lands, making a prosperous life for himself without benefit of title. It had been a grand and bold venture that had resulted in the former earl finding not only wealth, but also happiness with a commoner whose beauty he had extolled in each communication.

Ryan's thoughts were crowded with visions of Brianna. There was nothing common about her. The blood of the Irish aristocracy flowed within her veins, yet she had an unspoiled air about her, a self-confidence that challenged his own bold nature.

It became vitally important that he find a way to get her to accept his authority without crushing her spirit. Totally unorthodox in her behavior, she enchanted him as thoroughly as the sirens of the sea had enthralled the sailors described in Greek mythology.

"I fear, my little siren, your sweet song must fall on deaf ears. For I must be as Odysseus and sail a course, straight and true, without yielding to the pleasure of your persuasive entreaties."

Ryan burrowed deeper beneath the covers, his body filled with an overpowering desire to hold her once more within his embrace. "My enchantress of the sea," he murmured. "Sweet. So sweet."

Sleep claimed him. In a blanket of warmth, he was transported back in time to a dusty vacant cabin, a place where his eyes feasted on the soft, inviting curves of a sleeping maiden.

His hands gently caressed the silky swell of her hips, plunging into the valley of her diminutive waist. On she slept, unaware as he explored the smooth, flat planes of her belly, moving upward until his hand cupped the satin globe of a pink-tipped breast within his heated palm.

She had sighed, unknowing as she pressed closer to his

experienced touch, her own body seeking greater contact with the temptations offered.

He turned, uncomfortable as his conscience prodded him without mercy for his transgressions. He had not known. How could he know the beauty within his reach was the daughter he must protect? Mumbled curses spilled from his lips as heated desires waged war with obligations of honor.

He was Ryan Fleming, Earl of Tyrone. At all costs, he must protect and defend the virtues of his ward.

Brianna's face taunted him through fevered eyes, her hand cool against his brow. "Be gone, sweet siren. I'll hear not your song," he said, drifting into deeper slumber.

She stepped away from the bed, her face evidencing her puzzlement at his peculiar words. "Song?" she whispered.

" 'Pears to be out o' his head to me," Sudie offered, stepping up beside her mistress. "He done started thrashing and mumbling all sorts o' strange things. I thought it best to call you. Thought maybe we should send someone to fetch de doctor man."

"Yes, Sudie. I think we should. He seems to have a high fever. Tell Toby to send for Dr. Wells right away, will you?"

"Shore enough, missy. I is on my way. Don't you gets too near him while I is gone. Never know when he might gets a violent spell."

Heeding Sudie's advice, Brianna retired to the nearby chair, watching him with concern. Beneath the bandages, Ryan's face was a mask of pain. She yearned to ease the lines etched on his sun-bronzed face but was unsure of how to proceed.

All she could do was watch and wait until the doctor arrived. Time stretched onward, each passing minute increasing her anxiety. Her heart felt heavy within her breast.

Despite Sudie's warnings, Brianna returned to his side with increasing frequency, until at last she settled herself on the edge of the bed. Taking his hand in hers, she crooned words of encouragement until the doctor came to relieve her.

At Sudie's insistence, she relinquished her post, retiring only so far as the hallway to await the doctor's word.

"Will he be all right?" she asked the moment Dr. Wells appeared.

"He has youth and a good strong constitution on his side, Miss Brianna. With plenty of rest and care, there's a chance . . . a good chance. Of course, he will have to stay in bed a couple of weeks or so. Pneumonia is a dangerous ailment, but he does have a chance," he repeated.

"Thank you, Dr. Wells. We'll keep a close watch on him."

"Fine. I'll stop by in a couple of days and look in on him. In the meantime, I left some medicine on the bed table. Try to spoon some in him whenever he rouses. It will help break up the congestion, make breathing a mite easier."

"Yes, of course. I'll tend the matter myself."

The doctor stopped, eyeing her with consternation. "You best leave things to Sudie. She knows how to tend sick folks. No call for you to trouble yourself. Like as not, there will be enough talk once word gets around about you, a single lady, having a man not related in her home."

Brianna bit back a sharp reply. She didn't care what people thought. It was her house and she would do as she pleased. "Thank you, doctor."

Chapter 3

Rubbing her neck, Brianna stretched to ease the cramped muscles of her back, satisfaction overruling fatigue.

It had been a long night, one filled with frenzied activity as she tried to hold her thrashing patient within the confines of his bed. At last, he had fallen into a fitful sleep. She had maintained a worried vigil, alternating between pressing cool cloths to his brow and coaxing him to take the medicine during his brief moments of wakefulness. Only when the fever had broken had she dared to rest her weary body.

The morning sun streamed through the windows, the light adding a new cheeriness to the room and bolstering her spirits.

Ryan stirred, shifting positions as Brianna drew near the bed. His eyes opened cautiously, as though expecting to be assailed by renewed pain.

Brianna's face hovered near his. "Good morning, *M'sieur* Fleming. How are you feeling?"

"Monsieur? I thought we had established a friendship," he drawled, his words slightly slurred.

"Very well. Good morning, Ryan."

"That's better." He looked about, contemplating his surroundings. The room seemed awash in a hazy light. He strained, trying to gain his bearings. "Where am I?"

"You are at Lagniappe," she responded. "This is called the Blue Room."

His vision cleared. He studied the spacious room with a discerning eye. A variety of blues, blended and contrasted to create the aura of a cooling breeze upon a becalmed sea. "A logical name," he said.

Eyeing her speculatively, Ryan continued. "May I ask the cause of your presence in my chambers?"

"You were very ill," she began. "I was forced to spend the night in order to see to your needs."

A small smile played at one corner of his mouth. "It seems I am destined to have you in my bed at the most inopportune moments."

"I was not in your bed, sir, and I'll thank you to wipe that silly smirk from your face! If you must know, I spent a most uncomfortable evening there." Brianna turned, indicating the nearby wooden rocker with a wave of her hand.

"My sincere apologies, sweet siren. I appear to be once more in your debt."

"It is better that you be in my debt than I in your bed," she retorted. "And I am not your sweet siren."

Laughter rumbled from deep within his broad chest, cut short as he was wracked by a coughing spell that left him weakened.

"You must take care, Ryan," Brianna said, coming quickly back to his side, her anger forgotten. With practiced ease, she measured out his medicine from the near-empty bottle. "You have been grievously ill this past week."

"Week? But I just arrived," he protested.

"Take this." She held the spoon before him. Ryan complied, grimacing at the vile taste. "Your arrival was some eight days past," she answered as she replaced the stopper.

"Surely you jest." He leaned back on his pillow, trying to bring some semblance of order to his thoughts. He searched his memory, methodically listing the facts as he knew them.

He had been knocked overboard, sustaining a head injury. Checking the area of his temple, Ryan was surprised to find the bandage missing and a healing scab near his hairline. By means of which he knew little, he had found himself awaking to the soft warmth of Brianna's body pressed to his own. And now he was again cosseted alone with this angel of mercy. It was a circumstance he wished he was in a better position to appreciate. "A week, you say?"

"A week. After Toby put you to bed, you took a turn for the worse. We were forced to call upon the doctor. He told us you were suffering a case of pneumonia. For a while, I feared you might die."

"Feared? Would my death have caused you pain, my sweet siren?"

Brianna grew warm beneath his direct gaze, but she was unable to draw away. Her heart swelled within her breast at the thought that so vital a man might have perished. She swallowed with difficulty. It was foolish! She knew nothing of him save his occupation of sailor. He had been a continual bother since she had found him. Why, then, was it so important he fare well?

"To have a strange man meet his demise in my home would have been most inconvenient," she snapped, annoyed by the unreasonable effect he seemed to have over her.

Again the teasing smile returned. He appeared not the least concerned by her answer. "I would hate to inconvenience such a lovely hostess."

She waved away his words, flustered by his actions. "No matter. You are on the road to recovery now. Soon, you shall be well enough to continue on your way."

"Not too soon," he cautioned.

"But . . . but you cannot expect to stay. Already I have had visitors and many inquiries about your presence. It is causing quite a stir. Besides, the Earl of Tyrone is liable to arrive at any time now. He is already overdue, according to *M'sieur* Westman's calculations."

"I thought you were against the earl's arrival. Have you experienced a change of heart?" he inquired. Dare he hope she would accept his being the earl? Ryan wondered. Should he reveal his full identity?

"I have not. The thought of his presence at Lagniappe is abhorrent to me, but I was given no choice in the matter."

Ryan hid his disappointment behind a mask of casual interest. "Then why the concern about his finding me here?"

Brianna began pacing the room, relieving her anxiety with physical activity. "He may take strong exception to the presence of a stranger within my home. Although I do not like him, I cannot afford to alienate him, at least not from the very beginning."

"Ah, but you do plan to offer him every resistance," Ryan countered.

Brianna turned to face him, her hands braced against her hips in anger. "Do not try to put words in my mouth, *M'sieur* Fleming. What I choose to do is my concern, not yours."

Ryan offered a weak shrug of his massive shoulders. "I did not say I was concerned, merely curious."

"Why should you be curious about my affairs?"

"Everything about you stirs the curiosity. In the short time of our acquaintance, I have found you a constant source of amazement and contradiction."

A frown furrowed her smooth brow, tilting the corners of her mouth downward. "Contradiction?"

"But of course. One moment you are defiant, demanding I be given refuge within your home. Now you are vigorously protesting my presence."

Brianna lowered her eyes, avoiding him as she spoke. The words galled her, catching slightly within her throat as she tried to explain. "I have been thinking. Perhaps this earl may not wish to be at Lagniappe any more than I would wish it. If I can but persuade him that I am capable of managing without him, then . . ."

"He might choose to leave," Ryan provided. "Do you really believe such a thing possible?"

"It's worth a try."

"Brianna, if a man puts forth the effort and time to come all the way to Lagniappe from his own Irish home, it's not likely he will so easily abandon his duties once arrived."

"It is in his best interests," she asserted with vigor. "I shall not have some fancy dandy parading about the grounds of Lagniappe, posing as lord of this manor! This is my home, my birthright."

"Dandy? What makes you so certain he is a dandy?

You may find him to be intelligent and a man of sound practices."

"Men! You are all alike! You don't know him, either, but there you go defending his character with unwarranted enthusiasm."

"It's better than assassinating his character without cause," Ryan challenged.

"Ooh! Just recover your health and be gone with you, Ryan Fleming. I don't need you or any man telling me how to think."

She whirled on her heel, making an exit to his amused laughter. "How dare he mock me! I saved his life. . . . He owes me."

Stopping outside his door, she gave the matter her full attention. He did owe her, but how could that be of use in her present circumstance?

"There you is, missy." Sudie stopped at the head of the stairs. "I has been a-looking for you. That Massa Arlington is here to sees you again."

"Thank you, Aunt Sudie. Offer him some refreshment and tell him I'll be down shortly." Brianna retraced her steps toward her own quarters.

"Ain't no need to offers that gent'man nothing. Ever' time he comes in, he jest helps hisself to de liquors," Sudie mumbled to herself.

She watched her mistress retreat to her room, then made her way to the Blue Room. Poking her head through the door, she saw the patient was alert. Sudie entered, not waiting for an invitation.

"Lawdy, Massa Fleming. I shore is glad to see you looking more fit."

"Thank you, madam."

Sudie giggled at the prim formality. "Lawdy, but you

do has a way with words. I ain't no madam. You can jest call me Sudie."

"Ah, the celebrated Aunt Sudie, I take it."

Sudie frowned, her eyes narrowing with suspicion. "I don't know nothing 'bout cel . . . celebrated, but I is Aunt Sudie all right."

"Don't be offended. Celebrated is a compliment, I assure you," he said, offering a friendly smile that thawed her disposition considerably.

"Well, if it's good, then I reckon it's all right if you wants to call me Aunt Sudie."

"Thank you. I'm honored."

"Is you feeling better?"

"I thought so, but at the moment I'm not certain," he confided.

"What you mean?"

"I seem to have upset Miss Brianna somewhat, though I fail to find the cause of her disturbance. She left here somewhat irked with my presence."

"That's 'cause that fancy earl is coming, and Massa Westman done told her what-for is going to happen if he shows up and finds you here."

"I see, and do you know how my presence is supposed to adversely affect Miss Brianna's relationship with her new guardian?"

"This here is de South. Things be a mite different than how you is used to, Massa. There is certain things that's expected from the ladies of Miss Bri's raising, and she ain't been much on toeing de mark, if you know what I means."

Ryan flashed a broad smile. "I think I have a very good idea. She does seem a bit independent, shall we say?"

"Humph. Independent? That gal is as stubborn as an old mule, she is. Why, ever since she's been big enough to talk, she's thought she's as good as anybody and a sight better than most."

"And is that really so bad, Aunt Sudie?"

"It is when you is supposed to be a lady, like Miss Bri. All de other young ladies in these parts, they don't do nothing 'cepting a bit o' fancy sewing, gossiping, and always flirting with de gent'men what comes to call."

"Miss Brianna doesn't?" he inquired, growing more interested in the conversation with each passing minute.

"Lawd, no. Miss Bri don't go lolling about de bed 'til noon. She's up early and out there on that big black stallion o' hers checking de fields." Sudie paused, shaking her head in dismay.

"What's so wrong with keeping an eye on one's investments?" Ryan inquired.

"Nothing if you is a man. Ain't fitting a woman to go traipsing 'bout de fields. Them field hands is working out there beneath de hot sun and all. Why, most o' them ain't even got shirts covering their backs. Not a fitting sight for no lady to behold."

The thought of Brianna staring at bare sweat-glistening torsos aroused him. Would such a sight affect her as he had been affected by her own unclad form laying pressed against his?"

A spark of jealousy flickered within him. He found it most disconcerting to consider the possibility of those bewitching eyes lingering on another man's form. Perhaps it was time he made his true identity known. As the Earl of Tyrone, he could put a stop to her activities.

"Yes, of course," he said, offering what he hoped would be an acceptable answer to the formidable black woman who stood before him. "A lady must be careful of her reputation."

Sudie tilted her head to one side, eyeing him speculatively. "Seems I be doing all de talking, Massa Fleming. When is you going to tell old Sudie about you?"

"What would you like to know?"

"How come you is here at Lagniappe?"

"I thought Brianna would have explained my presence by now."

"She did, but I ain't buyin' it none. I is de one what washed yore things. Miss Bri thinks you is some kind o' po' sailor boy washed overboard."

"And you don't?" Ryan asked, his admiration for the woman rising.

"I don't, for shore. Them clothes o' yours don't go with no po' anything. Now, who is you and what for is you here?"

The friendly banter was gone. Sudie had now marked her stance and was firm in her determination to learn the truth. But could he trust her? Ryan decided to take a chance. He had to trust someone sometime, and if he could gain Aunt Sudie as an ally, his plans had a better chance of success.

"I was on a ship. And, I did go overboard during a storm," he began.

Sudie moved closer, her face evidencing curiosity mingled with suspicion. "I is listenin', but don't go expectin' me to believe you is a simple sailor."

"I won't," he answered with a wry grin. "I own the ship I was on."

"I knowed it. I jest knowed it for shore, but how come you let Miss Bri keep on thinkin' wrongheaded?"

"Can you keep a secret, Aunt Sudie?" Ryan leaned forward, his voice a husky whisper.

Sudie backed away, alarm rising. "I ain't going to keep quiet 'bout nothin' what can cause Miss Bri troubles."

"I don't wish to cause Brianna any trouble. I'd like to help her." His words were cut short by the opening of the door. Ryan leaned back, resting his head against the pillows as Brianna entered.

"I thought I heard voices," she began.

Sudie moved toward the bed, smoothing the covers as she spoke. "I is jest tryin' to coax Massa Fleming into takin' some food. A big man like him gots to eat or he'll jest plumb dry up and blows away."

Brianna smiled toward the patient. "Aunt Sudie believes food is the cure for everything," she explained.

"If that's the case, I'm willing to submit," Ryan acknowledged with a bold wink toward Sudie. "I wouldn't want Aunt Sudie to think I'm stubborn as a mule by refusing her advice."

Brianna arched a brow at the familiar phrase. "Aunt Sudie?" she said, her tone holding a question.

"I is busy, missy. You has best go seein' to yore company and let old Sudie takes care o' this man." She pulled Ryan upward, more forcefully than necessary, and vigorously pounded at his pillow. Ryan winced but said nothing of the rough treatment.

Brianna studied the pair momentarily but it became apparent there would be no forthcoming confessions. "Very well," she agreed. "You see to his appetite and I'll go entertain Jeffrey." She excused herself, annoyed by the transparent conspiracy of silence.

"Who's Jeffrey?" Ryan wanted to know as soon as he and Sudie were alone.

"Massa Arlington. He owns Belle Terre and if he gets his way, he'll most likely be ownin' Lagniappe, too."

The fires of jealousy flamed higher. Ryan hadn't considered the possibility of a suitor. "How does Brianna feel about him?"

"She don't say much to me. I s'pects that's cause she know I don't cotton to him. Him and his fancy struttin' about de place, like he done owns it and all what's on it."

"Ah, then you don't approve the match?" The idea pleased Ryan and he felt confident Sudie would make a perfect ally.

"I don't. 'Course, Miss Bri has a way o' makin' up her own mind 'bout things. Reckon if she do up an marries Massa Arlington, old Sudie is goin' to be sent packin'."

"You surely don't think Brianna would allow him to sell you?"

Sudie laughed, her bulky frame quivering with the action. "Lawd, Massa Fleming, ain't no way nobody is goin' to sell this chile. I is a free woman o' color, I is."

Ryan stared at the woman, contemplating her words with care. "I thought . . ." he began. "I mean, it never occurred to me."

"Don't fret yoreself none. Folks hereabouts don't figures I is any different than any other blacks and I guess I ain't. De big difference was Massa Calhoun. He was what was different."

"How so?" Ryan prodded, curious about the man who had chosen him as conservator of his estates.

"I belonged to de massa when he gots married. When his wife passed on, I is de one what took care o' Miss Bri. She was a handful, too!"

"I don't doubt it," Ryan answered with resounding agreement. "But please continue."

"Anyways, de massa weren't no southerner. He done come from cross de oceans. Don't know why, but he never did take to one man ownin' another."

A dark shadow crossed Ryan's sharp features. He thought of his father's stories of years past. Why couldn't he remember the reason the Earl of Kenney had abandoned his lands and removed himself to the New World?

Sudie continued her tale, her voice pulling Ryan back to the present. "One day, de massa ups and calls me in to his study. Said as how I was a fine and good woman. De next thing I knowed, he was handin' me papers and tellin' me I was freed. He said as how he would pay me for my services from then on. He did, too. Right up to de day he died, de massa paid me every month."

"And now?"

Sudie bowed her head, hesitant to continue, but Ryan was persistent. "Are you still receiving wages?"

"Not since de massa gone to his rewards. That lawyer man done says as how my services ain't needed and I can leave. Miss Bri fought for me, but it didn't change things none. 'Til de new massa gets here, that lawyer man's in charge o' de purse. He says he ain't partin' with a speck o' money for no worn-out mammy."

Ryan stiffened, his dislike for Westman intensifying. "When will Westman return?"

"Don't rightly know. He jest comes when he's a mind to. 'Course, if Miss Bri marries Massa Arlington, there won't be nothing different. If he takes hold o' things, I reckon Miss Bri won't have no choice but to tell old Sudie goodbye."

"Don't go packing your bags prematurely. From what I've seen, Brianna would be lost without you. I suspect you'll be around a long time."

Sudie beamed at his words. "Lawd, I shore do hope you is right, Massa Fleming. I'd be in a heap o' sorrow without my missy."

"You don't concern yourself," he said. "In the event Mr. Westman returns, I want you to bring him to me. I think it's time we have a little talk."

Sudie's eyes widened in surprise. "That ain't no good, Massa Fleming. I done told you, that man says you has got to leave. Him and Massa Arlington both done got Miss Bri riled up with their carryin' on. They allows as how you bein' here is a terrible scandal."

"Just bring him, Aunt Sudie. I'm sure I can persuade him to change his opinion." Ryan smiled, wondering what their sentiments would be if they knew of the intimacy he had shared with Brianna in the quiet cabin.

Sudie's eyes narrowed as she considered the man who spoke with such confidence. "I is beginnin' to think maybe Miss Bri ain't de only one round here what's stubborn as a mule."

"I think you think too much, Aunt Sudie. But for the time being, I'd appreciate it if you keep those thoughts to yourself. Now, how about providing me with some of that food you were discussing earlier?"

"I don't 'pose it can hurt," she grudgingly admitted.

"Food? Or silence?" he asked.

"Both. Jest as long as you don't forget, I'm goin' to look out for Miss Bri."

"Agreed."

Satisfied he understood and accepted her loyalty to the young mistress, Sudie bustled away.

Ryan leaned back against the pillows. Westman was no concern, but Arlington . . . What of him? Did she love him? he wondered.

* * *

"I am flattered, Jeffrey, but I must have more time to consider. Papa's only been gone eight months. I'm still in mourning." She indicated the traditional black frock with a graceful gesture of her hands.

"I can appreciate your circumstances, Brianna, but you must think of the full scope of your position."

She watched as he refilled his glass, curious as to his sudden nervousness. "To what position do you refer?"

"This business of the Earl of Tyrone," he said. "You know nothing of him."

Ryan's words echoed through her mind. I do not assassinate a man's character without cause, he had said. Was that what she had done? She pulled at her bottom lip with her teeth. It wasn't fair. She knew so little of her father's life in Ireland. Until Westman had revealed the contents of the will, she had never heard of the Earl of Tyrone. "What has the earl got to do with this?" she asked, forcing herself to concentrate on the matter at hand.

"Possibly everything. Many an inheritance has been squandered by careless management."

"You're concerned for my well-being? Or that of my property?"

Arlington downed the last of his bourbon, his hand shaking with suppressed anger. "Both. You're a beautiful woman, Brianna." He set his glass down on a table and came to her, kneeling before her on one knee as he took her hands in his.

"Beautiful women should be surrounded by beautiful things. If you marry me, I'll see to it you always have the luxuries you deserve."

"I have luxury now, Jeffrey."

He rose, running his fingers through his thick golden curls. "And the earl?"

"What of him?"

"Suppose he comes here and you wake up one day to find you no longer have your fortunes? Suppose he is a rogue, a scoundrel? Suppose he absconds with all you own?"

"Would that make a difference? Between us, I mean?" She could hear a sharp hiss as he exhaled. Brianna watched closely, unable to prevent herself from comparing him to the man who lay upstairs.

"Of course not, but you're not seeing the full context of the matter."

"How should I see it, Jeffrey?"

Arlington rose, taking her arm and guiding her to the settee. He spoke slowly, as though talking to a backward child. Brianna clenched her teeth, fighting back the urge to give him a severe tongue-lashing. Why had she not noticed his selfishness before? she wondered.

"Of course my feelings wouldn't change. I love you. I want you to become my wife, mother of my children."

Brianna tried to envision herself as mother of his children, but it was hopeless. Thoughts of Ryan kept interfering. He might not always agree with her, but he didn't treat her as a child. She remained silent, allowing Jeffrey to continue.

"Naturally, as parents, we would want the best for my heir. As you know, Belle Terre abounds the northernmost sector of Lagniappe. Should we marry, our children would inherit a sizable amount of land. Their future wealth would be secured for generations to come. You would want your children's future secure, wouldn't you?"

"Of course."

"Good. Then you agree we should be married before this earl arrives?"

"As I said, Jeffrey, I must have time to think. This is a big decision. I cannot answer so quickly."

Jeffrey smiled, his face smug with assumed victory. He leaned forward, lifting her hand for a kiss. "Very well, my dear. I must be content for the moment, but don't keep me waiting overly long. The earl cannot be much longer in making his appearance."

At the mention of the Earl of Tyrone, Brianna's heartbeat quickened. What if Jeffrey was right? What if the earl was an evil man, intent on robbing her of her precious Lagniappe? She must stop him! Her eyes sought Jeffrey's face. Was marriage the solution to her dilemma?

Already the puffiness under his watery eyes offered mute testimony to his fondness for drink. Would marriage to him offer any better security than abdication of Lagniappe to the unknown earl? "I . . . I must bid you goodbye, Jeffrey. There is much to do, and I fear I have spent too much time away from my duties," Brianna said, anxious for him to leave.

"Of course, my love. I understand." He rose, assisting her to her feet. His hand felt soft, almost flaccid to her own firm touch.

Brianna fought the urge to pull free, allowing him to guide her toward the door. "I shall return tomorrow," he said. "Perhaps you will have an answer."

"No. Not tomorrow. The doctor is scheduled to stop by and check on my guest."

Jeffrey scowled, his mouth pursing in a sullen manner. "That creature is not still here, is he?"

"He is not a creature," Brianna quickly protested.

"Whatever he is, I told you I do not consider it proper to have him abiding within the main house. Why haven't you had him moved?"

"He is injured."

"All the same, it isn't seemly and I won't have you become the object of gossip. I have a certain standing to uphold, and I can't have the Arlington name tarnished by your allowing him to remain at Lagniappe any longer."

Brianna bristled at his proprietary manner, her shoulders stiffening in protest. "Tongues may wag as they choose. I cannot concern myself with such foolishness. This is still my home, and I shall say who resides within."

"Very well," Jeffrey said, his manner turning cold. "I have tried to warn you. It appears I shall have my duties well cut out for me when we wed. I'm sure though, in time, you will come to see the wisdom of my decisions. Good day, my dear."

Brianna offered a curt nod as Jeffrey made his exit, holding her temper in check until the door was securely bolted behind him. "Such arrogance!" she railed, once alone. "Not one mention of my reputation. I have a name, too. It's Calhoun, and if Jeffrey Arlington thinks I'll trade it for the Arlington moniker, he's mistaken."

Her lips thinned into a pink slash across her pale face. "Your decision, is it? Well, we'll see who decides what." Lifting her skirts, Brianna headed for the stairway, her fury mounting with each successive step. "I'll make my own decisions. I won't have Jeffrey or the Earl of Tyrone telling me what I'll do. I'll show them. I'll marry who I want and when I want. I'll . . ."

She stopped, staring at the closed door before her. A smile filled her face, chasing away the stormy anger in an instant. "And why not?" she murmured.

He did owe her a substantial debt, she mused. Allowing him the opportunity to relieve himself of the obligation was only proper. With Ryan's help, no one would take Lagniappe from her . . . not even the Earl of Tyrone.

Her hand reached for the latch. He wanted to help her; he had even offered. Now she would accept.

Chapter 4

"You want me to what!" Ryan could not believe the words he had just heard.

"You don't have to yell, Ryan. A simple yes or no will be sufficient. Will you or won't you marry me?"

"I hardly consider your request a matter of simplicity, Brianna. While I'm certain southern customs differ from those in Ireland, I doubt they are so different as to assume it commonplace that a lady just walks into a man's chambers and proposes marriage."

In truth, she hadn't paused to consider how her actions might appear to him. How could she have been so rash? she wondered, inwardly regretting her impetuous nature. Brianna looked at the man before her, her confidence waning somewhat. Well, it was too late to back down now. Like it or not, she had to pursue her course. It was her only option.

"It is not commonplace, but I'm certain that at some time and some place, a lady has made such an offer."

"How comforting," he answered dryly, forcing himself to calm down. "And what leads you to believe there is any cause for repetition of such action?"

Brianna felt herself warming beneath his stern piercing look. "The Earl of Tyrone will be here most anytime. Jeffrey pointed out the possibility the earl might waste away Lagniappe."

A scowl darkened Ryan's face, sending shivers of apprehension racing along Brianna's spine. "You refuse to give him any consideration?"

She met his gaze with one equally determined. "Why should I? I know nothing of the man. Lagniappe is my home, and I must consider it first and foremost."

Ryan arched a dark brow, his tone sardonic as he answered. "Mercenary little wench, aren't you?"

Brianna's anger flared. She rose from her chair, eager to end the doomed conversation. "I'm sorry I bothered you with my proposal, *M'sieur* Fleming. I had hoped you would be pleased to have an easy manner in which you could discharge your debt."

"What debt? I owe you nothing."

"You owe me your life. You even mentioned it was quite valuable, too."

"Very well. I concede to the accuracy of your observation, but what makes you think marriage to you would be easy?"

"Ooh. You are impossible. Just forget I mentioned it. It is obvious you have no interest. I shall simply look elsewhere for a solution."

Ryan tensed, his muscles flexing as he challenged her choices. "And where might elsewhere be, my little siren?"

"*M'sieur* Arlington has offered the option of marriage." She afforded herself a smile in his direction. "You see, *M'sieur* Fleming, not all men find my attentions unacceptable."

Ryan chafed with anger. His eyes locked on hers, forcing her to meet his mesmerizing glare. "I did not say I find your attentions or . . . your proposal unacceptable."

Stunned, Brianna sat back down, watching him with wariness. "Are you saying you will agree to my proposition?" she asked with hesitance.

"No, but I am willing to listen. Once I hear all the details, I will decide what course I shall follow."

She clasped her hands together. Her entire body seemed to be quaking uncontrollably. Why hadn't she given it more thought before she had barged in, blurting out such an unlikely arrangement?

Her thoughts churned like an ever-increasing whirlpool, threatening her with its growing strength. Dare she trust him? she wondered. Scarcely had the question formed within her mind than Brianna knew she had to risk it. Jeffrey was her only other option and she refused such a union. At least Ryan was willing to listen. It was a start.

"Papa's will states that the Earl of Tyrone shall have conservatorship unless I am suitably wed."

"And you believe he will consider me suitable?" came the calmly posed question.

"Uh . . . er . . ." Brianna bit into her lower lip, shielding her eyes from his brazen appraisal. The silence hovered like a summer storm, threatening to unleash an angry flood at any moment.

"Am I suitable?" he repeated.

"Only a cad would deny suitability once the vows have been consummated," she blurted out. She gasped aloud at her own boldness, covering her mouth with one hand.

An amused smile touched his lips as Ryan seemed to peel away her clothing with his eyes. Brianna trembled, as much in fear of the heat growing within her own untried body as from the words just spoken.

"At least you give the poor earl benefit of some redeeming qualities. And . . . what are the terms if he finds you 'suitably' wedded?"

Brianna turned away, unable to bear his bold looks for another moment. She moved toward the window, glancing outward over her beloved plantation. "If I am married, then his duties will be discharged, and he shall have no reason to remain at Lagniappe."

"What then, sweet siren?"

Brianna turned, puzzled by the question. "I . . . I'm not sure I understand."

Ryan leaned forward, capturing her attention with the magnetism of his personality. "If I choose to accept your arrangement," he replied, "what will happen once the earl sails away?"

"Oh. Why, I haven't given it much thought," she confessed.

"Interesting. You enter my room, ask me to become your husband, and you give no thought to what destination will be reached from the course you have set. What of me?"

"What of you? You have nothing to lose in the bargain."

"Nothing to lose? What of my freedom, sweet siren? Marriage will definitely deny me the pleasure of my freedom."

Brianna felt herself grow warm. "I shall release you from the bonds of matrimony," she agreed, wondering why she found the words so difficult to say. There should be no reluctance to be rid of him once the danger of losing Lagniappe was past.

"Is the ending of marriage so easy in this land?"

She closed her eyes, berating herself once more for her impetuosity. "After a decent interval, you . . . you could go away . . . never return," she suggested.

"Yes, of course. I could simply vanish from your life. But what of the future? Have you given it any thought?"

"I would have Lagniappe. That is all I want."

Why did he ask so many questions? she wondered. Why didn't he just say no and be done with it?

"Should you find someone you loved, a husband might prove a little inconvenient, wouldn't you say?"

"I am not interested in love. I want no husband. This is merely a . . . a . . . temporary arrangement." Her heart seemed to lurch within her breast, leaving a strange ache within her. She pushed it aside, resolute in her decision.

"Perhaps not a husband," he said, rising from the bed, "but there is Lagniappe, and it demands an all-consuming love."

"What?" Brianna's eyes widened as she turned to find Ryan moving steadily toward her.

He wore one of her father's freshly laundered nightshirts. Even with the ties undone, the thin material stretched tightly across his muscular chest, exposing the dark bronze of his flesh against the snowy white material.

"Lagniappe," he repeated. "Something extra." He hovered closely, too closely, as he looked down at her, his expression unreadable.

"Something extra?" she whispered, staring at him, unable to move. Her fingers tingled, aching with desire to reach up, to bury themselves in the bed of black curls that swirled invitingly upon his chest.

"Oh, yes, sweet siren. That something extra which men and women only find together. It's like a powerful drug, carrying them ever higher until they lie, energies spent, upon the shores of blissful contentment."

Ryan reached out, grazing one soft cheek with the back of his hand. "It's called passion, and you are a woman made for passion. That is your true Lagniappe, my sweet siren. That is your 'something extra,' and you must have it to live, as surely as you must have the air you breathe."

Brianna felt herself growing weak with yearning, but she knew not for what she craved. What was wrong with her? Why did she feel this way? Dimly, she became aware of a subtle change within the man who held her so effortlessly within his power.

Ryan smiled, slowly removing his hand, allowing it to fall by his side. "Now I know how Odysseus must have felt. Hearing life's most tempting song, and being bound and unable to answer its sweet call. It is truly the most exquisite of tortures a man can bear."

Brianna watched, her throat too dry to speak, as Ryan distanced himself from her, returning to sit upon the edge of the bed. "I . . . I don't . . . understand your meaning, Ryan."

"Perhaps one day it will become clear." His face once more became stern, all business as he continued. "Now, if you will continue with your plan . . ."

Flustered, Brianna could only shake her head. "It would never work. Tomorrow, I will speak with Jeffrey," she murmured, turning to leave. With sheer force of will, she reached the door, her fingers finding comfort in the cool metal as they curled about the knob.

"I will marry you, Brianna."

His words came like a flood to a dry creek bed, crashing into every thirsty crevice of her soul, leaving her trembling in its wake. She nodded, acknowledging his vow, and walked slowly from the room without a word.

Sitting before her dressing table, Brianna stared at her reflection. It was done. When the Earl of Tyrone arrived, he would find her a lawfully wedded woman, no longer requiring the services of a guardian.

She stared at the image before her, her fingers touching the cheek he had so recently caressed. His touch had been sure, yet so tender. What manner of man was this who could have her burning with ire one moment, then wrap her within the bosom of an entirely different kind of heat the next?

Reaching for her hairbrush, Brianna pulled it through the long, shining curtain of deepest brown. In the light, it shimmered with russet highlights as she continued the measured strokes. Did he really think her beautiful? she idly wondered.

"Surely, I must be going mad," she grumbled, discarding the brush and eyeing herself critically. Eyes of pure jade stared back at her from beneath a thick sable fringe. Pink spots of color dotted her high-placed cheekbones, a sign of her agitation. She hated it that she blushed so easily. It had often been her downfall. Pretty? Perhaps, she decided, but that was at very best.

Ryan's words taunted her, giving her no rest, even in the privacy of her own chambers. He seemed to know everything about her, yet he remained a mystery. A mystery except for the single fact that remained undisputed.

He had agreed to marry her. Brianna worried her bottom lip, wondering at the wisdom of her decision. Ryan

Fleming seemed agreeable, true enough, but was he really what he seemed?

One by one, her mind posed questions that held no answers, only more questions.

She knew nothing of him save that he hailed from Ireland. Brianna closed her eyes, trying to recall her father's voice, the rare stories he had told of the old land. A frown pulled the corners of her rose-colored mouth downward. Odd that she had never noticed her father as being a part of those stories. It was as if he had been an outsider looking in. She shook her head, trying to dislodge the thought.

Surely he had been a part of the land of which he had spoken with such reverence. How else could he have painted such vivid pictures with his words?

A soft tapping at the door drew her attention. "Enter," she said, resuming her toilette.

"I done thought I best come help you dress for dinner, missy." Sudie bustled into the room, heading straight for the chiffonier.

"Hardly a cause of excitement. As I'm in mourning, there is only one decision," Brianna answered, the thought depressing her even further.

"Not tonight, there ain't. Tonight, you is goin' to look yore prettiest ever and wear de finest colors you has."

"Who says?"

"Massa Fleming, that's who. He done told me to pick out yore finest gown. Even said he preferred a green to match yore eyes or maybe ivory to blend with de creamy texture o' yore skin." Sudie chuckled as though remembering a private joke. "That man shore enough has good taste, I give em that."

"Well, that is more than I will give him." Brianna

twisted around in her chair, disdainfully eyeing the gowns being laid across the bed. "Put those away. Have you forgotten? Papa is scarce in his grave. It would be a sin to wear such things so soon."

"Been nigh close to nine months now," Sudie agreed.

"Eight," Brianna corrected before continuing. "Then you must know I can't appear in such finery. I shall wear black for at least a year, maybe longer. I can do no less in honor of Papa's good name."

"I done told Massa Fleming that, but he says different."

"He would. And just what did Master Fleming say, pray tell?"

"He allowed as how it might cause talk if you was to go cavortin' about in such attire, but this here is yore home. And he allows as how it couldn't do no harm for you to have a little less sadness and a little more color in yore own home and all."

Brianna could not find fault with his logic, try as she might. Hadn't she felt the same on so many lonely evenings? Black might be all right for older ladies, but she was not old. She was young and the past months had been especially trying. Surely a little color would not hurt? "Very well, but not the ivory. I would feel uncomfortable."

She eyed the gowns, selecting the deep russet.

"Massa Fleming says he favors green," Sudie reminded.

"Then let him wear the green," Brianna snapped. "The russet gown is far more suitable. It has color, yet it is not ostentatious."

For the first time since her father's death, Brianna found herself looking forward to dinner. She fingered the smooth satin, pleased with her decision. "I suppose once I'm dressed, I really should pay brief respects to *M'sieur* Fleming. At least let him see the gown," she added, looking to Sudie for agreement.

"That ain't going to be necessary, missy. De massa, he says he's going to be joinin' you in de dining room. I'se already told de cook to be fixing dinner real special for this evening."

Brianna tilted her head to one side, considering the prospect. "Is that a good idea?" she asked.

"Massa Fleming thinks so," Sudie answered.

"But is his health up to such strenuous exertion?"

Sudie shrugged, tightening the corset about Brianna's waist before answering. "I don't see as how there's anything so hurtful 'bout sitting' in a chair and eatin', less o' course he nips too much and falls out o' that chair."

Brianna giggled, unable to picture the sight of Ryan Fleming falling from such a common perch. "Then I assume he should be safe. I doubt *M'sieur* Fleming would consider anything so mundane as worthy of risk."

"He does seem de darin' kind, now that you mentions it. I s'pect that man shore do know a heap 'bout how life should be lived."

Brianna turned to face her trusted companion. "Do I, Aunt Sudie? Do you think I know how life should be lived?"

Sudie wrapped her arms around her, hugging her close. "Lawd, chile. You is too young to know too much about life. It takes a passel o' years to learn a whole life."

"But you said Ryan knows. He isn't exactly ancient. He couldn't be much more than thirty."

"Things is different with men, missy. They's gots more worldly ways than lady folks."

Brianna's lips formed a firm line. "You mean more freedom to make their own choices."

Aunt Sudie nodded her head, concentrating on the tiny hooks of Brianna's gown. "Guess you could say that. That's jest de way it is."

"I did say that, and the way it is isn't fair."

"Now, now, chile. Ain't no call to go gettin' yoreself all riled up."

"I can't help it, Aunt Sudie. Papa raised me to run Lagniappe. Me, not some stranger! Then he suffered a change of mind, deciding I couldn't manage on my own. Now the only way I'm going to be able to regain my rightful place is to marry Ryan."

Sudie's eyes widened. "You is what?"

Brianna bit down on her bottom lip. She hadn't meant to break the news so bluntly. She inhaled a deep breath. Now that she had, she might as well reveal her plan.

"Sit down, Aunt Sudie."

She led the shaken woman to a nearby wing chair, gently pushing her down into the comfortable seat. "I'm sorry. I didn't mean to be so abrupt."

"I don't wants to hear yore apologies, chile. I jest wants to know what makes you think you is goin' to marry Massa Fleming."

Brianna moved back to sit at her dressing table, buying a little time to shape her plan before speaking.

"I'se waitin', Miss Brianna Calhoun."

Brianna clasped her hands together, focusing her eyes just above Sudie's right shoulder. She couldn't bring herself to look the woman in the eye. "It's true, Aunt Sudie. I spoke with Ryan earlier this evening."

Sudie shifted, trying to pull her massive bulk upward. "I'se goin' to has myself a talk with that man. He ain't goin' to come in here and sweet-talks my missy into no marriage."

"Please. Sit back down and let me finish." The soft plea reached out, urging Sudie to stillness once more. "He didn't talk me into marrying him."

"Humph. I finds that hard to believe."

"It's true. As a matter of fact, I was the one doing the talking." Brianna smiled, recalling the look of shock on Ryan's face when she proposed. "Marriage was my idea."

"Lawd, chile. What's done happen with yore mind? Ladies don't go round askin' menfolk to marry up with them. They waits . . . real ladylike." Sudie leaned forward, emphasizing the lady part.

"There wasn't time for coy ladylike games. We have no idea when the Earl of Tyrone will show up. I can't take any chances. As it is, there is always the possibility he may arrive before I can complete my plans."

Sudie shook her head, her face evidencing her confusion. "I don't know what you is talking 'bout and I don't know why that Massa Fleming done agreed with you. I shore enough thought he'd a had better sense."

Brianna gave a sigh of resignation. "He didn't agree with me . . . at first. I had to resort to other tactics."

"What has you done?"

Brianna quickly explained Ryan's refusal and how she had mentioned her option of wedding Jeffrey Arlington.

"Goodness, Miss Bri. I can't see how you could even think o' marryin' that fancy man. He's so in love with hisself there ain't much love for anybody else."

"Oh, Aunt Sudie, I wasn't really considering Jeffrey. I just wanted Ryan to think I was. I was hoping he would relent and see things my way."

"Humph. And you was jest sayin' you don't got no time for games. For shame, missy. For shame! Massa Fleming figure out what you done pulled on him, I s'pects he'll have more than a few words to say on the subject. He don't strike me as the kind o' man to take kindly to bein' bamboozled."

Brianna had the good grace to look embarrassed, lowering her head as Sudie continued scolding. "And jest what would you have done if he didn't see things yore way?"

"Luckily, I didn't have to worry about it. The important thing is that I'm legally married by the time the earl arrives. Then he will just have to turn around and sail right back to Ireland."

"Uh-huh. And then what you goin' to do?"

"After a decent interval, Ryan will go away. Once he's reached a place he likes, he will send me notification and I'll arrange for a suitable amount of money to be forwarded to his bank."

"What if he up and decides he don't want to leave Lagniappe? What if he decides he wants a lot more than you is willin' to give, missy?"

"You worry too much, Aunt Sudie. We have all the details worked out. Everything will be fine. Trust me. I know what I'm doing," she lied.

"Oh, I trusts you all right." Sudie hauled herself up from the chair, heading for the doorway.

"Aunt Sudie? Where are you going?"

"I done heard what you has to say on this shameful matter. Now I'se goin' to pay Massa Fleming a visit and hear his side. Then, I'll know if I trusts him . . . and how far," she mumbled as she left the room.

"I declare. That chile is goin' to be de death o' me yet,"

Sudie said, continuing her one-way conversation as she made her way to Ryan's chamber. Curling her pudgy fingers into her palm, she pounded on the door, waiting impatiently for permission to enter. "My baby ain't got no business marryin' up with some ship's cap'n. Naw suh. I don't care how good-lookin' he be."

"Come in," Ryan called out in a firm baritone. He continued scrubbing his arms, never bothering to turn toward the opening door. "Glad you came back. Why don't you pour another bucket of water in the tub, Toby?"

Sudie walked toward the bucket, lifting it with the ease of one used to heavy work. Moving behind him, she tilted the pail, not slowing until it was empty.

"What the hell!" he roared, sputtering as the hot liquid spilled over his head and face. He wiped at his eyes, continuing his blistering tirade. "Have you lost your mind, you fool?" Ryan looked up, his face dark with rage.

"That's jest what I want to know, Massa Fleming. Has you done gone and lost yore mind or was I an old fool, thinkin' maybe you might be a gent'man?" Sudie waited for his answer, her own fierce scowl matching his.

Ryan stared blankly, stunned to find the woman not only in his room, but leaning over the tub looking as though she were more than slightly tempted to drown him. "What in the world is the matter with you?"

"Miss Bri is what's de matter. She done told me as how you two is gettin' married."

Leaning back against the tub, Ryan ran strong fingers through his dripping mane, pushing his hair back as he pinned her with a hardened gaze. "We are, but I hardly see where that should be any concern of yours."

"Everything 'bout Miss Bri is my concern. You can't go marryin' her. It ain't right!"

"According to Brianna, there isn't anyone to stop the marriage, at least not at the present."

"I'll stop it. I don't know how, but I will."

"Why, Sudie? I thought you liked me." Ryan leaned back, flashing a lazy grin. "Would you rather she marry Arlington?"

"I do. I did . . . likes you, that is," she corrected, "but that was 'fore all this marriage nonsense reared its ugly head, and you knows full well I don't want my baby marryin' that Massa Arlington." She pushed balled fists against her ample hips. "I don't wants her marryin' you, either. You gots to call it off."

"A gentleman would never go back on a pledge of marriage to a lady."

"That's jest my point," Sudie continued, undaunted by his calm manner. "You ain't no gent'man. You is jest some sailin' man she done dragged in from de beach. Miss Bri's been cartin' all manners of critters in here ever since she was knee-high to a grasshopper. It's no good and you is no good!"

"Are you quite finished?" Ryan asked, his voice wielding a hard, cold edge.

Sudie stood upright, stepping back from the tub as she returned his glare. "I is."

"Good. Then if you will be so kind as to hand me that toweling, I would like to get out of this tub."

"And if I don't?" she challenged, hands pressed stubbornly against each hip.

"Then I will be forced to rise without it. Either way makes no difference to me. I intend to get out of this damn tub. Since you are so concerned about propriety, I sought merely to avoid an unnecessary display which would further shock your sense of decency."

When Sudie made no move, Ryan began to pull himself upward, the water sluicing downward in glistening sheets across his muscular torso.

"Wait!" she cried, scurrying for the requested toweling. She shoved it at him and quickly averted her eyes, unwilling to test his threat any further.

The minutes crawled by before Ryan signaled the safety of turning around. "Now, if you can refrain from further outbursts, I will gladly explain."

He stood before her, the toweling wrapped securely about his trim waist. Pointing a finger in her direction, he continued. "I must have your word that what I'm about to tell you will go no further than this room."

Mutely, Sudie nodded, unable to summon the courage to protest.

Convinced of her sincerity, Ryan made his way to the chair where he had laid out fresh clothes. "I was as surprised as you when Brianna came to me. I didn't realize she resented me so much."

"Resent?" Sudie asked, her voice tentative.

Ryan nodded. "Yes. From the very beginning, she has made her dislike for having a guardian known. Only when she proposed marriage as a solution did I understand the full extent of her determination not to be plagued with enduring such authority."

"Lawd, Massa Fleming. That don't mean she got resentment for you."

He offered a rueful smile to the woman, his voice dropping to a conspiratorial whisper. "I'm afraid it does, Aunt Sudie. You see, I happen to be the Earl of Tyrone."

"That ain't so. You was washed up on de beach." She

puzzled over his words momentarily, then offered the only answer that came to mind. "Maybe that nasty bump you got on yore head done give you ideas that ain't so."

Laughter spilled across his lips, his face appearing younger with the effort. "Only you would seek such a conclusion, but you are wrong. I am indeed the rightful Earl of Tyrone, and as such, I am Brianna's guardian."

"Then why hasn't you told her so's she could stop frettin' herself about what kind o' man you was goin' to be."

"I haven't known her long but Brianna Calhoun does not appear as a lady quick to forgive and forget. You yourself told me she was as stubborn as a mule. Would my revealing my identity have changed her mind?"

Considering his argument, Sudie shook her head back and forth. "I s'pect you is right, massa. That girl done got it in her head what de earl . . . I mean you . . . is like and there ain't much chance she's goin' to be persuaded to de contrary. Least not for a goodly spell to come."

"Precisely my opinion. My only hope is that I can convince her there is nothing to fear, then she will see there is no reason to enter so hastily into marriage."

"And how is you figurin' on doin' that?"

"I have a plan but first I must get my strength back. Once that is done, I intend to go to the nearest city of any consequence and make some arrangements which might prove advantageous." He looked at Sudie, offering a dazzling smile. "I may need your help. Are you willing?"

"I'se willin' to do anything that is right for Miss Bri." She chuckled with delight. "Now that I knows who you really is, I'se even willin' to let you two jumps de broom if you's a mind to."

"Jump the broom?"

"That's jest another way for sayin' get married," she answered with a chuckle.

"Please, Aunt Sudie. I'm not sure I'm ready to take on the responsibility for any siren at the moment, no matter how enchanting."

"I declare, Massa Fleming. You shore do has a strange way o' sayin' things ever' now and then, but I can't help but likes you."

"The feeling is mutual. Now if we can just convince Brianna to see things through your eyes, perhaps success will be ours."

"Oh, I don't thinks you need go troublin' yourself on that account."

Ryan cocked his head to one side, waiting for her to continue.

"I'se got me a pair of real good eyes. When you was in that bed all dead to the world, I seen how she looked at you."

"And how was that, Aunt Sudie?"

Laughter gurgled free in a gruff avalanche of sound. "Naw suh. I ain't going to be tellin' all I knows. You jest take Aunt Sudie's word for it. My baby ain't exactly no fool. Could be she knows more what she's about than anybody can guess."

She shuffled toward the door, her massive frame quivering with delight. "Lawd, but I gots me a real deep-down feelin' that things is shore goin' to liven up about this old place. I shore enough does."

Chapter 5

Brianna admired the table, set with gleaming crystal and her favorite china pattern. It had been a long time since she had eaten in such a lavish setting.

Her thoughts drifted backward in time to happier days. It had been just before Papa had taken to his bed. Oh, what stimulating times they had, lingering over coffee and dessert as they discussed a particularly controversial book. Sometimes, they just enjoyed the quiet camaraderie of two similarly inclined personalities. They didn't have to exercise any effort to entertain each other. How she missed him.

"My apologies," the sinfully intriguing voice said.

Brianna looked up and smiled, unable to quell her pleasure at having Ryan join her for a brief period of time.

"For what?"

"Had I known you would be so punctual, I would have arrived earlier," he admitted, his own smile evident.

"You don't think a woman capable of punctuality?" It was a challenge. She knew it and wished she had made any other comment. His eyes answered with a predatory gleam; his mouth curled upward at one corner.

"Not and manage to be as breathtakingly beautiful as you," he answered.

"My compliments, *M'sieur* Fleming. I forgot for a moment your Irish blood." She inclined her head slightly, her words teasingly lighthearted.

A vibrant chuckle rumbled from deep in his chest, spilling over the lips she found to entreat her own to taste. "I believe we are a rather close match," he told her, stepping forward to raise her hand and graze it with a light kiss.

Heat seemed to leap from his touch, radiating through her like a flow of lava rushing from an erupting volcano. Her heart quivered, beating erratically.

Slowly, unwilling to allow him the advantage of knowing the strange effect he held over her, Brianna slipped from his easy grasp.

"And who is in the lead, *m'sieur?*" she gently queried as she moved toward her chair.

He followed, slipping one hand beneath her elbow to escort her. At the end of the table, he slid her chair outward, offering her a casual glance as she was seated. "Must there be a lead?"

It was hardly the answer she expected. Certainly, no other gentleman of her acquaintance would be adverse to suggesting that man should lead . . . at all times and in all matters. "I'm not sure," she answered truthfully.

Ryan retraced his steps, taking his own place at the far end of the table. She couldn't help but notice his proud stance, the way he moved with such confidence. Were all men of common breeding so content with their lot? she wondered.

A servant appeared, filling each glass in turn with a white wine. Brianna sipped hers, casting shy glances in his direction. To her surprise, he seemed completely at ease in the elegant surroundings, tasting his own wine with the manner of a connoisseur.

"Do you find the wine to your liking, *M'sieur* Fleming?"

"Please. I thought we had agreed. I'm Ryan and you are Brianna," he reminded her with a smile. "And in answer to your question, it is an excellent selection. I had no idea such pleasant amenities were available in your country."

"I think you will find we will offer many such pleasant surprises, *m'sieur.*"

A smile touched his lips, his eyes sparkling with undisguised interest. "No doubt, madam."

Brianna felt the familiar warmth coursing through her veins. Why did he persist in twisting her every word to suit his pleasure? "I was referring to the land and its people," she amended, taking a sip from her glass to silence the trembling of her nerves.

A dark brow arched in silent query. The heavy silence was relieved by the presence of the servants as they entered the room with the first of the steaming dishes of food.

Brianna lowered her head, her focus centering on the small cup of soup placed before her. If only she didn't have this nagging feeling that control was slowly slipping from her grasp, she thought as she pretended to ignore her companion.

Only an occasional sound could be heard from the direction of the nearby butler's pantry as servants continued their duties. The silence continued, awkwardly reaching into every crevice of the elegantly appointed room.

Brianna glanced toward the end of the table, her efforts met by the calm scrutiny of her guest. She quickly averted her gaze. How dare he stare so boldly, she inwardly fumed, her anger rising rapidly. She reached for her wine glass, draining the contents far more rapidly than intended.

"More wine for the lady," he told a hovering servant.

Brianna accepted the glass, drinking deeply to restore a measure of serenity. Pleased by her outward calm, she offered Ryan a tentative smile. "You have scarcely touched your wine. Is it not to your liking after all?"

"I find my interests diverted to more intriguing areas of thought," he replied with dry amusement.

"Such as?"

"You."

Brianna drained her glass, motioning for a refill. "Me? Why do I merit such concern?"

"I have known many ladies in my time, but I must confess that none have captured my imagination quite so completely."

Brianna frowned, fortifying herself with yet another swallow from her glass. "I suggest you might exercise more control over your imagination," she cautioned. "I fail to see reason for concerning yourself with my life."

"Ah, but there is, sweet siren. After all, if memory serves me well, we shall soon be married, and it is a man's duty to attend the welfare and happiness of the lady in his life."

"My happiness is Lagniappe," she said, pausing as she remembered his words on the meaning of Lagniappe. "My plantation, of course," she hastily amended.

"So you say."

"More wine," she said, indicating the bottle was to remain when the glass was filled. "You may leave," she murmured to the servant. She glared silently at Ryan until the servant had withdrawn and they were alone in the large room.

"Not that I object," he began, "but don't you think you are imbibing a bit more than is wise?"

"Your objections are of no consequence, *M'sieur* Fleming." Defiantly, Brianna hurriedly drank the contents and poured another drink. She leaned forward, trying to get a clear image of the man before her. He seemed to waver slightly from side to side. A smile of satisfaction touched her moist lips. He obviously had little tolerance for the fruit of the grape, she decided.

It was a comforting thought and she leaned back in her chair, the tension flowing from her taut muscles. "I suppose we should discuss the details of our arrangement, *m'sieur.*"

Ryan rose, holding the stemmed crystal glass casually as he made his way to her end of the table.

"What are you doing?" she demanded.

"If we are to discuss business, I should think it would be preferable to keep it confidential." He gestured toward the pantry with a nod of his head. "It would never do for the servants to be privy to our words. They might repeat them in the hearing of wrong ears."

A frown furrowed Brianna's brow. "To whom?" she asked, blinking as the room seemed to blur before her eyes.

"The Earl of Tyrone," he said. "Surely you would not have him learn of your . . . ah . . . proposal."

"Once the deed is done, he shall have no say in my life."

"But I am another matter," Ryan said, his voice a low sensual whisper that sent shivers skittering across her sensitive nerves in silent warning.

He lowered his powerfully built frame into the chair next to hers, refilling his glass with slow deliberation. "To other matters," he said, lifting his glass in a mock salute.

"*M'sieur* Fleming," she began.

"Ryan," he said, interrupting her shaky train of thought.

"Ryan," she firmly repeated. His eyes held a look of frank appraisal. Brianna lowered her lashes, desperate to organize her confused thoughts in some semblance of order.

"Of course, I appreciate your assistance in reclaiming my rightful inheritance, and I'm sure you will be pleased with the reward I'm offering for your services."

Ryan continued to watch her, his face revealing none of his thoughts. She lifted her glass to her lips, the once-sharp taste now mellow as it soothed her parched mouth and relaxed her constricted throat.

"I'm certain you shall be most generous," he agreed with just a hint of a smile.

Brianna cleared her throat, forcing herself to continue the painfully awkward conversation. "Naturally, I would expect you to remain at Lagniappe for a suitable period after the earl departs."

"Naturally," he agreed.

She stiffened her spine, her delicate face etched in anger. "It would not look well should you disappear directly after the earl. I intend to live my life here, and I do not care to rouse the suspicious natures of my closest neighbors."

"A wise decision," he said, sipping slowly as he continued watching her.

"Must you do that?" she asked with growing exasperation.

"Do what, sweet siren?" He presented the picture of innocence, further fueling the anger flaring heatedly within her breasts.

"It isn't necessary to be quite so agreeable, and I would appreciate it if you quit referring to me as a sweet siren. You know perfectly well my name is Brianna. You only seek to annoy me."

The room seemed to be getting increasingly warm. Brianna wished she had thought to carry her fan. It was so difficult to breathe! She glanced about. The room appeared to be shrinking, yet she knew such a thing was impossible.

"But we are supposed to be in love, aren't we? A charming pet name would indicate deep affection." He leaned toward her, his hand capturing hers lightly as he raised it to his lips. He saluted each finger with a feathery kiss before he took the tip of her little finger in his mouth.

Brianna closed her eyes, trembling slightly as she felt the warmth of his lips tugging gently at the entrapped digit. "No . . . no one expects love to be a requirement. There are many marriages of convenience," she stammered, pulling free from his grasp.

"True," he conceded, his eyes boldly caressing her, "but ours must appear to be one of true love."

"Why?"

His smile mocked her as he patiently offered his explanation. "You are without benefit of proper male guidance," he reminded. "It would be difficult to expect a lady to be directed by any reason beyond the calling of her heart in such a matter as marriage."

Brianna bit down on her lower lip, unable to refute his words, though they galled her. It was true. Hadn't she been witness to more than one of her friends being pushed into marriage for the sole purpose of increasing family land holdings? Hadn't she frequently told her father that only her heart would decide her future?

"More wine?" he asked, lifting the crystal decanter. Before she could respond, he filled her empty glass. She became aware of the presence of servants as the bowls were removed, replaced by warmed plates filled with various seafoods.

Brianna stared mutely at her platter, her confusion increasing with each breath. By her side, Ryan sampled the artfully arranged fare, spearing the snowy crabmeat and deftly twisting his fork in a singular motion.

"Do you feel ill, Brianna?" he asked.

His question forced her back to the present. "I . . . I . . . No. I'm just not hungry," she lied.

"An appropriate sentiment for a lady about to enter into marriage," he answered.

Marriage? Oh, Lord, how could she have forgotten, even for a single moment? Panic threatened to overwhelm her as she contemplated her actions. Even worse was having to acknowledge that her pending wedding would be no different from those she had witnessed. Her fervent vow not to emulate them had been in vain. Her eyes sought the man she had so recently engaged in her ploy.

"Ryan?"

"Yes, my sweet . . ." He stopped, affording her a slow smile. "Brianna," he finished.

"Perhaps we've entered into this agreement too hastily."

"Possibly. Do you wish to reconsider?"

His response struck her as somewhat eager, pricking her sense of pride. "No. I just feel we should discuss more fully the pertinent details." Why did she feel so empty inside? Brianna wondered as she struggled to banish the discomfort.

"I'm listening."

Brianna frowned. It was clear he had no intention of making anything easier. She had no choice but to continue. "The wedding should be held quickly. Should the earl arrive unexpectedly, it is likely he would disallow the proceedings."

Ryan nodded in agreement, offering no words of advice or even encouragement. Brianna reached for her glass, needing some diversion as she attempted to refine the details of her plan. "I suppose you would have to be moved into the suite next to mine," she began.

"Won't the earl be suspicious that we have separate rooms? We are supposed to be in love," he added.

"Love has nothing to do with it. It is customary among certain social classes to provide separate quarters to allow a degree of privacy. He'll understand."

"Ah, yes. I suppose someone of your elevated station in life would consider it rather plebeian to express any true human emotions."

Brianna chafed beneath his scathing condemnation. She had never considered herself different from others. He had no right to brand her as cold, without feelings. "Emotion is not the issue. You forget yourself, *m'sieur*.

Our marriage is solely for the benefit of my guardian. A temporary alliance which shall richly reward us both if we succeed."

"And how do you intend to reward me, sweet siren?"

A fluttering sensation began in the pit of her stomach, building in intensity as she was impaled by the disquieting tone of his voice. "Er . . . ah . . . I'm prepared to compensate you for your efforts . . . within reason."

His eyes darkened. His smile was slow in coming, as though he contemplated rewards far removed from Brianna's knowledge.

The tip of her pink tongue darted out, licking at lips so suddenly dry as to be incapable of allowing any form of speech. A tiny whimper rose from her throat.

The room changed before her eyes until it resembled the dark mysterious swamplands of Lagniappe—forbidding, filled with unknown danger.

Steamed heat swirled about her, making it difficult to draw a deep breath, yet the darkened recesses of unexplored regions beckoned with promises of adventure and indescribable excitement.

Brianna rose from her chair, her stance unsteady as the room seemed to tilt at an impossible angle. "If you'll excuse me . . ." she began, unable to finish her apology.

Ryan rose, reaching out to her. "Bri."

Her legs seemed to melt beneath her slight weight. Only Ryan's quick action kept her from falling. She felt herself being lifted, the burden of walking being taken from her. With a soft sigh of gratitude, Brianna leaned her cheek against his hard chest and surrendered to the oblivion that enveloped her.

Ryan looked down into her face, so soft and appealingly innocent. "My sweet, sweet siren. I fear you know

not the consequences of your rebellious heart or the
tempting allure of the rare beauty you hold before the
eyes of your intended victim."

Refusing to dwell too deeply on his quietly spoken
words, Ryan carried her toward the stairs. She was soft
and yielding to his touch, remaining unaware of his presence as he headed toward her chambers.

"Gracious sakes, Massa Ryan. What has you done to
my missy?" Sudie demanded, seeing him striding down
the hallway.

"What you see is the result of her own doing, Aunt
Sudie. Now stop gawking and open this door," he commanded.

Sudie instantly responded to his demand, following
him into the room like an overly worried mother hen.
"What you mean by that, Massa Ryan?"

He laid her gently on the bed, pausing to briefly trace
the outline of her full mouth. Then he turned his attentions to the anxious Sudie. "She exhibited too great a
fondness for wine."

Sudie's eyes widened in disbelief. "That's not de way of
Miss Bri. Why, she ain't hardly ever had more than a
small glass of sherry in all her borned days, Massa
Ryan."

Ryan grinned at the woman. "Well, then, all her
borned days did not prepare her for tonight. I can assure
you, she made significant strides in catching up this evening."

"You shore you didn't ply my missy with them evil
spirits?"

"My word of honor, Aunt Sudie." Ryan offered the
wary woman a solemn look. "I even took the liberty of

suggesting to her that perhaps she should desist with the libations."

"Uh-huh. And these li . . . liba . . . sions done put her in a swoon?"

Ryan's easy laughter filled the room, earning him a warning look from the confused Sudie. He took a steadying breath, once more exercising self-control. "Sorry, Aunt Sudie. It's just that I hadn't given it much thought until you expressed yourself so delightfully."

"You shore do have a strange way o' sayin' things, Massa Ryan. I don't see nothin' funny 'bout Miss Bri goin' into a decline like this."

Ryan placed a strong hand on each of the woman's wide shoulders, grinning at her with amusement. "A libation is a sip of strong spirits, my friend. When one imbibes to excess, there is a tendency to get . . ." He paused, searching for a word he felt Sudie would understand, yet hesitant to blurt out Brianna's condition in a manner that would be certain to offend the dedicated woman before him. "There is a tendency to get a bit disoriented," he said.

"You mean she done got fallin'-down drunk on her own and done fell plumb out?"

Ryan nodded, afraid to trust his voice.

"Why, I do declare. I don't know what's come over that chile. She always did have a wild streak in her," Sudie confided. "That was de old massa's doin's, but she ain't never done nothin' like this before, not ever."

"In fairness to Brianna, I do believe she was somewhat nervous." Ryan patted the woman's back in consolation. "I'm sure with the attention you have given Brianna, she must have found it somewhat awkward to find herself dining alone with a man who is a relative stranger."

Sudie beamed up at him, her strong teeth glistening whitely against the smooth ebony satin of her skin. "Lawdy, Massa Ryan. You do has a way o' makin' things right again. I s'pect that's jest what happened. My missy was jest too shy about de presence of a man not her kinfolk."

"I'm glad we're in agreement, Sudie." Ryan walked toward the door, relieved by Sudie's acceptance. "I'll leave you now to attend your mistress." He cast a final glance at the sleeping woman.

He could think of many descriptions for Brianna Calhoun, but shyness was not among them. Passionate. Yes. That was a more fitting word to ascribe to her.

She was very much like her beloved plantation. Brianna Calhoun was "something extra," and Ryan knew she had to be his.

"Yas suh, Massa Ryan. Don't you worry 'bout a thing. Old Sudie'll see to gettin' missy tucked in all proper like, jest like she was a little baby."

Assured Brianna was in good hands, Ryan made his way down the stairway to the study. Now was the perfect time to inspect the books.

Amusement tickled the corners of his mouth as he thought of Brianna blissfully unaware of his actions. He pushed aside thoughts of the time he would have to reveal his full identity. Given her volatile nature, it was a scene upon which he found himself loath to speculate.

The massive door opened to his touch, making nary a sound. He made a mental note that the household was at least in excellent shape.

Settling himself at the oversized desk, Ryan began

opening one drawer after another until his quest was complete. He leaned back in the chair, eyeing the thick leather-bound ledger. It would be a long night.

Hours slipped by swiftly as he examined the neat print on the pages. The flickering of the nearly empty oil lamp drew his attention from his work.

Ryan pulled his timepiece from his pocket, surprised to find he had been reading for the entire night. With a sigh of satisfaction, he closed the bulky ledger and returned it to its rightful place.

At least he was reassured that Lagniappe was in no danger of falling apart in the absence of a guardian. He thought again of Brianna's words.

If she was telling the truth, then Brianna Calhoun could not be faulted for her objections to having a guardian thrust upon her.

He had never doubted her intelligence but he had not expected her to be so thoroughly well versed in the daily business of running a profitable holding. Yet the evidence was clear.

Ryan puzzled over his findings, finally deciding it would be best if he continued his charade a while longer. He told himself it would allow him more time to gather facts, but there was more to his delay than that. Much more, and it annoyed him to admit how easily and completely Brianna Calhoun had inserted herself into his otherwise carefree life. "Damnation," he grumbled.

Blowing out the lamp, Ryan left the room and made his way quietly through the darkened house to his own suite of rooms.

Once inside, he discarded his clothes and slipped beneath the crisp, clean sheets. He needed sleep, he told himself. This was his first day out of a sick bed. Obviously, he was overestimating the enigmatic temptress due to overexertion.

A good long rest, and everything would be restored to its proper perspective. That was all he needed. Ryan stretched, forcing himself to relax. "Women," he muttered in the predawn twilight.

Brianna winced, automatically turning away from the source of her pain.

"It's time to rise and shine, missy."

Brianna pulled her coverlet higher. "Go away, Aunt Sudie. I don't feel well."

"Most people don't when they has done li—ba—ted too much for their own good."

Slowly, with reluctance to face the blinding light that spilled across the bed from the eastern window, Brianna turned to face Sudie. "Libated?" she whispered. "Where did you ever hear such a word?"

"Old Sudie hears lots o' words, missy. But don't you worry none, 'cause I'se understands how a lady o' yore gentle upbringin' could get so in a fluster by a man's attentions when you ain't got a proper chaperon an' all."

Her face etched with a pained scowl, Brianna forced herself into a sitting position. "It is becoming annoying to have everyone continue to point out the absence of a chaperon in my life. I will not tolerate allowing the fact to be used to excuse my behavior."

Sudie chuckled, ignoring the rebuke as she continued to lay out Brianna's riding habit. "I s'pect since you is goin' out to ride, you best wear yore black again." She shook her head in dismay. "I shore enough will be glad when yore mournin' period done over. Ain't natural for a pretty young woman to be dressed in such things."

Ignoring the comment, Brianna reached for a cup of coffee from the nearby breakfast tray. She shared Sudie's sentiments but there were some traditions even Brianna refused to ignore. Despite her father's actions, she had loved him and her loyalty would not allow her to banish him from her heart and mind.

Her red-rimmed eyes caught sight of the gown she had worn the previous night. It lay across the chaise lounge by her window, silently mocking her prim opinions in the harsh light of day. "Ryan," she murmured, her throbbing head forgotten.

"Did you say something, missy?"

"Where is *M'sieur* Fleming?" she asked.

"He's still abed, I reckon. Leastways, I ain't heard no sounds comin' from his room."

Brianna felt a twinge of pleasure. So much for the silly foolishness of men being the strong protectors of fair womanhood. She was certain she had drank far more of the wine than Ryan had, yet she was the one awake. He, on the other hand, lay abed like a sluggard, surrendering meekly to the slight inconvenience brought about by drink.

She rose, fortified by her new knowledge and began her morning ablutions. "Let him rest. No doubt *M'sieur* Fleming feels rather weakened this morning," she advised.

"Maybe you is right, but he seemed fit enough when he come carryin' you in here last night."

Brianna turned toward the woman, her mouth pulled downward in a puzzled frown. "Ryan was here? In my private quarters?" she asked.

"He was. Someone had to tote you to bed. You was done gone to this here world. It was all that libatin' you did, even after the massa tried to tell you it wasn't good for you."

"Will you kindly stop parroting Master Ryan. And I wouldn't be so quick to consider his advice as expert if I were you."

"Well, missy, is you tryin' to tell me you was in the best of condition when he come a-haulin' you up that great long old staircase?"

"I don't remember." Brianna tried to recall the previous evening but all that lingered was the feeling inside her, the one that defied all explanation of why something so simple as a look, a smile, the brief touch of a man's hand, could render her weak with yearning.

"Guess not," Sudie agreed. "Anyways, after Massa Ryan done seen to yore needs, he left."

"Left? Where? He hasn't changed his mind about our arrangement, has he?" A trace of panic weaved its way through her rapid-fire questions.

"Don't get yourself all excited, chile. I didn't mean he left Lagniappe. He didn't go no further than yore daddy's study. Must of been in there most of de night, I guess. Toby said this morning he had to put a new wick in de desk lamp 'cause de old one done burned down nigh to nothin'."

Brianna's anger sparked, flaring to new heights as Sudie's words penetrated the dull ache of her head. He had been prying in her affairs, no doubt trying to ascertain just how great a reward he could obtain for the small service she had requested, she thought.

She was jolted from her thoughts as Sudie tightened

the laces of her corset. She gritted her teeth with determination, her mouth forming a firm line of resolve.

Brianna hurriedly donned her attire, eager to finish her normal duties of touring the fields. Then she would return and have a talk with Ryan Fleming . . . a very long talk, she decided.

"I'll be back in about two hours, Aunt Sudie. If *M'sieur* Fleming arises, have him wait for me. I have urgent matters I wish to discuss with him."

She started for the door, her mind already at work on shaping the verbal flaying she intended to give.

"Yes, missy, but what if de massa ain't woke up?"

"Then wake him." Her command was punctuated by the sound of the door slamming behind her as she left the room. "The very arrogance of the man," she grumbled under her breath. "I'll deflate his monumental ego quickly enough."

Chapter 6

Brianna rode toward the north fields, her body moving in harmony with her powerful mount. The sun felt warm on her face, the fog already receding before its strength. It hovered as a pale mist blanketing the ground, swirling lightly before it kissed the verdant grass a dewy farewell.

This had always been her favorite time of day. Everything was quiet and peaceful, but for once, Brianna couldn't find peace in the solitude. *It is all his fault,* she fumed. Ryan Fleming. What right did he have to invade her father's domain? She had not given him leave to consult the books, nor would she do so.

"Come on, boy." She pressed her knees to firm horseflesh, anxious to finish her duties and return to the main house. Ryan's face taunted her, urging her to greater speeds.

The sight of the fields filled her vision. Brianna slowed, forcing herself to exert a picture of tranquility as she approached the foreman.

"Morning, Miss Calhoun," her foreman greeted.

"Good morning, Mr. Rawlings." She eased her stallion to a halt. "How is everything going?"

"Fine. We're somewhat ahead of schedule, and if the weather holds a while longer, looks like we're going to get ourselves the best yield Lagniappe's ever had."

Brianna scanned the fields in silence. The sea of white swayed before her gaze as far as she could see, but patches of brown were growing as the cotton bolls were harvested. "How much have you sent to the gin?" she asked.

The foreman scratched his head, trying to recall the previous day's tally. "Best as I can figure, there was nearly twenty full sacks yesterday. Like I was telling Mr. Fleming, your new system is real encouraging to the darkies."

Brianna's smooth brow furrowed as she frowned down at the man. "Mr. Fleming?"

"Yes'm."

"When did you speak with him?"

"Why, not more than an hour past. He inspected everything here and seemed mightily impressed."

"Impressed, was he?" Her voice vibrated with agitation. "And just where is *M'sieur* Fleming now?"

Rawlings's smile disappeared into a look of worry. "I guess he rode to the mill. At least that's what he asked directions for. Something wrong?"

Brianna inhaled deeply, forcing her turbulent emotions into a semblance of control. "Not at all, Mr. Rawlings."

"I hope I didn't do anything wrong in talking with him. Mr. Fleming introduced himself as your intended and said he would be coming by regularly."

Intended! Good Lord, but that popinjay was actually suffering under the delusion that he would be master of Lagniappe, she thought with rising anger.

Rawlings continued watching her, his own face growing more anxious with each passing minute. "Miss Calhoun?"

The sound of her name brought her back to the present conversation. "It's fine, Mr. Rawlings. It's just that *M'sieur* Fleming recently suffered a grave injury and I am concerned that he not overtax his energies," she smoothly lied.

Rawlings beamed back at her. "I don't think you need bother yourself, Miss Calhoun. He looked right healthy to me. Sits straight in the saddle and seemed strong enough to handle the task."

Brianna nodded, turning her mount with a flick of her wrist on the reins. "Good day, Mr. Rawlings."

She spurred her horse forward toward the gin. Ryan might not appear quite so ready for any task when she finished with him, she thought, her rage flaming to newer heights.

The soft alluvial soil flew from beneath the horse's hooves as she galloped westward. How dare he talk of their arrangement to the people of Lagniappe! He had no right to make such announcements to anyone. One by one, she mentally added up the number of his transgressions. The list grew as the distance between her and her unsuspecting quarry lessened.

The weathered gin and warehouses loomed ahead. She squared her shoulders, clenching her teeth in determination as she approached the structure. Her father's favorite bay gelding was tied to a post. *He has gall.* Brianna's temper mounted, her body quivering in response to the rage that threatened to explode within her slender frame.

Dismounting, she walked into the dim recesses of the

busy building. Pausing to allow her eyes to adjust to the hazy light, she took a deep breath.

"Good morning, sweet siren." The deep voice reached out to caress her.

Brianna turned toward the sound, her eyes flashing with a fiery gleam that boded ill will. "It's morning, *m'sieur,* but at the moment, I fail to see anything good about it. What are you doing here?"

One dark brow arched slightly. The corners of his full mouth tilted upward in amusement. "I thought it time I made my presence known, and still the rumors and gossip that Sudie assures me are becoming larger with each passing day."

"You flatter yourself. Your presence is of no consequence, *m'sieur,*" she snapped.

"Perhaps not," he agreed, "but a gentleman cannot allow rumors to touch the reputation of a lady such as yourself."

Brianna felt her face warming, a blush stealing across her cheeks. "You are not a gentleman and I am quite capable of handling my own reputation," she answered, her voice trembling with emotion.

His smile remained in place, only adding to her annoyance. "Did you know a Mr. Arlington has been making inquiries to your foreman regarding your male guest?" he asked.

Brianna blinked, her lips parting slightly in surprise. "Jeffrey? But . . ." she began, stopping to chew on her bottom lip in consternation.

Ryan's smile disappeared. His eyes studied the bewilderment on her delicate face. A touch of annoyance rose within him. Jealousy? he wondered, brushing away the fleeting thought even as it formed. Frequently, he had reminded her to call him Ryan. Yet the familiar Jeffrey rolled off her tongue with ease. "But what?" he asked, his question taking on a hard edge.

"Nothing," she said with a slight shake of her head. Rawlings had made no mention of Jeffrey's visit. Brianna pondered the situation, unable to find a logical explanation. And why had Rawlings told Ryan? She looked up into his face. "You had no right to speak to Rawlings," she blurted out.

"I shape my own rights," he answered quietly.

"Lagniappe belongs to me," she reminded him. "I shall decide when any information shall be given." Her chin tilted forward in defiance. "A gentleman would never be so bold as to make public the knowledge of impending marriage until all the details have been finalized."

The lopsided smile returned, bringing a fluttering sensation to the pit of her stomach. "Ah, but as you were so quick to point out, I am not a gentleman. And if memory serves . . ." He leaned toward her, his voice dropping to a mere whisper, ". . . we have finalized our bargain."

The hazy light cast the sharp planes of his face in contrasting shadows. It seemed unbearably warm. Brianna felt perspiration slowly trickle between her breasts. It was difficult for her to breathe with any comfort.

Thoughts of the sparse cabin swirled through her mind, twining with the memory of his firm muscular body pressed close to her own. Brianna eased backward, wanting desperately to escape. *Mon Dieu. Why did I not think of this before?*

The possibility that he might choose to seal their bargain by claiming all his rights as a husband filled her mind with new thoughts . . . thoughts that kindled an answering response in the very fiber of her being.

Ryan slowly followed as she edged her way from the entrance back into the morning light. "We have only to set the date for the nuptials," he added.

"We . . . we haven't reached agreement on final payment," she stammered. Her heart raced within her breast, and silently she prayed he wouldn't hear it pounding.

His maddening smile deepened; his eyes grew dark as his gaze swept the length of her body. "Payment?" he softly queried. "I'm sure we will find suitable recompense . . . a payment which will be mutually satisfying to both of us," he said.

Brianna gasped, the heat within her bursting into full flame. "Sir! You . . . you forget yourself. Ours is a business arrangement. Do not bandy words with me. You will receive nothing but that which you earn."

His face mirroring his amusement, Ryan watched her turn abruptly and walk toward her horse. "And no doubt, sweet siren, I shall earn all I receive." He followed at a leisurely pace.

Strong hands circled her waist, then lifted her into the saddle with ease. For a brief moment, one hand rested lightly on her thigh before trailing the length of her riding skirt.

Despite the barrier of material, Brianna fancied she could feel the heat of his touch. She knew the need to distance herself from him. "My reins," she said.

He held the reins loosely in one hand. "Are you going somewhere?"

"That's really none of your concern." She tilted her chin outward, trying to deny the evidence of the emotions whirling through her body.

"But it is, sweet siren. Everything about you concerns me. We are soon to be wed and there is much I would know."

"Such as?"

"I would know the places that called the child to play, the special treasures gathered by the young girl who knew Lagniappe as her home." The soft gray of his eyes darkened, melting into the unrelenting blackness of the glittering pupils. "Most importantly, I would know the secrets which lie sheltered in the dreams of so beautiful a woman as yourself."

Brianna's flesh rippled in response to his words. Her fingers felt too weak to make use of the reins he handed her. She remained motionless as she watched him mount her father's gelding.

"Ride with me, Brianna. Show me the Lagniappe which holds your heart."

Throughout the morning they rode, speaking quietly at times and enjoying a companionable silence at others. To her delight, Ryan demonstrated an affinity for the land that matched her own.

He challenged her with questions and ideas that offered new directions of growth for the plantation. So involved did she become in one lively discussion, she failed to notice her surroundings.

"Is that the landing where you load your goods?"

She stared at the now-deserted area. Boards, weathered by time and the elements, were laid to form a small loading dock. An empty barge was anchored to the wooden pier by thick ropes.

Brianna pulled back on the reins, bringing her stallion

to a halt. It had been years since she had visited this part of the bayou, not since . . .

The past crowded in on her, hurtling her back in time until she could see herself once again at the tender age of seven. Oh, how she had loved to come here then.

It hadn't changed. The water moved at a lazy pace, lapping at the pilings that supported the narrow pier that swept over the water. Thick clumps of Spanish moss dripped from the gnarled limbs of ancient oaks.

"Brianna? Is something wrong?"

Wrong? The word struck her like an anvil, robbing her of breath. The past swooped over her, distancing her further from the man who watched, concern hardening his face with lines of worry.

"Don't get so close to the edge, Brianna. Come back."

Her mother's voice called to her from the past, showering her with memories of images long buried.

Her own child's laughter trilled with self-confidence. "I'm all right, Maman. Watch me." With the agility of youth, she had climbed atop the bales of cotton, moving higher . . . higher.

"Come down this instant, Brianna. You'll fall!"

She executed a pirouette, then laughed as she leapt from her lofty perch. Her feet touched the bale, then faltered as the cotton shifted beneath her weight. Her fingers brushed the coarse burlap covering. There was a piercing scream . . . her own. She clawed at the air, frightened by the panic that threaded her mother's shouts.

Her leg scraped the edge of the pier moments before Brianna landed in the water. "Maman!" she screamed.

Water rushed into her mouth and nostrils, burning her lungs. "Maman! Help me." Her arms flayed at the water as she tried to gain some purchase that would lift her from the icy liquid.

"I'm coming, baby."

The words roared through Brianna's mind, to lodge painfully in the region of her heart. A harsh sob wrenched free from trembling lips.

"Brianna. Answer me. What's wrong?" Ryan hurriedly dismounted to reach her side.

Through tear-filled eyes, she stared down at him. "She didn't come."

"Who?" He reached up to grasp her hand.

She sobbed, choking on the dark reminders. Hands had reached for her, grasping, clutching. In terror, she had fought. Her foot struck something solid, then she was free. "Maman!" she screamed.

"Stop it," Ryan commanded. "You're hysterical." He tried to get a grip on her arms, but she fought him as though he were the devil incarnate.

"She's dead! I killed her!" came her agonized response. Her stallion reared, spooking Ryan's mount in the process. Brianna pulled free of his grasp and set her horse to a frenzied gallop. The gelding gave a shrill whinny and lunged away before Ryan could stop him.

Ryan was left stranded, hurling impotent curses in the suddenly-empty land. He pulled the air deeply into his lungs. He had to reclaim his frightened mount as quickly as possible. Visions of Brianna's face, paled by terror, haunted him. He had to find her, had to chase away the pain that had so unexpectedly stripped her of all reason. He wanted to comfort her, to hold her in the safe embrace of his arms. She needed him. And God help him, he knew he needed her.

*   *   *

The hooves of her horse thudded against the packed earth, the measured repetition of sound gradually soothing her frayed nerves.

Numb with exhaustion, Brianna slowed the lathered animal to a canter, then an easy walk.

By the time she reached the main house, her tears had all been spent, the unbearable pain once more dismissed to the deepest recesses of her memory as her instinct for survival surfaced to offer her protection.

"You wants me to take him?"

For a moment, Brianna stared down at the dark face of the stable boy who had come to greet her. Her eyes burned with dryness; her face felt stiff where the wind had licked away her tears. "Thank you," she muttered as she allowed him to help her dismount.

Her energy drained, she moved toward the main house with slow wooden movements. Tired, so tired, she thought.

"Lawd, but I is glad to see you, missy." Aunt Sudie's voice pulled her from the last lingering touch with the past. Brianna frowned.

"You are?"

"I shore is." Sudie leaned closer, lowering her voice. "You has company waiting in the parlor."

"I . . . I don't feel up to entertaining anyone. Give them my regrets."

"That won't do no good. It's that Massa Arlington. And this time he done brung that she-devil sister of his with him."

"Ivy's here? I thought she was in Europe."

"I don't know where she was, but right now she is

sitting in your parlor. You has got to go in there. I ain't going to be listening to the both of them."

"All right. You take some refreshments to them while I freshen up a little. I won't be long," she promised.

Brianna stood at the door, inhaling deeply to brace herself for the ordeal ahead. Forcing her lips into the semblance of a smile, she entered the parlor, interrupting the heated conversation in progress. Her presence brought a quick halt to the quarrel, as brother and sister stared at her as though she were the intruder. Ivy was the first to regain her composure.

"Oh, my dear Brianna," she cooed as she approached with outstretched arms. "I can't tell you how sorry I was to learn of your father's tragic demise."

"Thank you, but Papa suffered a lingering illness and I think he looked on death as more a blessing than a tragedy."

"No doubt. Do come sit down and tell me all about it." Ivy coaxed Brianna toward the settee, making sympathetic noises with her tongue.

"There isn't much to tell," Brianna answered once they were seated.

"Suppose you tell me about your newest patient then. I'm sure that would be interesting."

Ryan. She had completely forgotten about him.

"I would be more interested in learning about the Earl of Tyrone," Jeffrey interrupted.

"Why?" Brianna met his scowl with a bland smile.

"That should be obvious, Brianna. This entire business of your father appointing some stranger to oversee your inheritance seems rather mysterious."

"In truth, Jeffrey, the idea that Papa would deem a guardian necessary is a puzzle to me." She heard the soft opening and closing of the front door, but ignored it as her hurt and anger at her father's actions surfaced once more. "Throughout Papa's illness, I have managed Lagniappe by myself. I had thought he would see fit to allow me to continue. The land . . . the house . . . everything belongs to me anyway. Why should another control what is mine?"

"Bravo, my sweet," the deep sonorous voice cheered from the doorway.

She glanced toward her company, noting quickly their reaction to his unannounced entry. Jeffrey's face clearly evidenced his displeasure. More unsettling was the unmistakable look of interest that touched Ivy's porcelain features.

Brianna gave a small gasp as she felt the firm touch of his hands on her shoulders. Her flesh tingled in response. Waves of heat rushed over her, suffusing her in unbearable warmth as she felt his lips boldly brush the nape of her neck. "Ryan," she pleaded, her voice a whisper of sound.

"But of course, my sweet siren. Who else but your intended would greet you with such adoration?" His words were a silken flow, but instinctively, Brianna grasped his subtle warning not to deny his right to such open possession. "We'll talk later," he whispered as he relinquished his hold.

"Intended?" Ivy stared at the couple in open shock. "You never breathed a word, Brianna."

"How could she?" Jeffrey snapped. "You haven't stopped talking long enough for anyone to say a word."

Ryan made his way around the settee, standing by

Brianna's side, his bronzed face set in lines of amusement.

Brianna clenched her teeth together. His face held a mixture of unasked questions. If only she could understand him, she thought. Ever so neatly, he had placed her in an impossible situation. She must make public their position, or now deny it and be branded a common trollop before the sunset.

She could think of no explanation to extricate herself from his careless comment and had no delusions about the possibility that Jeffrey and Ivy would maintain a discreet silence.

Brianna found herself watching closely as Ryan welcomed Jeffrey and offered polite compliments to an entranced Ivy. Carelessness was not a trait she could believe Ryan possessed. He had deliberately made the announcement, but why? she wondered.

Only when he seated himself by her side did she become aware of a faint sheen of exertion about him.

"You appear tired. Have you forgotten your recent illness?"

Anger flickered in his eyes then disappeared as he seemed to study her look of innocent concern. He offered her a smile, its gentleness providing her with a peculiar sense of well-being. "Perhaps, but now that I'm with you, I'm certain my strength will quickly return."

She heard Jeffrey's voice penetrate the soft veil of serenity that settled about her. Ryan's hand found hers, covering it in a warmth that felt protective. She offered a tentative smile.

"I find it difficult to believe Brianna is engaged. We've been neighbors since her birth and I know you were never a guest at Lagniappe before *M'sieur* Calhoun's recent demise."

Brianna winced inwardly at Jeffrey's tone of disapproval, but the blunt words had no effect on Ryan.

"Brianna and I have only recently met, but you might say we're both people given to decisive action. In some ways, I feel I know her far better than anyone else."

Brianna gasped audibly at the boldness of his words. It seemed impossible that he would offer such an obvious reminder of their first meeting. The teasing light of silver that danced in his eyes left no doubt in her mind of his thoughts.

"Ryan, don't tease my friends so. They might take your words of jest to be serious. Such a thing would be unforgivable."

He scanned her face, his thick fringe of lashes shielding his thoughts as his gaze came to rest upon the gentle swell of her cleavage.

"Sorry, my sweet siren. I shall refrain from further explanations." One corner of his mouth twitched slightly before easing upward in a lopsided smile.

Her fingers fairly itched with the desire to slap his arrogant face. *How dare he openly mock me!* "I'm sure Jeffrey and Ivy would find it a terribly boring story." She ground out each word with terse precision, her look silently conveying her wrath. Ryan offered a slow smile in return.

Even in her state of mounting anger, Brianna found herself drawn to him. It was impossible. She positively loathed him. He was arrogant, incredibly brazen in his behavior, yet . . .

"I'm not at all bored," Ivy protested, her words bringing a sharp edge to Brianna's turbulent emotions.

"I'd be interested in learning a few more details myself," Jeffrey added.

Ryan shifted, resting his arm across the back of the settee. His fingertips caressed the back of Brianna's neck, sending shivers of anticipation chasing the length of her spine. "Do you wish to satisfy their curiosity, my sweet siren, or shall I?" he teased, his voice a mere whisper of sound that brushed across the sensitive lobe of her ear.

"Ryan, please." With a look, she pleaded with him for silence.

He raised his hand toward her face, tracing the outline of her lips with a single finger. "Brianna is correct. There are some memories too beautifully fragile to share with others."

"Oooh. I must confess I had never thought little Brianna's life was one which could possibly interest me." Ivy stopped, smiling coyly until she was assured she had her companions undivided attention. She leaned forward, affording Ryan a clear view of her generous endowments. "However, your words pique my curiosity."

"Not nearly as much as your presence piques mine," Ryan answered smoothly.

Brianna made a tiny choking sound in her throat. Ryan squeezed her hand in silent conspiracy. The small action relaxed her, banishing her earlier tension. This was the Ryan Fleming she knew, the one who parried words with the skill of a duelist with a sword.

She rewarded him with a dazzling smile, grateful that Ivy had unwittingly made herself the victim of his lethal charm.

Jeffrey's untimely intrusion prevented Brianna the pleasure of watching Ryan match wits with the woman who had so frequently exasperated Brianna during their lifetime as neighbors.

"We didn't come here to listen to flattering small talk."

"Why did you come, Arlington?"

Jeffrey gave a nervous cough in the face of Ryan's blunt query.

"I'm becoming concerned that Brianna's guardian has not arrived. He was expected some two to four weeks past. Isn't that right, Brianna?"

"I can't say for sure. Your information is probably more detailed than mine. *M'sieur* Westman seems quite willing to confide in you regarding my affairs."

"Westman? Your attorney?" Ryan asked, his full mouth turning into a grim frown.

Brianna nodded, wishing she had never mentioned Westman.

"Mr. Westman seems to be quite free with privileged information for an attorney," he observed.

Jeffrey stiffened at the thinly disguised insult.

"See here, Fleming. Oliver Westman served as the Calhoun attorney for years. That was Richard Calhoun's choice. When he died, it was only natural for Oliver to seek my advice."

"Why?"

"Belle Terre Plantation borders the Calhoun property to the north. We are neighbors. Brianna, Ivy, and myself grew up together. To anyone of reason, it would seem perfectly logical that I would be the one most likely to offer protection to Brianna."

"Do you feel in need of protection, my sweet siren?"

Invoking the use of his pet name for her had the desired effect. Ryan watched color flame to her cheeks. Her eyes glittered with indignation. He flashed a smile of amusement, pleased at her show of defiance. Whatever ghosts had visited her soul at the bayou were gone now, but he vowed to find out the reason for her earlier fears.

"I do not need anyone's protection." She bit back the urge to scream. Even to her own ears, the assertion lacked conviction. It was one thing to have Ivy fall prey to his Irish blarney, quite another to become a victim herself. She lowered her head, but not before she caught a glimpse of pleasure sliding across the strong planes of the man beside her.

Ryan directed his attention to Jeffrey. "You heard it for yourself. Miss Calhoun feels capable of taking care of herself, making her own decisions. The next time you see Westman, you might convey that information to him. I'm sure he will be relieved to know he need not concern himself with Brianna's welfare any longer."

"It is obvious you know nothing of our way of life, sir. This is the South. We do not burden ladies with matters of business. We prefer to pamper them, cherish them as the beautiful treasures they are. No man would turn his back on offering a lady his protection and still call himself a gentleman."

"Then consider the matter from a different viewpoint." Ryan's voice held an edge of steel that sent shivers down Brianna's spine. "As Brianna and I will soon be married, there is no longer a need for anyone to offer anything. Should she find herself in need of protection, I shall reserve the honor for myself."

Silence hung heavy in the room. For once, Brianna felt no desire to voice her opinion of self-reliance. She prayed Jeffrey's arrogance would not blind him to the quiet challenge of Ryan's words.

Cautiously, she risked a glance in Jeffrey's direction,

barely holding back a groan. His stance seemed less than stable as he concentrated on refilling his empty glass. Why must he drink so much? she wondered. She focused her attention on Ryan. His dark face held a look of disdain, bordering on disgust. With relief, she realized he would not take umbrage at the comments of a man so obviously intoxicated.

"Marriage." Jeffrey slurred the word, stretching it to almost comical length. "That is another problem."

One corner of Ryan's mouth tilted upward. "An interesting choice of words, Arlington."

Jeffrey bestowed a blank look on him, unable to follow the conversation any further.

"Do you consider marriage in general to be a problem, or are you suggesting that marriage to Brianna, in particular, will be a problem?"

Abruptly, Ivy laughed. The shrill sound grated on Brianna's nerves. Her temper flared. How dare he suggest she was a problem! "Swine." She spewed the accusation is a low, desultory tone.

He favored her with a sublime smile. "Welcome home, my lovely siren of the sea."

He watched with growing fascination as her mouth parted, enthralled by the full softness of lips that seemed to beg with forbidden hunger. He sought to spark her spirit, to return her to her former habit of protective defense. Now he realized that he faced a new and different kind of problem. Who would protect him from this siren's sweet song?

Chapter 7

She stood on the veranda, only her strong will holding her shattered nerves intact. Never had any afternoon in her life seemed so unbearably long.

How could Ryan maintain such incredible composure? she wondered. He had exceeded the most lenient boundaries of proper decorum she could imagine. But then, why not? she reminded herself. He was responsible for the fiasco that marked this day.

"How could you?" Brianna asked, waving and forcing a stiff smile for the benefit of their departing guests.

"How could I what, my sweet?"

"You know very well what. You implied to Jeffrey that I would . . . would . . ."

"Would what?" Ryan stared at her, his eyes boring into hers, perplexed by her growing anger.

"You know very well what, you rogue . . . you cad . . . you bounder."

Brianna stormed back into the house, furious that he had spoken with such open boldness to the Arlingtons. "Lord, but it will be all over Mississippi, even up to the Delta, before those two stop talking."

"Fine. So I'm a rogue, a cad, a bounder. Now, what has sparked you to such a state of fiery anger?" he asked, following her into the house.

"You told them I would . . . *submit!* Submit to the likes of you. Never! I've a good mind to toss you back on the beach and let you flounder about the seas like so much flotsam!"

Brianna headed for the stairs, her voice rising loudly to echo through the great foyer. Ryan followed close behind.

"I think I'm beginning to understand."

"Are you now? I thought I would perish of embarrassment when you made that horrible and totally untrue statement."

"Why was it so horrible? He impugned my honor, called me a liar when I said we would marry. I could have called him out for that."

"He only questioned that I would enter into so hasty an arrangement."

Ryan caught her wrist, halting her progress as he turned her toward him. "Not enter into," he corrected as he kissed her forehead. "He said you would not submit to such an arrangement." He punctuated his words with a feathery kiss to each cheek.

"Ryan . . ." It was a rasp of sound, the effort straining her throat.

"I merely defended myself by assuring him we will wed." Warm lips grazed hers in brief exploration. "And what you submit to . . ." Another kiss pressed to the velvet soft column of her neck made him pause. He savored the taste of her flesh, the smell of roses that seemed to cling to her. ". . . will most definitely remain our private affair," he finished. "Does submission bother you so greatly? I thought I was rather clever," he teased. "Your friend, Miss Arlington, seemed enchanted."

"Don't speak to me of Ivy Arlington. I was there. I saw. She was practically drooling at the mouth. There were a few brief moments when I thought she would fling herself at you without giving a thought to pride or decency."

"Is that the cause of your frustration, sweet siren? Does it bother you that another woman can show a desire for passion when you force your own to remain hidden?"

"How dare you!" she shrieked, raising her free hand and swinging in an arc toward his face. "Owh!"

Ryan caught her wrist, pressing it down to her side. He stepped up onto the stairway, his face but a breath away from her own. "Never try to strike me again, my darling Brianna." He spoke with a deceptive calm, but there was no mistaking the warning in his silken tones. "I am not like the hapless sailors of Greek myths. I do not easily surrender to my own destruction."

She matched his firm resolve, not caring about the consequences. "And I . . . *M'sieur* Fleming, will never *submit*. Now, if you will release me, I find myself weary and wish to retire to my rooms." Brianna forced herself to maintain a direct gaze into his face, a mask of cold civility in place over her delicate features.

A pained shadow crossed the deep gray of his eyes, lending an ebony cast that caused her to tremble within his grasp.

"Do not quake, sweet siren. I will never give you cause to fear, for there are far more wondrous things I would teach you." His thumbs rotated at the pulse of her wrist with a hypnotic persistence. Temptation called and the urge to answer flooded her being.

She could feel her resistance ebbing as surely as the evening tide, leaving her soul slick and naked, like the wet sand beneath a pale moon. She basked in the silvery light, moonbeams blending with heated flesh to leave her feeling languorous and submissive, despite her earlier protests.

Brianna felt his hands release her. A small whimper rose within her throat. Her lips parted in silent entreaty as his head bent lower. Oh, God, how she wanted him.

She closed her eyes, waiting until his lips touched hers. A kaleidoscope of color burst behind her eyes. The moon dissolved, replaced by a dazzling ball of fire. His kiss was a July-hot sun, his fiery touch searing her flesh, branding her as his when his mouth slanted across her lips. Waves of heat shimmered, twining around her nerves, soaking into her taut muscles to melt the last vestiges of her resistance. *Oh, God. What is he doing to me?*

Slowly, he eased away, his eyes surveying the depth of confusion mirrored within her own as sable lashes fluttered upward. "Perhaps you should rest now. Tonight we will talk," he promised. "There are many things of which we must speak." He studied her face with fierce intensity but could find no sign of the earlier trauma she endured. *Is it possible that she doesn't remember?*

Numbed, Brianna could only nod in agreement. Without a word, she turned, fleeing up the stairs, not daring to look backward for fear of finding him watching her. She couldn't bear it if his face held a look of mockery. Not now.

Reaching her room, she slipped inside, grateful to be alone. Her fingers traced the path of his lips.

It was inconceivable that one kiss could so profoundly touch her. It wasn't as though Ryan were the first. There had been others, but their touch was chaste, almost apologetic and hesitant. Ryan was no comparison.

There was no apology in his action. He had known what he wanted and had taken it without a single protest. *Submit? No wonder he had been nonplussed by the tirade. He had known.*

Tears stung her eyes. The inevitable, the unthinkable, had happened. She was in love, and for the first time in her life, Brianna Calhoun found herself without a single answer.

Assured that the mercurial lady of Lagniappe was indeed headed toward her quarters, Ryan set his own direction toward Richard Calhoun's study. There was a great deal of work to be done.

Closeting himself behind the polished doors, he put his mind to the task ahead. Methodically, he began checking the ledgers. The neatly placed entries in Brianna's hand told him more than he had dreamed possible. Every column balanced, every transaction made on behalf of Lagniappe for the past two years was meticulously documented.

He reached for a smaller journal, one of particular interest. A smile touched his mouth, erasing the harsh lines on his face. This was the most interesting aspect he had found to date. Brianna Calhoun not only valued her own freedom and independence, but she also had a high regard for the freedom of others, particularly the slaves of her beloved Lagniappe. He scanned the entries, impressed by her ingenious methods of determining values.

Aug. 1, 1856: Final indebtedness paid by Tobias Simpson. Freedom papers duly filed with Jackson Courthouse. Purchase price: 7/30/26, 300 bank notes. Value of service as house slave: 10 Bank notes each calendar year of service.

The door eased open, drawing Ryan's attention. "Come on in," he ordered. Sudie's round face appeared, then her ample frame, as the door swung on its hinges.

" 'Scuse me, Massa Ryan, but I done brung you a mite of food. I should think a big man like you would feel plumb weakened with hunger by now. Toby done told me you left 'fore de sun was up and ain't had nigh on a bite of food."

"Thank you, Aunt Sudie. I do believe you have the power to read my mind."

Sudie gave a pleased chuckle, her face wreathed in a broad smile as she ambled forward to place the tray on the desk. "Ain't no powers needed. Men jest naturally takes to eatin' real frequent."

"And ladies?" he asked.

Sudie made no pretense of not understanding. She met the question with forthright style. "Miss Bri done took up more bad habits than she should. That gal eats with indecent relish."

Ryan joined her amused laughter. "I would never have guessed. She is rather fragile in appearance."

"Don't set too much store in appearance where she's concerned, Massa Ryan. Miss Bri ain't always what she seems."

"On that, we are in complete agreement." Ryan poured himself a cup of tea. "Will you join me, Aunt Sudie?"

"Lawd no, Massa Ryan. I can't do that!"

"And why not? You're a free woman of color."

Sudie's eyes grew round, her mouth parting in stunned amazement. "You shore does has a powerful memory. I never knowed nobody listened to what's I got to say that good."

"I always make it a policy to listen when someone has something interesting to say." He gestured toward the comfortable wing chair across from the desk. "Sit down, Aunt Sudie. I have a few questions I think you can answer."

Cautiously, Sudie obeyed, her gaze never wavering from his face. "I'se sittin', but I ain't goin' to answer no questions what might hurt Miss Bri. Like you knows, I'se a free woman of color, and I don't have to do what I don't wants."

"Relax, Aunt Sudie. I'm not going to hurt Brianna." Ryan leaned back in the chair, pressing his fingertips together to form a steeple. "When I was out this morning, I chanced to meet Brianna. She gave me the grand tour. It was most enjoyable, until we arrived at the bayou where the barge is moored."

At the mention of the loading dock, Sudie's eyes widened. Abruptly, she rose.

"Is something wrong, Aunt Sudie?"

"Naw suh. I'se got lots o' work needs doin'. Old Sudie ain't got time to sits around listenin' to you spinnin' no yarns."

Ryan leaned forward, eager to learn more. "What makes you think it's a yarn? It could be the truth."

"Naw suh." She shook her head with vehemence.

"Why not?" His voice hardened with determination. "Why can't it be the truth, Sudie?"

" 'Cause my baby don't go there."

"Why not? It's rather picturesque. I would think it just the kind of place she would enjoy."

"I tell you, she don't go there, not since her . . ."

"Go on," he encouraged.

"I done said all I is goin' to say, Massa Ryan. The past is done gone."

"And Brianna's memory of the past. Is it gone, too?"

Sudie collapsed back into the chair. Hiding her face behind work-worn hands, she began moaning and weeping. "Don't be askin' no more questions, Massa Ryan. My baby done seen enough pain and misery. Don't go doin' it. It ain't right. It jest ain't right."

He waited until the harsh sobs quieted before he spoke. "It's all right, Aunt Sudie. I didn't mean to upset you. I'm only trying to learn more about Brianna, that's all. I want to understand her."

"She's got a kind and lovin' heart, Massa Ryan. That's all that counts."

His fingers tapped the cover of the plantation ledger. A smile touched his lips. "Let me ask you another question." Seeing the fear on her face, he hastened to explain. "Strictly business questions. After all, I am her guardian and it is my duty to manage her affairs."

"Affairs? Miss Bri is a gently bred lady. She ain't had no affairs!" Sudie's fear yielded to righteous indignation.

Ryan raised a broad hand, shielding the smile of amusement that could not be contained in the face of Sudie's outraged protest. "I refer to business dealings, Aunt Sudie."

The woman leaned back, relaxing somewhat upon hearing the brief explanation. "I jest don't want no mistakes."

"Nor do I." Ryan looked down at the journal, scanning the various entries. "Tobias Simpson. Is that Toby, the butler?"

Sudie nodded, her face reflecting her uncertainty as to where the questioning was leading.

"It appears several slaves have been provided papers proclaiming them to be free." Once more, the woman acknowledged his words with a nod. "When did Mr. Calhoun take to his bed?"

Sudie's mouth puckered, her smooth ebony brow furrowed as she tried to remember. "Near as I can 'members, it was most of two Christmases ago."

"And Brianna has been the only one making decisions since that time?"

"She has." Sudie's face took on sullen lines, her black eyes watching him as though he were a snake, near ready to strike.

"Since then, not only have no additional slaves been purchased, it appears Brianna has released nearly twenty slaves which were the property of Lagniappe."

"What Miss Bri done ain't illegal, is it?"

Ryan shook his head, offering the woman a reassuring smile. "Not at all."

"Then you ain't all het-up mad at Miss Bri?"

"No reason to be. According to the records, even though there is less human property at Lagniappe, the profits have steadily increased over the last year and a half." He watched Sudie, studying her reaction with a quiet intensity. "Would you have any idea as to why this is so?"

" 'Course I does. Don't matter none where you from or what color yore skin is, everybody always finds de strength to do more when they has gots a stake in things."

"And what might the stake be for the people of Lagniappe?" he asked, leaning forward in curiosity.

"Freedom. Miss Bri done give her word that she'll lets everyone on Lagniappe earn their freedom. That's a powerful stake, for shore."

"Very powerful," Ryan agreed. "What happens when the slaves earn their freedom? If I remember correctly, you said Mr. Westman refused to pay wages after Calhoun died. Yet you remained. Did the others leave right away?"

"Naw suh. They is still here. At least, most of them is."

"Here? Where?"

"Lapniappe is a good-sized plantation, Massa Ryan. There is a whole section to de west what never been put to use. Miss Bri done sets it aside for de buildin' of places for de folks what wants to keep workin' here at Lagniappe."

"What about the money owed them?"

"They knows Miss Bri will makes everythin' all right jest as soon as she can. Good Lawd willin'," she added.

"And how can they be so certain, Aunt Sudie?"

"Miss Bri." Sudie smiled, her ample breasts seeming to swell with maternal pride when Brianna's name was spoken. "Miss Bri is loved by everyone on Lagniappe. She's what makes this home, and I s'pects most of those what gets freed stays on 'cause it would be plain too hurtful to say goodbye to her. She done gives her word, and that's good enough for most folks."

Ryan gave an answering smile. "I can see where leaving Brianna might prove somewhat difficult," he admitted.

"Does that mean when you marries with Miss Bri, you is goin' to make it permanent?"

"Has anyone ever accused you of too much curiosity?" he asked.

Sudie gave a deep chuckle, her ponderous breasts heaving with the action. "Miss Bri says I is downright meddlesome, she does."

"Well, it is a comfort to know Brianna and I agree on at least one thing," he said, giving a teasing wink to soften his words.

"Lawdy, Massa Ryan, you shore is a caution. It done looks like Miss Bri has near enough bit off more than she can chew. I s'pect I is goin' to enjoy raisin' them young 'uns." Sudie hauled herself up from the chair, shuffling toward the door.

"Young 'uns?"

"Yas suh. Young 'uns. You knows what I mean. De sweet little babies what you and Miss Bri is goin' to make." The stunned look that touched his face filled her with laughter that refused to be denied. The sound burst forth, bubbling with pure joy. "Land's sakes alive, I shore enough figured you to be a man of de world. Thought you'd know all there is to know 'bout babies . . . leastways, de makin' of them."

"Get out of here, woman, before I start looking for ways to refute those damn freedom papers you're so proud of," Ryan said, trying his best to assume a stern pose.

Sudie's continued laughter as she departed showed her lack of concern.

Babies? The thought of being a father had never really occurred to him before. Ryan rose, walking toward the well-stocked bar. He needed something a lot stronger than Sudie's herb tea. Pouring himself a generous amount of bourbon, Ryan downed it in one swallow. He refilled his glass and returned to the desk.

What would it be like to father a child by Brianna Calhoun? he wondered. He indulged himself in a stiff swallow of the amber liquid, forcing himself to relax as it burned its way down into his still-empty stomach.

"Damnation." It was much more than he had bargained for. His eyes caught sight of the journal. Freedom. Love of freedom. That was something he could understand.

His lands, complete with castles that had stood for centuries, meant little to him. He had often left them in the hands of servants while he had chosen to sail the seas. His vast wealth continuously mounted through his shrewd investments, but held no meaning beyond the challenge that contributed an ever-increasing bounty to his coffers. Freedom was what he valued. The rightful choice of every man to determine the direction his feet would trod. That was what life was about.

That was the reason he had hesitated to allow this slip of a woman to coerce him into anything as confining as the state of matrimony.

And what of women? he wondered. Brianna? Her actions showed how greatly she valued freedom for others. And herself? His memory was jolted by recollection of her angrily flung gauntlet. Never submit, she had said. "That's it."

Ryan allowed himself a moment to savor the feeling of satisfaction. Now he understood. Brianna was her father's daughter.

Richard Calhoun had shown the same defiance toward the Crown. His protest of the harsh treatment meted out to the people of Ireland had brought swift retribution.

Quick thinking had allowed Calhoun to transfer his vast properties into Jason Fleming's name before he left the country.

For years, Jason held them in sacred trust until Calhoun had been proven innocent of treason and it was safe to transfer title back to his old friend, Richard Calhoun, Earl of Kenney.

Only on his deathbed had Jason revealed the true story to Ryan. Calhoun was not a traitor. He had happened on the group of conspirators on his way home from a party. They quickly ran, but not before Calhoun recognized them. That had been his only crime against the Crown.

When questioned by authorities, Calhoun had steadfastly refused to name a single man among them. This led to the cowardly charges that cost Calhoun his life in Ireland.

"But he forged a life here," Ryan muttered, his thoughts turning toward the willful woman who would soon be his wife. "Perhaps his gains far outweighed his losses."

Brianna's words returned, reminding him of their brief altercation. *"I will never submit. Never!"*

That had been her vow. Ryan closed his eyes, reliving the feel of her soft lips on his. He could still see the slight swollen look, the dewlike creaminess of her flesh and the misty, slightly confused pools of jade that had unflinchingly met his own appreciative appraisal.

The proud father clearly lived on in the heart of his daughter. It was an undeniable fact. Unfortunately, it appeared pride was not their only common bond. Just as Calhoun's life held secrets, so did Brianna's. But this time would be different, he vowed. He would uncover the secret locked deep within her. This time there would be no reason for a Calhoun to flee a way of life held dear.

A soft rapping at the door interrupted his private musings. "Come in," he said.

" 'Scuse me, Massa, but de Arlingtons has returned," Toby announced. "Massa Arlington wishes to speak with you."

"Very well. Send him in."

A few seconds later, Jeffrey Arlington entered the study.

"Sorry to barge in on you, Fleming, but it seems Ivy and I have had a bit of bad luck." Jeffrey remained standing, although he appeared unsteady on his feet and his face held a pasty pallor.

"How's that?"

"We hit a blasted chuckhole in the road and broke a wheel on our carriage. I'm afraid I had to leave poor Ivy at the scene and return for some help."

"I take it the servants are seeing to repairs."

"Oh, yes. That old man Brianna insists on keeping has sent a buggy to fetch Ivy back here. He assured me Lagniappe has a fine wheelsmith who can make virtually any repairs needed." Jeffrey leaned forward, lowering his voice. "Of course, you know how these simpleminded blacks are. They tend to exaggerate everything."

Jeffrey's face mirrored his obvious disgust. "I have no idea why she keeps that fossil. He outlived his usefulness years ago. That kind of foolishness will soon come to an end. Plantations don't make money on sentimentality." He rocked forward, then caught his balance.

"Sit down, Arlington, before you fall down."

"Believe I will." Jeffrey collapsed in a chair.

"Toby seems both proficient and dedicated to his position in the household. In fact, since my arrival at Lag-

niappe, I've found everyone I've met to be quite knowl-
edgeable and efficient at their duties. I see no merit to
your complaint."

"Ah, well, I expect that's Brianna's doings. I've told
her she will get herself in trouble with the local constabu-
lary if she's not more careful." Jeffrey eyed Ryan's half-
empty glass, his tongue licking at his lips.

"Care for a drink, Arlington?"

"I do believe I could use a little refreshment if it's not
too much trouble."

"Not at all." Ryan rose, returning to the bar to pour
himself another drink and provide his unwanted guest
with one. "Is bourbon all right, or would you care for
something else?" he asked.

"Bourbon's just fine. Straight, if you please."

Without comment, Ryan filled the glasses, returning to
resume his place behind the desk before he spoke again.
"I'm curious, Arlington. How will the servants being
intelligent and skilled create problems for Brianna?"

"We have laws here in Mississippi. It's illegal to teach
the darkies an education."

"A trade at increasing the profits of Lagniappe hardly
qualifies as an education, does it?"

"Not usually, but haven't you noticed anything different about the slaves on Lagniappe?"

"You'll have to forgive me, but I'm afraid our situation in Ireland doesn't use this particular type of labor."
Ryan leaned forward, offering a tight smile of encouragement. "Perhaps you can enlighten me as to the differ-
ences."

"The people here . . . well . . ." Jeffrey paused, trying
to put his thoughts into words. "At Belle Terre," he said,
beginning anew, "I have a foreman who handles the

populace. Now, Roderick has a great many years' experience in plantations and he knows the only way to get enough work out of these people is to keep a sharp eye and a handy whip." He stopped, availing himself of the bourbon, not pausing until the glass was drained. Ryan offered a refill, waiting until Jeffrey was ready to continue.

"No argument? Perhaps you'll learn, old man," Jeffrey said with a tone of smug satisfaction.

"Oh, I intend to learn everything I can. Please continue."

"Have you had a chance to meet Rawlings?"

Ryan nodded, his introduction to Lagniappe's foreman clear on his mind. "As a matter of fact, I met him this morning. Seems a likable fellow."

"That's just my point. He's likable. Certainly not the type to be able to handle those heathens if they decide to stir up trouble."

"And do they frequently stir up trouble?"

Jeffrey shook his head from side to side. "Not too often, but once in a while some young buck gets real wild and that seems to set all of them to acting crazy. Only recently, the owner of Willowgreen had a problem with one of his best breeding bucks. Went plumb loco trying to bust loose. Attacked the foreman, he did."

"And do you know the reason for his behavior?" Ryan chose his words with care, not wishing to rouse any undue suspicion.

"Fargus, the owner of Willowgreen, had a chance to make a good profit on selling one of his female slaves and he took it. Seems that buck had a thing for her or something and when he found out she had been sold, he just went crazy."

Ryan's hand slid across the journal he had been studying. With casual indifference, he closed the cover and continued probing. "What happened?"

"What happened? Why, Fargus did the only thing he could do. He hung him, naturally."

"Naturally," Ryan echoed, his voice revealing none of his true feelings.

"If something like that were to happen here, Rawlings couldn't handle it. He's much too soft, I tell you. Of course, Brianna won't listen. But then, women can't be expected to have a head for business, now, can they?"

Ryan gave a smile, the effort never reaching the pewter-gray of his eyes. Silently, he refilled Arlington's now-empty glass. "Speaking of women, what happened to the female slave?"

The question brought a snicker and a sly smile from Jeffrey. "You know, Fleming, you're not such a bad sort after all. You catch on to the way of things real quick. I got that hot little number stashed out in a secluded shack on my place. When I tire of her, I can always get my money back by selling her elsewhere."

"Really?"

"Yes." Jeffrey stirred, twisting around as though to check for spies before continuing. "Now, just between us men, what's the real truth here at Lagniappe?"

"I'm afraid I don't know what you're talking about."

Jeffrey laughed, a thin trickle of bourbon spilling from his lips to course down the corner of his mouth. He wiped it away with the back of his hand. "I've known Brianna Calhoun since birth. She's always had a cussed stubborn streak about her. Never was much at doing things like other females. Once she gets a proper husband, though,

I've no doubt she will settle down and become quite an asset."

"I quite agree and I look forward to our upcoming marriage with eagerness."

Ryan's words were met with a dark scowl of disbelief. "You can't be serious? Surely you don't intend to wed Brianna. I don't know what your purpose of this masquerade is but I know how you came to be at Lagniappe. Word has a way of getting around."

"Ah, but I do intend to wed Brianna and the sooner the better. And I take strong exception to anyone gossiping about her."

"Sir." Jeffrey rose from his chair, placing both hands on the desk as he leaned toward Ryan. His words were cut off as a knock sounded at the door.

"Enter," Ryan commanded, never taking his gaze from Arlington's flushed face.

"Beg pardon, Massa, but Miss Arlington is waiting in de parlor. Shall I have someone fetch Miss Bri?"

"That won't be necessary, Toby. Miss Brianna retired to her quarters, no doubt to get some much needed rest. She shouldn't be disturbed. Have Aunt Sudie show Miss Arlington to one of the guest rooms."

Ryan stood, executing a slight bow in Jeffrey's direction. "It will most likely take several hours of hard work to repair your carriage. In Brianna's absence, I shall offer you and your sister the hospitality of Lagniappe. Perhaps we can continue our discussion over dinner this evening."

Not giving Jeffrey an opportunity to respond, Ryan started for the door. "Toby, escort Mr. Arlington to a guest room also. I'm sure he will wish to rest. See that Sudie provides our guests with anything they might require."

"Yas suh. I shore will," Toby answered. Politely, he held the door open, waiting for Jeffrey to depart the study.

With long strides, Ryan made his way toward the front door, eager for a breath of fresh air. After his conversation with the insufferable Arlington, he found himself appreciating Brianna's actions even more.

"Lord, and to think I almost allowed Brianna to accept marriage to that insufferable beast." He had been forced to exercise every shred of his self-control to avoid indulging in the self-satisfaction of fisticuffs.

With deprecating humor, he wondered if he might have a bit of scoundrel in his veins after all. How would Brianna react should he take the liberty of trouncing her lifelong neighbor? It was a question he felt strongly inclined to explore.

Ryan leaned back against the thick pillar, allowing his mind to drift. Common brawling was hardly the sport of the aristocracy. The épée or even the finely crafted pistols available were preferred.

He reminded himself that he wasn't dealing with the aristocracy. He was dealing with a crude drunkard who wanted to claim Brianna Calhoun.

Ryan pressed the knuckles of a hard fist into the palm of his other hand. "Too late, Arlington," he whispered. "She belongs to me, and what is mine, I keep."

Chapter 8

Brianna watched with wry amusement as Aunt Sudie laid her finest black ensemble across the bed. "I thought you approved Ryan's choice of a bit of color within the walls of Lagniappe," she said.

"I does, but not tonight."

"What's so special about tonight?"

"You and Massa Ryan is entertainin', that's what!" Sudie bustled about, gathering all the items she would need to prepare her mistress for the evening ahead.

"Entertaining? I don't recall sending any invitations to anyone. It isn't suitable."

"Naw, missy, but Massa Ryan done give de hospitality of Lagniappe for this night."

"How could you allow him to take such undue privilege?"

"It weren't 'cause he had a mind for company, and from the look I saw on his face, I don't think he considers it much of a privilege, either."

Brianna's lips pulled together in a thoughtful pout as she pondered Sudie's words. "Maybe you best explain as to how we happen to be such apparently reluctant hosts, then," she quietly suggested.

Sudie stopped, facing her young mistress as she related the ill fortunes that had returned the Arlingtons to the front door of Lagniappe.

Despite her desire to find fault with Ryan's every action, Brianna could not voice a complaint. Had she been available, no doubt she would have been obliged to extend the same offer. Still, his behavior surprised her with its touch of courtesy. After all, she knew his opinion of Jeffrey.

Brianna brushed aside the thought. She entertained no doubts as to his opinion of Ivy. Hadn't he fawned over her? Exerted an unnecessary amount of charm? *No doubt he only did it to annoy me.* She had hardly been discreet in her feelings regarding Ivy Arlington's presence. Brianna shuddered to think of the evening ahead.

Jeffrey would avail himself liberally of her father's stock of bourbon while Ivy would engage in outrageous flattery and flirtation with Ryan.

Ryan. A mischievous smile curved her lips upward. *Ah, yes.* The arrogant Ryan Fleming would find much use of his skills tonight. Perhaps she should watch and learn, Brianna mused. She might even decide to follow his example. Jeffrey would not be adverse to a little flattery. Of that much, she was certain. A soft chuckle bubbled over, lightening her mood. Dinner promised to be a most interesting affair.

"You best be studyin' on gettin' yourself out of that water or you is going to be shrunk up like a prune, missy."

Startled, Brianna dropped the sponge in her bath. Feeling about with her toes, she nudged it, then leaned forward to recapture the dripping mass. "According to Ivy, it would scarcely be noticed. She thinks I've grown quite thin," Brianna confided.

"Don't go payin' no attention to that woman. You is put together nigh perfect."

Brianna laughed, squeezing her sponge and watching the water trickle down one soap-covered leg. "I think you're somewhat partial when it comes to me, Aunt Sudie."

"Maybe, but Massa Ryan ain't partial."

"What's he got to do with this conversation?"

"I seen de way Massa Ryan looks at you when he don't know no one's around. That man has a good eye for beauty and he thinks you is jest right."

"Has he been talking to you about me?" Brianna questioned, all senses alert.

"Why would he ask old Sudie anythin'?" the older woman hedged. She moved toward the tub, lifting the bucket of rinse water as she climbed upon the stool.

Brianna stood, sighing as the tepid water sluiced down her naked body, washing away the remaining bubbles that were clinging to her. Accepting the toweling Sudie offered, she wrapped it tightly about her as she climbed from the tub. "I don't know," Brianna admitted. "But where Ryan is concerned, I'm beginning to learn not to take anything for granted. I've also noticed that you have made no objections to the upcoming nuptials. Surely you don't approve the match. Whatever happened to your lament about a poor sailor man not being a proper husband?"

"Massa Ryan ain't jest a sailor. He was de cap'n o' that ship."

"Captain?" Brianna's lips pursed into a thoughtful

frown. "He never said anything to me about being a captain."

Sudie watched her, carefully refraining from comment as she assisted in toweling the younger woman dry. With more effort than necessary, Sudie began dusting powder over her body, stirring up a cloud of fragrance that set Brianna to sneezing.

"Take it easy, Aunt Sudie. Gracious, but the way you're carrying on, a body would think you've got secrets to hide."

"I ain't hidin' nothin', and I don't think you should go hidin' nothin' either," Sudie answered, attempting to change the subject.

"And just what am I hiding?" Brianna demanded.

Sudie fixed her with a stern eye. "That glorious body, for one thing. And I also seen how you looks at him. Only you is too stubborn to lets him know what you is really feelin' inside. How does you s'pects poor Massa Ryan to know what you has got to offer if you don't even let him gets a glimpse?"

Brianna felt her face warm. *A glimpse?* The cabin sprang to mind as quickly as though it were waiting to remind her of her brief lapse of decorum. *Ryan had seen far more than a glimpse! He's seen me totally without a scrap of clothing.* A chill skimmed her flesh and she shook off the warning. She couldn't fall in love . . . certainly not to anyone as arrogant as Ryan Fleming. There were more important things to consider.

She had to save Lagniappe from the clutches of Lord Tyrone. Thinking of Ryan and the unknown earl was more than she wanted to contemplate. With a glance at Sudie, Brianna decided to steer the conversation to safer territory. "Are you suggesting I dress in the same manner as Ivy?"

"Naw, I ain't. That woman is downright indecent with de way she wears clothes. They is more flesh showin' than she has hidden."

"Then what are you suggesting, Aunt Sudie?"

"I'm jest sayin' it won't hurt none if you show maybe a little hint of yore hidden charms." Sudie spoke with unaccustomed gruffness, her irritation causing her to cinch Brianna's undergarments more tightly than usual.

Brianna glanced down, observing the swell of her pert breasts above the lace-covered bodice. She bit back her complaint. Maybe a little cleavage would be all right, she silently decided. He wouldn't be able to see within her heart. The unbidden thought brought a feeling of hollowness to the pit of her stomach.

"Actually, I find it . . . er . . . shall we say rather too convenient that the near-drowned man Brianna found on the beach has become the man she chooses to spend her life with." Jeffrey downed his bourbon with eagerness, reaching for the crystal decanter to replenish his glass.

"Stranger things have happened. Sometime . . . somewhere," Ryan added with a mischievous grin in Brianna's direction.

Her breath caught in suspense. Surely he won't tell them of my proposal, she hoped. Ryan continued speaking, making no comment on her sudden lack of color.

"You might take into consideration that Brianna is responsible for saving my life. That in itself is worthy of my deep appreciation. She is also a beautiful woman. What man would not fall in love with her? How could any man resist the temptation of dreams which promise a lifetime of contentment?"

"Yes, yes, of course," Jeffrey snapped, waving one hand in dismissal. "I still find it too coincidental."

Ryan shrugged, finding a measure of pleasure in the other man's discomfort. "Would you have preferred it if I had been the Earl of Tyrone?"

"I wouldn't," Ivy answered.

Ryan turned his attention toward the woman entering the parlor in a flurry of red satin. He watched with interest as she made her way across the room to where he stood.

Ivy extended her hand, her voice a soft purr as Ryan granted the perfunctory kiss. "I find your presence far preferable to that of some stuffy old earl."

Ryan afforded Brianna a look of droll amusement. "Old and stuffy sounds like a description I've heard before. I think you have been listening to the wrong people."

Ivy slipped her arm through his, guiding them toward the settee. "Quite likely, but ladies do enjoy a little gossip now and then, and Brianna has such a lively way with words."

"Oh, I see," Ryan commented. "Would you care for a glass of sherry?" he asked, once she was seated.

"That would be delightful, and then I want you to sit right here beside me and tell me all about yourself."

Ryan poured the sherry, dutifully taking time to see that Jeffrey's drink was also replenished in the process. His eyes went toward the doors.

Never had he realized how late dinner was served at Lagniappe. Given the unusual reticence of his intended, Ryan felt as though he were alone in dealing with the

Arlingtons. He refilled his own glass, the muscles along his jawline tightening at the prospect of the long hours ahead.

"Would you care for a small glass of sherry, sweet siren?"

Brianna declined with a shake of her head, her eyes widening at the mention of spirits. "No, thank you."

One corner of Ryan's mouth tilted upward, his eyes gleaming in delight as he recalled the previous evening's finale. "As you wish."

Ryan watched as she fussed with smoothing imaginary wrinkles from her skirts, unable to meet his gaze. She looked so small, sitting in the chair that had obviously been constructed for a large man.

He retreated to the settee, positioning himself where he could watch her without appearing conspicuous. To his annoyance, Ivy moved closer.

"Forgive my curiosity," Ivy began, "but I've heard you refer to our dear Brianna as a sweet siren before. Is there some special meaning to the term?"

Panic wriggled to life within the pit of Brianna's stomach. She looked toward Ryan, her eyes pleading for his silence.

"Only in a literary sense," Ryan said. "Brianna and I both have what you might call a fascination for Greek mythology. Don't we?" he asked, directing his attention to Brianna.

"Yes." She stared at him, certain he would reveal in detail their night spent in the deserted cabin, trying to prepare herself for the worst. *How could he?*

"As I own several ships and enjoy sea voyages, it seemed apt that I would be compared to Odysseus. It is rare to chance upon the sirens of the sea . . . almost as

rare as it is to be rescued by one as lovely as Brianna."
He lifted his glass in salute.

"Oh," came Ivy's flat reply. "How charming, utterly
charming. You call her a sea siren because she saved your
life."

Brianna stared at Ivy, finding it difficult to comprehend that the woman had traveled the world and yet
knew virtually nothing, nothing at all.

"I suppose you could put it that way," Ryan answered,
not bothering to correct or elaborate on the story.

"Well, that's very nice and all, but I find it simply
appalling that Brianna was out and about in such a
storm." Ivy shifted, looking at the other woman with
disapproval evident on her heavily powdered face.

"It wasn't storming when I left. I got caught. You
know how unpredictable our weather can be sometimes,
Ivy."

"Maybe, but I have never been caught so unprepared.
Why, it must have been terrible trying to get poor Ryan
back to the main house. Goodness knows, I'd never have
been able to find such muscle to perform the task."

"I had help getting him here. Toby and some of the
field hands were able to lift him quite nicely." She tried
to ignore the implication of Ivy's statement. Still, she felt
awkward and definitely lacking in femininity. Ivy had
always had a knack for making her feel less than acceptable, she mused.

"Oh. Then you weren't alone?"

Brianna took a short breath of surprise. *It was a trap.
All the time, Ivy had been planning to eke out some vicious
scandal to spread.* But why? she wondered.

From years of observation, she knew Ivy Arlington to
be a creature of habit. Cruel comments, vicious rejoin-
ders, words of destruction, were all part of Ivy's style, but

always, she had reserved such behavior for women she considered to be competition.

She felt Ryan's hands press firmly on her shoulders and wondered briefly how he had managed to rise and come to stand behind her so unobtrusively.

"I can assure you, Ivy, Brianna was not alone for a single moment," Ryan said. Brianna felt the warmth steal across her cheeks.

Mon Dieu! It is Ryan she covets. She felt the urge to laugh at the absurdity of it all, but the impulse quickly died. *She cannot steal what is not mine.* The thought proved painful, but Brianna knew not why. She concentrated on Ryan's response. On the surface, she was forced to admit it sounded gallant, protective almost.

But she knew the truth. She hadn't been alone. It was what he left unsaid that brought the uncomfortable warmth surging to her face. *She had been with Ryan Fleming . . . in an unoccupied cabin . . . naked as the day she had been born!*

"Dinner is served." Toby's timely arrival prevented any further questions.

"Thank you, Toby," Ryan said. "Ladies. Arlington. Shall we adjourn to the dining hall?"

Brianna allowed Ryan to escort her, seething inwardly that he could be so calm when she was fast approaching a nervous breakdown. It was so unfair, but try as she might, Brianna could not help but admire his composure and wished she could emulate it.

Throughout the evening, Brianna retreated deeper into silence, barely touching her food as her companions conversed with ease.

She tried to concentrate on the conversation but found

her mind wandering to other occasions when the Arlingtons had sat at this table. Had Jeffrey ever before been so boring or Ivy so empty-headed? she wondered.

"Speaking of royal blood . . ." Ivy's voice reached out to her from afar, pulling Brianna's attention back to the present. "I heard frequent mention of Lord Tyrone while in England. I gather that despite his Irish heritage, he is quite a favorite among the English aristocracy . . . particularly the ladies."

Brianna felt a tightness forming within the pit of her stomach. "Perhaps that is why he is so late in making his arrival," she ventured. "No doubt he is engaged in a dalliance with one of his admirers." She turned toward Ryan, waiting for his expected protest. He had defended the absentee earl frequently enough.

"Perhaps." Ryan sipped his wine, maintaining a casual disinterest in the habits of the earl.

His answer left her increasingly agitated. Is there no predicting how the man will react? she wondered.

"Have you ever seen Lord Tyrone?" Ivy asked.

"I have," Ryan said. "A rather dashing sort of fellow from what I observed."

Brianna chafed at the smile of superiority he cast in her direction.

"I understand he has never married," Ivy probed.

"No doubt his disposition is such that ladies shun the thought of such a union," Brianna suggested.

Laughter vibrated within the depth of Ryan's chest, forging a path past his lips. "Ah, my sweet siren. You must not be too hard on the gentleman. Not every man can be so fortunate to find a lady of such devotion as I have."

She fairly choked on his choice of words. Never had

she known anyone possessed of such ego. Brianna slanted him a glance that clearly indicated her disapproval.

"Shall we retire to the parlor for coffee?" Ryan asked, rising even as he spoke.

Mechanically, Brianna rose from her chair. She refused to continue the charade. "If you'll forgive me, I feel rather tired. I think I shall retire to my room," she began, only to find Ryan hastening to her side with undue concern.

"You're not ill, are you?"

"No."

"Then you must join us. The evening is only made worthwhile by your presence," he said, his voice a seductive whisper that tantalized her senses, evaporated her ire.

"If Brianna isn't up to entertaining, we'll understand," Ivy interrupted, smiling at the couple. "Don't worry. I'm sure I can entertain Ryan."

"I'm sure Ryan will find your concern most gratifying." Brianna felt his hand squeeze her arm in silent warning. For a brief instant, she thought to defy him. She felt sickened at the sight of Jeffrey with his overindulgence of spirits. Ivy and her viper's tongue tested her own sensibilities too far.

And then there was Ryan. Ryan . . . with his enticing smile that beckoned her to cross the lines of polite society. Ryan . . . with his smoldering eyes that promised such intoxicating pleasures, she dared not dwell on his gaze too long, lest she succumb and be lost forever.

She held her silence, instinctively knowing this was a conflict she could not win.

"I'm sure with your affection for Brianna, both of you

would share my disappointment in the absence of such a fair hostess."

"Here, here," Jeffrey bellowed, raising his glass in salute. "You must remain in our company, fair Brianna."

"Stop it, Jeffrey. You're dreadfully sotted."

"True, my dear sister, but I still enjoy Brianna's company, unlike others I know." He staggered past Ivy, bowing before Brianna with an exaggerated flourish. "Allow me to escort you to the parlor, my dear."

"Whoa." Ryan reached out, holding Jeffrey in a grip of steel. He tottered, his body weaving back and forth as Ryan continued to offer his support. "I think it best that you concentrate on getting yourself safely into the parlor."

"No problem," Jeffrey assured him. "I know my way about this place as well as my own. Follow me." He staggered forward, lurching so erratically, Brianna found herself forced to accompany him and assist Ryan in assuring his well-being.

Once positioned in a comfortable chair, Jeffrey stretched his legs and heaved a heavy sigh. "Fleming, have you seen the charms of Lagniappe yet? Truly magnificent." Only the familiarity of the words made it possible to follow his speech, which was pathetically distorted by drink.

Ryan smiled down at Brianna. "I find them irresistible."

Brianna felt her face growing warm. She tried to move away from the casual touch of his hand at her elbow, yet Ryan maintained a firm but gentle hold.

"I'm referring to the charms outside the main house," Jeffrey added, staring at Ryan through a red-rimmed glaze.

Ryan nodded toward the man. "But of course. As a matter of fact, I took the liberty of riding through the fields only this morning and was beginning an inspection of the cotton gin when I was . . . ah . . . distracted by the charming picture that presented itself."

At his side, Brianna gave a small whimper. How could she possibly have forgotten? She had intended to flay him with words of rebuke, but had left in a maelstrom of confusion. She risked a small glance in his direction as she took her seat, but found no sign of mockery upon his face.

"Lagniappe seems to be rather self-sufficient," Ryan continued. "I understand there is a virtual village of services to be found on the plantation. A remarkable feat."

"No doubt," Jeffrey agreed with a hint of boredom.

"You approve of the way business is handled here at Lagniappe?" Brianna asked.

He met her gaze with a boldness that caused her breath to catch within her throat. "What I have seen meets my complete satisfaction."

Her spine stiffened, her guard instantly aroused by the double meaning of his words. Did he refer to the plantation? Or to herself? She grew more nervous, unable to find a satisfactory answer to her questions.

The conversation continued, leaving Brianna to speculate on his intent. The cabin seemed to haunt her memory, evoking strange feelings from deep within her. If only she knew more about life. If only she were a man, she wouldn't find herself beset by such vexing thoughts.

"Have you set a date, Brianna?"

Brianna gasped softly, her thoughts propelled forcefully back to the present by Ivy's question. "Date?" she asked.

Ivy's shrill laughter exploded and Brianna curled her fingers tightly into small fists. Why hadn't she paid more attention?

"A date for the wedding, dear child."

Brianna offered a tight smile, the effort causing her face to ache. "Child? Why, Ivy, there is a scant six months' difference in our ages. You really should take more care with your choice of words lest Ryan assume you're beyond the age of being considered marriageable," Brianna cooed.

Her confidence rose as she heard Ryan make a small choking sound. Brianna maintained her composure as she watched Ivy's face grow pale beneath her artificial coloring.

"Why, I never . . ." Ivy sputtered.

"Really?" Brianna asked, then hastily bit into her lower lip to refrain from further comments. It was unthinkable that she would insult a guest in her own home, but Brianna was unable to deny that she had done so now. She dared to glance in Ryan's direction, tilting her chin upward in defiance.

She didn't care. Ivy had been allowed too much leeway with her spiteful comments. It was time she had been put in her place. With a look, she dared Ryan to make objection.

Ryan lifted his glass in silent salute, his full mouth curved upward in a most intriguing manner.

Brianna felt her heart lurch, then gather speed, beating to a dizzying tempo within her breasts. *It is his fault!* He had entrapped her with so many words that now she was following suit. What would Aunt Sudie think of her?" Brianna lowered her head, knowing full well the tongue-lashing Aunt Sudie would have delivered had she been present.

As it was, only Ryan was there to witness her lapse of genteel behavior. Brianna shifted her gaze toward Jeffrey, then Ivy, who was struggling to regain her balance.

His eyes were dulled as though he were far removed from the events at hand. The result of her waspish tongue, she wondered, or the effect of too much drink? She couldn't tell. Tensions rose higher until Brianna was certain she would explode in a tirade and order them both from her home if the silence continued.

"I think Brianna was only seeking to point out your own beauty," Ryan smoothly intervened. "It would never do to be remiss in complimenting one's guest on her personal attraction."

"Oh. Er . . . yes," Ivy stammered, her anger evaporating with his words of flattery. "I suppose I do have a tendency to think of Brianna as being younger since my own life is one of so much more . . ." She paused, seeking the perfect word.

"Experience?" Brianna supplied, groaning quietly as she realized her lapse. Good Lord! Maybe Ryan was right in referring to her as a sea siren. For some peculiar reason, she seemed bent on wreaking havoc, inviting her own personal destruction.

"Actually, I believe *sophistication* would be a better word," Ivy coyly amended.

"Of course," Brianna answered, her manner demure. She found herself watching Jeffrey, almost envying him his dazed stupor. There was no use in attempting any form of flirtation. He appeared beyond reach. If only she had retired to her rooms when she had wanted. "I'm afraid I'm more accustomed to earlier hours and my conversational skills are somewhat lacking as time passes."

"The hour does grow late," Ryan interrupted. "Perhaps it would be best if we all retired. No doubt you will wish to resume your journey homeward at an early hour in the morning," he said, leaving no room for disagreement.

"Yes. Yes, to be sure," Jeffrey agreed, clearing his throat. "Of course, that's not to say a little nightcap would be refused." He raised his empty glass.

"I shall have someone bring a fresh decanter to your chambers," Ryan said.

Assured of further drink, Jeffrey readily started for the foyer, pausing only long enough to bestow a wet kiss upon Brianna's hand.

Ivy lingered to brush her cheek to Brianna's and offer effusive praise to Ryan for his companionship of the evening. She repeated the same ritual of touching her cheek to Ryan's.

Ignoring the burning pain gnawing at her, Brianna watched as Ivy pressed her breasts to Ryan's chest, her body swaying in an oddly erotic rhythm. Jealousy tightened its hold.

"If you'll excuse me, I believe I shall retire," she began.

His movement barely perceptible, Ryan caught her wrist. While Ivy plied her wiles on him, Brianna remained a captive witness.

"I look forward to seeing you later," Ivy purred, smiling up at Ryan.

He smiled, forcing Brianna to break the silence as he watched Ivy climb the stairs. "Let me go," she said.

"I think we should have a talk first," Ryan suggested.

"It can wait. I really am exhausted."

Ryan slipped his hand beneath her elbow. "No doubt, my lovely little siren. Your repartee this evening would have left far more experienced she-cats faint from the effort."

Brianna gave him a withering look as he guided her toward the privacy of the study. "I'm not entirely to blame," she pointed out.

"I never suggested you were," he answered. "Though I was somewhat taken back by your . . . mmm . . . shall we say, unorthodox behavior?"

Brianna stepped into the study, her anger fueled by his rebuke. He had no right to chastise her for anything she said or did. This was her home, and she was free to do whatever pleased her. She thought of the look of shock on Ivy's face and surrendered to the laughter that lurked beneath the surface. "Unorthodox? Maybe, but definitely effective. Ivy Arlington was deserving of her come-uppance."

"And you certainly gave it to her. Had I not been there to intervene, no doubt there would have been a devilish scratching, spitting, hair-pulling brawl."

Brianna stared at him in astonishment. "How dare you suggest . . ." she started, only to have her words cut off in mid-sentence.

"I don't suggest anything, Brianna. I'm simply trying to point out that if you wish to be successful in your attempt to rid yourself of Lord Tyrone, you will have to be far more circumspect in your behavior than you have been this evening."

Brianna frowned, her brow furrowing at the mention of the earl. "What's he got to do with this evening?"

"Everything," Ryan said, striding toward the overstuffed chair that was placed by the fireplace. "He is supposed to be your guardian."

Brianna nodded, waiting for him to continue.

"As such, I assume he will be most interested in how you conduct yourself."

"How I live is none of his business," she snapped.

"Ah, but it is." Ryan leaned back, pressing his fingers together to form a steeple with his hands.

Brianna stared, her imagination stimulated by the thought of how those strong hands would feel upon her body. The room felt overly warm. She stepped back, distancing herself from the fire and . . . Ryan. "In what way?" she asked.

"Most likely, the gentleman will wish to assure himself that you are properly settled before he departs for his homeland. In that case, he will surely wish to check with those who know you best, to ascertain that you have assumed your proper place in society."

Brianna shrugged, feigning indifference, though honesty forced her to admit the validity of Ryan's words.

"And what will he hear?" Ryan continued. "You have an attorney who will testify as to your skills at horse theft, and neighbors who will verify the wicked sharpness of your tongue."

Brianna winced, unable to refute the charges. "You've made your point, Ryan. Until the earl departs, I shall refrain from any further display of temper. I shall be the soul of diplomacy, exuding charm and grace to all." His rebuke chafed, and her words held a sharp bite of sarcasm to dim the pain that would not go away. "Now, if you are quite finished, I wish to retire." She didn't want to argue, not with him.

"Does that generosity extend to me?" His voice

reached out to her in a soft caress. His eyes watched, admiring the way the light caught the soft waves of her hair when she tilted her head, as though cautiously considering his suggestion.

"Are you implying you will provide your own testimony to the earl if I don't?"

"Please, my sweet siren," he drawled, suppressing a smile. "I'm not a total cad. I am offering nothing more than a truce. Since we are agreed to this charade, it will be more convincing if we try to get along."

It was a sensible suggestion, one difficult to deny. "Very well. I will keep my temper under control, but . . . don't provoke me," she warned.

"A fair bargain," he agreed, offering her a deep bow. "That only leaves one question unanswered."

"Only one? I must be losing my touch," Brianna answered, evoking a slow smile from him.

"Have you chosen a date for our wedding?"

"Sunday afternoon."

One dark brow arched in question. "So soon?"

"If the Earl of Tyrone arrives within the next three days, I fear it won't be soon enough."

Ryan nodded, his gray eyes serious as he studied her face. "Then you still refuse to consider the possibility that the earl might not be the tyrant you imagine?"

"I cannot afford the risk. Lagniappe is all I have left. To surrender it to the keeping of a complete stranger would be to betray my very soul."

"I understand."

Brianna moved toward the door, the soft rustling of her skirts the only sound within the room. Her fingers on the doorknob, she turned, her voice hesitant. "Ryan?"

"Yes," he answered, his eyes mating with her own.

"You won't . . . won't change your mind, will you?"

He shook his head from side to side. "No, my sweet siren. If this is what you must have, I won't desert you."

"Thank you." Turning away, she hurriedly left the room, relieved that her freedom from the Earl of Tyrone would soon be reality.

Alone, Ryan turned toward the fire, watching the yellow fingers of flame curling about the logs, breaking free to dance in gay abandon before disappearing into wisps of smoke.

Like Brianna, he brooded. She reveled in what she believed to be her course to freedom but courted that which she sought to defeat. Was there no way he could let her know his full identity without earning more contempt?

Ryan reviewed their time together from that first moment of his awareness of her presence. She had been a sight like none he had ever beheld. Undeniably sensual in her state of nakedness, he had also beheld the innocence that was captured in the softness of her face while asleep.

Brianna Calhoun was a rare gift from the gods, and with a small, wry smile, Ryan knew he would risk everything to possess her.

Chapter 9

"You can't stop me, *M'sieur* Westman. There was nothing in Papa's will that gives you the right to restrict any decision I might make regarding my personal life."

Brianna clasped her hands together, sitting primly on the edge of her chair. She tilted her chin upward in a show of determination as she faced the man who paced back and forth across the wide veranda.

"Now, see here, young lady. I don't need you telling me what rights I have. Why, if it hadn't been for young Arlington, I might not even have known of your latest escapade until it was too late."

Westman stopped in mid stride, taking a fortifying breath before continuing. "I won't allow you to make such a momentous decision without benefit of proper counsel."

"The decision is mine to make and it is done." Brianna glanced across the horizon, wishing Ryan would appear. He would put an end to *M'sieur* Westman's autocratic behavior.

"The decision as to when . . . and to whom you will be wedded belongs to the Earl of Tyrone."

"As you well know, *m'sieur,* the earl has not seen fit to make an appearance. I can only assume he cares not a whit for any decision involving Lagniappe or myself."

"Then it is my responsibility to act in his behalf." Westman cleared his throat, the lines on his face deepening with stern reproach. "I forbid you to marry this man!"

"You forbid?" Brianna's voice rose with indignation. "By what authority do you forbid anything? You were not so eager to assume responsibility for the daily task of maintaining Lagniappe. You may have temporary control over my inheritance, but that control does not extend to my personal life."

"It is my opinion that your father overindulged you. Well, I do not intend to perpetuate his behavior. As I was your father's lawyer, it is my duty to protect your interests until such time as Lord Tyrone arrives to assume his duties as appointed guardian. Until that time, you leave me no choice but to cut off funding of Lagniappe."

"Really? Your sense of duty seems rather selective, don't you think?"

"I don't know what you mean, but I will not tolerate your insolence."

"I believe the lady is referring to your lapse of duty when her mount returned to Lagniappe without her." At the sound of Ryan's voice, Brianna's heart swelled with relief. The blood began to surge through her veins in a warm flow.

Westman turned, his eyes widening at the sight of Ryan striding toward him from around the corner. "Who . . . who are you?" he stammered.

Ryan elected to ignore him, moving purposefully to Brianna's side and bestowing a chaste kiss to one flushed cheek. "You look radiant as befits a young bride-to-be."

"Thank you, Ryan."

"I trust my absence has not caused you undue stress," he said.

The words she would say lodged within her throat. Brianna stared at him, absorbing the strength of his presence. For so long, she had shouldered the burdens of being solely responsible. Now, this self-assured stranger stood before her, patiently waiting. He offered her the choice of sharing those burdens with broader, stronger shoulders.

Her smile brightened. *"M'sieur* Westman, may I present *M'sieur* Fleming, my intended."

"So, you're the rapscallion who has turned this young woman's head," Westman charged.

A dark brow winged upward. His eyes held a wintry chill as Ryan surveyed the portly attorney. "I doubt anyone can turn Brianna's head. As I'm sure you have discovered, she has a mind of her own, and"—he paused for effect—"I have found her quite capable of using it to protect her best interests."

"Nonsense," Westman said, his manner growing more flustered with each passing minute. "Richard did her no service by filling her head with notions of not needing a man to guide her. It's ridiculous! It is a man's duty to protect women from their own impetuosity."

"Protect? You speak of protection, *M'sieur* Westman, yet when Brianna was left stranded, you did nothing to try to find her. You left her in circumstances which were totally unknown." Ryan stepped closer, his mouth forming a firm line that slashed across the hard planes of his sun-bronzed face.

"I . . . I . . . I had no reason to assume she would be

in need of assistance," Westman stammered as he stepped backward, eagerly seeking some distance between himself and Ryan's growing wrath. "She knows every inch of this property and I thought her capable of finding her way home without my help."

"Then you have no reason to assume she is in need of your assistance now, sir. She is also quite capable of knowing her own mind and if not"—again he halted to emphasize his next words—"I can assure you, I do know my mind. We are agreed to this marriage and no one shall stand in the way of our commitment."

His assertion brooked no room for further discussion. Brianna watched, her confidence soaring with the knowledge that she had truly made the right choice. He would keep their bargain and when the time came, he would depart and leave the destiny of Lagniappe to her. With a sinking heart, she contemplated the inevitable end to this peculiar strategy she had devised.

Leave? Why does the thought of Ryan's leaving fill me with disquiet? Brianna forced herself to concentrate on the conversation. She would not . . . could not think of Ryan leaving. Not now . . . not yet.

"Very well, sir. I see you are quite determined to go through with this farce. I feel it is my duty to warn you though the properties of Richard Calhoun shall remain in the control of the earl until he shall relinquish them. I doubt you will find him easily swayed to your opinions."

Ryan's mouth slid into a smile of relaxed insolence. "I imagine I shall be able to deal with the earl quite nicely."

"Then I leave you to reckon with Lord Tyrone. I wash my hands of this entire business." Westman turned toward Brianna, offering a stiff bow. "Good day to you."

Ryan and Brianna watched quietly as Westman made

his way hurriedly down the stairs to his waiting carriage.

"Didn't you mention something about drawing and quartering *M'sieur* Westman?" She flashed an impish grin at the unrepentant man who stood by her side, his hand pressing possessively at the small of her back.

"Drawing and quartering is too good for him," Ryan commented with casual indifference.

Laughter bubbled from her lips. "Judging from the way he's lashing that poor animal, I've a feeling *M'sieur* Westman is adverse to any suggestions you might have for his future."

Ryan's easy laughter joined hers, mingling in a light-hearted conspiracy to evaporate the tension. "I'm glad to see his presence didn't depress you."

"M'sieur Westman never depresses me but he does have a tendency to inspire a goodly amount of temper," she confessed.

"Ah, yes. But are you certain it's Westman or could it be that your Irish blood is responsible for your low tolerance of the gentleman in question?"

Brianna wrinkled her nose in disdain. "I find that question difficult to answer, *m'sieur,* and in truth, I thought I handled myself most admirably. I didn't raise my voice. Well . . . not much," she conceded. Laughter laced each word as she continued. "You were hardly a model of restraint."

She leaned forward, her eyes sparkling with mirth. "Tell me, kind sir, were you lurking about, waiting for the opportune moment to descend upon him like an avenging angel?"

"I was not lurking," he countered in amused protest.

"I watched, in hopes of seeing you ride in."

"I am pleased to know my absence was noticed. Dare I hope it is a sign you missed me?"

"Perhaps. A little," she added. "Where did you ride?"

"Toward the eastern boundaries of Lagniappe. That is why you did not see my return. It was mere accident that I stumbled upon you and Westman."

Brianna's smile disappeared, replaced by a somber look of curiosity. "The east? Why did you go that direction?"

"It seemed appropriate. I've seen the cane to the south, the cotton to the west. North and east were the only directions remaining."

Ryan settled himself into the chair next to her, stretching his long legs before him as he tilted his head back in a relaxed pose. "The east fields seem to have been recently stripped," he commented.

"The vegetables are harvested first. The women spend most of a month with drying, canning, and preserving. As you remarked last night, Lagniappe is self-sufficient."

"Like its mistress?"

"Perhaps Lagniappe is more so," she answered with a trace of hesitancy. "Of course, Lagniappe has been here much longer than I."

"Then you lack experience?"

Brianna started to speak but held her tongue, unsure of the full meaning of his carefully worded phrase. There was experience, and then . . . there was experience. She recalled her hastily spoken words of the previous evening. *Experience* was the word she has applied to Ivy. Did Ryan suggest she was . . .

"I'm capable of managing my affairs," she stated with caution.

Her answer evoked a deep chuckle from her companion. His obvious amusement only served to incense her temper.

"You find it humorous to think of me as capable?"

"Not at all, but according to Aunt Sudie, you're a gentle-bred lady and have had no affairs."

"Oooh. Honestly, Ryan Fleming, sometimes I think you set about to embarrass me with your continual barrage of double entendres."

"Not me, sweet siren. I was merely quoting Aunt Sudie and I might point out, you were the first to mention affairs." He shifted positions, leaning his weight against his arm as he drew closer to her. "Is Aunt Sudie in error?"

He could hear her sharp intake of breath; he watched the pupils of her eyes dilate as she continued to stare at him. Her lips slowly parted, delectably tempting in their sweet softness.

Brianna's heart quickened its pace, the sound throbbing in her ears like the incessant pagan beat of voodoo drums late at night. Her throat ached with an almost painful dryness but there was another, different kind of ache building within her.

She moved toward the whitewashed railing, careful to keep her back to him. Would she always respond to his careless taunts thusly? Brianna wondered.

She heard not a sound, knew nothing until that moment his hands pressed against the flesh of her arms as he gently forced her to turn toward him once more.

"You haven't answered my question, sweet siren." His voice was a low vibration, sending shivers of anticipation racing through her already-quivering body. "You said you watched for my return. Have your eyes perhaps searched the land at another time, waiting for another arrival?" Once spoken, the thought left a bitter taste in his mouth but Ryan pressed on. "Has one before me supped of your sweet nectar? Felt the passion rising within you? Are there rivals I must vanquish for your affection?"

Brianna felt waves of heat rush to her face. Her voice abandoned her, leaving her tongue thick and useless within her mouth. *How can he ask such a question? Is he so blind he cannot see what is in my foolish heart?*

Her silence pierced his flesh, a deadly rapier plunging deep within his belly. His muscles tensed, growing rigid under his sun-darkened skin as his eyes tried to bore into her soul. Jeffrey's arrogant face bedeviled him. *Had Sudie been wrong?*

A vague illness invaded him, his stomach twisting into hardened knots as he envisioned Brianna lying in Arlington's arms.

Without warning, he bent over her, capturing her lips with his own in a bruising motion meant to punish. Too late he realized he was the victim. A groan arose from the depths of his throat as he felt her tremble then melt into his embrace.

He eased away, far enough to see the surrender on her face. He reclaimed her lips with feather-light kisses, tracing the full scope of her acquiescent mouth.

Brianna melded her body to his, the hardened nipples of her breasts straining the material in search of his flesh. Her fingers went on their own quest, moving upward over the hills of pulsating muscles to twine about his neck. Her tongue made tentative explorations, touching, tasting his own more experienced endeavors.

The flickering flames within her burst into a raging inferno and she felt the thick, moist swell of her passion erupting in answer to his entreaties. It became an agonizing torment that threatened to shatter every myth she had ever heard.

"Noo, nooo," Brianna whimpered as she realized he was retreating.

Her lashes fluttered upward, allowing her to see his passion-darkened gaze. She was overwhelmed by a sense of incredible weight pressing down upon her, rendering her weak and helpless. Her hands slid down his massive chest, unwilling to break contact.

Vaguely, she became aware of his own heartbeat, strong but rapid. "Ryan?"

"Never forget, my sweet. You shall sing your siren's song for no other man, for it shall surely invite their destruction."

A chill swept across her, setting her to trembling. *A warning?* She pushed the question away. Surely not. Ryan had made a bargain with her and their agreement made no mention of . . . *Of what? Love? Passion? A real marriage?*

She made no protest when he stepped backward, a mixture of regret and relief blending together in her confused mind. She needed time to think and Ryan's presence made it impossible to do more than feel.

Wordlessly, Brianna took her leave, the only sound the soft rustle of silken petticoats brushing against the stiffer material of her morning gown of black.

Ryan watched her retreat, steeling himself not to follow. Surely she had not surrendered to the likes of Jeffrey Arlington, he reasoned. Even worse, he was forced to reconcile himself to waiting.

"You are her guardian, sworn to uphold her honor," he sternly said aloud, his voice harsh to his own ears. Running long fingers through his thick ebony mane, Ryan tried to steady his shaky nerves.

Never had one woman so affected him. There had been many who tried, but Ryan had found no problem in distancing himself from any real involvement . . . until now.

"Ah, my sweet siren. So tempting. You would lure me to your warm embrace with your song of enchantment. But at what price?"

The front door opened. Ryan watched, scarcely daring to breathe. It wasn't Brianna, but Aunt Sudie who stepped out, eyeing him with curiosity. He relaxed, motioning her forward.

"Massa Ryan?" she inquired haltingly.

"Yes, Aunt Sudie."

"Has you and Miss Bri done been fussin'?"

"No. Why do you ask?"

"Well, she's acting mighty peculiar-like, that's all."

"Peculiar-like?"

"Yes suh. She's done gone all closed-mouth on old Aunt Sudie." The old woman shook her head in dismay. "Ain't like her. Ain't like her at all."

A slow smile tilted one corner of his mouth, understanding Brianna's actions, if not his own. "No," he agreed, "I doubt if Brianna is accustomed to being unable to express herself."

He thought of the way she had fitted her slender body to his, how her arms had wound their way around his neck as her lips mated so seductively with his.

"Don't let it bother you," he advised. "Brianna is a

woman, and sometimes women must have private musings to ponder upon the direction of their destiny."

"I s'pose," she said, though the doubtful look she cast toward Ryan told him his answer was hardly satisfactory. "There ain't been no more changes, has there?"

"Changes? Of what kind?"

"I mean . . ." Sudie bit her lip, twisting her face in consternation until her almond eyes disappeared behind the plump mounds of her cheeks. "You ain't done called off de weddin', has you?"

"The wedding is still scheduled as planned," Ryan answered with a wry laugh. "Though I have doubts about the marriage."

"Doubts? What kind o' doubts is you havin', Massa?"

Ryan shook his head, denying Sudie access to the thoughts that plagued him. "Never mind." He turned his back to her, staring out over the landscape. "You better tend your mistress. She will need help in dressing for dinner."

"Yes suh," Sudie answered with unaccustomed meekness.

"Sudie?"

"Yes suh?"

"Does Brianna have a gown of soft green? Maybe one the color of the sea when a storm is brewing?"

"Naw suh, but her mama had one that de massa had special made from a bolt of silk he brung back from that China country. It's a powerful strange gown, goin' from nigh black to deep greens and blues when de mistress would move. And when de candlelight would touch it, those silver threads plumb shown like ribands of stars."

She shook her nappy head, remembering the sight

Brianna's mother had made in the creation. "Hmm, mmm. That shore was some kind o' special gown."

"Where is it now, Aunt Sudie?"

"Why, I packed it away, real careful-like, when de mistress died. Ain't never had it out o' de trunk since."

"Find it. Tonight, I want Brianna to wear it."

"But, Massa, that ain't de kind o' thing for a young female like Miss Bri. Why, it ain't de style for this here part o' de world, and . . ."

"No *but*'s, no *and*'s," he told her. "See that Miss Brianna wears it this evening."

"Yas suh. I shore hope you ain't 'spectin' no folks to be joinin' you."

"No. Miss Brianna and I will be quite alone."

Ryan stared upward, watching in fascination as Brianna descended the staircase, the Chinese silk clinging to her form in tender adoration. He had seen similar gowns worn by Oriental women, but never had he appreciated the graceful symmetry as much as this very moment.

"Aunt Sudie said you wanted to see my mother's gown," Brianna offered, her voice unusually shy in tone.

He took her hand in his, grazing her fingertips with his lips. "She made it sound so intriguing with her description," he answered.

"Are you . . . you disappointed?"

"Disappointment would be impossible. It far surpasses my expectations, though I suspect the lady who wears it has greatly contributed to its beauty."

Brianna offered a tentative smile, her eyes more luminous than he had dreamed possible. Tonight, he silently vowed. Tonight they would have a quiet meal and become better acquainted. He would tell her who he was, explain that he would continue the use of her methods of managing Lagniappe, a method that included hired labor.

"My sweet, sweet siren," Ryan murmured, leading her toward the dining hall.

"I've never worn anything belonging to my mother," she began. "I had no idea she possessed such exotic taste."

"You don't admire it?"

"Oh, yes." Brianna turned toward him, her eyes wide with surprise. "It's just . . . unexpected. I remembered her as a beautiful lady . . . always serene."

"And now?"

Brianna felt herself relax. It seemed the most natural thing in the world to speak openly to the man who escorted her to her place at the elegantly appointed table. "And now, she seems as though she was somewhat mysterious."

"And perhaps a little bold and adventurous?" he asked.

A soft smile touched her lips. "Yes, though it is difficult to attribute those qualities to one's mother."

"Like mother, like daughter," Ryan murmured, pulling back the chair and waiting for Brianna to sit.

Her lashes fluttered upward, forming a thick lacy fan beneath finely arched brows. "Do you think I'm like my mother?"

"I only know I find that you possess all the qualities of which we speak." Ryan moved away, his eyes never leaving her face as he took his own place at the table. Silently, he blessed Aunt Sudie for preparing the table in a more intimate setting.

Throughout the meal, they conversed, quietly exploring each other's interests; their hopes, dreams, and plans laid open and expanded through the sharing of their thoughts.

Brianna found herself intrigued by Ryan's stories, listening with rapt attention as he told of Ireland. "I think I would like your country," she said when he finished.

"It's not just my country, Brianna. It's part of your heritage, too."

A tiny frown furrowed her brow. "The thought never occurred to me. I suppose you're right, but I've always considered Lagniappe my heritage."

"Then consider yourself doubly blessed. You have two heritages to remember."

"That's true."

"Speaking of remembering . . ." Ryan paused, uncertain how to broach the troublesome subject. "I was thinking of our ride through Lagniappe."

"Yes." She smiled. "It's always beautiful but I think I like it best in the fall. It's still warm but there's a freshness not often found in the sultry climate of our summers."

"I agree. I particularly admired the quite beauty of the bayou."

The corners of her mouth turned downward. Her eyes reflected a hazy mist. "Bayou? I wouldn't know," she said. "I never ride near the bayou."

"Never, Brianna?"

"No. And you shouldn't either, Ryan. It's much too near the swamp. The mosquitoes are most bothersome and it's easy to get sickness." Her frown deepened. "I call it *Bayou de Mort* . . . Water of Death."

"Is that where your mother died?" He thought of her panic when she saw the pier. He could vividly hear her tortured screams: *"Maman, Maman."*

"Maman died when I was very young." She shrugged, offering an apologetic smile. "I don't remember the circumstances."

"I see." He sipped his wine in thoughtful silence. What were the circumstances? he wondered. Recalling Sudie's plea, he decided it wise to change the subject . . . for the moment.

"I shall ride to Biloxi soon to secure the services of a priest. Do you have a preference?"

"No. We seldom left the plantation with Papa's many projects to be tended. That's why he built the chapel. When we were fortunate, we would receive the blessings from those who traveled past. The rest of the time, we contented ourselves with the lighting of candles . . . a prayer."

"Plantation life does present a solitary existence."

"Yes, but it's a good life, one I love. That is why I am so anxious to insure Lord Tyrone does not have a chance to spoil it."

"The earl figures prominently in your life of late. I only wonder if the title would be perhaps less offensive if it belonged to someone for whom you cared."

"Why would I have cause to care for some Irish earl?"

"Maybe because he's Irish. Didn't you tell me your father was Irish? You cared for him."

"He was my father. I have no cause to care for Lord Tyrone."

Ryan nodded, his manner casual, almost indifferent as he continued. "I suppose you're right. Tell me, my sweet siren, from where in Ireland did your father hail?"

"He was born and raised in Kenney. Why do you ask? Have you been there?"

"Ireland is considerably smaller than here. It is difficult not to be familiar with most of the land and its owners."

"I didn't know."

"Did you know that only two properties border Lord Tyrone's land? Those of Kildare and Kenney."

"What are you saying?"

"Only that I think you should consider your father's wishes more carefully before you cast them aside. There may be many things you don't know." Ryan watched the effect of his suggestion from half-closed eyes. Confusion followed by indecision flickered across Brianna's expressive face.

"I cannot imagine anything that would change my opinion."

"Maybe your father was himself a part of the aristocracy. It would explain his decision to choose the earl as your guardian; a man he could trust, a man like himself."

Nervous laughter spilled from her trembling lips. "Such a thing is not possible! My father? Part of the Irish aristocracy?"

"Would it be so bad if there were truth in my story?"

"I don't know. I mean . . . it's not true. Were my father an earl, he would have told me long ago."

"Would he? He didn't tell you of the Earl of Tyrone."

Brianna's defenses rose, her back stiffening at the mention of the name. "Must you remind me of him? It has been a most enjoyable evening. I see no reason to spoil everything."

"I'm not reminding, only asking. Has your father never mentioned his life in Ireland?"

Brianna shook her head, her face reflecting a brief

shadow of sadness. "Papa sometimes told stories, but it was as though he were apart from them somehow. Telling only what he saw through a looking glass." She sighed, her breath a soft whisper. "At least it seemed so to me."

He thought of her observation, so different from his father's views. Jason had spoken of courage, honor, a man who would prefer death to betrayal of those whose convictions he shared.

He glanced at Brianna. *And the sweet siren would never have lived to sing her song.* He felt gratitude that Richard Calhoun had escaped.

"Ryan? Is something wrong?"

At the sound of her voice, he shook off the disturbing thoughts. "No. I was just thinking of the past. Nothing to trouble yourself about, my sweet."

"Does it have anything to do with the Earl of Tyrone?" she asked.

"Not really. Why do you ask?"

"I frequently worry that he will arrive too soon."

"You might find his arrival to be timely. Being an earl does not necessarily make him evil."

"It doesn't matter. By Sunday, we will be married, and if and when he arrives, there will be little to do but set sail back to Ireland."

"Very well. Since you can be persuaded to no other course of action, I shall leave early in the morning to make the final arrangements."

"Arrangements?"

"Have you forgotten the need of a priest so soon?" A teasing grin brushed across his mouth. "Or can it be that marriage in this land is as unique as proposals?"

"Ryan!" Proposing to a man had never been among

her desires, but it had happened. It appeared to be a circumstance he was loath to allow her to forget. Discomfort drew heat to her cheeks, adding to her embarrassment as she found herself without defense against his jest.

"Sorry, my sweet. It seems I have a weakness for enjoying the charming blush of color which steals across your cheeks."

"As I have no wish to remind you of your weakness, I shall make every effort to avoid further demonstrations of blushing," she retorted, annoyed by his words.

"Even on our wedding night?"

The wedding night! Brianna's eyes widened, panic rising as she met the gaze of her dinner companion. She watched in growing fascination as his eyes darkened with passion. "No . . . I mean . . . we won't be having a wedding night."

"Are you certain?"

"This is to be a business arrangement. I have agreed to pay you a set sum for the temporary use of your name . . . and your presence. That is all."

He lifted his glass in a mock salute, his eyes never wavering in their bold appraisal. "True, my sweet siren, but then . . . there is always the matter of interest."

Chapter 10

"And what are your plans while I am gone, my sweet?"

Brianna quickened her pace, trying to keep up with Ryan's long stride. "The usual, I suppose. I'll ride to the fields and check on the progress with *M'sieur* Rawlings. He thinks we will be able to start sending our barges out sooner this year than last."

"Yes. Lagniappe has increased the yield, and in less time than previous years. No doubt, your ingenious plan for the slaves purchasing their freedom is responsible for the extra output."

"You know?" Brianna stopped, staring up at him in amazement.

"Of course I know. I have had the opportunity to look over the ledgers. I'm very impressed with your business acumen."

"You didn't have the opportunity. You took it," she retorted, unable to summon up any real anger at his actions. *He approved of offering everyone on Lagniappe the chance to earn their freedom.*

Ryan chuckled, not bothered by her accusation. "So I did. But little would ever be learned if not for those willing to take what they desired." He turned toward her, his face mirroring his true thoughts.

"Do you always take what you desire?" The question slipped out, but once spoken, Brianna found herself waiting breathlessly for his answer.

"Not always. There are some treasures that become priceless only when offered freely. For such a gift, I have infinite patience."

"You . . . you must be . . . be careful on your journey," she stammered. "The roads are not always safe for a lone traveler." She was anxious to change the subject before her emotions propelled her into his arms, wrenching forth declarations that she knew were impossible. *This is a business arrangement, nothing more.* She clenched her teeth, silently acknowledging the obvious. More and more, she craved less business and more arrangement.

"Don't worry, my sweet. I'm accustomed to taking care of myself. I shall return in plenty of time for tomorrow's wedding."

Brianna smiled, feeling strangely shy at the mention of the pending wedding.

Together they entered the stables, greeting the groom as he brought their mounts forward. Ryan assisted her, his touch lingering in her memory even as he prepared to mount the bay he always rode. "Give Mr. Rawlings my regards, and Brianna . . ."

She looked at him, committing his face to memory as she waited for him to continue.

"Please try not to create too much havoc in my absence." He flashed a teasing wink her direction, his full lips tilted in the now-familiar lopsided grin. Her melancholy mood vanished, vexation replacing it with alacrity.

"I don't create havoc," she answered in a huffy tone, reining her animal next to his.

"Then don't encourage it," he murmured, leaning across to give her a lingering kiss before she could respond. "Remember your promise to control that Irish temper of yours."

All thoughts of a proper rebuke shattered at the touch of his lips on hers. Caught in the throes of pure tactile sensations, she could only savor the moment.

His expression was etched with regret, his eyes drinking in every delicate feature of her finely sculpted face. "I'll see you tomorrow," he promised, wheeling his horse around and spurring him into a gallop.

Brianna sat motionless, watching the dust billow upward, forming hazy brown clouds about the horse's hooves. "It's bad luck to see the bride on her wedding day," she whispered. She blinked, trying to hold back the tears that welled so unexpectedly.

Why did she have to love a man she had vowed to release? The irony of her situation was not lost, even in her confusion. Slaves she could emancipate with a few strokes of the quill. But herself? Would she forever be ensnared by the poignant memories of his embrace?

And what of Ryan? she wondered. Would he feel such pangs of remorse at bidding her farewell? The memory of his vigorous protest at giving up his own freedom taunted her. "No doubt he will return to his carefree ways before the earl's ship is beyond the horizon."

The words tasted bitter upon her tongue, her intended attempt at indifference twisting her efforts of laughter into heartrending sobs. "Oh, Ryan. Don't leave. I love you," she wept, her plea finding no ears but her own.

* * *

Brianna tried to concentrate on the report, but the image of Ryan kept intruding, pushing all else aside. "Yes," she muttered, assuming *M'sieur* Rawlings's last words required some answer. He stared at her, his face a picture of bewilderment.

"Are you feeling unwell, Miss Brianna?"

"Hmmm?"

Rawlings was slow in answering, the worry lines on his face deepening, even as Brianna tried to recall what he had said last. "Maybe you should return to the main house. It is awfully sultry today, and you look somewhat pale," he suggested.

"Perhaps you're right. I do feel a bit tired," she agreed. She grasped at the suggestion, wanting to abandon everything for the chance to be alone.

"Don't concern yourself with operations here. Mr. Fleming left instructions and I'll see that they are carried out while he's gone."

Brianna could only offer a wan smile as she departed. No longer did she take offense at Ryan's intervention in the business of Lagniappe. She could not deny his apparent knowledge, and in truth, Brianna knew she had savored the few times they had joined in lively discussions, inspired by his forays.

He seemed to care for Lagniappe in much the same way she did and she would not deny herself the pleasure of that opinion.

Moving at an easy canter, Brianna allowed her thoughts to drift at will. The tiny cabin sprang to mind. *Would it be so wrong to be married in every sense of the word?*

The thought of waking to find Ryan by her side was far from distasteful. He was very handsome, she reminded herself. And despite the times he had troubled her with his boldness, Brianna was forced to admit she found it preferable to his absence.

"Brianna! Brianna, wait up!"

Hearing her name, she reined in her horse, turning in the saddle to locate the disembodied voice.

From the north, a rider came galloping toward her at full speed. Forcing an overly bright smile that brought an ache to her cheeks, she prepared to greet him. "Good morning, Jeffrey. I didn't expect visitors so early in the day."

"I've had a few problems. Been up most of the night." He answered absently, swiveling about as though searching for someone. "Where's Fleming?"

"He's gone to Biloxi. Is your problem serious?"

"Not really. Just a few of my people have taken it in their heads to find . . . religion," he said, his voice curling the final word into a sneer.

"There's nothing wrong with religion."

"Depends on who—or maybe I should say what—they worship. In this instance, it's more a case of voodoo." His horse shuffled in agitation, distracting him as Jeffrey concentrated on bringing the animal under control.

"Voodoo?" The words struck terror in her heart. Even on Lagniappe, there were practitioners of the mysterious rituals. There was Greshna. She had heard whispered comments in the past about the woman being some kind of priestess. "What have you heard?"

"I never should have bought those damn bucks from Haiti. I knew where the hell they came from." He spoke more to himself than to her and Brianna's voice jerked him from his ruminations.

"Stop mumbling, Jeffrey. Has something happened?"

"Never mind, Brianna. I didn't mean to say anything. Must be more tired than I realized."

"No need to apologize. I want to know more details about this trouble and how it involves voodoo."

"Good heavens, Brianna. Surely you don't think me so ungentlemanly as to fill your ears with such talk!"

"What's wrong with telling me? You would willingly share the information with other plantation owners, wouldn't you?"

"Yes," he sputtered, his annoyance shading his pallid skin a dull red. "And in absence of a proper gentleman in charge of Lagniappe, I did ask to see Fleming. I know my duties."

"Ryan doesn't own Lagniappe. I do," she pointed out. "And since Belle Terre borders my property, I suggest you advise me of the nature of the problem. It is Lagniappe most likely to be affected by any danger."

"As I said. I know my duties, and I do not consider putting you in a state of hysteria to be among them."

"Hysteria? I'm hardly the type for such nonsense. You are talking foolishness."

"You are a woman."

"Congratulations on recognizing the obvious. What does my gender have to do with the subject at hand?"

"It's a well-known fact that by nature, women are often apt to be irrational. Many people hold with the idea that such tendencies make a woman more susceptible to things like voodoo. It's a nasty business and I won't jeopardize your safety by involving you. This is best left to be tended by men."

Control your temper. Ryan's earlier admonition echoed within her head. She took a deep, calming breath but it didn't relax her. Rather, it inflamed, firing her wrath to greater heights. "I see. Then I will leave you to your business, Jeffrey, but I'll thank you to stay out of my affairs."

"Where are you going?"

Offering an honest answer was far more courtesy than Brianna felt he deserved. She hid the truth behind a tight smile. "Home. I have a wedding to plan and there is much to be done before tomorrow."

"Tomorrow? Good God, Brianna. You don't mean to marry that Fleming person so soon, do you?"

"Indeed I do."

"But that's preposterous!"

His shocked indignation spurred her on. "How could you expect otherwise, dear Jeffrey? Didn't you just say that we ladies are prone to irrational behavior?"

"Your action only proves my point," he snapped.

Her back grew rigid, her shoulders squaring in defiance. "Think what you will, Jeffrey Arlington, but know this. Tomorrow I will become Mrs. Ryan Fleming despite all your objections."

"Don't count on it."

"Ah, but I do. And in the meantime, I remind you that you are on Lagniappe property. Don't bother any of my people in your search for those poor souls who most likely only seek relief from the injustices meted out by that barbarian you call an overseer."

With a snap of her riding crop, Brianna set her stallion into motion, racing across the fields, putting distance between herself and Jeffrey as quickly as possible.

She kept the brutal pace until she reached the stables,

her anger somewhat lessened by the vigorous ride. Relinquishing her lathered mount, she headed for the house, wishing again for Ryan's soothing presence.

Brianna stopped, wondering at the peculiar desire. "What's wrong with me? No doubt Ryan would find the entire episode highly amusing."

She slapped the crop smartly against her thigh, the limber leather making a dull thud as it connected with her riding skirt. "Men are all alike and I trust none of them!"

The door slammed behind her, punctuating the vehement proclamation. "Aunt Sudie? Where are you?" Brianna started for the stairway. "Aunt Sudie!"

"I'se heared you de first time, missy. What for is you hollerin'? That ain't no way for a lady to act."

"Then don't think of me as a lady. Think of me as the owner of Lagniappe . . . your employer . . . the one who wants to talk to you . . . now . . . upstairs." Sparing the briefest of glances toward the older woman, Brianna started the upward climb, questions multiplying in her head with each step.

Sudie lifted her eyes heavenward. "Lawd, but you has best give old Sudie a little help here. That gal is in a powerful vexed state. If that man o' hers done riled her up, then I ain't shore I can be makin' everythin' right. Massa Ryan ain't jest any man. He can gets that gal fired up quicker than I ever thought possible."

She paused, grinning with open pleasure before continuing. " 'Course, there is some fires what needs stokin', not puttin' out."

"Sudie!" The sharp reprimand got her attention, and Sudie abandoned her one-sided conversation as she lifted her skirts higher.

"I'se comin'. I ain't as spry as I once was. You gots to have patience."

Sudie's eyes widened, her mouth growing slack as comprehension settled like a heavy cloak about her shoulders. "Voodoo? What for is that man troublin' your head with things like that?"

"You sound like Jeffrey. I don't consider it trouble . . . at least as long as it doesn't bring harm to the people here on Lagniappe."

"Then what you askin' me all these questions for? I ain't got no use for that kind o' thing. It scares de wits out o' me."

"I need information. I don't want Belle Terre's problems becoming my problems. How can I protect Lagniappe if I'm kept ignorant of the facts?"

Brianna began pacing, her agitation growing. Her fertile mind gave birth to yet another question but she waited for Sudie's answer.

"I don't know de troubles at Belle Terre, missy. I don't want to neither. I s'pects they is caused by that Massa Arlington bein' a pure fool, and that's his business, not mine."

"I won't argue the point, Aunt Sudie." Brianna settled herself on the edge of the bed, leveling her gaze on Sudie's stubbornly set face. "I still want to know all you can tell me about voodoo."

"Naw." She shook her head in firm refusal. "I ain't fillin' yore head with sech things. You shouldn't ought to fret yourself."

Sudie beamed at her, trying to get out of the awkward situation. "Why don't you takes yourself a nice nap?

When you wakes up, we can gets everythin' ready for tomorrow. That handsome Massa Ryan will be here and he can handles any little old problem there might be. You jest needs to think on lookin' yore best for him."

"If Ryan were here now," Brianna began, "I'll wager you wouldn't be so evasive."

"Now, missy, you knows that ladies don't go wagerin'. What would Massa Ryan think?"

"He'd probably think I had a winning bet," she retorted. Brianna stood up, planting a hand on each hip with her legs slightly spread in a stance she had often seen young men use when challenging one another. "Are you going to answer me or not?"

"Not." Sudie's lips pursed together in stubborn silence. "I ain't goin' to talk about it and that's that. So you best be takin' a nap."

Brianna headed for the door. "I'm not taking a nap until I have some answers!"

"Where is you goin', chile?" Sudie started after her, breaking into a run as she tried to catch the young mistress of Lagniappe.

"If you won't help me, I know someone who will." Leaving the cool quiet of the house, Brianna set out for the stables.

It had been years since she had seen Greshna but if anyone would know the truth, she would. Only once since the death of her mother could Brianna recall the old woman being in the main house.

She tried to remember the circumstances but could only recollect being ill. By the time she had recovered, Greshna was gone. There had been whispers that she lived in the swamp, mixing potions and praying to some voodoo god called Dambella.

Were the rumors true? she wondered. Had Greshna been a high priestess of voodoo?

Mounted, she set her course for Freedman Acres. When she had first begun freeing the slaves, Brianna realized they had no place to go, so she'd designated a few acres of the western-most property as their community. She allowed herself a moment of pride. It had been the perfect location. Surrounded on three sides by Lagniappe land and backed by the swamp, it was a safe haven.

They were far enough from the main house to enjoy their freedom, yet close enough to insure none of them fell prey to unscrupulous men who would sell them into slavery again. A careless word, the slip of a name, had alerted her to the fact that Greshna had forsaken the swamps to live among them.

At the time, it hadn't mattered. But now? Brianna couldn't help but wonder if Greshna could be behind this voodoo. *If only Ryan were here.*

She slowed her mount as she neared the growing rows of wooden structures. None of the houses were larger than a single room, but it was obvious the people who owned them were careful about their possessions.

Despite the lack of whitewash or other amenities, the buildings were in good repair. The small planked dog-trots were swept clean and appeared to be freshly scrubbed.

In several places, the attempts to grow greenery were being met with varied success. Three or four azalea bushes showed healthy signs of growth. Bougainvillea twined about the corner post of one house and tiny saplings dotted the dirt-packed common grounds.

Naked children stopped their play when she approached, staring at her with rapt attention.

Brianna guided her horse toward the center cabin, the fine hairs on her arms rising as she felt herself the object of scrutiny from every window. She couldn't stop now. She had to know the truth.

Ground reining her stallion, she moved toward the house with firm determination. She raised her hand to knock but the door swung open before she could move.

"Morning, *mam'zelle.*" Despite the intervening years, the soft French accent was the same; so precise, so assuredly proper.

"Greshna. I didn't know this was your house."

"I have been waiting for you." The withered old woman stepped outside, motioning Brianna toward one of the two straight-backed chairs. "I have cool water for your thirst," she offered.

Obligingly, Brianna accepted the chair and waited, hands clasped demurely on her lap while Greshna filled the canning jars that served as glassware.

Taking the offering, Brianna sipped slowly. There was no need to question. Greshna had known she would come. She would know the questions and when the moment was right, Brianna was certain she would have her answers.

"The cooling balm of fall will be late this year. It does not wish to be upon the land."

Brianna's brows knitted together in puzzlement. "Why?"

"The spirits are displeased. Their wrath hovers over this place in heavy oppression, like a storm building strength to vent its powerful revenge."

Brianna swallowed the tepid liquid, keeping her gaze

upon the common grounds that were now empty of children. "It's not angry spirits but humidity which oppresses. This is hurricane season. It will pass. There are no spirits."

"Then you did not hear the drums calling on Dambella last night."

"Drums?" Brianna softly queried.

"Yes, *mam'zelle*. They spoke of Belle Terre. They told of pain and a fierce anger that put flame in the heart and set wings to the feet. The spirits cry out in agony. They roam the land in search of revenge."

"I don't understand. Will the unrest at Belle Terre touch us?"

"You are white. How can you understand? You have never been torn away from your home, those you love. You do not know what it feels like to be treated as a dumb animal."

"Being white does not keep me safe from madness. Have I not lost my mother? My father? Even now a stranger nears who will take control of my home. I have come seeking answers and am met with riddles and spurned as one without understanding."

Greshna nodded. "For one so young, you show great promise. I will answer your questions." She leaned her arthritis-plagued body back, her bony shoulders pressing into the wood of the rigid chair.

For a brief instant, Brianna likened the old woman to a queen holding court in order to indulge her lowly subjects. *"M'sieur* Arlington said some of his people fled into the darkness last night. He thinks they may be hiding on Lagniappe."

"When men run, they must hide. Only with rest will they become strong enough to defend."

"Are they here, Greshna?"

"Only freed men and women live here."

"At the moment they are free. You have not answered my question." Brianna was determined not to overlook any possible meaning to Greshna's answers. She knew the woman was shrewd and she vowed to be more so.

"In this land, many will flee. Some in search of freedom, some in denial of the very reason for their existence, *ma petite.*" Greshna's intense gaze set Brianna to trembling inside.

"What . . . what do you mean? Are you saying some people are meant to be claimed as the property of others? Do you believe there are those who should be slaves?"

Greshna grinned, exposing a wide space of gum between yellowed teeth that reminded Brianna of fangs. "Slaves? Not all who flee will have skin the color of coffee. Chains can hold a body in bondage, but chains can be broken; then there is freedom." Her husky contralto rippled in laughter. "There are other ways to trap, to enslave, if you will."

"You're talking in riddles again."

"Some traps ensnare the very soul, *ma petite.*"

"Foolishness." Brianna wanted the disconcerting conversation to end. She had come to learn of the missing slaves from Belle Terre. Why did she feel the talk was of herself? She was no slave. She was not fleeing. "If . . . if chains can be . . . be broken," she stammered, "then there is escape from other traps."

Greshna's laughter came, the sound sharp and harsh in the still air. "When the soul is captive, escape is only possible when the heart is surrendered. You guard your heart well, *ma petite.*"

Brianna rose, eager to be away. Belle Terre's missing

slaves were not her concern. *Why did I come here?* Greshna wouldn't tell her anything. "I will assume you know nothing of the missing slaves. If you learn anything, send word to the main house."

"I have told you what I know. The trap is set, and the little rabbit's heart flutters with . . ." She broke off, laughing at some inner thought Brianna knew nothing of.

Remounting, Brianna gave a final warning. "Let none of Lagniappe's people become involved with the runaways. There is nothing I can do for them."

"I know, *ma petite.*" Her voice dropped, the words barely audible. "You cannot change destiny any more than you can stop the fluttering of a heart that must follow its own frenzied song. Do not run too far, little rabbit."

Her riding boots made sharp clicks on the wood as Brianna climbed the curved stairway to the veranda. Her efforts had been wasted in riding to Freedman Acres. If only Ryan had been here. *Ryan.* Her hopes dropped as quickly as they had soared.

It was much too soon for his return. If only he hadn't gone for the priest. *Priest! Wedding!* How could she have forgotten?

Brianna quickened her pace, hurrying into the house and mentally preparing herself for the scolding she knew Sudie would have waiting.

"There you is." The booming voice reached out to her from the main parlor. Brianna stopped, trying to summon her brightest smile as Sudie approached.

"Have you been looking for me, Aunt Sudie?"

"I has. There is a heap o' plannin' to be done and I can't does it all, missy. What's Massa Ryan goin' to think when he comes home and finds there ain't no weddin' ready?"

"Don't worry about Ryan. I don't feel an elaborate wedding is in order, what with my being in mourning. I will send Eli to The Pillars. The Maxwells will be delighted to stand as witnesses. That is all the church requires. The small upstairs parlor will do nicely for the ceremony and we can celebrate with a late luncheon."

"Massa Ryan might wants somethin' a mite more fancy than that."

Brianna shrugged her shoulders. "I doubt it, but I'm sure he will see things my way."

"Yes 'm. But after tomorrow, Massa Ryan jest mights be seein' things a whole lot different way."

"Nonsense. Ryan has no say. I've explained this before. We have a business arrangement. We are going through with this farce to ensure my continued management of Lagniappe."

"Uh-huh. And I s'pects Massa Ryan is goin' to has himself a time managin' de likes o' you."

Brianna stiffened her spine, giving Sudie the sternest look she could manage. She had always been Brianna's most trusted ally. "Hush that talk. We're both adults and we know what we're doing."

She swallowed the lump that seemed to be growing within her throat. Was Sudie abandoning her to the unpredictability of Ryan Fleming?

"At least one of you does," a grumpy Sudie retorted, lifting her heavy skirts to follow Brianna up to her room.

Even absent, Ryan seemed to be everywhere. Brianna breathed deeply, reminding herself of the clean rainwater scent of his flesh. Tremors filled her slight frame as she recalled strong arms cradling her in a protective embrace. Brianna carefully kept her back to Sudie, lest the blush she knew stained her cheeks give rise to the old mammy's curiosity.

"I thinks you ought to be callin' in de dressmaker. Don't seem fittin' to gets married without a proper gown and all."

"It's too late. I'll just have to make do with what's available."

"If you say so, missy."

Brianna stood at attention, allowing Sudie to relieve her of her riding attire. After her unfruitful discussion with Greshna, not to mention her earlier confrontation with Jeffrey, Brianna was forced to acknowledge her exhaustion. Maybe a nap before lunch was a good idea, she decided.

"Is I jest talkin' to myself here?" Sudie demanded.

"I'm sorry. I guess I'm tired. What did you say?"

"I asked about de massa movin'."

Panic sliced through her like a rapier. "Moving? But he can't. He promised."

" 'Course he can. You don't s'pects him to stay down de hall once you is married, do you?"

"No. Of course not," she agreed. "He will be far more comfortable in the adjoining rooms. They're much larger."

"I don't thinks that's what de massa has in mind."

Brianna's senses sounded in alarm. "What do you mean? Has he told you something, given you specific instructions on this move? What do you think he wants?"

"I don't thinks, I *knows*. And Massa Ryan don't has to tell me nothin', missy. I'se got eyes."

Sudie stooped to retrieve the garments from the floor, continuing her lecture. "I done seen him . . . de way his eyes follows you when you ain't lookin'. That man is like de thunder. Jest a rumblin' low whilst de lightnin' makes great slashes across de sky."

She looked at Brianna, her eyes wide with excitement. "Then, when you least expects it, de big boomin' comes, so fierce it plumb makes de earth shake and sets a body's heart to poundin'."

Sudie shook her head to and fro. "Yas suh. That man's been a-rumblin' for you ever since he come. De big boom is comin'. I knows it."

Brianna rubbed her hands across her arms, hugging herself in an effort to stop the chill sliding across her flesh. Fear of the ominous unknown? Or could it be eager anticipation? "Wicked. You're talking wicked, Aunt Sudie. I don't want to hear any more. Go see to the preparations and leave me to my rest."

"If that's what you wants, but don't go sayin' old Sudie didn't try to warn you."

She shuffled toward the door, her skirts making a soft swooshing sound as she crossed the carpet. Brianna kept her face averted, trying to ease the pained breaths that were so fast, so shallow.

"Sweet dreams, missy." The whispered wish was followed by a distinct click as the latch fell in place with the closing of the door.

Brianna threw herself across the bed, moaning in confusion. "Dreams, or are they nightmares?"

Chapter 11

"Oh, Ryan! You're back. It's so good to see you." Brianna threw herself into his arms, not caring how it might look or what he might think.

It had proven to be a nightmare after all. But he was back. Surely he could do something to make everything right again.

"Had I known my return would be met with such enthusiasm, I would have left long ago," he told her, his voice aquiver with amusement.

"Don't make jokes. It's not funny. Nothing is going as planned. It was supposed to be a simple wedding. I sent Eli to the Pillars. I thought the Maxwells could serve as our witnesses. Now this."

She stopped, waving an arm in a graceful arc to indicate the bevy of excitement.

"So I see." He grinned down at her, his hands loosely encircling her waist. "It would appear you managed to create a great deal of havoc in my short absence, my darling Brianna. Are my pleas forever to fall on deaf ears?"

"I did not create anything. It was all Ivy's fault. She acted behind my back."

He glanced about the immediate area, taking in the sight that threatened to approach pandemonium. "Maybe we should go to the study, where we can discuss this with some degree of privacy."

Brianna nodded, suddenly conscious of the many people moving about. "Yes, of course." She relinquished her hold about his waist, trying to affect a belated appearance of propriety. Wordlessly, she accompanied him to the solitude of the empty study.

Once the door was bolted behind them and they were settled, Ryan probed for more details.

"First, I would like to hear what part Ivy Arlington plays in this flurry of activity."

"I had scarcely awakened from my nap yesterday, when she came barging in here, telling me that I had given her no notice at all. She sent runners to every family that could possibly make their way to Lagniappe in time for the wedding. She never consulted me at all. She just took it upon herself to issue invitations to our wedding."

"That couldn't be more than one or two at most, could it?"

She sank back into the chair, her shoulders slumped in abject misery. "Three, but *M'sieur* Fargus was entertaining several relations, and . . ." She winced, unable to continue.

"And they are all coming en masse," Ryan said.

She nodded. "And Lawyer Westman is currently a guest of the Arlingtons."

"Is he here now?" A frown tugged at the corners of his

mouth. Westman's hasty departure had prevented his having the earnest discussion he desired.

"No. He's out with Jeffrey and some of the other gentlemen. According to Ivy, though, they shall all descend upon Lagniappe in ample time for the festivities."

"I do believe I detect a vague note of sarcasm. Perhaps you are entertaining second thoughts after all."

"Oh, no. Truly I'm not. It's just that Ivy has made such an elaborate affair of everything. All we need are witnesses and the priest." She looked at Ryan, the beginnings of a new worry forming.

"The priest! You did get a priest, didn't you? I didn't see him."

"Relax, my sweet. I would not be here otherwise. Father Paul was most anxious to see the Chapel. I had Toby show him the way."

"How nice. No doubt by now, Aunt Sudie has probably thrust a broom in his hand and has him sweeping the place. She's gotten as carried away with this nonsense as Ivy."

Ryan's laughter sounded, rich and full, in the quiet of their sanctuary. "I can't imagine Aunt Sudie following Ivy's example."

"It's true. You should have seen the two of them last night. They were pulling out every gown I own, trying to decide what I will wear for the ceremony. They didn't even have the courtesy to ask my opinion. Can you imagine!"

Ryan shielded the grin on his mouth behind an upraised hand. "I find it difficult that anyone could do anything without hearing your opinion, my sweet."

"They heard my opinion all right. They heard it very clearly. They just didn't listen. Ever since then, people have been scurrying about, polishing, moving. Even the children were set to work, gathering ferns and late blooms for 'atmosphere,' as Ivy calls it."

"So much for controlling your temper."

His gentle reminder stilled her frustration, bringing a trace of regret for her behavior. "I'm sorry, Ryan. But you weren't here; you didn't experience the myriad of problems that rose to tempt me beyond tolerance."

"Of course I wasn't. Maybe that's why I still have a few questions."

She tilted her head to one side. "I've told you everything. Surely you know what is going on. Our wedding has been turned into a social event."

He nodded, still struggling to restrain his mirth. "Yes, but how did it begin? When I left, Ivy knew nothing of the time chosen. She had to get the information from someone. You and I were the only two privy to the information. Since it wasn't me . . ." He let the sentence dwindle into silence.

"Jeffrey told her. I suppose I let it slip when I spoke with him last. He made me furious."

The mention of the man brought a tightness to his spine. His shoulders squared as he studied the new information. "When was this?"

Brianna answered without hesitation, revealing Jeffrey's appearance in the fields and relating the purpose of his visit.

"As loath as I am to admit it, I'm inclined to agree with Arlington this time. What he said makes sense. I don't want you riding out alone again until this matter is settled."

"Surely you jest." Her own body tensed, her senses acutely aware of the impact of his words. He was actually ordering her about! "Do you suggest that I am prone to bouts of hysteria?"

"No, my sweet. Your weaknesses are far more dangerous. You are more susceptible to trouble. That is why I must insist. It sounds as though we have enough trouble at the moment. Should you wish to go anywhere, I will be happy to accompany you."

"I was born on Lagniappe, lived every day of my life here. I am perfectly safe going where I choose by myself."

"You can't know that for certain, Brianna. Slaves on the run are desperate, and desperate men are not always rational. They could be anywhere, and I won't have your safety jeopardized."

"They aren't on Lagniappe." She held her head high, defying him with a look of cold hauteur.

"You appear to be certain of this."

"Greshna told me." She gasped, clasping her hands to her mouth. It seemed impossible that she had blurted out the information, but she had.

"I don't believe I've met this Greshna." Ryan leaned forward, entwining the fingers of his hands as he continued in a deceptively calm voice. "Suppose you tell me more, my little siren."

Brianna bowed her head, unwilling to speak of her visit with the old woman. She was still troubled by the conversation and felt more than a little reluctant to confide in him. He didn't know her world. How could he possibly understand?

"Very well. Since you don't wish to talk with me, I have no recourse but to find my answers elsewhere."

Ryan struggled to control his frustration with this new turn of events. He had thought he was making progress, slowly coming to the point where he and Brianna could trust each other. Her behavior proved otherwise.

"What are you going to do?"

"That is not your concern. In the meantime, remember what I have said. You are not to leave the safety of the main house without an escort." He rose, his long strides taking him quickly toward the door.

"She's a witch woman." The words were torn from her in a rushed confession.

Ryan turned to stare at her, his face a reflection of his disbelief. "A what?"

"It's true, Ryan. She took care of Maman's needs. Then Maman married Papa. That was when Greshna came to Lagniappe. When Maman died, she went away. Everyone says she is a voodoo priestess, a witch woman."

"And you believe this?"

"No. I . . ." Her lashes fluttered downward to shield her from the brooding intensity of his gaze.

Other images appeared behind the dark curtain. Candles, hundreds of them, burned, their tiny flames eking out pinpoints of light in her memory.

Her blood pulsed in her ears with a steady cadence, like the dull faraway throbbing of drums.

Slender fingers sought the circle of lace that felt so tight around her throat. *So hot. So very hot.* She pulled at the fragile fastenings, releasing the material with a soft gasp.

Ryan came to kneel by her side, his hands closing over hers in a gesture of comfort. "Brianna." Her skin felt like satin, cool and so incredibly soft to the touch. "Brianna," he whispered. "You can tell me."

"Can't tell. My fault. Papa will . . . will banish me. No," she said, her voice a tortured rasp of sound.

Ryan lifted her into his arms, carrying her to the sofa, where he gently laid her down. With an economy of motion, he poured a small glass of bourbon and tried to coax her to drink.

It slid down her parched throat in a fiery trickle. She coughed, strangling on the unaccustomed taste.

She watched him through a blur of tears, confused by his appearance. "Ryan?" Her hand reached up, her fingers touching his lips in tentative exploration. "When did you return?"

"Damn," he swore softly. *So close.* Yet he didn't doubt for a moment that she was innocent of trickery. Twice the truth had been snatched from his grasp. In exasperation, he tunneled his fingers through the thickness of his hair.

"Have I offended you?" Her eyes held a look that mingled pain with confusion. He sought to reassure her, offering a slow smile.

"Nay," he said, adding an Irish lilt to his voice. "A siren whose song is so sweet it would tempt the gods, whose face is so fair it makes the heart swell with joy in the beholding; such a treasure could never offend."

Her lips parted in a soft smile. "Aunt Sudie is right. You do have a way with words, *M'sieur* Fleming."

His hands pressed to her face. Slowly, he traced the path of her high-placed cheekbones with the pads of his thumbs. "Could it be I hear approval from the fair lady, or do you seek to make light of my moment of weakness?

She stared, her look of stark innocence causing him to be breathless with anticipation. "I do not consider such expression a weakness when it offers so much happiness."

"Then trust in me, my sweet, and this night I shall

teach you other expressions, those which transform happiness into heaven itself."

Trust. The word twisted like a sharp knife within the pit of her stomach. She had trusted her maman to be a loving force in her life, but that trust had been betrayed in death. She couldn't even remember the day she had left. Had she not trusted in Papa to know she would honor the efforts of his lifetime? He, too, had betrayed her.

Lagniappe, the only part of her life that remained untouched, could, at any moment, be denied her. Such a gift as trust could not be given lightly. Experience had taught her well. The price could be more than she would pay.

"I will try," she whispered, unable to meet his gaze.

As though sensing her reluctance, his hands relinquished the gentle caress of her face. "Maybe that is the secret of marriage, my sweet; two people always trying."

"Marriage." She pushed him away, struggling to return to an upright position. "Oh, Ryan. There is so much to be done before tonight. I cannot imagine why I am lying about as though I have nothing to tend."

"Easy," he cautioned. "There is no reason to upset yourself. I'm certain Aunt Sudie has everything well in hand." He favored her with a teasing grin. "And if not, I'm sure Ivy shall happily offer her own formidable services to ensure everything goes smoothly." He firmly pushed her back into a reclining position.

"I am truly sorry that you returned to find such a spectacle."

"Don't concern yourself. I want you to rest."

"How can I rest? Guests will be arriving most any hour. They must be greeted, made welcome to Lagniappe. The service is not until ten o'clock this evening."

"Why so late?"

"Actually, it is an acceptable time. Travel is often uncomfortable, and guests expect a proper interval for rest. Then, of course, there are gowns to be considered. They must be tended to remove wrinkles. And the dressing . . ."

He held up his hands in mock surrender. "Say no more, my sweet. I think ten o'clock is a perfect hour to wed."

She offered a shy smile. "Aren't you even curious as to the rest of Ivy's plans?"

"There's more?"

She gave a solemn nod. "There's the bridal supper. Ivy has scheduled it for midnight. Then, of course, there will be dancing."

"Of course."

"You aren't angry?"

He chuckled, his breath ruffling across her face like a warm breeze off the Gulf. Then his lips touched her, brushing with light strokes to tease her senses. "Not at all, but it does prove my point."

"What's that?"

"That you should rest." He rose, his long legs unfurling until he towered over her. "You stay here where it's quiet. You're less likely to be disturbed."

"And what of you?"

"I have a few things to attend."

"And our guests?"

"Don't worry, my sweet. I'll be finished long before they arrive. We'll greet them together."

She accepted his word, drifting toward peaceful sleep

even as he slipped from the room, closing the door quietly behind him.

Directing the moving of furniture, Toby started by him, stopping instantly at Ryan's command.

"Yas suh. What can I do for you this glorious day?"

"Tell me where I can find a woman called Greshna."

"I don't know about this, missy. You shouldn't be goin' downstairs, minglin' with de guests and all."

"Why not? I am their hostess."

"You is also de bride. It's powerful bad luck for de bride to be showin' herself before de weddin'."

"Somebody has to do it. I can't leave Ryan to fend for himself among a roomful of strangers. And besides, he approves. He told me himself that we would greet our guests together."

"I'll be glad to see that Ryan has proper introductions, if that's what worrying you, Brianna."

Brianna glanced over her shoulder, grinning in spite of the provocative sight before her. "Thanks, Ivy, but this is a duty I've reserved for myself."

Ivy gave a pretentious shudder, coming closer to inspect Brianna's gown. "Duty is something reserved for a time when you can do nothing else."

Behind her, Sudie gave a snort but said nothing.

"Some duties are more pleasant than others. Besides, it would be a pity for you to have all your time taken up by a man who is already taken."

"You is all fastened, missy. If you is set on presentin' yourself, you best be gettin' about it."

Ivy studied Brianna's appearance like a hungry cat sizing up her next meal.

"Thank you, Aunt Sudie." Brianna smiled at her neighbor. "Are you coming?" The look on Ivy's face sent confidence flooding through her frame. She pushed Sudie's warning of bad luck aside. At the moment, she couldn't recall a more lucky moment in her life.

Outside the door, Ryan waited, engaged in quiet conversation with Jeffrey. At her appearance, he abandoned the discussion to step forward and take her arm in his.

"You look radiant, my sweet."

"Thank you." She took her time, admiring the way he appeared in formal attire. Although Ryan was slightly taller than her father had been and boasted a more athletic physique, she was pleased with the results. Privately, Brianna gave thanks that she did possess a certain skill with needle and thread.

The hours she had spent altering her father's clothes while Ryan was ill had paid off. Never had she known a man more handsome, more intriguing than her soon-to-be husband.

Together they descended the stairs, prepared to greet the newly arriving carriage.

To her delight, the first to arrive were the Maxwells. Lifting her skirts, Brianna hurried down the steps to the carriage. "Mara," she called, laughing as her best friend clambered out of the conveyance.

"Brianna the Impetuous," she greeted, her laughter signifying her easy acceptance of the situation.

"I take it you know my sea siren quite well." Ryan's comment held a hint of amusement.

"Sea siren?" Mara looked at her friend, her generous mouth parting in a broad smile at the blush that stained Brianna's cheeks.

"It's nothing."

"Of course," Mara answered, quickly introducing herself to Ryan, then turning back with a sly wink. "It's nothing."

Henry's jovial appearance delayed Brianna's response while more introductions were made. Servants arrived to unload the portmanteau and bandboxes. The two couples started the upward climb, allowing Brianna the opportunity to elaborate on Ryan's comment.

"We have similar interests," she whispered, not wishing to intrude on the gentlemen's conversation.

"Mmmm. And from what I see, I suspect you will have even more interests after tonight." Ignoring Brianna's outraged gasp, the cheerful matron continued. "Oh, Brianna, you have no idea how thrilled I was when your man arrived with the news. Uh-oh."

With the unexpected warning, Brianna looked up just in time to see Ivy embracing Henry without any concern for his obvious discomfort. "Don't get in a snit, Mara. Even Ivy can recognize that Henry is so in love with you, he's practically blind to other women."

"I know. It wasn't me I was thinking about, Bri." She took Brianna's hands in hers, stopping on the veranda for a moment's privacy. "Is that the way your Ryan loves you?"

The question pierced her, inflicting a pain so poignant that she felt light-headed. *Love. If only it could be.*

"Ladies." Ryan's voice called her back to reality. "Surely you would not abandon us so quickly."

Mara's infectious laughter greeted him. "Certainly not to the tender mercies of Ivy Arlington," she quipped as she hastily followed her husband into the house. "Good evening, Ivy," she said as she sailed past the woman into the parlor.

Ryan lingered behind, tilting Brianna's face up with a gentle nudge under her chin. "You seem rather pensive suddenly."

"Ryan?" She stared into his eyes, admiring the silvery lights that glinted so brightly. She felt an overwhelming need to touch the sensual contours of his mouth, to feel his lips on hers. If only . . .

"What is it, my sweet?"

She forced herself to smile. "Nothing. It's nothing. We better join our guests."

Throughout the early evening, carriages turned off the main road to journey the mile-long drive that led to Lagniappe.

First came the Fargus family, followed in close succession by other relatives: the Blanchards, the Wilmots, and the Roucheaus. To her astonishment, even the Fontaine family managed to make it in time. Brianna surmised their presence could only be credited to Mara. They both had a fondness for Elyese Fontaine. Oliver Westman proved the last arrival, preferring to remain at Belle Terre until the last moment.

He acknowledged Ryan with a stiff bow, then focused his attention on Brianna. "I had not expected to see you until the ceremony."

Ryan's resonant voice intervened. "That's part of Brianna's irresistible charm. She is inclined to do the unexpected."

His quick retort filled her with a warm glow, which lingered even when she was obliged to withdraw to prepare for the ceremony.

At the top of the stairs, Brianna paused for one final look. She could see Ryan's dark head move as though nodding in agreement with another. "Ivy." The woman stood close, her hand resting lightly upon Ryan's arm. Her face tilted upward, clearly revealing her excitement of the chase . . . another conquest. "Damnation," Brianna muttered as she forced herself to turn away.

So intent was she on thinking of Ivy with Ryan that Brianna was down to her smallclothes before she noticed the gown carefully arranged across the poster bed. "Aunt Sudie, where did this come from?"

"One of de boys. Don't rightly know which one."

She fingered the batiste material. Soft with age, it held a tint of ivory to highlight to perfection its old-fashioned elegance. "I think you do. Tell me, Sudie."

Gone was the affectionate term of *Aunt*. Her voice trembled with emotion.

"That there gown was sent here from Freedman Acres."

"Greshna." It was a guess, but the moment she said the name, Brianna knew in her heart she was correct.

"Yes'm."

Without a word, Brianna turned away. "It will be time soon. We better get my bath finished. Even with the fire, it will take a while for my hair to dry."

The ritual was performed in total silence. Words presented too great a risk. Brianna turned inward, her thoughts a mixture of memories that posed questions but offered no answers, no solace as she strived to understand this latest happening.

Help me. The terrified plea screamed in the distance of her past. Her hands pushed away the rose-scented bubbles to reveal the clear water beneath.

In this land, many will flee. Some in search of freedom,

some in denial of the very reason for their existence, ma petite.

Greshna's prophesy rose to taunt her. Is the call for help a cry of freedom? Or the plaintive wail of a soul entrapped? She wondered.

Brianna started at the touch of Sudie's hand on her shoulder. Glancing upward, she watched as Aunt Sudie climbed atop the sturdy stool with her water-filled pail.

Motionless, she stood waiting while Sudie sluiced the contents of the bucket over her body. Frothy bubbles burst on her skin, slithering down her slick flesh to plunge into the bath water where they were hopelessly crushed beneath the burden of a stronger force.

Accepting her wrapper from Aunt Sudie, Brianna donned it quickly and cinched the tie about her waist. She reached for the hairbrush Sudie held. "I'll do it."

"Yes'm." Without protest, the old mammy left the room, allowing Brianna the solitude she craved.

Exercising the same patience she had often observed in Sudie, Brianna pulled the brush slowly through the wet tangle. "One, two, three," she counted. Each stroke received a number, until the heavy skein lay in submission over one shoulder.

Curled up close to the fireplace, Brianna began the arduous task of brushing small sections toward the heat. Time passed unnoticed as she concentrated on the task.

She didn't want to think. To think required seeking the answers to all the riddles that plagued her. How she feared the pain those answers might bring.

"Your hair has long since dried, *ma petite*. It is time to prepare yourself for the rest of your life."

"Greshna!" She stared at the woman standing so regally in the middle of her room.

A turban wound about her head, accenting skin the color of coffee richly laced with cream. A long multihued robe hung loosely about her gaunt frame to touch the floor. A strange assortment of necklaces adorned her, shielding the faintly visible remains of withered breasts from full view.

"There is no call to fear, *ma petite*. Come. There is much to be done before you see your man."

"You shouldn't be here. You must leave, return to your home before anyone learns of your presence."

"But my presence is already known. It has been known for many years that I would be here on this day."

Further objections lodged on her tongue, unable to find voice. The words made no sense, but she knew they were truthful. She could hear it in the melodic sound of her French accent, could see it in the clearness of black eyes that watched her with a wisdom known only to those who had seen life in all its shapes.

As one in a trance, Brianna obeyed, moving toward the gown that lay in fragile splendor upon her bed.

"Maman wore this when she married Papa." Brianna stared at her reflection in the oak-framed glass that stood in the corner of her room.

"Oui, and on that special night, I dressed her just as I have dressed you. It was then I pledged to dress the girl child I had seen in her future."

"I didn't know they had a night wedding."

"It was a night much like this."

"Was she . . . was she very beautiful?"

"Her hair hung down her back in a thick mantle that rivaled the sky with its blackness. The stars littered the heaven like a king's treasure trove of diamonds." Greshna paused, chuckling softly to herself before continuing. "But it was a display that received only trivial notice. The starlight in her eyes knew no worthy match. She was very beautiful, just as you are this night."

"Papa always said he loved Maman as much as life."

"It was so, and she loved him."

Brianna stared at her reflection. Her own mahogany tresses gleamed, but not like the sky. They held the glowing amber found in a carefully banked fire. Eyes of pure jade peered back at her. "There are no stars in my eyes. Perhaps it is because there is no love. Not like Maman and Papa."

"Love is a curious thing, *ma petite*. When a person finds love, she has two choices."

"Two? What are they?"

"She may hold it tight, hoarding it deeply within her heart."

"Don't speak to me of the heart. The heart is a source of pain."

"True, but how does one recognize joy if she has not experienced pain?" She smiled, reaching out to touch Brianna's arm. "Come, *ma petite*. It is time. You must not keep your future waiting. Sudie is downstairs. She will take you to the Chapel."

At the door, Brianna stopped. "You said there were two choices. What is the second one?"

When no answer was forthcoming, Brianna turned back, needing to know. Across the trunk that sat at the end of her bed lay her wrapper, neatly folded. The covers of her bed were turned down in preparation of occupancy. At the far end of the room, the flames burned low in the fireplace.

In the dark of night they cast shadows across the width of the room. Shadows. Nothing but shadows meet her gaze. "Greshna?"

She was alone in the room.

"Oh, Greshna. I love him. I must know the second choice."

Chapter 12

"You is de most beautiful bride this county has ever seen," Aunt Sudie announced, beaming broadly as she surveyed the results of Greshna's effort.

"You're biased," Brianna answered. Her nerves jerked and twisted throughout her body, making it impossible to give credence to anything beyond her own emotional state.

"Don't know what that biased thing is, but I say you is beautiful and you shore enough is. You look just like your mama."

Her mouth dropped into a worried frown. "Greshna said Maman had stars in her eyes the night she married Papa. I looked in the mirror. I saw no stars in mine, just eyes."

A dark scowl dissipated Sudie's smile. She dropped to her knees, intent on spreading the circular train of Brianna's gown. "Don't you be worryin' none about such things. You jest wait. Massa Ryan will be puttin' stars in your eyes soon enough."

"I hope you're right."

" 'Course I is." She twisted about, looking up at the

pensive young bride. "You ain't thinkin' about changing yore mind, is you?"

Brianna shook her head. "No. Even if I wanted to, I couldn't. I must think of Lagniappe."

Sudie gave a snort of derision. "You best be thinkin' on de massa." She rose, pulling her bulky frame upright with slow deliberation. "You just has yourself a peep through that curtain. You'll see what I mean."

Slowly, Brianna moved forward, taking care not to be seen as she inched the heavy cloth aside to view the interior of the private chapel.

From the cool dimness of the vestibule, she could see the entire gathering. The tiny sanctuary was full despite the hasty invitations.

A low murmur of voices could be heard among the gathering as they chatted while waiting for the candle-light service to begin.

Ferns spilled in profusion from recently placed vases and an arrangement of white roses provided an elegant centerpiece.

For all the rush, it looked as though every detail had been carefully planned months in advance.

A lone figure stood to the right of Father Paul. He waited in solitary magnificence, no trace of impatience or nervousness evident on his face.

"Ryan." She spoke his name in an awed whisper. The rest of the world ceased to exist as her attention focused on him. Brianna admired the proud tilt of his head, the broad expanse of squared shoulders. Her inventory continued with increasing boldness until she found herself clutching the velvet drapery between trembling fingers.

Forcing herself to exert a self-control that did not

extend beyond an outer facade, she stepped back. The curtain dropped into place.

Her wayward thoughts seemed to take on a life of their own. It was a prospect she found both frightening and . . . promising.

Soft laughter rumbled within the ponderous confines of Sudie's breasts. "That man is waiting for my baby. Don't go makin' him waits too long, else his patience might wear too thin."

Moving to one side, Sudie pulled the heavy cording that parted the drapes. "You go on now, missy. Don't look back."

She took the first step forward, only faintly aware of the woman's encouragement. Scarcely had the velvet parted when Ryan's eyes searched out her own rapt gaze.

A second step, then a third followed, each move bringing her closer to him. As she approached the altar, her step faltered.

His arm stretched toward her, his hand taking hers in a firm grasp of assurance.

No longer was it an obscure plan, designed with the purpose of defeating the intentions of an unknown earl. It was real. It was now.

With solemn dignity, they took their places before the black-robed priest. Father Paul began reciting the time-honored words, his voice firm and clear.

She paid scant attention, her thoughts directed toward the man who stood by her side. *What if he doesn't want me? What if he demands the freedom I so foolishly offered?*

Her thoughts were cut short by the vibrancy of his voice. ". . . I take thee, Brianna, to be my lawful wedded wife."

Moments later, she echoed his pledge. Like a mist-shrouded dream, the service continued until they knelt before the altar, heads bowed.

". . . by the power of God . . ." The words hung in midair as if frozen in time. Brianna glanced up to find the priest poised to speak, his mouth gaping wide.

Behind her a low hum of voices, all speaking at once, could be heard. *But why?* She turned to Ryan. He answered with a smile that spoke more eloquently than words.

It was then she heard them. The drums. From miles away came the muted sound. They called to her, but the pagan voices were not menacing. She felt no fear. Their incessant throbbing pulse invaded her lithe body, filling her with a welcome warmth. She returned his smile with one of her own.

"Continue, Father." His command, quietly spoken, lured the priest from his trance.

The voices stilled as Father Paul picked up his speech, his voice rising as he continued until the final "Amen" was uttered.

In a single motion Ryan rose, pulling Brianna up with him to stand at his side.

His face drew near. She could see her reflection in the glittering light of his eyes. Mesmerized, she waited, her lips slightly parted in growing anticipation.

So sweet was the exquisite pain she felt that it swiftly tested her endurance.

His lips caught hers, demanding, then giving with breathtaking wonder. The throbbing rhythm renewed itself, but this time the sound came from the region of her heart.

* * *

Wish You Were Here?

You can be, every month, with Zebra Historical Romance Novels.

YOU'RE GOING TO LOVE GETTING
4 FREE BOOKS

These books worth $18, are yours without cost or obligation
when you fill out and mail this certificate.

*If the certificate is missing below, write to: Zebra Home Subscription Service, Inc.,
120 Brighton Road, P.O. Box 5214, Clifton, New Jersey 07015-5214*

Complete and mail this card to receive 4 Free books!

Yes! Please send me 4 Zebra Historical Romances without cost or obligation. I understand that each month thereafter I will be able to preview 4 new Zebra Historical Romances FREE for 10 days. Then, if I should decide to keep them, I will pay the money-saving preferred publisher's price of just $3.75 each...a total of $15. That's $3 less than the publisher's price. (A nominal shipping and handling charge of $1.50 per shipment will be added.) I may return any shipment within 10 days and owe nothing, and I may cancel this subscription at any time. The 4 FREE books will be mine to keep in any case.

Name _____

Address _____ Apt. _____

City _____ State _____ Zip _____

Telephone ( ) _____

Signature _____ LP1294
(If under 18, parent or guardian must sign.)

Terms, offer and prices subject to change without notice. Subscription subject to acceptance by Zebra Books.
Zebra Books reserves the right to reject any order or cancel any subscription.

An $18 value.
FREE!

No obligation
to buy
anything, ever.

ZEBRA HOME SUBSCRIPTION SERVICE, INC.

120 BRIGHTON ROAD

P.O. BOX 5214

CLIFTON, NEW JERSEY 07015-5214

Everyone crowded about them, pressing closer as they added their best wishes for happiness. Brianna watched the scene as though in a daze. She scarcely remembered the words spoken by the priest.

It was done. She was Mrs. Ryan Fleming. She stole a sidelong glance in the direction of the groom, only to find him watching her, a half-smile on his lips.

"Ryan?" she queried.

"Yes, my sweet siren?"

She smiled back at him. Why the phrase no longer offended her, she could not say. Brianna only knew she found an odd sort of comfort in hearing him say the words, knowing they were meant for her alone. "What do we do now?"

He leaned closer, whispering in her ear. "What do you want to do?" he asked.

She grew hot beneath the dark intensity of his scrutiny. There was no denying the meaning behind the seemingly innocent question he had posed. "I . . . I . . . th . . . ink we should lead our guests back to the main house," she stammered.

The answering gleam in his eyes caused her to begin a desperate search for some rational reason to justify hurrying back to the house. It would never do for him to think she was eager to reach the marriage bed. "I'm sure our friends must be famished for food."

Ryan's deep laughter filled the room, causing several in attendance to exchange knowing looks, which added to Brianna's discomfort. "My sweet, how you wound my ego. We are only minutes joined in matrimony and your thoughts are for food. I am deeply pained."

The words seared her heart. "Oh, Ryan, I didn't mean . . ." She halted, caught by the mirth that danced with silvery lights in those oh-so-mesmerizing eyes. "You rogue," she whispered. "You really are wicked."

"Don't worry, my sweet. It will remain our secret," he countered, his gaze darkening with repressed passion. Turning his attention to the crowd, Ryan deftly took possession of Brianna's arm and guided her forward.

The merry guests moved aside, laughingly falling in behind the bride and groom to form a winding procession back to the main house.

Outside, Brianna saw Aunt Sudie hugging Toby when they appeared. Behind them, the people of Lagniappe joined in a song of jubilation as Ryan and Brianna led the way back to the main house.

From the corner of her eye, Brianna thought she caught a brief glimpse of the witch-woman, Greshna. She turned for a better look but saw nothing.

"Looking for someone, my sweet?" Ryan asked.

"Not really," she said, unable to explain the words Greshna had spoken. She turned her attention to the growing crowd.

Everywhere she looked, Brianna was greeted by shouts of approval and unrestrained joy. As they climbed the stairway to the veranda, she knew there would be a great celebration throughout the quarters tonight. Before her, the doors of Lagniappe opened wide in welcome.

To the encouraging cheers of the merry throng, she felt herself being lifted into Ryan's arms and carried across the threshold. How long would such unbridled joy continue?

In the distance, she could hear the drums once again beating out that pagan rhythm. All around her was laughter, but within the depths of her heart, Brianna

Calhoun Fleming could not help but wonder what life would hold when the drums stopped.

"I tell you, gentlemen, it was a most impressive occurrence."

Ryan listened intently to the discussion, offering no comment as Fargus held the attention of the small group of men.

"I suppose you must maintain your authority," Henry ventured, "but hanging seems extreme. The man's crime was loving a woman. It is the natural way of things."

Jeffrey slapped him on the back, ridiculing his sentiments in a loud voice. "That's the main problem with your thinking, Maxwell. The woman—as you call her—is property. And that property did not belong to that temperamental buck."

"That's right," Fargus answered. "Anyway, you missed the point. He struck a white man." Others muttered in agreement. "Anytime some damn slave gets so uppity he thinks he can commit such an atrocity, he deserves to find a rope about his neck. You can't coddle them."

"Here. Here." Jeffrey raised his glass in salute. "That's the same thing I was trying to explain to Fleming." He darted a sidelong glance at his host. "Of course, I suppose a man who spends his life at sea can hardly be expected to understand what it takes to manage a plantation."

All eyes turned toward Ryan. He met their curiosity with casual indifference. "I find the sea air cleanses the mind . . . allows a man to think more clearly. You should try it some time, Arlington."

Ribald laughter greeted the suggestion. Maxwell rewarded Ryan with a companionable slap on the back. "I do believe you'll learn the way of things quick enough."

"Well, I am delighted you gentlemen are enjoying the evening." The feminine voice brought an immediate halt to the conversation as men bowed in respectful greeting. "But what of the dear ladies?" Ivy fluttered her lashes in bold flirtation. "I put forth a great deal of effort to make this evening possible and here you are huddled in a group discussing whatever men discuss when you should be dancing with the ladies."

She offered Ryan a smile. "Surely the new master of Lagniappe does not intend to slight my generosity by neglecting to honor me with one little dance."

He offered a courtly bow and after making polite excuses to the gentlemen, Ryan escorted her to the adjoining room where the furniture had been cleared for the occasion.

Reminded of their social obligations, the others broke off the conversation and obediently trailed after them.

"That Miss Ivy certainly knows how to gain a man's attention." Sissy Wilmot's plaintive observation sparked Brianna's interest.

She abandoned her private musings in time to watch her neighbor's grand entrance into the hastily arranged ballroom.

Several gentlemen followed in her wake, meandering off in different directions once they arrived, but it was Ivy's escort who held her rapt attention. *Ryan.*

She tried to quell the feelings of discomfort that invaded her. Not once had he complained as they greeted the well-wishers in the lengthy receiving line. She reminded herself of his attentiveness throughout the supper feast. He had even done his duty by leading her in the first dance of the evening.

It was not enough. Her discomfort increased, threatening to evolve into pain. Ryan whirled the smiling woman around the floor while Brianna continued to watch them. A part of her ached to feel his arms about herself.

The music stopped. Ivy curled her arm around Ryan's, steering him toward the heavily laden refreshment table . . . and away from Brianna.

"Where are you going?"

Brianna turned, a tremulous smile touching her lips as she answered Mara. "It's rather stifling in here. I think I'll step out for a breath of air."

"An admirable idea. It's been a most hectic day. You're probably beginning to feel the strain of all the excitement." Mara gave her an impulsive hug. "Don't worry. I'm confident your husband will treat you gently. It's natural for every bride to experience a twinge of anxiety."

Brianna lowered her head, hiding the truth she knew would be reflected upon her face. "You're a good friend." Lifting her skirts, she hurried away as quickly as possible without drawing more attention to herself.

Strain? If only she knew, Brianna mused.

The night air touched her face, soothing, calming the churning thoughts that threatened her reserve. "My husband," she said, testing the words with her tongue, listening to the sound as the declaration reached her ears. "Mrs. Ryan Fleming." How strange it sounded. "Brianna Fleming."

"Please spare me the tedium of repetition, my dear."

Brianna whirled about, startled to discover she was not alone on the veranda. From the shadows, he pushed himself away from the support of the wall, propelled toward her with an unsteady gait.

She stepped back, forced to stop as she felt the press of the solid railing against her back. "Jeffrey."

"Correct, my dear. Your obedient servant."

He leaned forward, his hands grasping the railing on either side of her to effectively bar further retreat. She smelled the distinctive aroma of bourbon upon his breath.

"I . . . I thought I was alone."

"Perish the thought. You can never be alone." His face moved forward. She turned her head aside, then felt the moistness of his mouth touch her cheek. "Haven't I always been here for you?"

"Don't," she warned. "I'm . . . married."

"To the wrong man." He raised a hand, entwining his fingers within the inviting lushness of her unbound hair. "I'm the man you should have married."

Brianna tried to pull away but found her tresses entangled around unyielding digits. "You're hurting me."

He laughed, the sound slurred by overindulgence. "It is I who have been hurt. For years, I have assumed you would be mine, share my name, bear my children. Can you imagine how it felt to watch you marry another? Have you no pity for my position?"

"I'm sorry, Jeffrey."

"Then prove it. Come away with me tonight. Leave this vagabond from the sea before it's too late. You can never belong to him. You're mine . . . mine." With unexpected swiftness, he captured her lips, forcing her to accept his attention.

She pushed her hands against his chest. Nausea rose from the depths of her stomach. Her breath was trapped, burning with searing intensity within her lungs.

"There you are, my sweet siren."

Release proved instant. Brianna took deep reviving gulps of air. With difficulty, she sought to control the quaking of her body, to bring coherence to her thoughts.

"Well, well, well. If it isn't the lucky bridegroom." Jeffrey propped himself against the railing, smiling benignly.

"Arlington."

Brianna cringed at the dark look he gave her, even though he addressed her in the most civil of terms, making no reference to the scene he had witnessed.

"I've been looking for you, sweet siren. It's getting late."

"I . . . I stepped out . . . for a breath of air. It was hot inside."

"Mmmm. I got the same impression out here. It seems quite warm . . . for the season."

The thinly disguised accusation wounded, then angered her. It was not her fault. If he hadn't been so completely occupied with the charms of Ivy Arlington, she would likely not have ventured forth from the room.

Jeffrey's harsh laughter infringed upon her indignant thoughts. "Come now, Fleming. Surely you don't begrudge me a kiss from the bride. A farewell kiss, as it were."

Ryan looked at her, his lips curling into a desultory smile that never quite reached his eyes. "Of course not." He held out his hand in silent indication for her to join him.

She stepped forward, her muscles taut, her movement

unnaturally stiff with tension. His hand curled about her forearm, fingers biting painfully into her flesh.

"Just make certain you remember it is farewell," he warned. "I am not a man given to sharing what is mine."

How dare he! He spoke of her as though she were no more than property. Wrath burgeoned to life, swelling to fill her with a desire for revenge.

Rage choked back response, feeding on the turbulence of her emotions as Ryan guided her through the throng of merrymakers toward the stairway.

"Where are you taking me?"

"As I said, it's late. It's been a long day and I find it senseless to prolong it."

"We have guests."

He glanced about, calmly surveying the revelers who continued their quests for entertainment, unmindful of the couple. "I doubt they will notice our absence. Shall we?" He gestured toward the upper story.

The fingers of her free hand coiled about the smooth polished wood of the banister. "No." His earlier warning reminded her of how easily men thought to subjugate a woman. Hadn't her own father been guilty of the same crime? She refused to be humiliated by such treatment. "No," she repeated. "Our agreement doesn't include . . ." Small, even teeth caught at her bottom lip, halting her speech.

"Include what?" he queried.

She looked at him in silence, her tongue growing thick within the confines of her suddenly dry mouth.

"Say it," he demanded. He reached out to press the palm of one hand to her pale cheek. "Tell me precisely what our agreement doesn't include."

"You know."

"Do I, my oh-so-delectable siren? My seductive little sea witch."

"I . . . I don't want to go with you. I won't," she hastily amended. Brianna burned with shame. Her body developed a will of its own, boldly denying her refusal.

His eyes glowed, transformed into hard spheres of metal. "Relax, sweet siren. You have nothing to fear." He leaned near, holding her gaze in a searing heat.

Her lips parted, whether in silent supplication or to call back the denial, she could not say.

"I have no desire to claim a mercenary heart, no matter how sweet the siren's song. I would sooner find surcease in the doubtful charms of a woman like Ivy. At least she can appreciate my efforts."

In sharp dismissal, he released her to climb the steps alone.

She stared after his retreating form, the full impact of his harsh condemnation penetrating slowly. Her wounded pride swelled with the burning infection of new and greater humiliation. He had spurned her! "How dare he!" she fumed, lifting the hem of her skirts to follow. "Ryan," she called.

He never paused, the wide expanse of his back held ramrod straight as he continued his upward course.

She quickened her pace, determined to catch him. "Ryan. Don't you dare walk away from me," she said, her earlier anger cast aside. She wanted to scream, to throw something.

A new, more powerful rage emerged to imbue her with a burst of strength, enabling her to reach his side as he started down the corridor. Reaching out, her fingers curled about the top of one wrist.

His face an image of cool indifference, Ryan stopped, watching, waiting for her to speak.

The unexpected exertion had taken its toll, leaving her to stand before him, pale and shaken as she gasped for breath. "You . . . can't . . . I . . ." she began. Her eyes filled with moisture, turning them to deep pools that reflected her confusion and misery. "Oh, Ryan."

Instinct pushed her forward, seeking the protective safety of his powerful embrace.

In quiet reflection, Ryan held her. Losing control was not a part of his nature, but honesty forced him to accept the facts. Finding her in the arms of Jeffrey Arlington had come as a severe blow. It had taken all his willpower not to throttle the life from the smirking drunk and claim her for himself on the spot.

He breathed in the rose scent of her, wondering at his own behavior. How would he ever get her to accept the Earl of Tyrone if he failed to gain acceptance as Ryan Fleming?

Sliding one hand up her back, he laced his fingers through the long, cascading waves of mahogany tresses.

Feeling a gentle tug when his fingers caught in a tangle of curls, Brianna risked a tentative glance at him. "I'm sorry."

She knew the words were contrary to her earlier actions, but she no longer cared. She wanted him, and nothing else seemed to matter.

"Not nearly as much as I," he muttered, his emotions still guarded by the chiseled granite of his somber expression.

"I . . . I need time, Ryan. I've never been . . . married," she said, her stumbling confession bringing a slight smile to the sensual fullness of his mouth.

"Nor have I, my sweet tempting siren."

"But, I mean . . ." He placed one finger to her mouth, stopping any further explanation.

"I know what you mean," he answered. His mouth came closer, enveloping the waiting petals of her lips with a warmth that spread like wildfire through her untried body.

"My, my, my," the feminine voice purred, the sound parting the couple as Brianna hastily pulled free from the heated embrace.

"Ivy, what are you doing here?" Brianna asked.

"Yes," Ryan added as he slid his arms about Brianna's minuscule waist, gently pulling her backward to rest against his chest. "I would think you would be busily garnering the glowing compliments from every gentleman on the premises."

Ivy gave a husky chuckle, her eyes grazing Ryan with undisguised appreciation and desire. "Words can only soothe the savage beast so long," she countered. "Isn't that right, Captain?"

"Ivy!" Brianna stared at the woman in shocked surprise.

"Oh, come now, Brianna. Surely you don't think the captain expects to tuck you in like a little girl and settle for a small peck on the cheek, do you?"

Brianna felt Ryan's chest vibrating with repressed amusement. She knew the urge to strangle both of them—Ivy for her brazen tongue, and Ryan for his continued silence in the face of Ivy's blatant ridicule.

Without hesitation, she raised one dainty foot, swiftly bringing the heel back against Ryan's unprotected shin.

"Humph." The muffled sound crashed into her ear in a heated breath of air. Brianna inhaled deeply against the involuntary tightening of his hands about her waist. She felt as though a heat wave, heavy with breath-stealing humidity, had come surging through the hallway to wrap itself about her.

Searching the vast hall, her eyes scanned every shadow. She needed to find a sanctuary, someplace safe from prying eyes. Why hadn't she realized she was so exposed? So vulnerable?

As her logical nature began to assert itself, her surroundings took shape. Brianna realized they were standing outside the door to her own quarters. Ivy's outrageous comment began to make sense, in a warped sort of way.

"We were about to retire for the evening," Ryan offered, his rich baritone sending tiny tremors bounding across the responsive chords of Brianna's acutely sensitive nerves.

"I would wish you a pleasant evening," Ivy cooed, "but knowing our sweet Brianna as I do, you will most likely occupy separate rooms."

Faintly, Brianna heard Ryan make a small choking sound. Anger rose, fueled by a twinge of jealousy as she studied the hopeful invitation Ivy was so clearly issuing to Ryan. "Don't be foolish, Ivy. Separate rooms are for women who can't hold a man's interest for more than a brief period."

It was Ivy's turn to gasp, giving Brianna a measure of satisfaction as she watched the color drain from her rival's face.

"We'll see you in the morning," Brianna sweetly intoned, her face tilting upward to receive Ryan's appreciative gaze. "Maybe."

He shrugged, bowing from the waist to the woman.

"Good night, Ivy." With a disarming smile, Ryan followed Brianna into the bedchamber. The door closed softly behind him, barring all but the lively nymph before him from sight and mind.

Passion swelled as he watched the gentle sway of her hips as she crossed the room. Her agitated stride set the lustrous length of her hair into provocative motion. Like a paintbrush applying the finishing touch to a masterpiece, the tips of her mane stroked the delightful curve of firm buttocks.

The outside world vanished in the wake of far more interesting pursuits. His smile deepened. The first stirrings of pleasure yet to come awakened desire that refused denial.

Chapter 13

"It appears my sea siren not only sings, she also scratches," Ryan said. He propped his foot on the edge of a nearby chair, raising his trouser leg to examine the small wound made by the sharp heel of Brianna's slippers.

She whirled about, her eyes wide with astonishment. "You're in my room."

"After what you said to your . . . ah . . . friend Ivy, I'm afraid you made it impossible to be anywhere else."

His smile was evidence that the situation was not one he found onerous. Brianna recalled waking up one morning to just such a smile.

"I'm certain you will agree," she began, squaring her shoulders. "I didn't have much choice in the matter."

Again he offered the same lazy smile. "You could have maintained a polite silence."

"Like you did? No thank you, sir. There is no way I would let her get by with the outrageous behavior she was suggesting."

"What was she suggesting, my sweet?"

Rose-flushed lips opened, then closed. She certainly

couldn't point out that Ivy had very nearly invited him to share her bed instead of remaining with Brianna. The thought set her stomach to churning with an exquisite agony. *Oh, no*. Telling him the truth . . . that Brianna Calhoun Fleming felt desire for her husband . . . was out of the question.

He had said nothing of love, of the future. She tilted her chin outward, straining to retain her pride. That and Lagniappe were all she had.

"I may have led a somewhat sheltered life, Ryan, but Ivy was hardly discreet. I am not stupid."

"I don't recall ever saying you were."

She thought of his earlier display of self-confidence. His casual demeanor that echoed the sentiments of male perception, the age-old perception that woman was but chattel and man the victor. *To the victor belong the spoils.* Anger roiled hotly within her veins.

"You don't have to say the words when actions speak so eloquently, sir."

A winged brow arched in question. "I would be most interested in what you think my actions say, Mrs. Fleming."

Brianna ignored the reminder that she was legally bound to this man. "Men view women as jewels to collect and display before their peers, striving to prove their masculinity. There is no thought for a woman's feelings in the matter, and God forbid a woman should have intelligent thoughts. So unseemly."

"I am not all men, Brianna. Never forget that fact. I treat each person, be they male or female, according to the behavior they exhibit. As for Ivy Arlington"—Ryan paused, offering a casual shrug of his massive shoulders—"she delights in being considered a jewel."

"Well, I don't."

"No, but at the moment, your actions could well be considered along the lines of a spoiled child." He moved closer, his hands reaching out to cup her face in his upturned palms. "An overly imaginative and somewhat jealous child," he added.

"I'm not the least bit jealous," she hotly denied.

"I'm glad. You have no reason to be."

Her anger wilted beneath the warmth of his smile and the heat that glowed in the silvery depth of his eyes. "I . . . I'm not jealous," she repeated.

"Then it would appear this discussion need never be broached again." Despite his quiet tone, she sensed the firm finality of the situation. Brianna took a calming breath, grateful to hear her own voice sounding so composed. "As you wish, *m'sieur.*"

"I wish. Now tell me something, my little siren. What do you wish?"

The last vestiges of anger dissipated like the morning fog before a brilliant sun. "I don't know," she answered simply.

"Then perhaps we should relax and discuss it," he suggested.

Ryan looked about the room, quickly spotting the crystal decanter and two glasses on the bedside table. He advanced to fill each glass with a generous amount of brandy. Recalling her earlier attempt to imbibe of strong spirits, he knew the liquor was a new addition, one he surmised had been made by Aunt Sudie.

"Would you care for a drink?"

"A drink?" Her eyes widened as she saw the tray. "No. I don't drink . . . much," she added.

One corner of his mouth tilted into a half-smile. "I

know. It has been a difficult day though. It might serve
to calm you."

"I doubt it." Nothing could calm her. She was ada-
mant on that account. Ryan was in her room and there
was little doubt that he intended to stay.

Even worse was the knowledge that a part of her was
glad he would stay. "Maybe a small one," she relented.

He returned the top to the container, then made his
way toward her. "Shall we sit down, get comfortable?"
Without waiting for an answer, he led her to the comfort
of the lounge, taking care not to move too quickly.

She had no idea what would happen next but Brianna
was anxious to learn, and God help her, she wanted
Ryan to teach her. There was no resistance as he gently
pulled her down before him, tugging until she was reclining, her back against his chest.

She could feel the steady thump, thump of his heart
against her spine, the whisper of each breath brushing
her cheek.

Every fiber of her being tensed as his hand slid the
length of her rib cage, then moved forward, coming to
rest on the flat planes of her stomach. She dared not
move, trying to remain calm by focusing on the flicker of
the fire recently laid to ward off the night chill.

Ryan sipped slowly of his brandy, making no further
move to claim what was rightfully his. He inhaled the
fresh fragrance of her hair, dreamed of tangling his fingers within its silken thickness.

A sturdy log gave a sharp cracking sound within the
hearth. A yellow flame shot upward. Brianna swallowed
the golden liquid within her mouth, briefly closing her
eyes against its scorching trail.

Small patches glowed whitely within the log and rays

of colored lights danced in midair. So strong, yet the thick log was bending, yielding, being consumed by the relentless flames licking at it with determination. Brianna felt its searing heat within her own flesh.

She wanted to move, to say something, but was unable to act. The huge log shifted, sending a spray of ash spiraling upward to be caught in the heat of the flame. Her tongue slid over her lips, offering brief moisture to the dry petals. She brushed her fingertips across the smoothness of her arm, imagining her flesh to be as vulnerable as the nearby log to the conflagration building from within.

With infinite patience, he eased her forward, allowing himself room to unhook the tiny fasteners that held the bodice of her gown closed.

There was no protest when his hands caressed the silken wall of her back. His fingers splayed outward, gliding across the surface until the bodice slipped free, exposing her bare shoulders.

The garment continued easing downward under his gentle guidance until it reached her waist. He pulled her backward, breathing deeply as her bare flesh pressed to his.

An unexpected liquid coolness trickled into the soft indentation formed by her clavicle. Brianna closed her eyes, sighing softly.

Fascinated, Ryan watched as each droplet of brandy spilled from his tilted glass. The liquid shimmered, the color deepening to a rich golden hue against the creamy softness of her bare flesh.

He dipped his head, his tongue laving the fiery nectar from the true object of his quest.

"Hmmmm." The contented sound rippled within the

confines of her throat as she turned to her side, lifting her face to his. Her lips parted slightly, the dampness glistening in the flickering firelight. "Ryan . . ."

His own hungry mouth caught hers, tentatively exploring, then boldly possessing as his passion mounted. Her hands traveled upward, tightening about his neck. Trembling fingers sliced through the full texture of his dark mane. She moved closer to accommodate the experienced fingers tugging gently to free the bothersome hooks that sheltered her heated body from his touch.

Like the delicate ashes lifted by the breath of flame, Brianna felt herself spiraling upward in weightless ecstasy.

The silken gown slithered across her burning flesh as Ryan released her from the fragile barriers. Lacing broke, freeing her from the final restraints.

He rose, lifting her slight weight in the circle of his arms, then carried her toward the bed that sat like an inviting island.

She rubbed her cheek across the ruffled silk of his partially opened shirt, anxious to touch the rough texture of his flesh. Not a word was spoken.

He laid her tenderly on the bed, quickly divesting himself of his own garments before joining her.

Arching her back and tilting her head, she exposed the slender column of her neck to his fevered kisses. Every muscle, every nerve stretched toward him, crying out silently for the ministrations of his touch.

"My sweet, sweet siren," he muttered, raining kisses upon her as his hand boldly captured the soft globe of one waiting breast. His lips traced a searing path downward, nipping lightly as he ensnared the waiting nub with the moist heat of his mouth.

Of their own accord, her hands explored the hard planes of his form, finding delight when her fingers brushed a vulnerable spot that quaked beneath her whispered touch. The fires within her burned higher, taking her to dizzying heights. Her blood curled, then surged through her body.

The flower of her womanhood quivered beneath the tender onslaught, then blossomed, its moist petals vibrating to render her breathless and weak with the most exquisite of agonies.

The pain yielded, her flesh sheathing his throbbing fullness in exaltation. She met each thrust without restraint, surrendering to the passion that was hers.

Exhilaration was hers as she rode higher, higher, crying out to Ryan. "Yes, oh yes," she screamed.

The storm faded into a warm soothing mist and Brianna lay still, trying to hold the memories close. "I never thought it could be so . . ." she began, stopping when she realized she knew no words to adequately express the enormity of the emotions pulsing within her.

Ryan smoothed a damp auburn tendril back from her face, smiling tenderly at her open expression of wonder. "So right?" he ventured.

With sudden shyness, she nodded, her lashes shielding the glowing jewels of her eyes from his scrutiny.

"Don't hide your feelings from me, my sweet. It is natural to appreciate the finer aspects of relationships. There is no cause for shame."

"I'm not ashamed," she protested, "only somewhat bewildered."

Laughter rumbled within the depths of his chest. Her hand reached out, her fingers lightly pressing the damp bed of ebony curls that laced the hardened muscles.

"Don't make fun of my ignorance," she implored.

He caught her hand, pulling it upward to place teasing kisses on each pink fingertip. "I would never be guilty of such a thing," he told her. "A man can only cherish a woman who can surrender so completely to the passions of love."

"Ryan? I've never been in love. I'm not sure what love is."

He pulled her into a light embrace, placing a kiss upon her forehead. "Nor I, my sweet. It's a world we shall explore together. Agreed?"

"Yes. I would like that." With a burst of emotion, she confided, "I hope the Earl of Tyrone never arrives."

Ryan stiffened slightly, the muscle alongside his jaw tensing. "Would his presence be so terrible?"

"It would. In truth, the thought of anyone intruding into this new world we have found would be most distressing."

"Ah, my siren of the sea."

Her eyes met his, unable to deny the growing passion within the darkening orbs of gray that seemed to penetrate her very being. "My husband," she whispered, her heart aching with the sweetness of the sound which no longer sounded alien to her ears.

He caressed the soft velvet of her cheek. "Your siren's song has a melody that cannot be denied, my sweet. Its haunting refrain pierces the soul. It lingers as a beacon of enchantment to call even the strongest of men to your tantalizing shores. I fear I am lost in its exquisite symphony."

Placing a kiss on her shoulder, Ryan breathed deeply of her delicate scent, his hand stroking each rib, dipping into the valley of her small waist before it began its deliberate ascent over the soft swell of her hip.

The night passed in wondrous splendor, until at last they lay spent on the quiet shores of contentment. Greshna's words of warning lost their sense of urgency. Surely nothing could every touch the magic Brianna had found with Ryan.

Her muscles relaxed, allowing sleep to lay its blanket about her. Her heart and mind knew peace as she lay in his protecting embrace.

The dull thudding sound increased, forcing Brianna to groggy wakefulness. Disoriented, she moaned, burrowing deeper into the warm comfort of masculine flesh.

"Go away," a deep voice grumbled.

"I can't rightly do that," the voice called from beyond the door's barrier. "I got your breakfast, and Miss Bri don't take too kindly to her morning victuals being late."

Brianna winced, her nose wrinkling in a pixieish manner that brought a chuckle of amusement to Ryan's lips. "Then you best enter," he relented. He reached out to touch the tip of Brianna's nose with one finger. "I prefer to keep my lady in a kindly mood."

Aunt Sudie bustled in, keeping her eyes averted from the bed. "I think you has done made a wise choice, Massa."

Brianna wriggled out of Ryan's embrace, pulling the sheets more closely about her as she tried to present a dignified appearance.

Her actions exposed the muscled expanse of his torso to her view and she gave a whimper of frustration. There was more to life than food, she decided.

Ryan afforded Brianna a mischievous grin. "I'm sure Brianna appreciates your concern, as do I. It would be sinful to deny a lady her desires."

She felt a heated flush racing toward her cheeks and gave him a withering glance as Sudie arranged the tray. It seemed as though her husband had the power to read her very thoughts.

Even worse was knowing her body was rapidly responding to his veiled suggestion with wicked eagerness.

"Yas suh. I'se tried to tell Miss Bri that ladies mostly sleeps late and when they does wake, they has little appetite. She don't pay no attention to Aunt Sudie though."

Laughter rumbled, reminding Brianna of Sudie's reference to his being like the thunder. She flushed before his candid appraisal, his antics earning him a scorching look from his annoyed companion.

"If it will free me from such foolish nonsense as this, then I may well cultivate more ladylike habits of having meals at a later hour," Brianna said.

Giving no sign of recognizing the testy tone of the suggestion, Sudie handed each of them a steaming cup of chocolate, her round face wreathed in smiles. "That's good to hear. I done knew de massa would be good for you. I guess you won't be needin' yore ridin' clothes this mornin'."

Brianna's lips parted in protest, her face mirroring a brief flicker of pain. Ryan's hand closed over hers, gently squeezing it as she caught her bottom lip with her teeth to hold back her objection.

"Do you ride every morning, my sweet?"

She nodded, unable to trust her voice.

"She shore does," Sudie said. "Even when she was a

little girl, she was up with de sun to ride with de old massa. Been doin' it ever since."

"Then you best lay out Miss Brianna's riding attire," he instructed. "And send word for Toby to bring our mounts to the front in an hour."

"Thank you." Her acknowledgment was so soft, he wasn't certain he had heard correctly but there was no denying the look on her face.

"You're very welcome. I would never deny you pleasure," he murmured. "I only wish to share your desires."

Her heart halted, like a hummingbird selecting one special bloom. With a flutter, it renewed its efforts at a faster pace. Dimly, Brianna took note of Sudie's grumbling protest but it was of no importance. She wanted to concentrate on the man at her side. She wanted seclusion, once more to hear the rhapsody of wild songs he so easily plucked from her responsive flesh.

"I can see why you were loath to surrender your morning rides." Ryan sat atop his favorite bay, viewing the tranquil scene spread before him.

The unusually warm fall had preserved the luxuriant green of unplowed areas. The morning haze was pregnant with the rich smell of the earth, seasoned with a touch of brine carried inland from the Gulf waters on a gentle breeze.

Stately pines and venerable oaks dotted the rolling landscape. Waxy foliage of the magnolia trees formed giant umbrellas of shade against the buttery rays of the sun which was slowing pushing the cool fog from the land.

"Lagniappe is beautiful. I can see why you hold it so

dear." He cocked his dark head to one side, a carnal smile touching his lips as he continued. "Though I doubt it can ever rival the beauty of its mistress."

Brianna bowed her head. "Ryan, please. You embarrass me with such bold words."

"Then I fear you shall suffer frequent mortification, my sweet. I find you most desirable and it gives me pleasure to express my appreciation. Surely the gentlemen of your acquaintance have told you such things before?"

She shook her head. "After Maman's death, I spent most of my time with Papa. When he was away, there was Aunt Sudie to occupy my time. When I reached the age to attend soirees, I'm afraid my outlook on life was somewhat of a shock to the male population." She shrugged her shoulders in dismissal of her detractors.

"There have been no serious beaux in your life?" Jeffrey's image hovered at the perimeter of his memory.

"Not really. With Papa's illness, I found the perfect excuse to eliminate the frivolous gatherings from my schedule."

Ryan coaxed his mount into a slow walk, continuing the conversation. "Then, my sweet, it is another chapter we shall have to explore. I shall enjoy twirling you about the dance floor while the gentlemen admire your grace and charm."

"I have no desire to expose myself to the parsimonious minds of my neighbors."

He raised a brow in question. "Parsimonious? Do you consider all mankind to be stingy with opinions and praise?"

"I have found that men are wont to hear only that which applauds their own sense of self-importance. It is my opinion that conversation without substance can only stagnate the mind, and experience has taught me that men prefer ladies who never venture beyond the area of flattering the male ego."

"A somber observation," he said, a wry smile tilting one side of his mouth. "And do you feel I slight your intelligence in favor of other . . . attributes?"

"Don't mock me, Ryan. I speak earnestly." She waved one arm toward the expanse of land before them. "Many years past, the Gulf water flowed inland. It became trapped within earthen boundaries, no longer moving. Time passed and scum settled over the once-clear liquid, smothering what life remained. It became an uninhabitable swamp. I believe the mind is like the water. When it is confined within narrow boundaries, it becomes lifeless. I will not be so confined by the petty dictates of an intolerant society. I want to learn, to experience, to live life to its fullest."

Ryan reined his mount to a halt, facing her, his clear eyes seeking the very windows of her soul.

Brianna waited, her breath caught painfully within her throat. This man held control of the very life of which she spoke. Would he deny her? Her lungs ached. Her mouth grew parched, but still she waited in fearful anticipation of his rejection.

"Then, my sweet, we shall chart our course toward the sea. I shall teach you to steer beneath full sail, and together we shall fly across only open waters."

A trembling smile touched the pink buds of her mouth. Her lips parted, allowing her breath to escape into the hushed silence; her smile broadened. Her heart thumped within her breasts like the roar of thunder. She felt she would burst with joy. Unable to speak, Brianna jabbed her knees into her stallion, spurring him into a hasty gallop.

Across the fields she flew, the pins flying from her thick tresses to allow her hair to flow freely on the wings of the wind.

Ryan followed suit, the resonance of his laughter reaching her ears as he galloped past her, stirring her to greater efforts.

The impetuous action was exhilarating and she laughed gleefully, unperturbed by the ultimate loss of the impromptu race she had sparked. Tugging at the reins, she brought her lathered horse to a halt by the stream where Ryan was dismounting.

"I thought you would never arrive, my sweet," he teased as he stepped forward to assist her.

"At least have the decency to calm your breathing before you make such rash statements, sir," she boldly countered.

He lifted her from the saddle, slowly bringing her quivering body down the length of his own hard frame as he set her on the ground.

She sought his face, astounded by the ease with which his touch could excite her. "We will sail the seas together. He shall never find us."

Jealousy flickered. "Who?" he asked.

"Lord Tyrone," she said. "Not even he can touch us or change our course."

He pulled her close, stroking her tangled tresses in quiet contemplation. "Never be certain . . . of anything, Brianna. The sea can prove a cruel mistress. It is this truth which ordains there be but one captain to a ship."

She eased back, searching his face for answers to the puzzling words. "But you said . . ."

"I know what I said, and I shall enjoy every opportunity to know what thoughts you entertain. I only caution you to heed the power of the sea and to understand that when the storm comes, there can only be one hand at the helm." He looked deeply into her eyes, willing her to accept what must come.

This charade could not continue forever, he knew. The day would come . . . and soon . . . that he must reveal his full identity. He could not deny her feelings, but he could not deny his own birthright, either. How would she react, knowing nothing would change?

She was a part of him and he would never let her go. "Remember, my sweet. I am the captain of our ship."

"And what am I?" she asked, her face revealing a new wariness to his gaze.

He smiled down at her. "You are my most valuable first mate. And it is said that no captain worth his salt would undertake the rigors of life at sea without a truly competent first mate."

"Is that true?" she asked.

"It is." His lips hovered near her own in supplication. Slowly, the breach was spanned and flesh melded to flesh, his touch searing her with the unmistakable brand of his mastery.

An anguished groan emanated from deep within his throat. His fingers tightened possessively about her arms, coaxing her down onto the carpet of grass.

Willingly, she yielded, her mind relinquishing its fragile grip on the troubling nature of the words he had spoken. *Later,* she silently promised herself. There would be time to probe and ferret out the true meaning of his veiled warning.

It was enough to know that they were together, and

she refused to consider that any storm could rend the bonds being so intricately woven by their spirits. With a gentle sigh, she surrendered to the wonders he brought, the passion they shared.

Passion. It was the only storm she wished to know, and she reached out to welcome it with open arms.

Chapter 14

"My stars, where did you two come from? We thought you were still in your quarters." Mara's cheerful observation flustered Brianna, and she could feel the familiar heat coursing over her pale skin.

"Good morning." She kept her eyes averted, fearful the true nature of her recent activities would be all too easily revealed. "Er . . . uh . . . you remember Mara Maxwell, don't you, Ryan?"

He chuckled, amused by her suddenly shy manner. "How could I forget anyone so charming," he answered, offering a bow toward the young matron.

"I assure you the feeling is mutual, sir."

Brianna felt an inane urge to laugh. Never had she seen her friend play the part of coquette, yet here she stood, prettily plying the art on Ryan. "Where's Henry?"

She asked on impulse, she told herself, but her sense of honesty compelled her to admit it was vaguely disconcerting to find other ladies drawn to Ryan . . . even when those ladies were good friends.

"Where else would my dear husband be but at the buffet. As always, he awoke with a voracious appetite, and thinking we were the only ones up and about, I fear we took the liberty of sampling the fare available at the buffet."

Ryan's easy laughter filled the hall. "It sounds like he has something in common with my bride. I've discovered she has something of an . . . hmmm . . . appetite, too."

"Ryan!" From the moment the vows had been taken, he had swept her into a new world. Now, it seemed, her devilish husband was to inflict the nerve-racking game of double entendres upon her at will.

"Yes, my sweet?" He offered a look of total innocence, the effort giving an almost boyish handsomeness to his lean face.

She inhaled deeply, striving for composure. "Perhaps you should follow Henry's example and partake of adequate sustenance." She tilted her head to one side, teasing him with a saucy smile. "I should hate to think of your own strength wilting from lack of proper nourishment."

He made a choking sound, then grabbed her in his arms to twirl her about, caring not a whit that his action had an audience. "Never fear, my sweet siren. I've a hardy constitution and my strength has never been in question."

With deliberate slowness, he released her, smiling at her soft gasp. He could feel her nipples come to rigid attention when they brushed against the hardness of his chest.

"You rogue. Miscreant," she hotly accused, the huskiness of her voice betraying her barely controlled passion.

"Ah, have you ever seen a lovelier bride, Mara?" he asked, the joy in his voice offering no option but agreement.

"Nor a happier, more satisfied one, unless my eyes are failing," she answered.

Brianna frowned in disapproval at Ryan, then conveyed the same message to her friend. "And Aunt Sudie accuses me of failing to behave as a lady. I am shocked by the both of you."

"Sounds as though my arrival is too late as usual," the jovial voice boomed, getting the attention of the trio.

"Henry. I'm grateful for your arrival, late or not." Brianna stepped forward, rewarding Maxwell with an affectionate hug. "I'm in need of a sensible ally."

"What's the matter, my dear? Is Mara making a nuisance of herself?"

"I'm never a nuisance," Mara snapped.

"Then what are you doing?" He reached out, playfully tweaking her upturned nose.

"I'm doing what best friends are supposed to do, being utterly charming to Lagniappe's new master."

"And succeeding most admirably," Ryan chimed in, reaching out to shake hands with the other man. "Pay no attention. Brianna is a bit peeved." He flashed a warning grin. "Though I haven't any idea why."

Joining in the lively banter, Henry stroked his beard, appearing to give the matter deep thought. "I daresay she's probably distraught at being out of bed so early this day."

"Henry Maxwell!" His wife gave him a playful jab. "For shame! You forget yourself. This man barely knows us and your speech must be shocking."

"I'm rarely shocked, but I do confess, of late my humor is in excellent spirit."

"He may not know us, my dear, but last night I decided it would definitely be an oversight soon corrected.

We might as well begin our friendship with honesty." He threw back his head to unleash a robust laugh.

"I must have missed something, Henry." Brianna doubted the wisdom of her comment, but found herself in favor of satisfying her curiosity. She wanted to know everything about Ryan. Everything.

As they walked toward the dining room, he filled her in on the way Ryan had turned the tables on Jeffrey's attempted slur.

The reminder that others were in her home caused her to hesitate. Brianna glanced down at her disheveled appearance. She couldn't face guests looking like this. Not once, but twice, Jeffrey had attempted to besmirch Ryan. Her unseemly appearance after their hectic ride and . . . well, she told herself, she didn't wish to give Jeffrey a chance to use her to get at her husband. "Ryan, I should change."

Tucking her arm under his, he gave her hand a pat. "Later, my sweet." He leaned closer, lowering his voice so only she could hear. "If you're very nice, I may be persuaded to help you change."

"Ooooh." He chuckled as he watched her eyes widen, glittering a deeper, more mysterious shade from beneath a thick veil of lashes.

"No fair," Mara objected. "You shouldn't have secrets. It's not polite, particularly when my own spouse sees no need for decorum."

"Have you forgotten so soon how the first days of marriage are?" Henry's blunt question stilled her lively tongue. Brianna felt a kinship with her friend as she watched the flush of red stain her golden cheeks.

"Are you recently married?" Ryan asked as they walked toward the dining room.

"We're soon to celebrate our second anniversary, but some memories linger longer than others," he said.

Ryan turned to study his own wife's somber face. Could they hope to share such easy camaraderie . . . once he made his full identity known? His mood darkened as he pondered the troubling question.

After his recent discussion with the witch-woman, he knew he must soon face the issue. They would have no future until the truth was told and . . . there *would* be a future. Of that he was certain. He pressed his hand to hers, his mind willing her to love him.

Conversation shifted from one subject to another as they enjoyed their coffee. In the brief span of time, Mara gave him a glimpse into his wife's younger years. "Precocious child, weren't you, my little siren," Ryan chuckled.

"I was not at all that way," she retorted in a prim manner. "I simply recognized what needed doing and did it."

Amid affectionate laughter, Henry chimed in. "I will vouch for that trait. Are you still continuing your plan to release all the slaves of Lagniappe, Brianna?"

"I am."

"Do you disapprove?" Ryan asked, curious to know more about local opinion.

"I confess to harboring doubts, but I've recently learned information which may force everyone to do what Brianna does so willingly."

"That sounds interesting. I'd like to hear more," Ryan encouraged as he sipped his coffee.

Henry cleared his throat. "Being a banker, I have a great deal of contact with the North through other bankers. One acquaintance recently sent me packets of newspapers." He shrugged his shoulders. "They are several months old, but I find them useful. It was that way with the article on Anthony Burns."

Brianna puckered her lips in concentration but could not summon any recognition. "I don't recall ever hearing that name before."

"Not surprising, my dear. He was a runaway slave from Richmond."

Runaway. Ryan and Brianna shared looks filled with concern. A vague fear prickled her skin on hearing the word. Ryan urged Henry to proceed.

"According to spokesmen for suffrage groups and abolitionists in the city when he was arrested, the federal officials in Boston attempted to frame him for theft."

Frame? Her muscles tensed. It sounded harsh to her ears yet vaguely familiar. The stirrings of memories rose, curling like wood smoke through the corridors of her mind. She could hear them clearly as old refrains were again renewed.

"You are grieved, m'sieur. I would never allow harm to befall mam'zelle." From the past, Greshna's voice called out to profess her innocence.

"You lie, you lazy no-account bitch!" A sharp cracking sound punctuated her father's roared accusation.

Greshna sprawled so near the child's hiding place, she could see the blood stream from her nose. Brianna's small arms hugged her body more tightly, wishing to disappear. But there was no hiding from the dark, knowing eyes.

The woman vanished, brutally yanked upright by her furious master. *"Would you point the guilty finger at my own daughter?" he demanded. "Would you charge a child with your willful neglect?"*

"Don't tell!"

"Don't tell what, Brianna?"

She started, her coffee forming a muddy stain on the tablecloth as it spilled from her tightly held cup. "Noth . . . nothing, Ryan. I must have been daydreaming."

One dark brow winged upward, but he said nothing. Only his eyes probed for the truth.

"My apologies," Henry interrupted. "My wife often rebukes me for my lack of social skills." He smiled at Brianna. "Having grown accustomed to Brianna's own outspoken ways, I fear I sometimes forget she is a lady whose delicate sensibilities can find offense."

"No," she began. "It's not anything you said. It's . . ." She provided a wavering smile. "It's just that my mind wandered to other matters. That is all. You haven't offended. Please continue."

"Are you certain?"

"Yes. You said he was . . . framed. Then what happened?"

"Throughout Boston, the church bells tolled to mark the event and buildings were draped in black. A large number of soldiers and policemen were called upon to guard the streets when Burns was taken to Long Wharf to be returned to Richmond." He turned his attention to Ryan. "It cost over one hundred thousand dollars to return one runaway slave."

Ryan nodded in understanding. "The cost of slavery does seem high."

"It may prove too high. The people of Kansas have

drawn blood in the issue of slavery. The Topeka Constitution went so far as to outlaw slavery." He shook his head. "I fear it is not a matter easily resolved."

"I agree. I've been reading Mr. Christy's book *The Economical Relations of Slavery*. It does pose some interesting questions. People like Jeffrey Arlington will never be convinced to accommodate any theory that denounces slavery."

Ryan's mention of Jeffrey renewed Brianna's quest to freshen herself before anyone else put in an appearance. Her fingers brushed the top of his hand, the action drawing quick attention.

"Yes, my sweet."

"I really must be excused, Ryan. I'm in need of a bath and fresh attire."

A slow provocative smile gave proof of his thoughts. "I'll join you," he suggested with quiet intimacy.

Brianna felt herself growing uncomfortably warm as she hastened to glance at their companions. The couple chatted easily with each other, oblivious to the whispered conversation. "Our guests . . ."

". . . won't object," he added with confidence. Not giving her a chance to respond, Ryan made brief apologies and escorted her from the room amid indulging smiles.

The house held an air of expectancy despite the silence that prevailed as they climbed the staircase toward her room. His hand, poised at the small of her back, offered both comfort and a peculiar sense of excitement.

"It appears someone anticipated our return," he said, nodding toward the filled tub that occupied the area before the fireplace.

"That's mine," she said.

"How can you be so certain, my darling?"

"Aunt Sudie always has my bath drawn and waiting when I return from my ride. No doubt with our dawdling downstairs, it has grown quite cold." She wriggled free from his embrace and went to test the water with her fingertips.

"Still hot enough?" The whispered query was so near, his warm breath stirred a loose curl at the nape of her neck.

"It . . . it's fine," Brianna stuttered. She set about to dispel the tension that seemed to fill her at his presence. "I shall send for Aunt Sudie."

"Why?"

"She must wash my back . . . help me with my hair."

He reached forward, loosening the thick mass of curls from their pins. The rich mahogany skein fell across her shoulders, framing the delicate oval of her face with soft waves. "We have no need of her services," Ryan murmured.

He moved closer, his hands burrowing through her hair, his eyes glowing with unspoken desire. "I will wash your hair, my sweet." He bent to place a kiss on an exposed earlobe. "I will wash your shoulders." A feathery kiss seared her shoulder as he slid her jacket from her quivering frame.

"Ryan." Her breath caught in expectation, the word issuing in a husky whisper. She could feel the skillful probing of his fingers as he loosened the jabot, pushing it away to reveal the satin of her throat.

"Hmmmm." The sound reached her ears, echoing her own emotions. Her blood bubbled within each vein, hotly pulsing through the complicated maze of nerves and muscles that seemed to compete for the attention of his touch.

It was indecent, she knew, but with his mastery, her body had no will of its own. No protest was heard as he stripped away the layers of clothing until she stood in naked splendor before his avid gaze.

Intent on performing the task he had assigned himself, Ryan lifted Brianna into his arms, placing her carefully into the waiting water.

Vapors of rose-scented heat filtered upward to fill his nostrils. His hands reveled in the slippery silk of her flesh. A sigh of pleasure warmed the petals of her passion-swollen lips. "Ryan."

He needed no other invitation. With bold efficiency, he peeled away his own riding garb. His massive frame hovered over her, then joined her within the cramped confines of the tub.

Water sloshed over the rim, soaking the Aubusson rug. Bubbles rose, covering the shimmering cream of her flesh with a lacy froth. He watched, fascinated by the fragile prisms that glittered in a kaleidoscope of pastels before melting to reveal her gentle curves to his smoky survey.

Arched toward him, Brianna sought the magic of his touch, rejoicing in the rough texture of his hands as they skimmed across her body. Her nerves jerked, then quivered uncontrollably as they exploded in a pagan dance that blinded her to all but the tactile sensations he evoked.

Ryan shifted positions, manipulating her pliant body until she found herself atop him. Unschooled in the variety of intimacies available, she was hesitant, uncertain as to what was expected.

He chuckled, delighting in the wide-eyed innocence of

her expression. A smile touched his sensual lips as he gave his attention to the dark curtain of hair that sheltered the swollen globes of her firm breasts. Gently, he separated a thickened strand, leaving it to curl downward into the foam-covered liquid. He pushed the remaining mass of wet curls over her shoulders, removing the last barrier to his heated gaze.

She waited, poised in breathless wonder, watching his every movement.

He raised the thick rope of hair, idly inspecting the tip as water gathered to form a heavy droplet before plunging back into oblivion. Like an artist studying his masterpiece, he focused on the velvet swell of her breasts.

Touching the water-laden tip of her hair to one mound, he traced the pale-blue veins that throbbed beneath the translucence of her flesh.

She gasped, the small sound encouraging further exploration. Closing her eyes, she wanted to capture the moment within the deepest caverns of her soul. Her insides seemed to undulate, twisting and twining with an exquisite agony that set her skin aflame.

With an expert touch, he continued to wield the sodden tress like a paintbrush, swirling it in ever-tightening circles around the aroused nipple which stiffened in anticipation.

Her tautly held emotions surged upward, a fountain of desire that demanded release. She wriggled forward, a half-smile touching her mouth as she felt the hardness of him pressing, pushing urgently like a ship whose course is set. Headlong he would steer into the eye of the building storm and she yearned to ride the wild waves with him.

Brianna pressed her palms to his chest, startled to feel

twin nubs hardening beneath her touch. A surge of power swept through her, intoxicating her senses. Like the wanton sirens of the sea for which he had named her, she cried out in sweet entreaty.

His penetration was swift, thrusting deeply within the tight moistness of her, ripping a gasp of pleasure from her parched throat. The song of the sea roared through her ears, its lure beckoning her with each forceful stroke. Over and over she answered the wild tempest, until at last she lay spent upon the warm sands of contentment.

The tepid water licked at her heated flesh, soothing her as Ryan rose from the tub, his arms sheltering her within his protective embrace.

She pressed her cheek to the damp curls that shadowed the bronze hardness of his chest. "I would hold this time forever if I could," she confessed as he lowered her to the nearby lounge.

He smiled down at the open expression on her up-turned face, reaching for the thick square of toweling as he spoke. "And what makes you think it impossible to capture this time for all eternity?"

"Lord Tyrone."

He stiffened, his movements becoming brusque as he toweled her dry. "Must he intrude on our every moment?"

"I'm sorry. It . . . it's just that I have no knowledge as to if or when he might arrive. He looms like a dark specter over the future."

Ryan chafed at the hurt expression on her face. She did not know how cruelly her words twisted within his heart. He was the one who maintained silence. Always he had spoken the truth, yet now he seemed possessed by some devil that denied him the speech to set him free. "You worry beyond reason for the appearance of a man you do not know, a man who has done no wrong nor given you cause to fear."

"I suppose you are right, Ryan. My worries may be for naught. The earl may well be lost at sea."

He stretched out beside her on the narrow lounge, his body pressing close to her own. "Lost is an apt description, my sweet." He held her tight, breathing deeply of the rose fragrance that was so much a part of her. "I fear he is lost to the haunting strains of the siren's song, his destiny forever claimed by enchantment which holds the heart captive."

She lay quietly, puzzling over the poignancy of the words which struck a responsive chord within her own heart.

A vague sense of unrest settled over her as recognition evaporated into an illusive fog, even as she reached for it. Her hand came to rest in the region of his heart. Closing her eyes, she willed her body to absorb the steady cadence of his heartbeat.

Gradually, she became aware that his pulse seemed to beat in harmony with the muted sound of drums.

Voodoo worked outside the protective walls of Lagniappe. She could sense a restless discontent in the throbbing sound carried on the damp winds of winter.

We will have tomorrow, she silently promised herself. *And then?* How many tomorrows would be theirs to claim? she wondered.

Greshna's warning words echoed in her memory, her body trembling with a sudden chill.

Strong arms pulled her closer, protecting her from the unknown. Brooding thoughts of tomorrow yielded before the promise of today, and she reached for it with an eagerness not to be denied.

Various conversations cluttered the air when they quit the privacy of their room. Belowstairs, trunks, bandboxes and an assortment of portmanteaus waited to be transported to carriages.

Brianna smiled up at Ryan, earning quick comment.

"Our guests appear on the verge of bidding farewell."

"So they are." Gratitude welled, forcing her to concentrate on self-control. It mustn't look as though she anxiously wished their departure. She traversed the stairs with a light spring to her step, eager to perform this last duty. Then she would be alone.

Not alone, she corrected. Alone with Ryan.

Reaching the foyer, Brianna found herself besieged by females, each hugging her as though they were long-lost relatives. First in line came Ophelia Blanchard, then her daughter. She paused to speak a few words to Elyese Fontaine before another matron interrupted.

She glanced about in search of Ryan, paying little attention to what was said. He was busy shaking hands, listening politely as various men shared a few thoughts with him.

It seemed impossible that they had been married even a mere twenty-four hours and they were on the verge of having peace and solitude. The thought buoyed her spirits.

Festivities were infrequent and distance such that it was normal for guests to remain days, even weeks, before giving thought to leaving. Brianna made a swift inventory of the faces, praying all were accounted for.

"As usual, Bri, it's been exciting."

She grinned at Mara's choice. *Exciting. If only she knew,* a delighted Brianna thought. *If only she knew.* "I'm glad you're pleased."

"Definitely. And to prove it, I've persuaded Henry to invite Father Paul to accompany us and take lodging tonight at the Pillars."

Brianna couldn't hold back the giggle. "Henry and a priest. Now, that should prove an interesting evening."

With an answering laugh, Mara agreed, then added, "Not as interesting as some people's evening, but then . . ." She discreetly omitted the rest of the sentence, her pleasure evident. "Be happy."

Offering a final hug, Mara Maxwell departed, her place quickly filled by another.

Ryan fought impatience, smiling as each guest presented himself with more well-wishes and warm invitations that the couple call in the near future. From years of practice, he maintained a calm facade, responding with flawless courtesy. At last he found himself standing before Oliver Westman.

"Mr. Westman. Before you leave, I think we should have a conversation. Will you join me in the study?"

"Sorry, Fleming. I've arranged to join the Roucheaus in New Orleans and they are already in the carriage."

"Really? I was unaware you were friends with Charles."

"We have a passing acquaintance," the man admitted. "I'm not going for a visit. I have business in New Orleans."

"Profitable, I hope."

"I don't know yet. Jeffrey told me that his cousin spoke of several ships which have docked this past month

. . . ships which were damaged in the same storm that brought you to Lapniappe."

"I had no idea you were interested in ships."

"Only one. If I am fortunate enough to find Lord Tyrone, I shall be shortly returning to Lagniappe." He ended with a stiff bow. "Until that time, sir."

Ryan's smile broadened, one corner of his mouth tilting at an upward slant. "I shall look forward to it."

Gradually, the crowd thinned as families ducked out of sight within their carriages. Ryan escorted his wife onto the veranda to wave final goodbyes.

One by one, the drivers set the rigs into motion to form a caravan which meandered along the winding drive toward the road. A heavily ladened wagon lumbered past, filled to overloading with an assortment of baggage.

"I suppose they will party the next few days at Willowgreen," she mused.

"Perhaps, but it will likely be without the company of the Roucheau family."

She tilted her head to one side. "I trust there has not been a family squabble that I missed."

He threw back his head, laughing heartily at the image of his wife missing any kind of excitement. "Sorry, but it's nothing so dramatic." Looping his arms around her waist, he pulled her close. "Westman told me he is traveling to New Orleans with them today."

A frown of puzzlement touched her mouth. "Odd. I hadn't thought you would be his confidant."

"I'm not." Staring down at her, he knew this was the opportunity he'd been waiting for. He should . . . *must* tell her the truth. "He's searching for a ship, the one on which Lord Tyrone sailed."

"No."

"He hopes to find the earl and bring him to Lagniappe."

"No!" She pulled free, her eyes bright with panic as she stared at him. "He can't. I . . . I hope the earl is dead . . . *dead!* Do you hear me?" Racing for the door, she swung it open and disappeared inside.

"Brianna. Come back." He started after her.

"Massa Ryan! You gots to come quick. They gots Eli."

Whirling toward the yelling youth, Ryan muttered an oath under his breath. He knelt down on one knee, grabbing the boy's shoulders. "Who's got Eli?"

"The bounty hunters. They says he's one of them runaways. They's goin' to hang him. You has got to come."

Ryan rose, bolting toward the stable and leaving the boy to follow as best he could. When he arrived, a stable boy was leading his bay outside. Mounting, he pointed the horse toward the child and scooped him up before him on the horse.

"Which way?" he curtly demanded. Chubby fingers pointed to the west.

Dust billowed but Ryan refused to slow his pace. He could hear the drums add their distinctive tattoo to the sound of hooves pounding into the ground.

"Damn!" Off to the left he saw them. With a twist of his wrist, he urged his mount toward the riders. Tied by his wrists to a long length of rope, Eli stumbled along behind them.

Yanking back hard on his reins, Ryan pulled to a halt. The child sitting in front of him slid off and scrambled to a safe distance.

"Who are you men and by what authority are you on Lagniappe?"

A heavily bearded man riding lead answered. "We're paid by the master of Belle Terre to round up runaway slaves."

"Round them up?" Ryan dismounted and ground reined his animal. "I heard you're hanging them."

A snicker from one of the three men met his observation. The bearded one squared his beefy shoulders as Ryan approached with the wary stealth of a big cat. "That's right. Mr. Arlington says he don't want them back, claims they're pagans not worth keeping alive."

Ryan's fingers casually caught the leather throat latch. "What makes you think any of Arlington's people are on Lagniappe . . . mister?"

"Name's Hacker," the leader said, leaning forward, his sneer displaying yellowed teeth. "And this place is the most likely for those bucks to run."

"I disagree with your opinion, but in this instance, you are definitely mistaken." He nodded toward Eli. "I know this man. He's a Lagniappe slave, so you can let him go and look elsewhere for your money."

A stream of tobacco shot from the man's mouth, landing at Ryan's boot with a dull splat. "The way I see it, the only one who could likely identify this buck besides his mammy is the owner of this place."

"And of course, you and the owner of Lagniappe are well acquainted."

Bawdy laughter ensued. Ryan remained motionless, waiting patiently for his answer.

"Not likely. Hell, I ain't never laid eyes on her." He scratched one furry cheek. "'Course I might change that one day when I've got more time. I hear that little split-tailed gal is quite a looker."

With the speed of a cottonmouth, Ryan grabbed the

man's shirt, yanking him from his saddle. As he fell, Ryan relieved him of the hunting knife that protruded from a scabbard strapped to his hip. "I wouldn't get too excited," he warned his two companions.

The tip of the blade rested against the base of the bounty hunter's jugular vein.

"Easy, boys! Don't move!" Sweat beaded on Hacker's forehead.

"I suggest you have them release the prisoner."

Seconds, then minutes passed. "You better hope your friends have a high regard for your life, because as far as I'm concerned, you're good for nothing but alligator bait."

"Ya'll hurry!" The sweat began to roll down his face, spilling into eyes reddened by too much whiskey.

Eli stumbled into view, exhausted from the punishment he had so recently endured.

"Fetch that shotgun from his horse and bring it to me," Ryan said. He glanced at the two who remained astride. "Keep your hands where I can see them. Let's keep this a friendly transaction."

Adequately armed, Ryan released the man and stepped back, taking care to keep the muzzle aimed at his stomach. "Since you gentlemen have overstayed your welcome, you better ride north. Tell Arlington none of his slaves are on Lagniappe."

With a snarled oath, Hacker remounted, glaring down at Ryan with a twisted sneer. "That's my gun."

"You can pick it up from Arlington in a couple of days. Oh, one more thing you should remember, Hacker."

"What's that?"

"If you ever get any more ideas about calling on the

lady, make sure your personal affairs are settled." His eyes narrowed in warning. One finger tightened over the trigger, drawing Hacker's undivided attention. "If you ever come near my wife, I'll kill you."

Lowering the muzzle, he fired. Hacker's horse reared in terror. Ryan stepped aside, never flinching as the animal bolted past to carry its rider out of reach.

A hard glance from Ryan and his two partners urged their own horses into fast retreat.

"I shore does thank you, Massa Ryan. I thought I was goin' to meet my maker. You is a fine gent'man."

"Don't mention it, Eli."

He thought of Brianna, of her violent reaction when he mentioned Lord Tyrone. It seemed the more he learned, the less he knew. The marriage was legal. No reason remained for her to care one way or the other when the earl might arrive, yet she acted even more upset than ever before. Then there was the matter of her disturbing memory lapses. If only he could have gotten some information out of Greshna instead of all those senseless phrases. If only she thought him a fine gentleman, would thank him.

He started for his bay. "Damn!"

The tears had long since dried. Brianna lay quietly on her bed, staring at the high ceilings. She never wanted the Earl of Tyrone to come. His continued absence held a new urgency.

Once he arrived and found her wedded, he would leave. She gave a choking sound. Then Ryan would leave. Brianna felt as though a heavy weight were falling on her, pushing her under. Flames burned, searing her lungs, scorching her throat until it seemed more than she could possibly bear. "Ryan." In a small croaking sound she called his name. *"Ryan, I love you!"*

Chapter 15

Idyllic days blended into tempestuous nights as Ryan and Brianna savored their time of solitude. They explored their mutual interests, finding delight in shared beliefs.

Even the times when they differed proved exhilarating, reminding Brianna of the awesome lightning displays that sparked the imagination, when powerful bolts glowed whitely over the churning waters of her beloved Gulf.

Together, they rode the fields of Lagniappe until they lay barren of further yield. They shaped new plans to improve and build upon the dreams they shared for the land.

Only when the barges were loaded for shipping did she absent herself from his side. Even her growing desire for his company could not persuade her to visit the bayou, the place she called Water of Death.

"Very well, my sweet. I shall return as soon as possible," he said. He sipped his morning coffee, brooding over the circumstances as he studied his wife's face. His need to reveal his identity paled in light of the increasing bouts of memory loss that plagued the woman he held so dear.

"If we are to call on Mara and Henry tomorrow, I have much to do." It sounded weak, even to her own ears. She pushed aside the feelings of foreboding that nibbled at the edge of her mind. "In her note, Mara mentioned the Fontaines will also be there."

He gave a wry smile. "Sounds like she plans to turn our visit into an event. Do you suppose she thinks we grow weary with only each other for company?"

The gentle query kindled a warmth inside her, bringing the recollection of the delights that had greeted her with this day's dawn. "I'm sure she gives no thought to our . . . our life."

"Then she misses a great deal. I find my own thoughts increasingly intrigued by the prospect of how best to pass the hours."

A hot glow touched her cheeks, worsened by the inner knowledge that she shared his thoughts. "You are wicked," she accused without rancor.

He gave a throaty chuckle. "You may be right, my sweet siren. I have been accused of being by the devil possessed a time or two."

"Don't say that!" Devils . . . spirits . . . they flooded her with unreasonable fear. Had Jeffrey been right? Could it be that women were more susceptible to such things?

"My apologies," he murmured as he brushed a light kiss atop her head. She looked up at him, uncertain as to how he came to be by her side.

Propped up by thick pillows, Brianna remained in bed, watching while he finished dressing. Her flaky croissant remained untouched on the tray. Her only thoughts were of Ryan . . . her husband.

She never tired of watching him, the liquid fluidity of his movements striking chords of intensity in her that so frequently rose to feverish heights. It added to her distress to realize that some unseen force kept them apart, even as they sought closeness.

Only in the throes of passion could the chasm between them fade into oblivion. She hungered for that passion, that "something extra" to lead her into the glorious light where she could drink her fill of him.

"I've instructed Mr. Rawlings to organize a work force of some of our more trusted people to prepare the main house for winter."

"I don't understand. All of our people are trustworthy, are they not?" Brianna tried to concentrate on more practical avenues of thought.

Ryan smiled, regret tingeing his words. "I'm afraid not, my sweet. Those drums seem to beat continually now. It's natural they will reach the most impressionable."

The corners of her mouth pulled downward. He spoke the truth, she knew. So accustomed had she become to the sound of them that Brianna rarely gave it thought. All that mattered was that everything on Lagniappe remained unchanged. The people continued to work toward their freedom. No signs of unrest had been noticed. "Has there been some trouble?"

"I'm not certain it could be classified as trouble, but Mr. Rawlings reported that two nights past, five of the men disappeared from the quarters."

"Runaways?"

He shook his head, the morning sun glinting on his ebony locks in such a way as to lend a blue-black cast of color. "No. They reported for work as usual the next morning, but . . ."

Stepping to the side of the tester bed, he paused to claim her mouth in a tender kiss. ". . . I don't want to take any chances on the safety of my favorite sea siren. To be denied the sweetness of her song would be to deny life itself." He caressed her cheek with the back of one hand. "Stay close to the house, my sweet. I shall return before you know I'm gone."

"Be careful, Ryan," she called in parting. He answered with a reassuring smile. The door closed softly behind him. "For I would surely perish if you were gone from me forever." Her whispered vow was met with a steady increase of sound. The drums spoke loudly, overpowering the rapid thump, thump of her fearful heart.

" 'Scuse me, Miss Bri, but you has a caller." Toby stood uncertainly at the parlor door.

"Who is it?" She had spent the better part of the afternoon engaged in needlepoint, an art that severely tested her patience. The prospect of an interruption was gratefully received.

"He says his name is Abercrombie, but he ain't got no proper callin' card. He don't looks like no kind of gent'-man to be callin' on a lady neither."

Amusement touched her mouth with an indulgent smile. She could feel Ryan's touch in the solicitous behavior of those who closely touched her life. "What does he look like, Toby?"

"He look like a common man of the sea, that's what."

The sea. She pushed back the hint of nausea that frequently visited her of late. *Lord Tyrone?* The thought sent a shaft of dread shooting through her. Exercising firm determination, she discarded it.

It had been nearly four months, she calculated, and the earl had not arrived. Westman's trip to New Orleans had proven a waste. No one had heard from him. "Send him in." Laying aside her work, Brianna rose to greet her guest.

"I'll be begging yer pardon for intruding, m'lady, but the time has come and I can be putting off me duty no longer."

She dipped into a polite curtsy and offered him a chair. Once she had settled herself, she wasted no time in inquiring as to the nature of his visit. "What can I do for you, *M'sieur* Abercrombie?"

"Folks call me Abby," he said. "I be more than a mite discomforted by more formal ways."

"Very well, Abby." Despite the rough appearance and nature of the man, she found herself liking him. Short and stocky, he moved with a birdlike quickness that reminded her of the descriptions given by her father of Ireland's leprechauns. "What business brings you to Lagniappe?"

He shook his head, his craggy face twisted by pain. "A sad one, to be sure." Clutching his hat in hand, he leaned forward, beginning a faltering explanation.

"I be the first mate of the proud ship *The Peregrine,* late of Ireland."

A constricting band wound itself about her heart, making the simple task of breathing difficult. "Ireland," she repeated. "You're a long way from home."

"Aye, that's the truth of it, m'lady. Would that we'd have stayed there, and I would not be forced to the telling of such sad happenings that has fell me lot."

The earl. He has come. She yearned for the comfort of Ryan's arms. A heaviness settled upon her like a dark thunder cloud waiting to release its burden of rain. *Once the earl is gone and a reasonable time has passed, you will leave Lagniappe.*

Her bargain reared like an ugly specter to torture her. And what is a reasonable time? Never, her heart answered. But what of Ryan?

In desperation, Brianna considered her time with Ryan, clinging tenaciously to a single hope. Perhaps he no longer wished to leave. "Please continue, Abby."

He cleared his throat, clearly ill at ease with her request. "Aye, m'lady. As I said, we sailed from the Isles, setting our course for this land. Me cap'n, a fine a sailor as they be, steered us a true course, he did."

Sudie entered the room, carrying a tea service that she placed on the table in front of Brianna. Abby halted his tale, watching and waiting politely until the woman was gone.

"Tea, *m'sieur?*"

"I thank ye, m'lady. A wee taste may take the dryness from me tongue at that."

He remained silent while she served. Taking her own refreshment, Brianna held the fragile china saucer in a tight grip. "Your captain had steered a straight course," she coached. "Please continue."

"We were nearing our destination when a terrible storm set itself upon us. For two days and nights it tossed us about in fury. We were snatched up by giant waves, then pitched down again with such force, I felt certain we would be dashed to splinters any moment. There was no way to be telling where we might be. The ship rocked,

tilting this way and that, rolling about without pause."
He used his hands in demonstration.

A queasiness invaded her stomach, threatening her
dignity. She interrupted the drama. "Excuse me,
m'sieur."

Brianna left the room without explanation, hurrying
to her private quarters with as much haste as she could
manage.

She knelt on the floor, poised over the chamber pot.
Her body trembled in response to the violent retching
that had overtaken her. Tears filled her eyes and her
throat ached. "Oh, Ryan," she sobbed. "Where are
you?"

Silence was her only answer. She sat motionless, fearful the least movement would unleash a fresh torrent.
"Nerves," she muttered, trying to convince herself. It had
to be nerves.

Cautiously, she pushed herself upward, moving slowly
toward the washstand. Pouring a small amount of water
into the flower-painted bowl, she sponged her face and
neck. Glancing in the mirror at her pale reflection,
Brianna acknowledged the truth with a sinking heart.

Her plaintive cry held no hope. "Why now?"

She could no longer avoid the issue. In her parlor sat
the messenger who would destroy her future . . . her
happiness . . . her "something extra."

He would announce the inevitable news and leave,
soon to be replaced by the arrival of the Earl of Tyrone.
Mentally, she forced herself to go through the subse-
quent steps.

The earl would satisfy himself that she was suitably wed and relinquish his authority to Ryan.

Ryan would go through the motions of continuing their business arrangement for a decent interval. Then he, too, would depart, leaving the legacy she had so craved in her sole control.

A tear slid down her cheek. Angrily, she brushed it away. There was nothing she could do to change the facts. She had made a bargain. To deny it would be to deny honor itself. Ryan had given too much to, be cheated now.

She would keep her secret, she decided. She owed him that much. Tilting her chin a little higher, Brianna squared her small shoulders and returned to her guest.

With grim determination, she continued the interview. "I must apologize for my abrupt departure, *m'sieur*. I've been feeling a touch of illness of late."

"It is I who should be begging forgiveness, m'lady. 'Tis unlearned I am in the ways of proper behavior in the presence of a lady like yourself."

With a wave of her hand, she stilled his words. "It is of little importance, but I believe the person of whom you speak is important. Can you tell me when I might expect Lord Tyrone to arrive?"

His eyes widened, his mouth opening in a show of surprise. "Begging your pardon, m'lady. That's the sad news I've been trying to tell ye. M'lord won't be arriving."

"I . . . I don't understand. Why not?"

"It happened near the nooning of the first day, it did. The sky darkened sudden like, as though the night was coming. The ship was taking a fearful beating and m'lord—" he took a steadying breath, "m'lord was taken overboard. He lies at the bottom of the sea, lost to the mortal world. He bides with Lord Neptune now." Abby bowed his head, making a respectful sign of the cross.

Brianna waited for the numbness to recede. *Dead. The earl is dead.* Appalled by the joy and relief such a thought brought, she hastily signed the cross. "I . . . offer my . . . sympathy," she said.

"And it's a kind heart ye have in the doing. M'lord was a fine, truly grand man. It was proud I was to serve him." He shook his head. "Since his passing, I find I no longer have a heart for the sea as I once did. 'Tis much the same for the rest of the crew."

His words brought a twinge of sympathy for his personal loss. The thought that she might lose Ryan had caused a suffering she had not known possible. It still seemed too good to believe. Miracles had never been a part of her life.

She broached the subject with caution, not wishing to inflict further pain on the man before her. "Is there any hope the earl might be alive?"

"None at all, m'lady. There were witnesses that saw the bow of the boat pass over his lifeless body. Even with the knowing, we made a search."

"And you found nothing?"

"Nay, but then, we didn't expect to be finding anything, either. Like I told ye, he was lost near the beginning of the storm. By the time it ended, we'd been pushed most a hundred miles from our course. The damage to our ship was great, and we spent the best part of a month or more on a distant island making what repairs we could."

"How dreadful."

"It was that, to be sure. The men were not much better off than the ship. Most everybody had injuries of one kind or another, but we Irish be a tough lot." Abby grinned at her, restoring a measure of her own good humor.

"I believe you," she said.

He picked up his tale, appearing eager to finish. "When we finally set sail, we were uncertain as to where we should be heading. Only this last month did we finally limp into port at New Orleans."

Brianna smiled. No wonder the frustrated attorney had been unsuccessful in his quest, she mused. His visit had been most premature.

"While proper repairs were being made, we took turns going out to search. We had hoped the sea would at least yield up his body so that we might be giving him a proper burial. But it wasn't to be."

She thought of the day she had found Ryan . . . the cabin. Gratitude filled her to overflowing. The sea may have held on to one poor soul, but she had kept it from claiming a second.

"Brianna! Where are you?"

The sound of his voice sent her spirits soaring, only to plummet to the pit of her stomach the next moment as she stared at her visitor. She mustn't let Ryan see him. He would learn of the earl's death . . . would know the danger was past and he was free to return to his carefree ways, unfettered by a wife.

"Excuse me," she said. With a speed born of desperation, she headed for the door, determined to prevent Ryan from meeting Abby.

"I'm here," she answered as she closed the double doors in a whirl of skirts and petticoats. She met him halfway across the foyer, throwing herself into his arms. "I hadn't expected you so early."

He laughed at her eagerness. "I told you there would be no time to miss me, my sweet." He tilted her face to his, slanting a kiss across her slightly parted lips.

Her heart gave a queer little lurch. A tiny quivering sensation fluttered to life in her stomach. For all time to come, he would be a part of her life. She smiled up at him. *He is my life.* Such a wondrous realization put her in an expansive mood.

She reveled in the deep resonance of his sudden chuckle. "You seem in a good mood," she commented.

"I am, although I should scold you for not waiting for me."

He made no sense. She tilted her head to one side. "Waiting?"

Ryan nodded toward the doors of the parlor, never loosening the hold he had on her waist.

Balancing a tray of food on one arm, Aunt Sudie was struggling to open the doors Brianna had so recently closed. She emitted a soft gasp. "Sudie!"

"I was jest going to . . ."

"Yes, I know," she interrupted. "I appreciate it, but . . ." She groped for something . . . anything that wouldn't rouse his suspicions. "Master Ryan is home. You must see that his . . . bath water is drawn."

"I'm in no hurry, my sweet."

"Oh, but Ryan, you can't possibly be comfortable. You're covered with dust." She brushed vigorously at the barely visible powder clinging to his riding coat. Ryan watched her, amusement written on his face as she continued to nervously prattle. "You will feel much better . . . once you've bathed. And . . . you must be hungry . . . famished. I'll have Aunt Sudie prepare you a tray. We'll eat together . . . in our room."

"Mmmm." He dipped his head to nibble at her exposed neck. "That does sound tempting."

"It's settled, then." Wriggling free of his grasp, she looped an arm around his, propelling him toward the stairway while Sudie watched, a dazed expression on her round face.

Waiting until he was halfway up the stairs, she sighed with relief, then turned her attention to Sudie, going to her and trying to take the food-filled tray. "I'll see to this. Have Ryan's bath readied and tell Cook to prepare two more meals. We'll eat upstairs tonight."

Sudie held fast to the tray, her eyes narrowing as she squinted at her.

"Stop staring, Aunt Sudie. Do as I say."

"Is you ailin', missy?"

"Of course not. I'm fine."

Sudie shook her head from side to side. "Lawd, but I hopes your condition ain't what's making' you act all funny like."

"Condition. What condition?"

"You know what I is talkin' about. I done seen that chamber pot sittin' there in de middle of yore room."

"Oh, no. I forgot." Panic threaded through her nerves.

"Jest calms yourself. There ain't no cause to worry. Old Sudie done cleaned everythin' up and puts it back where it belongs."

"Thank you." Relief washed through her, leaving her weak.

"You is welcome. Now, why don't you tell me jest what's goin' on here? How come you don't want Massa Ryan to know there's a man sittin' in yore parlor?"

Fearfully, Brianna glanced upward, then back at Sudie. "Can you keep a secret?"

"I s'pects I can keep one as good as the next body."

"The man inside is off the same ship as Lord Tyrone."

Sudie's eyes widened, shining whitely against deep chocolate flesh. "Oh, Lawdy."

"He told me the earl died at sea. That's why I don't want Ryan to know he is here."

"Lawdy," she repeated.

"If he finds out the earl is no longer a threat, he might decide to leave Lagniappe. He mustn't know. Please, Sudie. You've got to help me."

Sudie's gaze traveled toward the upper story, her face torn by indecision. "This is shore enough a terrible mess."

"It doesn't have to be if you'll help me. Will you?"

Sudie bobbed her head up and down. "What does you wants me to do, missy?"

"Have Ryan's water drawn right away. I'll take this tray." She relieved the woman of her burden. "Then I'll go up and make sure Ryan stays upstairs. As soon as *M'sieur* Abercrombie is finished eating, you send him on his way."

"What if that man wants to pay his respects before he leaves?"

"Tell him . . . give him my apologies. Tell him I'm feeling poorly and have retired for the evening."

"You thinks he's goin' to believe old Sudie? What if he says he won't leave without seein' you personal?"

With a sigh of exasperation, Brianna tried to explain. "There is no reason not to believe you. I did fall ill earlier and was forced to excuse myself. He won't be a problem. Just open this door for me and go do as I told you. And don't forget to close the door once I get inside."

"Yes'm." Sudie released the latch, pushing one side of the double doors open. "But I shore hope you knows what you is about."

Ignoring her, Brianna stepped into the room, offering her guest an overly bright smile. "You should have a decent meal to fortify you for your return trip," she announced.

Abby jumped to his feet, quickly taking the tray from her and placing it on the table. " 'Tis thoughtful ye be, m'lady. Truth be told, the worry of me mission did keep me from the table this day."

Noticing that he remained standing, she motioned him to a chair, quick to encourage him to begin. "I'm glad to help." She glanced toward the door, half expecting Ryan to enter. The tension was barely tolerable.

"Aye, and sure ye've done that. Are ye certain ye won't be joining me?" He favored her with a kindly smile. "Has been a long time since I've had the pleasure of such gentle company."

"Thank you, but . . . er . . . I'm afraid I'm feeling somewhat . . . ill again." She put one hand lightly beside her temple, praying that he wouldn't suspect. "I think it would be wise if . . . I . . . say my farewells now."

Concern etched deep grooves in his weathered face. "Shall I be calling someone, m'lady?"

"Er . . . no. I just need to rest."

"Of course, m'lady. Don't ye be giving meself another thought. As soon as I've eaten, I'll be shoving off. You just go along and be seeing to yer proper health."

"Thank you." Guilt pricked her conscience. At the door, she briefly halted. "Oh . . . Abby, for your sake, I'm truly sorry about Lord Tyrone."

He rose to his feet, bowing politely. "I'll be thanking ye for the kind words, m'lady, and for yer hospitality."

She hurried from the room, unable to continue facing him in light of her subterfuge. Lifting the hem of her voluminous skirts, she continued toward the bedchamber, not daring to take a deep breath until she had Ryan in her sights.

His coat and shirt had already been removed in preparation of the promised bath. The sight of muscle and sinew so perfectly shaped beneath bronzed flesh sparked immediate admiration. Her hands twitched, developing an independent need to feel the texture of taut skin, the tickle of coarse curls.

"Come here, my sweet. The hours this day have been long without you by my side."

She obeyed, anxious to feel his strong arms about her, his mouth on hers. She was possessed by a passion for him that seemed without limit.

His lips caught hers, drinking deeply of her sweet nectar. Their bodies molded themselves to each other in wild abandon. Of a single mind, they sought what would most please, deriving pleasure in the giving.

He pulled her down into a chair, holding her on his lap as his hand cupped the firm swell of one breast. "Ah, my sweet siren, how greatly you please me."

"Then I am content."

He held her apart from him, staring deeply into her

eyes. "Are you, my sweet? What of the earl? Are you no longer troubled by thoughts of him?"

She pressed trembling fingers to his lips. "Please, Ryan. Do not speak of him. I want only to experience you now. I would have all my thoughts be of you."

The door opened to admit three boys weighted down by large pails. Steam curled up from the buckets to evaporate in the cool air.

Freeing herself from his easy grasp, Brianna moved to another part of the room, wondering if Ryan had somehow learned of her visitor. *Impossible.* The thought gave her courage. By the time Ryan finished his bath, Abby would be gone, she reasoned. If per chance he still lingered . . . Quickly, she calculated the added time it would take Ryan to eat. Yes, she decided. She could keep him upstairs long enough.

Closing her eyes, Brianna willed herself to remain calm. Nothing could go wrong. Only Sudie knew who the stranger was and the purpose of his visit. She would never tell. Forcing a smile to her face, she turned back to face him.

Ryan was busily searching the pockets of his coat. "Damnation," he grumbled, then started for the door.

"Where are you going?" Terror introduced itself with a breath-stopping force.

"Just to the study, my sweet. I thought I would enjoy a cheroot and a brandy while I bathe."

"I'll get it." Her offer was made in haste, born of panic. "You . . . can't go parading about the house. It isn't dignified. You have no boots." She indicated his bare feet. "And . . . no shirt."

He laughed at her obvious frustration and couldn't resist teasing. "If I didn't know better, my sweet, I would swear you are jealous that some poor female may see something they shouldn't."

Heat swept through her in a rush. Pride refused to allow her to acknowledge her embarrassment, demanding she counter his charge. "To borrow your own phrase, sir, I simply do not take kindly to sharing what is mine."

His laughter grew bolder, the deep resonance pouring forth in an intoxicating flow. "Touché, my sweet siren. As you wish." He executed a sweeping bow. "You may bring my cheroots."

Ryan held the door open, his free hand playfully swatting at her behind as she fled past him. Brianna bit her lip, never slowing as she continued onward. *Hurry. Hurry. Hurry.* The words pounded in her head, keeping time with the muted tempo of distant drums. *Hurry. Hurry. Hurry.*

"Ah, 'tis blessed I am to be telling ye goodbye in person."

Brianna skidded to a halt, gasping for breath as she turned to face the man with the Irish song in his voice. "I thought you were gone," she said, her eyes pleading with Sudie, who stood beside him.

"A heartbeat later and I would've been, m'lady."

"Brianna. Wait up."

Ryan. She grabbed the man's hand. "I won't delay you, sir." She tugged insistently, urging him toward the front door.

"Brianna!" Ryan's voice bellowed through the halls, nearer this time . . . much nearer.

Abby's eyes widened, the color draining from his face as he looked upward.

Brianna knew what she would see, but she followed his

gaze. From the top of the stairs, Ryan stared down at them, his own face wearing a shocked expression.

"May the saints have mercy on me poor worthless soul. 'Tis himself, risen from a watery grave, he is."

His awed words drew her attention. She stared at him blankly, unable . . . unwilling to comprehend. "What did you say?"

Abby hastily signed the cross. "I said that be himself, m'lady." He pointed toward the stairs. "M'lord, the Earl of Tyrone."

Past lips numbed by shock, the words tumbled free. "Ryan? The Earl of Tyrone? No! He can't be! He's . . . my . . . husband."

"Aye, but it's the truth I be speaking. They be one and the same. Ryan Fleming is the Earl of Tyrone."

Chapter 16

With serpentine swiftness, pain struck and buried its sharp fangs deep within her heart. Venom spewed freely, tainting every emotion she possessed with the poison of betrayal.

Every nerve in her grew numb, each muscle tightened to deny her the ability to move. She waited, a statue devoid of life, and watched as he approached.

The ceaseless drums heralded each measured tread as he descended the stairs with an agonizing slowness.

"M'lord, Cap'n," Abby said as he ran forward to greet him. "Sure and begorra, the saints have heard me prayers. I've been sorely tested with thinking ye dead these past months."

"As you can see, I'm alive and well, thanks to the intervention of my wife." He nodded toward Brianna.

From the first moment Ryan caught sight of her stricken gaze, he had clutched it. He held it now, silently willing her to understand.

The pain that had twisted and turned within her when she learned of her father's action was so much less as she faced this latest perfidy. How could she have been so blind as to give her heart to the very man she sought to defeat?

Abby continued to ramble, blissfully unaware of the tension in the joy of reunion with his beloved captain.

Outside, the monotonous drumming ceased, their silence releasing her from inertia. No longer able to bear the pain of his presence, she walked away, her movements stiff, as if governed by some unseen force.

His jawline hardened, the muscles in his neck tightening with repressed anger. He should have been here instead of out searching miles of land for runaway slaves. He should have listened to Greshna. "Brianna. Wait."

She ignored him, continuing up the stairs in search of a safe place to hide. *Don't run too far, little rabbit.*

Greshna's warning sounded in her memory. It had made no sense then. It made none now.

There are other things to concentrate on now, Brianna admonished herself. First the right foot, then the left. She kept moving upward, away from the man who watched.

"Damn!" Ryan swore as she disappeared from sight. He would give her time to compose herself, he decided. Then they would talk.

"Cap'n. I'm right sorry to be barging in on you and the lady like I done." Abby's apology intruded on his thoughts.

In his frustration at the given message, he had forgotten the messenger. "It will be all right, Abby."

"Are ye being right certain of that?"

Ryan grinned, his agitation easing. "Not really. Brianna has a stubborn streak in her, and it will take some doing to get her to see things my way."

"Mmmm. Sounds as if the wee lassie has a touch of Irish in her blood."

"More than a touch. She's the daughter of the Earl of Kenney."

"Kenney, did ye say?" The seaman followed as Ryan headed for the study. He needed a stiff drink.

"Me uncles, Sean and Kevin, worked the land at Greenleaf. Said he was a grand man, they did. It will please them to hear he sired such a fine lassie as the lady."

Ryan filled his glass to the brim, then swallowed it in one punishing gulp. The fire burned its way down his throat, giving a small measure of solace to his guilty conscience. Refilling his glass, he poured a second one, offering it to Abby. He slumped into his chair, letting his first mate find his own comfort.

"Is Lady Calhoun his only heir?"

"She is, but her name's not Calhoun. It's Fleming. We were married some three months ago."

"Then I'm doubly repentant for the troubles I seem to have brought. Honest, Cap'n, I didn't know the way of things. Still don't," he added, his downcast eyes staring into his empty glass.

"Then allow me to enlighten you, my friend." Ryan reviewed the events that had transpired since that fateful moment he had been cast overboard.

Omitting his personal feelings for the woman he had taken to wife, Ryan focused on explaining Brianna's love and dedication to Lagniappe and her aversion to giving up her authority.

Abby emitted a low whistle, shaking his head in amazement once the tale ended. " 'Tis a vexing situation, to be sure, Cap'n. No wonder the lady disbelieved me words."

Having wandered to the window during the conversation, Ryan stared out over the landscape, silently acknowledging the truth of Abby's statement.

It was more than vexing. Ryan Fleming and the Earl of Tyrone were one person, with one heart, one love. Couldn't she see that? Regardless of name, he loved her, and in his heart, he knew she loved him.

"Begging your pardon, Cap'n." Still brooding over the unexpected turn of events, Ryan turned toward his first mate, waiting patiently for him to continue. "Now that Lady Tyrone knows your identity, what do ye plan to do?"

"Do?" One brow arched, a hovering bird of prey outlined against sun-darkened skin. "I intend to remain at Lagniappe."

"I see. Do you think Lady Tyrone will permit it . . . I mean, now that she knows who ye be?"

A slow smile emerged, one that held a mixture of amusement and determination. "Permit? I am her husband. Although she is too distraught to realize it at the moment, it is a fact that cannot . . . will not be changed."

Nervously, Abby cleared his throat, his face a picture of sympathy. "She seems a kind soul. A wee bit fragile, if you know me meaning."

"Save your pity," he advised, thinking of Brianna's sharp retorts to Ivy's bold trespass attempts. "Kind she is, but I can assure you, fragility is scarcely a part of her personality. "Brianna is . . ." He paused, the hard lines of his face softening as he sought an adequate description of the woman who scorned him. ". . . a true sister of the seductive sirens of the sea. She can lure a man so completely as to have him oblivious to all purposes save one . . ." His voice dropped to a whisper. ". . . complete possession of the exquisite soul she shields within such an enchanting package of beauty."

"But, Cap'n, like I said, she does seem very upset. Women can be unpredictable, and she might not be willing to continue being Lady Tyrone. You did say she is most opposed to the aristocracy."

A frown replaced his smile, his eyes darkening as he glared at Abby. "Willing or not, she is my wife, and what is mine, I keep."

Safe behind locks, Brianna leaned against the heavy barrier. Once more, her world had been torn asunder by forces she was unprepared to face.

"Oh, Ryan. How could you deceive me so?" Tears trickled down her pale face as she relived the arrival of the messenger from the ship.

She strained to recall the words. *The Peregrine.* That was the ship's name she had been given. It was the property of the Earl of Tyrone.

Her heart beat dully within her breast. Her arms and legs seemed like leaden weights as she walked toward the chaise lounge by the window. *He had lied!* But why?

Lord Tyrone and Ryan Fleming were one and the same. Brianna leaned back against the velvet headrest, closing her eyes to the truth.

"Why did you come to Lagniappe, *M'sieur* Abercrombie?" she whispered in the silence of her room. Her heart felt as though it were being crushed.

She examined the memories, hoarded like precious gems to be taken out and polished with loving care. One by one she lifted them forth.

The morning ritual of riding the land. Beginning with

the lively exchange of ideas, it often culminated with Ryan holding her . . . loving her so perfectly as to defy description.

"Lies. All lies."

Again her thoughts drifted, the black velvet of darkness beckoning her to review more intimate times. The still nights, when they traversed the uncharted terrain of sensuality. Happiness so complete, it had erased her fears of the absentee earl. Memories magnified, hovering over her, taunting her without mercy.

Her anger stirred, dragging her from the pits of despair. "Of course." She rose, pacing the floor as she sorted out her latest thoughts.

As guardian, the earl would only hold sway over the fortunes of Lagniappe until a suitable match was made. Then he would have no position of power. "So that was his purpose," she muttered, her fury building to new heights. "As the earl, he knew I would reject him. As Ryan Fleming, he became my husband . . . master of all I own."

She whirled toward the closed door, her fingers curling into tight fists. "The scoundrel. The blackguard!" A tight smile hardened her lips with firm resolve. "We will see how well you enjoy marriage, *M'sieur* Lord Tyrone. I vow you will rue the day you chose to set your wicked ways in the path of Brianna Calhoun."

"Sudie!" After more than a week of not seeing Brianna, Ryan's patience was wearing thin, and it showed in the gruffness of his call.

"Yes suh?"

"Where is Brianna?"

"She's still in her room."

"Perhaps you can answer a question for me."

"I'll try, Massa Ryan."

"How long do southern ladies pout? Or is she planning on languishing behind locked doors until she withers away?"

"Miss Bri ain't in no danger of witherin' nowheres, Massa. I can't rightly speak on the poutin' part, though. You done got her in a powerful fit of anger."

Strong fingers plunged through the thick locks of hair. "You don't have to remind me, Sudie. I'm fully aware of my part in this fiasco."

"Yas suh. I figured you was."

He scowled up at her, his attention on the heavy tray she carried. "Take that back to the kitchen."

"But suh. This here is Miss Bri's dinner. Surely you don't means to starve that poor chile?"

He was unable to repress a sly grin. "Ever hear of a gentleman named Shakespeare?"

She shook her nappy head back and forth. "No suh. I don't thinks I'se made his acquaintance. Does he live around here?"

For the first time in ten days, Ryan laughed, the sound reverberating through the halls of Lagniappe. "No, Sudie, but I think it is time I borrow a bit of his philosophy."

"I don't exactly knows what that is, but if you is plannin' on bringin' it to Lagniappe, I thinks you best be speakin' with Miss Bri first. She's already powerful upset, what with findin' out you ain't who you said you was. She shore ain't goin' to take kindly to you borrowin' things from folks. She's got her pride."

He watched the woman make her way carefully down

the stairs, stopping when she reached him. "Sometimes, Sudie, pride can be a fearful companion. It can keep people apart when they are meant to be together."

"Like you and Miss Bri?"

"Yes. It may take a little time, but with your help, I think Brianna will come around. Can I depend on you?"

"What you want old Sudie to do?"

He nodded toward the tray. "There is to be no more food taken upstairs."

Sudie's eyes widened and her generous mouth formed an O shape. "I won't be no part o' starvin' Miss Bri. She needs her strength."

"A tempting thought," he admitted. "Perhaps in a weakened condition, she would be more prone to listen to reason. But she doesn't strike me as having a temperament suitable to enduring such a test. I merely intend to entice her downstairs."

He placed an arm around Sudie's broad shoulders, guiding her toward the kitchen exit as he explained his plan.

"Have Cook prepare every dish she can think of that gives off the most succulent of aromas for this evening's meal."

Sudie nodded, her round face mirroring her puzzlement. "If you says so, Massa." She glared toward the hapless Abercrombie who wandered into the hallway. "Is you going to be having guests for dinner?"

"No. Tonight it will be just me and . . . my wife."

His answer brought a wide grin to her mouth. "Then I'll be sure and tell Cook to make everything extra special." She bustled away, eager to relay the instructions.

"Beg pardon, Cap'n, but I couldn't help but overhear yer conversation." He glanced up the stairway. "Do you really think m'lady will join you? She hasn't left her room since I arrived."

"I know," Ryan tersely answered. "But tonight she will either join me or go hungry. One way or another, I intend to breach this wall she has built, even if I have to batter it down with my bare hands."

Abby frowned, confused by his captain's behavior. "It don't seem fitting and proper to allow a lady to go hungry."

Ryan's laughter sounded again and he slapped his first mate heartily on the back. "I'll wager Brianna will agree, my friend. I know it is difficult to fathom but my spirited wife has an appetite that would rival the hardiest of sailors aboard *The Peregrine.*"

Thoughts of his wife brought a warm smile to his face. Food was not the only thing for which she had a appetite. God how he missed her!

"If you say so, Cap'n." His look belied his words.

"I say so. I do apologize for being unable to extend the hospitality of the table to you this evening but I'm sure Cook will be happy to provide you a fitting repast in the kitchen."

"I understand, sir. I would not intrude for the world. I feel bad enough knowing I be the cause of yer troubles with yer wife. Had I known ye was still alive, I'd have never come barging in. And your sudden appearance took me completely by surprise. I thought I'd seen a ghost, I did. Couldn't help blurting out your name."

"I must accept full blame. I should have spoken with Brianna before the wedding."

"Why didn't you, if you don't mind me asking?"

"My wife's vehement rejection showed me a side of myself I didn't know existed. It seems, in some ways, I'm quite the coward." *Rejection.* That was the monster that caused him to shake in his boots. He couldn't bear her rejection. Wouldn't bear it, he amended.

The crusty seaman scratched his head. "I won't be calling ye a liar, m'lord, but I never did see ye as a man to back down from a fight."

"Brianna has no use for following the rules of a proper fight as it were. She uses weapons we don't possess . . . and make no mistake." He shook a finger in warning. "When a lady decides to fight, she will challenge the Furies with all her considerable wrath. I fear my wife can be a most formidable opponent."

"If she dislikes ye so fiercely, then why did she marry up with you? Was it a part of the writing in the will?"

"No. Our marriage was more a part of destiny, I believe." Ryan paused, thinking of that day she had walked so boldly into his quarters with her scandalous proposal. "And destiny cannot be denied. She is my wife and she will remain my wife."

"Aye, Cap'n. That do seem to be the way of things when a man and woman takes the vows. They be bound together for as long as they lives."

"He did what? Of all the audacity!" Her petticoats swished loudly as Brianna whirled around to glare at Sudie. "He has forbidden you to bring food to my quarters?"

"Surely did. Said if you is of a mind to eat, you'll bring yourself downstairs and take yore food at a proper table."

"What makes him think he has the right to tell me when and where I may eat?"

Sudie stepped behind her, trying to unhook the catches on her gown. "Stand still," she said. "I can't get you out of this gown if you keeps on tryin' to sashay about de room."

Brianna halted, stiffening her back, her manner growing more belligerent with each passing moment. Concentrating on her chore, Sudie continued with her message.

"He says as his wife, you owes him de courtesy to make yore appearance."

"Oh he did, did he? Well, you can just tell *M'sieur* Lord of the Manor I don't intend to be his wife much longer, and . . ." She turned to face the older woman. "I don't owe him a damn thing!"

Sudie sucked in her breath sharply. "Now, you ought not be sayin' sech things. It ain't ladylike to carry on with all that man talk. What will Massa Ryan think if he hears you swearin' like some common street woman?"

Brianna offered a grim smile. "Maybe he should hear precisely how I feel. He duped me into marrying him with all his lies. A marriage built on fraud is not worthy of maintaining, and I intend to rectify the error as soon as possible."

"If I 'members rightly, you said you was de one what did de askin', an' I don't recall him tellin' no lies. He just didn't see no cause to add his entitlements, is all."

"That's beside the point."

"Is it?" Sudie placed her hands on her ample hips, affixing her ebony gaze on Brianna's flushed face. "And just what does you intend to do about that other matter? Is you goin' to call it one of them error things?"

One hand flew protectively to her stomach and Brianna gulped uncomfortably. The child within her . . . a mistake? "My baby has nothing to do with this."

Sudie stepped forward, catching Brianna's hands in her own. "If Massa Ryan knew, he'd likely have a difference of thinkin'."

"He doesn't know . . . and he won't."

"I ain't goin' to tell. That's one thing you two has gots to work out yourselves."

"There is nothing to work out. He doesn't love me . . . or the baby."

"Does you think you can keep it a secret forever, chile?"

Brianna shook her head, her earlier ire melting into misery. "No. Oh, Aunt Sudie, I don't know what to do."

Wrapping beefy arms about her, Sudie offered what comfort she could. "Now, now," she soothed. "You can't go gettin' yourself all upset. It ain't good for de baby."

She forced herself to take deep calming breaths, stilling the sobs that wracked her body.

"That's better," Sudie encouraged. "I know things looks bad, but you has gots a good head on your shoulders. You'll think of somethin'. I jest knows you will."

"I've tried. There is only one answer I can find."

"What's that?"

"He's got to leave Lagniappe . . . and soon."

"Don't rightly see how you is goin' to manage that. He don't acts like he is plannin' on goin' anyplace soon."

"He has to, Sudie. He has to leave. There's no way he can stay now."

"Why not?"

Brianna bowed her head in dejection. "He doesn't love me. He only wanted Lagniappe. I was the guarantee he would have it . . . permanently."

Sudie squeezed her hand, offering a sympathetic

chuckle. "Lawdy, chile, but I s'pects that man loves you more than life itself. 'Course, him bein' a man and all, I guess there is a chance he don't know jest how much. He can learn, though."

"Well, if he doesn't know it, I'm certainly not going to tell him," Brianna said.

"Tellin' a man anything don't do a bit of good. They is so dense, you has practically got to show them everythin' if you hope to get it in their skulls."

Brianna tilted her head to one side. "You may have a point, but at the moment, there is a lot more I intend to show Ryan Fleming than love."

"Uh-oh." Sudie shook her head. "I has done seen that gleam in yore eyes before and it don't look good. You best not be pullin' any of yore stunts on de massa. He ain't likely to take real kind to any of yore foolishness."

"Foolishness." Fire flashed from the younger woman's eyes, causing Sudie to cringe. "He tricked me. Just like Papa, he made a big show of how I'm as capable as a man, but when it came down to the bottom line, he proved that he wouldn't put any faith in a woman."

"There ain't no use in talkin' to you, is there?"

"No." Brianna grew sullen as Sudie busied herself in changing her gown.

While combing Brianna's long tresses, Sudie tried to broach the touchy subject again. "Does you know what you is goin' to do to de massa?"

"I haven't given it much thought as to the exact method, but I intend to teach him to respect my rights as an individual."

"That may not be none too easy. Men ain't used to bein' ordered about by their womenfolk. You might find you will has a easier time if you uses yore lady charms. They has worked for women for many years."

"Charms? You mean like the potions Greshna makes?"

"Naw, missy. I mean the charms like the old massa never thought you had any use for. The kind Miss Ivy uses when she has her cap set for a man."

Brianna gave a grimace, drawing a chuckle from Sudie. "I'm not setting my cap for him. I'm trying to get rid of him."

"Yes'm. Only, whilst you is gettin' rid of him, you best make sure you wants to. Once you has known a man, times can gets real lonesome without him."

"He tricked me, lied to me."

"I ain't sayin' he's perfect, but then . . . you ain't perfect yourself."

"I . . ." She bit down on her bottom lip, unable to refute the charge.

"Now you is plottin' to bring a baby into this world without no rightful daddy to teach him things."

"I can teach her everything she needs to know," Brianna answered, stressing the use of the feminine gender.

"He needs his daddy," Sudie countered, accenting the *he* with equal vigor.

"Of course. And for what? To teach him how to subjugate a woman, lie to her, bend her to comply with his every whim?"

A vibrant chuckle heaved Sudie's ponderous breasts up and down. "Them whims can be right pleasurable."

Brianna's eyes widened on hearing the implication of Sudie's words. A quick glance into the chevel glass revealed the evidence of telltale dark pink spots coloring her cheeks. "You're wicked, Sudie."

"If you says so."

"I do." Impatient to put an end to the awkward conversation, Brianna waved the woman away with her hand. "That will do. I don't want Ryan to think I dress for his pleasure. We're only having dinner." She glared at Sudie through the glass. "Something I wouldn't have to endure if not for the man's unreasonable attitude."

Sudie offered no argument, quitting the room to allow Brianna to consider what she should do . . . and how.

Try as she might, she could find no answer. Honesty forced her to concede one point to Sudie. After knowing Ryan, she was lonesome without him. Never had she known the nights could be so long or the days could blend together with such boredom.

And there was the pain, she chided. That never-ending pain that his betrayal created. If he knew of her pain, would he understand? Would he even care?

Her laughter greeted the unvoiced questions, a ragged sound that tottered on the edge of tears. Brianna looked into the mirror, her reflection peering back at her like a ghost. The small chin tilted outward.

"I won't cry. *I won't!* It's not good for the baby."

The unfairness of it all seeped in like the slow advance of the incoming tide. Ryan had inflicted a deep wound on her spirit. In turn, that wound could easily prove a threat to an innocent child not yet born. Why should he escape?

"Of course." Gradually, a plan evolved. The lines of worry faded from her face.

He demanded her presence at the table. She would provide it. He insisted on continuing with the charade of two people in love. She would oblige. She would offer conversation, smiles, laugh at his clever sayings, do all that was required . . . to a point.

Smiling into her mirror, Brianna gave voice to her plan. "I will employ your own weapon, m'lord. I will take your trust . . . your heart . . . your love. Then I will bolt the door to you. You may not understand or care now, but you will. You will learn. I will return the agony of this pain in full measure. You will experience my torment within your own deceitful heart. Then I will be free!"

The drums that called throughout the land beat with a dirgelike pattern, winding a path through her softly spoken vow. A damp chill permeated the room.

With a shiver, Brianna abandoned her one-sided conversation. It was done. She would not dwell on her decision nor would she question the method she had chosen.

She walked to the window, concentrating on the pagan melody that swelled, then faded. Her eyes searched the darkness. In the distance, she thought she detected a tiny pinpoint of light.

An open fire, she guessed. For cooking? Or could it be for some mysterious ceremony?

Brianna closed her eyes, speculating on the possibilities. From Sudie, she had learned more of her people now left their quarters in the dark of night to answer the wild call of the drums.

Images of reedlike shapes gleamed darkly in her imagination. She could see their half-naked bodies, slick with sweat. They dipped and swayed, undulating to the pagan rhythm set by the drums. Their voices raised in the fever pitch of chants that called upon their heathen gods.

A whimper, torn from her own throat, called her back to reality. Dampness slithered between the ripe globes of her breasts in tiny droplets. Her hands trembled as she pressed them to the aching throb of her temples. Straining for release, her breath came on shallow wisps of air.

Never had she heard any talk of such things. Although she had made extensive use of her father's library, Brianna could not recall a single mention of anything that might be responsible for the vivid images summoned forth from her mind.

There was no denying the vision. It was so clear, so real. So very, very real. The knowledge brought new fear.

A tear streaked down her cheek. *"Mon Dieu.* What is wrong with me? What lurks within me so horrible it cannot reveal itself? Is this why Ryan denied me true love?"

Chapter 17

Waiting at the elegantly appointed table, Ryan sipped his brandy, trying not to believe the doubts that crept closer with the passage of time. Surely she would come.

Given her fiery spirit, it seemed unlikely she would remain within the confines of her room without food just to avoid him. No, he decided. Inflicting pain upon herself in such a case didn't fit her personality.

A wry smile touched his mouth. "She's more apt to attack me." The thought amused, lifting his spirits. God, how he had missed her saucy manner, her quick wit, her . . . "Mmm."

Elegantly gowned in a watered silk of forest-green, she chose that moment to appear, ending his more provocative thoughts. Framed in the archway, she reminded him of a well-defined painting, a true masterpiece that could only be properly appreciated by the most discerning of patrons.

"I'm delighted you decided to join me, my sweet."

"I didn't realize I was given a choice."

He ignored her cold restraint, coming forward to escort her to her chair. "You look lovely."

"How nice of you to approve . . . your lordship."

At her use of his title, he winced. She's here, he reminded himself. It's a start. As he took his place, Ryan offered her a benign smile, determined her barbs would not rile him. "Cook has prepared a special meal for the occasion."

Brianna sipped her water, saying nothing. The mention of food set off a tiny rumble of protest in her stomach. Not since breakfast had she eaten, and most of it had surrendered to the persistence of the queasiness that plagued her.

"Would you care for a glass of sherry?"

Nausea fluttered in warning. She indicated refusal with a demure shake of her head.

Ryan leaned back in his chair, studying the paleness of her flawless complexion. His own sense of guilt plucked at his conscience. *I must get her to ride again, get out of this house.*

A servant arrived to set a bowl of steaming gumbo before her. Her stomach voiced its appreciation. Brianna glanced at her companion, relieved that he appeared not to hear her bodily protests. Lord, if he knew, he'd use food as a weapon for everything, she thought uncharitably.

She sampled the fare, barely containing a sigh of joy at the spicy taste. Tense muscles relaxed, warmed by the heated liquid that coursed down her throat.

Watching, Ryan found himself fascinated by the expression on her face. He envied knowing that something as simple as a bowl of gumbo could give her such pleasure, while he had managed to inflict so much pain into her life.

"I had the remainder of the stalks in the fields torched

yesterday," he said, eager to correct his own mistakes. "Once the ground is turned, I've instructed Rawlings to start the planting of a legume crop. It will be good for the soil."

"What of the . . ." She bit back her question. So easily, he could make her forget . . . take the most common of tasks and lure her into detailed discussion.

"Of course, the field hands will enjoy a couple of day's well-earned rest first," he said.

Has he the power to read my mind? Brianna asked herself. Past harvests had always marked a time of rest and celebration at Lagniappe. Regret at missing it this year was mixed with the knowledge that at least he would retain the tradition that made life a little easier. "Thank you."

The words were out before she realized it. Silently, she berated herself. She wasn't following her original plan at all!

"You're welcome."

Brianna bowed her head, staring into the thickened concoction before her. The effect of his smile proved to be more devastating than she had expected.

Woo him, then spurn him, she told herself. *But how?* His voice reached out to her, curling each word into an invitation with its resplendence. Her own body threatened to betray her, prodded by too many memories that refused to fade, despite his perfidy.

A change in tactics seemed the only solution. Maybe if the conversation could be aimed in more serious directions, she could restrain her wanton emotions. Brianna blotted her lips with the tip of her napkin, trying to marshal her thoughts. She had to try.

Ryan watched, entranced by her graceful action. He

yearned to feel those lush lips on his own. The memory of those slender hands gliding across his bared flesh brought a heated response from his loins.

"Aunt Sudie tells me more of the people are leaving their quarters at night."

He frowned, struggling to focus on the nature of her comment. "Er . . . yes." It wasn't the direction in which he had hoped this evening would lead. At least, we are communicating, he thought with some consolation. It was worth continuing. "Last night, I counted seven slip away."

"You counted?"

"Yes. Rawlings and I set up posts outside the quarters and watched. When they came out, we followed."

Her heart raced with fear. "But . . . wasn't that dangerous?"

His massive shoulders lifted in a dismissive shrug. "Not really. Since we had no plans to intercept them, it was easy to keep them in sight while remaining at a safe distance."

"I don't understand. If you didn't want to catch them, why follow?" Her anger began to flare. Much of her self-imposed confinement had been spent looking out the windows of her room.

She had seen the fires at night, had heard the threats within the ominous drums. It wasn't her imagination, she told herself. Each day had brought more riders to the doors of Lagniappe, owners coming to consult about the growing threat of violence.

"Stopping one or two won't end the matter, my sweet. We must find the source of the problem if we are to solve it."

"And did you?"

He shook his head. "I'm afraid not. We followed them to the loading dock. They had a crude canoe hidden away. Once boarded, they paddled north toward the swampland."

Relief coursed through her body, slowing the rate of her heart to a more normal level. Then anger flickered with new vigor. He could have been injured . . . killed. "You mustn't do that again."

A dark brow cocked in a curious slant. "And what would you suggest, my sweet?"

"Tell them if they leave again, they will lose the right to earn their freedom."

His laughter rumbled like distant thunder. "Well spoken, but I regret to say, it is not practical."

"Of course it is. No one would risk losing a chance at freedom."

"Exactly my point. You are offering freedom in the future. This present movement offers it now."

"But it's risky. It's a great uncertainty."

"Life itself is a risk, my sweet. Every life, every relationship is filled with uncertainty."

The conversation was no longer impersonal. She could read the intimacy reflected in his eyes, could hear it in the timbre of his voice. "I . . . I don't want to talk about . . . it."

Ryan leaned forward, reaching out to take her hand in his. He raised it, saluting her fingertips with a light flurry of kisses. "We must talk, my sweet. There is the future to consider."

He wants to leave Lagniappe. "If you don't mind, I have lost my appetite." Pushing her chair backward, Brianna rose, eager to return to the safety of her room.

"But I do mind, my sweet. I mind very much." He

grasped her wrist, halting her retreat with a steely clasp.

Forgotten was her assertion that he must leave. This was real. He would leave her. There was no recourse but to salvage her tattered pride. "Take your hands off me, m'lord."

"I am not your lord," he snapped, angered by her cold retreat.

Her lashes fluttered upward, her eyes gazing boldly into his. "No. You're not. You're not my anything, Ryan."

Her words hit him, a vicious brutal slap. His hand dropped to his side. He could say nothing. He knew it; he saw it in the icy cold of her eyes, felt it as each hard word sliced into his flesh. "I believe I'm beginning to understand, m'lady."

Too distraught to speak, she turned away, desperate to leave him before she disgraced herself with tears. His words stopped her anxious retreat.

"Perhaps I mean nothing to you, but to the law, I am your rightful husband."

Dazed, she faced him, unable to believe his callous attitude. "Husband?" The shaky query added another log to the fires of humiliation flaming within her breast. How dare he denigrate the sacred relationship of husband and wife with such mockery!

"Don't you mean *master?*" she hissed.

Strong hands reached out to imprison her shoulders, pulling her close until her breasts pressed into a wall of muscle and sinew. "Vent your anger as you will, my sweet. But remember, nothing can last forever . . . not even your hate."

His mouth descended with swiftness, capturing her lips in a punishing kiss that left her weak with wanting.

The firm pressure yielded, melting into teasing little nips that sent tingles of excitement across the fullness of her lower lip. Of their own volition, swollen lips parted to allow him greater access.

His tongue teased the inner lining, lightly tracing the sensitive curves, then plunged deeper to feast on her sweet nectar.

Choking back a whimper of pleasure, Brianna sought to resist his tender assault. She told herself it was the land he wanted, not her. She was but a vessel to be used to satisfy his carnal desires.

His mouth slanted across hers, transferring attention to the creamy softness of her neck.

Straining against the pull of her own burgeoning desires, she eased out of his grasp, leveling a remote look of disinterest at him. "As you say, m'lord, nothing lasts forever. Good night."

Not daring to wait for a response, she fled the room. Tears blurred her vision but she could not stop. Too great was her fear of surrender.

Rejected, he watched her retreat. A chill invaded the room, seeping into the very marrow of his bones. "We are not finished, my sweet. You are still my wife."

From her bedroom window the following morning, Brianna watched Ryan mount the bay and ride off in the company of waiting plantation owners. She recognized the owners of Belle Terre, Briarwood, and Glenbrook among them. The horses galloped west toward Willow-green.

With Ryan gone, she wasted no time in availing herself

of use of the premises. It had been agony waiting for his departure.

The annoying malady that recently blighted her life had disappeared as abruptly as it had begun. This morning she had been ravenous when she awoke. It felt wonderful to be more like her old self again. Her needs had nearly caused her to relent in her vow to avoid him as much as possible.

Hurrying downstairs, Brianna piled her plate with food, not caring that it was cold. "Sudie?" she asked when the woman walked by the entrance.

"Yes'm?"

"Do we have any strawberries?"

"Strawberries? Is you pulling my leg, missy?"

"Hardly. I'm quite serious. I would like a bowl of strawberries with cream."

"What you likes and what you gets ain't likely to be the same thing. There ain't been no strawberries since early summer. In case you has forgot, it's gettin' close to Christmas."

"I didn't think. Her lips puckered in a thoughtful pout. "I suppose I should do something for the season." With a laugh, she admitted her lapse. "The weather has been so mixed up this year, I don't recall our even having a proper fall."

"Don't rightly guess we did. It got plumb uncomfortable warm, even in de early part of November, it did. If you asks me, that's a bad sign, when a body can't tell one time from de next."

"Don't get gloomy on me, Aunt Sudie." Brianna whirled toward her, her happiness spreading her mouth into a broad grin. "I know. We'll decorate the main parlor. Maybe I'll even send out a few invitations for an impromptu dinner party."

Sudie shook her head. "You might be askin' de massa first. Things is gettin' in a fierce uproar here lately. Don't know as how folks would be feelin' about gettin' out for some kind of party and such."

"I don't think I need to ask him anything." Brianna leveled a somber gaze on the old mammy. "I'm asking you. What's happened now?"

"They has had more runaways."

"Oh no. When? Did anyone see where they went?"

"They not only seen, one of them got himself catched."

Sudie ambled into the room, drawing near and lowering her voice to a husky whisper. "One of de men from Willowgreen done hightailed it several days past. Last night, he went sneakin' cross Belle Terre."

"Belle Terre?" A frown furrowed her brow at the news. "There are only two ways someone can get to Jeffrey's from *M'sieur* Fargus's. They had to go through Briarwood or . . . Lagniappe."

"That's de truth of it, missy."

"Which one was it? Do you know?"

"No, ma'am, I don't. That's what all those men is tryin' to find out. They's done gone to Willowgreen now to see if they can find out what direction he lit out."

"That's ridiculous. Why didn't they ask the slave?"

"Can't. That Massa Arlington done sets his dogs on him."

"He didn't!"

Sudie's eyes grew wide with fear. "Yes'm. He did. By de time he called them off, there weren't nothing left but a few scraps of sackcloth and blood. There was lots of blood . . . and bone."

Brianna set her plate aside, her hunger destroyed by the gruesome events. "Oh, Sudie. Surely he didn't have to—"

"Didn't have to kill him, but he did."

Her head bowed, Sudie shuffled out of the room, her broad shoulders slumped in defeat.

The world seemed to be in such a muddle. Never could she recall violence touching the land in this way. There had to be an answer somewhere. Belle Terre seemed the most likely place to look.

Hurrying, she went up to change. It was time to pay a social call on Ivy anyway, Brianna told herself. She had never properly thanked her for arranging her wedding.

Handing the butler her calling card, Brianna followed him into the parlor. Once alone, she allowed herself a smile.

The man had exhibited the same lofty attitude of his master and mistress. She knew it wasn't in good taste to present herself at the door, but then, there had been little choice since she had refused to make use of a driver.

Idly, she wondered what Ryan would say when he found out she had gone calling without a proper chaperon. In a fit of irritation, she dismissed the thought. Why would he care? Hadn't he already taken to riding off into the night without so much as a word?

She tilted her head at an upward slant. If he could come and go as he pleased, then so could she.

Wandering across the room, Brianna looked out the window. Winter seemed more in evidence here than on her own Lagniappe. The grass was flattened into mats of drab brown. In the distance, a stand of pine trees provided evidence of a recent fire.

"My dear. What a surprise." Ivy's sultry greeting caught her attention.

"I apologize for the hour. I hope I haven't intruded on your lunch."

"Lunch? My dear, I haven't even had breakfast yet. I was still abed when my girl told me of your arrival." She scanned the room, peering over Brianna's shoulder to look out the window."

"Are you looking for someone?"

"Yes, of course. Where is that charming husband of yours?"

"Sorry to disappoint you, Ivy. Ryan isn't with me."

Jealousy pricked at her with nervous energy. Brianna bit back a waspish retort. She would never get information if she got in an argument with Ivy. Smiling, she continued. "He joined some of the other owners for a ride to Willowgreen. I thought you knew. Jeffrey was with them."

A servant arrived with the coffee service, setting the silver on a low table in front of the settee.

Brianna eyed the flaky pastries on the tray, her mouth watering with anticipation. Then she noticed the slight tremor in Ivy's hand. "Are you ill?"

"No. It's just that I had a very vexing night. If it hadn't been for Ryan, I would have never made it. He was such a comfort."

"Ryan?"

Ivy glanced up, a catlike smile on her lips. "I hope I didn't speak out of turn. I thought you knew."

"Knew what?"

"Why, that Ryan was with me last night, of course."

Fighting back the urge to wipe the satisfied smirk from her face, Brianna forced a composure she didn't feel. "Of course. How could I have forgotten?"

The answer had the desired effect. Ivy's smile tightened. Coffee splashed onto the service tray. "Damnation. Ellie! Ellie! Get in here!"

The shrill screams of agitation were like a balm to Brianna's bruised spirit. *Ryan and Ivy. How could he?*

Wide-eyed, a thin black girl scurried into the room. With her small rag, she tried to repair the damage. The threadbare cloth only smeared the brown liquid.

"Clumsy fool."

Brianna winced when Ivy's hand whipped across the girl's cheek. Her heart went out to her in sympathy. She was so young, just a child really.

"You're even more useless than the last one. Get out of here." The girl looked up, saying nothing.

Icy fingers clutched at Brianna's heart. Where once fear marked the smooth, youthful features, there was nothing but a blank impassiveness. Her eyes glowed with onyx hardness. There was no mistaking the hatred they harbored for the mistress of Belle Terre.

In an instant, she was gone. Ivy mumbled under her breath. "All alike, lazy and useless."

"Don't let it upset you, Ivy. There's been no real harm."

"Why shouldn't it upset me? This whole business—thefts, runaways, voodoo—it's enough to upset anyone. Don't tell me that you sit home and never stop to think about whether or not they will murder you in your bed."

"No, I don't. I see no reason the problems here should affect Lagniappe. There's no connection."

"No connection, you say. Surely you jest." Ivy paused

to take a deep swallow of her coffee. "Of course they're connected! Why do you think Jeffrey and the others came to Lagniappe this morning?"

"I assume because we are neighbors."

Ivy's laughter came in jerky spasms, the effect sending shivers of apprehension racing along Brianna's spine. "It's true that our slaves may be getting more fractious, but those damnable drums are the cause. They're heating up their blood."

She couldn't deny the accusation. Sometimes, she felt that those very drums were calling to her, urging her toward a certain destination. But where? What could they possibly say to her? "Very well. I concede they do represent a certain amount of annoyance, but there is no call to suggest they are a danger to anyone at Lagniappe."

"How idealistic you are, my dear. Perhaps Ryan's presence has a far more soothing effect than I realized."

Brianna felt the blood rush to her face in a heated flow. "Ryan has nothing to do with it." She felt her muscles knotting, twisting into tight balls at the mention of her husband.

First he had betrayed her about his identity, and now? Now he had betrayed her with Ivy Arlington. She wanted to make him pay. He compounded his wrongs with more wrongs. Why, then, was she so miserable? "Everyone at Lagniappe is well treated."

Her tongue felt thick in her mouth, but she had to remain calm. She refused to allow Ivy to see how much Ryan's behavior hurt her.

"There is no reason for anyone to wish me harm."

"If they are so happy, then why the drums?"

A frown pulled at Brianna's mouth. "The drums?"

"They are coming from Lagniappe."

She had the peculiar feeling Ivy had kicked her in the stomach. But that was impossible. Ivy was still propped on the settee in a regal pose. "What makes you think they are on Lagniappe?"

"Ryan mentioned it."

"I don't believe you. Ryan would never speak to you of such matters."

Beneath her sharp gaze, Ivy fidgeted, then gave a blasé shrug. "He didn't tell me specifically."

Brianna leaned forward, every fiber of her being taut with strain. "Maybe you better start at the beginning. And . . . don't leave anything out, Ivy."

"Beau was visiting and . . ."

"Beau Randolph of Glenbrook?" she interrupted.

Ivy nodded. "Yes. He was here when our overseer stopped by. He told Jeffrey that he overheard a couple of bucks talking about some runaway passing this way. Jeffrey and Beau decided to ride out and see what they could find."

Aunt Sudie's description returned. "They took the dogs with them." She fought the taste of bile that rose.

"Yes. With the dogs, tracking would be so easy."

"It wasn't easy for that runaway."

Ivy's face took on a scowl, adding a hard cruelty to her perfectly sculpted features. "Who cares about some runaway? Do you want to hear this or not?"

"Of course. Please continue." Brianna forced herself to remain silent and absorb every word of the story being laid before her.

"Shortly after they left, the drums started again. I was . . . frightened. I didn't know which way Jeffrey had gone. That's when I sent for Ryan."

She sent for Ryan. Brianna sighed in relief. It wasn't an assignation after all. Ryan had not betrayed her—this time, she reminded herself. With this latest burden lifted, she listened with new calm. Ivy droned on, unaware her attention wandered.

". . . checked the security of the house. I was still frightened . . . terrified, in fact. I begged him to remain until Jeffrey's return."

"I'm sure Jeffrey was displeased when he found Ryan waiting." She had no doubt he waited. Ryan would never abandon someone in need. *And me?* But I'm not in need, she silently chided. *I own Lagniappe.*

Again Ivy gave an elegant shrug of her shoulders. "A couple of drinks and he calmed. Besides, he was too excited about catching up with that runaway to overly care about anything."

She tried to visualize Jeffrey in such a state. She had always thought him rather stiff-necked, but cruel? It left her unsettled.

"Beau got in a discussion with Ryan and said something about those drums. Ryan casually mentioned they were coming from the edge of the swamp on Lagniappe."

"You were eavesdropping."

"There is no harm in paying attention when someone is speaking," Ivy heatedly defended.

Brianna found it difficult to disagree. Ryan had told her of following some of the men from Lagniappe. They had headed for the swamp. If only she hadn't been so upset. If only she had asked more questions.

Rising, Brianna tried to appear calm. "Thank you for the coffee, Ivy, and please accept my apologies for calling so early. I shall try to remember to observe protocol next time."

Ivy stood, patting her hair with one hand. "Yes, of course. Although I enjoy company, five o'clock is a more civilized hour to entertain."

"Of course." Brianna walked toward the hallway, anxious to be on her way.

"Speaking of calling," Ivy began. "I had thought I would have received an invitation for dinner before now. Surely, Ryan isn't keeping you occupied that much."

The innuendo was clear, bringing a quick flush to Brianna's face. "I was speaking to Aunt Sudie about that just today. With the problems that have developed . . . er . . . with the runaways, we thought it best not to rush things. We wouldn't want our neighbors taking any undue risks of attacks."

Ivy wrapped her arms about herself, giving a visible shudder. "I approve of your decision. I hadn't given it much thought. I guess I am having a problem adjusting to this sort of thing."

The look on her face gave mute testimony to the fear she felt. Sympathy surfaced and Brianna extended a hand to offer a reassuring pat. "Try not to think about it."

"That's easy for you to say. Jeffrey's either gone or too drunk to be of much use if something did happen. There are times I feel so alone . . . vulnerable."

Odd, Brianna thought. Until now she had never considered Ivy vulnerable to anything. "Please call on us anytime. Ryan will be glad to assist."

The offer was made on impulse, guided to life by a rise of compassion. Once made, Brianna found she had no regret.

The butler opened the front door. They stepped out onto the veranda. Brianna drew her cloak more tightly about her slender frame. It had grown more chilly since her arrival. "Looks like we may have a winter after all."

"I despise cold weather. Everything looks and feels so dead."

In the distance, the drums began to whisper their strange chant, adding to the negative description.

"Nonsense." Brianna forced a certain amount of cheer into the word. "The land is just taking a nap, reviving itself for another spring."

"Maybe." Ivy frowned, looking out across the drive. "I don't see your driver. Probably off nosing about. Perhaps we should step back inside. I'll send someone to fetch him."

Brianna reached out to stop her. "That's not necessary. I . . . I don't have a driver."

Ivy's eyes widened. "But you must! You can't go careening about without some protection, not the way things are."

"The way things are . . . is pretty much unknown. I've always driven myself. I enjoy it."

"It's not safe."

"I got here without incident."

"Let me send someone with you to act as a bodyguard."

Brianna thought of the young girl, of the naked hatred shining in her eyes. "That's not necessary. I'll be fine. Now I really must go."

Before Ivy could protest, she hurried down the steps and climbed up into her buggy. Picking up the reins, she looked at the afternoon sky.

A gray overcast dimmed the cold light of the sun. She thought of the trip ahead, of the narrow road with its countless ruts. An odd feeling passed over her. *Someone's walking on a grave.* Within seconds, the morbid thought withered away. "Maybe I should have brought a driver," Brianna mused.

Chapter 18

Brianna's hands trembled slightly as she flicked the reins, signaling the big black to start. She winced as one wheel dropped into a dip. "Lord, but Belle Terre is ill maintained," she muttered under her breath. The wheel creaked in protest and Brianna turned her concentration to the road. She couldn't afford to become stranded.

"All right, Papa. Maybe, just maybe, I do need someone to share the task of decision making. Not a guardian, mind you." Thoughts of Ryan intruded on her one-sided conversation. "I admit I haven't exactly handled matters as best as should be." She glanced up at the steadily darkening sky, as though her father would somehow answer her. "A partner would be all right." A fat droplet of rain splashed onto her upturned face.

"Wonderful." She resigned herself to the fact of not making it back to Lagniappe in time.

The promise of rain kindled new thoughts, memories really, of another rain . . . another place . . . another time. If only she could start anew.

"Why Lord Tyrone?" The anguished query tore free in

desperate search of an answer. Surely she deserved to know that much, she thought.

The silence continued. Taking stock of her present situation, Brianna felt regret that she hadn't elected to use a driver. At least she would have been protected from the weather, instead of riding down the narrow deserted road in a small open buggy.

She strained to see the road ahead, moving forward at a cautious pace. The sun hid behind billowing clouds of dark gray, adding to her feeling of foreboding as she studied the stretch ahead.

Tall pines and oaks stood in tight lines, casting the narrow dirt road in total darkness.

With stubborn determination, she plunged onward. She had to reach Lagniappe. "It will be all right. It will."

Occasional branches reached out like grasping talons, clawing at the inadequate tarplike hood of her buggy. The scraping sounds grated on her raw nerves. Her heart beat faster and she couldn't help but wish she had remained within the safety of her own parlor.

An eerie feeling crept through her. "Get along, boy." She flicked the buggy whip across the swaying rump. The sound of her voice emphasized how alone she really was. "Faster."

Not a bird chirped. Not a single squirrel could be seen scampering in the trees. It was as if . . . "Stop that," she sharply scolded herself. "Don't let your imagination get out of control."

She thought of Ivy, of the stark fear that twisted the normally controlled features of her face. Then there had been the drums. "Where on Lagniappe?" she asked. No longer did she doubt the source.

Silently, she berated herself. Wrapped up in her own

misery of personal betrayal, she had failed in her duties to Lagniappe . . . her people. She could only hope Ryan would be able to solve the problem before it was too late.

"Ryan." The thought of him, the sound of his name, brought tears to her eyes, blurring her sight.

Her horse snickered, then gave a high-pitched whinny of terror. Brianna blinked, tightening her grip on the reins.

Unseen hands grabbed at her heavy cloak, pulling her off balance. "No," she cried in automatic response.

Her fingers curled about the slim length of the buggy whip, but her wrist was being twisted. She cried out against the sharp pain, struggling fiercely as she felt herself being dragged from the now-motionless buggy. The whip was snatched away.

A rush of adrenaline gave her a new spurt of energy. "Unhand me." She wrenched one hand free, flaying wildly at her attacker.

Her nostrils flared. Nausea threatened as she inhaled the fetid stench of unwashed bodies. Blindly, she beat her fists at the seemingly endless number of hands that groped at her in a frenzy of motion.

A heavy weight lifted as her cloak was torn away from her. An unexpected gust of cold air washed over her to steal her breath. "Ryan!" she screamed.

On and on she fought, her nails gouging into unseen flesh. *So dark.* Brianna kicked, knowing a brief moment of satisfaction when she heard a pained grunt.

Cruel fingers dug deeply into her flesh as her hands were once again imprisoned. Everything, everyone was a blur of movement.

"Kill her."

She twisted her body, trying to lash out at the voice.

Pain sliced through her lower back. One hand found freedom.

"Flay her white hide off," another voice demanded.

"I wants her first. Never had no white woman."

She writhed frantically, desperate to escape.

"Me neither. Their menfolk done had our women, though. Let me have her."

So many hands. So many voices. Even in the jumble of sound, she recognized their intent. Pain tore through her arm as it was twisted behind her back.

She was roughly pushed to her knees. Bits of rock and dirt cut into tender flesh.

My baby. Have to protect. Must save my baby.

"Ryan," she called, struggling to keep the encroaching darkness at bay.

Breaking free of a slippery grasp, she cried out. "Leave me alone. Go away." The air, thick with sweat, threatened to suffocate her. Each breath became a painful struggle that left her heaving in ragged gasps.

Dark hands pushed, pinning her flat on the ground. She was losing. "No." Her heart raced with fear. A grotesque face loomed in front of her. Closer, closer it came. The smell made her want to gag. She twisted her head to one side, trying to get away.

Through the ruckus, she heard it, a steady pounding that grew louder and louder, each throbbing sound increasing as her meager strength ebbed.

"Run!"

"Hear that? Sounds like horses."

"Run, I says."

She heard the words, tried to obey. Oh, God, but how she wanted to run! The oppressive weight on her body lifted. She half raised her body from the ground. It was raining, harder now. The cold liquid slapped at her face, stinging her body with icy pinpoints.

Something hit her near the corner of her mouth. She didn't care. Trying to rise again, Brianna stumbled, falling prone, her face resting in the sticky shifting mud. The pounding was incessant.

Thunder? she thought, her mind detaching itself from the melee. Rain splashed onto her face, running down her skin in tiny rivulets and spilling onto the soggy mass that mushroomed around her.

Voices raised, releasing sharp shrieking sounds.

Struggling to her feet, she blindly sought escape. A callused band of flesh grabbed her arm, then hurled her aside. Buffeted by a sea of bodies, it proved impossible to gain her balance. She staggered, lurching forward. *My baby.*

Her hands clutched at the firm bulwark that suddenly met her touch. She heard a roar of sound. Her name? She didn't know.

With a quivering breath, Brianna filled her nostrils with the scent of soap and fresh rain. *Familiar. So familiar.* She felt safe. "Oh, Ryan. You came." Taut aching muscles turned to liquid, darkness wrapping her in oblivion.

He kicked at the door with a force that threatened to unhinge it. Almost instantly, it opened. Toby's eyes widened as Ryan pushed past him, Brianna cradled in his arms.

"Sudie! Where the hell are you?" he bellowed.

"I is comin'." Sudie's heavy steps could be heard as she

hurried into the foyer. "Oh, Lawd. My baby! What's done happened?"

"Never mind the questions. Get her bed turned down."

Sudie ran for the stairs, moving with a speed that belied her ample girth. "Fetch the doctor man, Toby," she called out.

His angry tread echoed through the house as he followed, taking the stairs two at a time.

"I'll gets her out of those wet clothes," Sudie volunteered.

"I'll do it. Go fetch some brandy," Ryan commanded. "And send someone in here to get the fire going. She feels half frozen."

"Yes suh." She bustled out to do his bidding, leaving him alone.

Staring at the still figure of his young wife, Ryan cursed himself for not being with her.

So pale, he thought, tenderly touching a wet cloth to her face. The mud and blood disappeared, revealing the swollen area at the corner of her mouth. Ryan cringed as his eyes took note of the bluish smudge that marred her creamy perfection.

"Bastards," he swore.

With grim determination, he gathered her in the curve of one arm while he removed the torn remainder of her bodice. An angry red furrow slashed across a bared breast, increasing his rage against the entire human race.

He cursed the arrogance of the South, railing against them for their mockery of human decency as they preened within the confines of their own decadent society.

With equal fury, he vowed vengeance on the runaway

slaves who had dared attack his beloved in a blind frenzy of hate. If she died, he swore those responsible would pay with their lives.

Lost in his own pain, Ryan refused to spare himself for what had happened. "You were right, my sweet siren," he muttered, his fingertips caressing one soft cheek. "I did deceive you, but no more than I have deceived myself. You believe yourself trapped in a loveless marriage, yet I know I am imprisoned by far stronger bonds. Love itself holds me in shackles, and I am powerless to free myself from your spell. Don't die," he quietly pleaded. "You are my life."

"She's dead! She's dead because of you." Her father's voice reached out to her from the corridors of time, screaming in harsh condemnation.

Brianna's arms and legs curled inward, huddling toward the center of her shivering frame. *Cold. So cold.* The injured woman disappeared, leaving behind the seven-year-old girl, alone and frightened.

The doors of the past slowly swung open, releasing the hurts, the fear, the agonizing loneliness that was so much a part of her. Nightmares drifted toward her from the dark recesses of her mind, growing bolder with each word, grabbing, clutching at her with dark hands.

"I did not kill her, *m'sieur. Mam'zelle* was my own joy. It was the river that took her." Pain etched Greshna's voice. Brianna could hear it, though she was unable to see the woman's face.

"You claim to be a high priestess. You have great powers," Richard Calhoun raged.

"I claim nothing, *m'sieur*. I did all I could. It was not to be."

"You did nothing. She is dead."

"Your daughter lives. Have you not thought of her?"

"I can think of nothing but my wife, and she is dead. Leave my sight, woman!"

His voice sounded hollow, a deadly tread marking each word. "I will bury my wife . . . mourn her. Then I will return. I will send you to the grave to bear her company."

Brianna crouched behind the forgotten trunk that had remained in the hallway since her mother's recent return from New Orleans. She trembled in fear of her father's threat.

The door of the master suite slammed shut.

From her cubbyhole, Brianna jumped, then winced. Other voices rose to replace her father's.

"Run, Greshna."

"You must hide . . . the swamp."

"Hurry. Go now."

"Won't find you there."

Footsteps rumbled through the corridor, moving farther away until Brianna found herself surrounded by silence.

Peeping cautiously around the corner of the large trunk, she could see no one. Her heart pounding, young Brianna ran to her room, hiding behind her closed door.

"Run. Run." Brianna sat up in the bed, her eyes filled with terror."

"Shh." Gentle hands pushed her back, lowering her head tenderly on the pillows. "It's all right, my sweet siren." He smoothed her hair. "You don't have to run."

She gripped his hand, ignoring his reassurance. "Don't tell. He'll kill me."

"No one is going to lay a finger on you." His voice rose in angry denial.

Her head tilted to one side, her eyes glazed as she studied him. "Oh, yes. I heard him. He must never know." Her voice dwindled into a weak reedy whisper. "Will bury me with Maman."

"What?" He frowned, unable to understand. How had her mother gotten involved?

His hand pressed her forehead. So hot. So dry. Rising from the side of the bed, Ryan went for more water. For three days, the fever had raged.

"Massa Ryan?"

He turned toward the door. "What is it?" he asked in a hoarse whisper.

"I brung you some food."

"Take it away. I'm not hungry."

"You has got to eat, Massa, and you needs to sleep, too. You ain't stirred from this room since you done carried Miss Bri in here."

He stretched, grimacing in pain as his cramped muscles protested. Not answering, he walked toward the window. A light frost covered the ground. "Looks like winter has decided to pay a visit after all."

"Don't go changin' de subject, Massa Ryan." Sudie pursed her lips, her thick brows forming a deep V as she scowled at him. "Instead of lookin' out that window, you best be lookin' in that glass. You is plumb a mess to behold, and you ain't goin' to be doin' Miss Bri no good if you ups and takes sick yourself."

Obediently, he studied his reflection. Dark smudges

covered his face, the result of ignoring his personal toilette. Ryan raked his hand across the thick stubble. Shadows underscored his eyes, offering testimony to the sleepless hours spent by his wife's side.

There was no denying the truth. It haunted him from reddened eyes that brimmed with deep, remitting pain. "You win, Sudie."

He relieved her of the tray. "You stay with Brianna. I'll take this to my room."

"That's a good idea. I'll sponge Miss Bri and puts her on some fresh clothes." She wrinkled her broad nose in disdain. "While I is at it, I'll have Toby see to fillin' a tub for you. A bath won't hurt none."

Despite himself, a wry grin of amusement touched his mouth. "What's the matter? Don't you like my fragrance?" He still wore the riding clothes he had had on when he'd rescued Brianna.

"Can't say as I does. And when Miss Bri comes to her rightful self, I don't think she'll be none too pleased about it, either."

The mention of her name called back the sadness. He looked toward the bed. "If she comes back."

"Don't go talkin' like that. Miss Bri ain't give up yet. You can't give up, neither. She may be lookin' all small and dainty-like, but she's real strong. I knows she's going to be all right, and you has got to knows it, too."

"I hope to God you're right."

Sudie followed him to the door that connected the two suites, opening it for him. "I is. Now you go on and let old Sudie tends things here."

* * *

The food held no appeal to him, but he forced himself to eat. Each bite coursed down his throat in a knotted lump, lying heavily upon his stomach. He had to admit, though, that the effort somewhat revived his energy. Across the room, his bath waited, steam rising to evaporate in the chilled air.

The door that opened into Brianna's room beckoned more strongly. Moving quietly so as not to disturb her, Ryan eased it open.

Sudie hunkered over the bed, stroking hot flesh with loving care as she bathed her patient. She spoke in low, crooning tones. "Don't you worry, chile. Those evil men ain't never goin' to hurt my baby again. They has done paid for their sins."

Ryan's frown deepened. He had received no word that the culprits responsible for her injuries had been captured. He held his position, listening carefully as Sudie continued.

"Yes suh. They can't bother you none. That old swamp has done got them. Old Greshna done took care of everythin'. You just gets yourself well."

Greshna. The name seared itself into his mind. Only once had he seen the old woman, but his visit to Freedman Acres was well remembered.

How clearly he recalled riding out to confront her. Instinct told him she was involved with the inexplicable lapses of memory that visited his wife.

A formidable adversary, she had countered his questions with rhetoric that found him departing with nothing but more questions. She held the key. He knew it. Resolve firmed within his chest. No one would cheat him of what he possessed, and Brianna belonged to him as surely as he belonged to her.

Making no sound, Ryan closed the door. He didn't know whether the old sorceress was friend or foe. It didn't matter. "Prepare yourself, Greshna. We are not finished yet. There are answers to be had, and by damn, I will have them."

"Maman!" The word cracked, barely escaping her parched lips.

"Shh, my lovely sea siren. Shh." Ryan tucked the covers more tightly about her. Sweat beaded on the pale satin of her face. Strands of burnished mahogany clung damply to her skin. He brushed them away, tenderly applying a cool cloth to her forehead.

The restless movements seemed to still, and Ryan resumed his vigil as the deep rumbling tones of her father's voice, a faint Irish lilt touching the words, beckoned her backward in time.

Heat burrowed to the very depths of her bones and Brianna felt certain she was being delivered to the fiery pits of hell for her crime.

She knew the truth. She was there; she knew in her young heart her father would never forgive her. Why should he? She couldn't forgive herself.

Her eyes opened. A familiar face hovered at the edge of her vision. "I killed her."

"Sip this. You need nourishment."

Her throat constricted, causing coughing spasms that wracked her body. *Water.* She was sinking into a watery grave. "Noo," she moaned.

Had to get air. Hands grabbing her, pulling.

She began thrashing, twisting the bedcovers as Ryan tried to restrain her. "Brianna. Brianna."

"Nooo. Help me." Her head twisted from side to side. She had to get free. All tangled. Must be her petticoats. With all her might, she gave a kick, feeling her captor's hand slip away. She was free! She wouldn't die.

High priestess. Witch, her father had said. Greshna knew and she watched. Everywhere Brianna looked, she could see the woman's eyes watching. She would tell.

Brianna's heart beat a rapid tattoo within her breast. It was an unbearable pain. Greshna would tell Papa. His word was law. Hadn't she heard him say so?

"No. Please, Papa. I'll be good. I'll be anything you want me to be," she murmured. Perspiration glistened, sliding into the thick tangle of mahogany that fanned over her pillow. "Don't tell, Greshna. Don't tell Papa." A thin sheen covered her trembling body, soaking into the fabric of her bedclothes.

Her cries brought Sudie scurrying into the room. "Massa Ryan?"

He offered the anxious woman a weak smile. "Everything is fine. Her fever has broken."

"Praise de Lawd."

"She needs a fresh gown."

"I'll gets it."

Standing by the bed, Ryan brooded over Brianna's words. *I killed her.* He rejected the confession. It was time for the truth—time to vanquish the ghosts that kept them apart.

"You sent for me, *m'sieur?*"

Ryan looked up, pausing to study the aged figure that waited respectfully at the doorway. Despite her advanced years and the ravages of time on her body, Greshna still exuded a sense of unbowed pride.

He felt a brief twinge of regret, then pushed it aside. All that counted was helping Brianna. "I did." He waved one hand toward a nearby chair. "I have some questions to ask."

The old woman glided toward the chair, her movements denying any infirmity. In silence she sat, keeping her back ramrod straight.

"You know of the attack on the mistress of Lagniappe," he began. It was a statement, for one look convinced him that nothing happened on the plantation that the woman did not know.

She nodded, waiting for him to continue. There was not a hint of nervousness in her manner. She met his scrutiny without fear. She knew why he had summoned her. Of that, he was certain.

"How did Brianna's mother die?"

"She drowned, *m'sieur.*" There was no sign she found the abrupt change of conversation unusual.

He leaned forward, his determination growing. "That much I already know. I want you to give me the details of the drowning."

"How would I know such things?"

"You were there."

"And you are here, *m'sieur,* but that does not mean you know all that happens."

A tiny glimmer of a smile touched her withered lips. "You love *la petite fille* very much, *n'est-ce pas?*"

The question startled him. He had said nothing of love, yet she spoke as though she knew what was in his heart. And why did she call Brianna a little girl? he wondered.

"It is good, *m'sieur*. I have long waited for one such as you to come. Perhaps now she can be as a woman whole instead of clinging to useless burdens."

"Explain yourself, woman."

"Explanations are but words, *m'sieur*. They offer nothing. The truth can only be found in the heart and soul."

"Do not seek to evade my demands," he warned.

She leaned forward. Greshna lowered her voice to a guttural whisper. "You cannot demand, *m'sieur*. You must be patient. The answers will be known, each in their own time. That is the way of life."

"It was not life that attacked Brianna." Ryan pounded one fist on the desk in growing anger.

Greshna leaned back, shrugging her bony shoulders. "It is done. *Ma petite* will soon forget. It will not happen again."

"How comforting." Sarcasm hung heavy in his observation. "I have no assurances of that. There has been no word that the perpetrators have been caught." He laced his fingers together, meeting her look with a hard one of his own.

"They have not gone unpunished, *m'sieur*."

"How were they punished?" His hands went up, preventing an answer. "Never mind. Let me guess." He parroted her earlier words. "How would I know, *m'sieur?*"

A smile touched the thin lines of her face, softening the ravages of time. "You are a wise man."

"Hmmm. A wise man knows that he must continue learning or he will soon fall into the pit of ignorance."

She spoke with hesitation, choosing each word with infinite care. "There have been . . . rumors."

"Tell me what these rumors are."

"Those who attacked *ma petite* were not of Lagniappe. They saw her only as being white, a symbol of all they had come to hate."

"A sacrifice to feed their desire for revenge?"

The old woman nodded. "Perhaps."

"Continue."

"Her innocence was her protection. The gods would not allow vengeance to visit itself on those who have no guilt."

"And what of her attackers? Did these bloodthirsty animals find escape from their crimes by the benevolence of these same gods?"

"No, *m'sieur*. They fled in fear to follow the path of the wind."

In silence, he picked through each word, eager to solve the riddles of her nonanswers. "The wind . . . or . . . the drums?"

Neither confirmation nor denial was issued. She sat before him, proud, unyielding in her silence. He smothered the urge to beat the answers from her, instinct guiding him to more prudent methods.

"And can you tell me where these . . . winds led them?"

"Mais oui, m'sieur."

Yes! At last, an uncomplicated answer. It was more than he expected. "Where?"

"The rain fell in thick sheets of silver. It blinded them to their surroundings. The ground turned to mush before their feet. It was only natural they could not tell where the land ended and the swamp began. Everything appeared the same in the storm's darkness."

"Understandable."

"Yes. They will not harm again."

"I cannot help but think on the possibility that they

may one day emerge to wreak havoc on another unsuspecting traveler."

"Have no worry on the matter. The swamp does not lightly tolerate unwanted intrusion. Those who trespass find that their presence, once known, becomes a presence that cannot be revoked. The swamp embraces them, holding them tightly to her bosom."

"You returned." One brow arched in question. "Another rumor, I suppose."

Greshna rose, squaring her shoulders to indicate an end to the peculiar interview. "It is possible. There are always rumors. Some true . . . some not. It is up to each man . . . and woman . . . to separate them."

"I am not finished!" Ryan roared, no longer able to contain his rage.

"We shall talk again." Her voice held a calm certainty.

"We shall talk now."

She continued toward the door, calling back to him. "That cannot be, *m'sieur*. *Ma petite* has need of you. You must go to her."

Brianna. His ire vanished, replaced by an overwhelming fear. She was all that counted. With the agility of a big cat, he bolted past Greshna, racing for the stairs. He had to get to his wife. "Dear God," he said, "protect her from this madness."

Chapter 19

"I was so afraid."

Sudie patted her hand. "Everything's goin' to be fine now. De Lawd was sure lookin' after you. Massa Ryan got there in time to stop them from . . ." She hung her head, hiding her embarrassment.

"Defiling me. That's what you mean, isn't it, Aunt Sudie?" Shivers of fear set her to trembling as she recalled the vicious attack. It seemed impossible that such a thing could happen on Lagniappe.

"Don't matter what I mean, missy. All that counts is you is safe and your baby is safe. Once Massa Ryan knows you is back to your senses, then he will be safe."

"Safe?" New fears blossomed within her breast. Vaguely, she recalled seeing his face through a blur of pain. Had it been real? Was he there? Did he save her from horror, only to be injured himself? "From what?"

"Jest calms yourself. De massa ain't got no bodily hurts if that's what you is thinkin'."

"Then what is it?" Her hands curled into tight fists, fingernails digging into her flesh. "Does he know about the baby?"

"No, but he . . ."

"Brianna!" The door whipped open. Ryan stood at the entrance, a look of panic on his sun-darkened face.

"He's got a case of de worries, chile." Sudie leaned closer to her patient. "That man has near lost his mind these last days jest worryin' himself about you."

He stared across the room, his eyes devouring her as she sat propped up against the pillows. "You shouldn't be sitting up," he scolded, his face mirroring more relief than disapproval.

Taking his time, he walked slowly toward her as though fearful that any sudden movement might send her into a swoon. "You . . . you've been quite ill."

Brianna offered a weary smile. "So I've been told." *So near.* She wanted to reach out, take his hand, feel its rough texture.

Standing before her, he studied her face, committing every detail to memory. The wanting to hold her, to breathe the rosy scent of her, to feel the creamy softness of her flesh, nearly overpowered him.

"And now? How do you feel now?"

"Weak and terribly sore," she admitted.

Sudie moved away, allowing Ryan to take her place next to the bed.

She tried to make light of her ordeal with a smile but it came out as more of a tremor.

"You've been through a great deal but you're safe now." He knelt beside the bed, taking her hands in his. She made a tiny grimace of pain.

With infinite tenderness, he turned the palms of her hands upward. Small scabs dotted the surface, covering the deep abrasions she had sustained in the fray. He knew her knees would look much the same.

God, but she had been a bloody mess when he reached her. The sight of her had nearly driven him mad. He wanted to tear her attackers to pieces with his bare hands.

Exercising utmost care, he began a visual examination. Her left hand still showed signs of swelling. Angry streaks of red mingled with purple bruises up the length of her arm. "Does it hurt?"

"Only when I try to move it."

He carefully laid it in a flat position. "Then don't try. I'll get you anything you want. You don't have to do a thing, except lie here and get well." He favored her with a slanted smile. "You do have to get well."

"Mmmm. That sounds like something I can handle."

"Then it's settled. Now, what would you have to assist you in handling such an assignment, my sweet?"

Her eyes widened, thick lashes making sooty frames around the jade ovals. "Food."

He choked back a laugh. "Ah, Brianna. I had forgotten how truly delightful you can be."

Solemnly, she looked at him. "I must be easy to forget."

"Nay, my darling Brianna. You can never be forgotten. You shall live on into eternity." He looked deeply into her eyes, his own gaze dark and serious. "Your charms are so numerous, it is difficult to call them all into mind at once. I am but a mere mortal."

Her head lolled heavily against the pillows, her meager energy becoming depleted. "Then . . . when I'm . . . stronger, I shall . . . remind . . . you of your . . . oversights."

His hand touched her face in a tender caress. "And I shall look forward to that time, my sweet."

Turning to Sudie, a teasing smile found its way to his mouth. "You heard the lady, Aunt Sudie. She is hungry. Bring her a tray."

"I shore will, Massa Ryan. I'se on my way."

Shuffling past him, her ample backside provided a tempting target for the suddenly-playful Ryan. He swatted, his palm connecting with a resounding whack.

"Massa Ryan!" She turned about, glaring at him. "Don't you go takin' advantage of old Sudie's good nature. I might think you has done been li-a-batin' too much for your own good."

His head reared back. Laughter gurgled through the thick column of his throat and spilled free with a deep rumble. "And right you would be, madame. But not from anything as mundane as spirits. This day I drink from the fountain of life itself, and it flows in abundance. The taste is sweet and pure, a touch of heaven."

Sudie peeked past him, nodding at Brianna. "I done thinks we is too late, missy. 'Pears this man has done worried himself into a good case of de crazies. Humph!" Shaking her head, she continued on her errand. "Things about this place ain't been the same since he plopped himself down here."

Still weakened from the fever, Brianna could only offer a soft sigh in answer, but she lingered over the feeling of peace that surrounded her.

"You're tired. Close your eyes and try to get some rest," he commanded.

"Not . . . now. I've had days . . . of rest. I want . . . to stay . . ." Her words fluttered away into nothingness, her lashes falling lightly over her eyes.

He reached out, tracing the contours of her face with gentle fingers. How delicate she looked, yet he knew beneath the outer fragility waited a woman of incredible spirit and strength.

"Welcome home," he whispered. "My lovely unpredictable siren."

"You can't be doin' like this, missy." Sudie's voice rose in a roar of protest.

"I most certainly can. If I stay in this bed one more day, I'll become quite mad." She fumbled with her wrapper, trying to get her arms through the sleeves.

"Get yourself back in de bed before Massa Ryan done finds out."

"Finds out what?" Ryan opened the connecting door, casually entering the room.

"Oh, fiddle. Sudie says I should stay in bed. I'm tired of lying about, looking at nothing but these walls." Brianna stepped forward, waving one arm about the room as she vented her displeasure.

A smile teased his mouth as he caught sight of her. Never had he seen such a lovely vision of indignation.

Her hair hung loose, flowing in rich tangled profusion about her shoulders. The silken wrapper was cinched snugly about her waist.

He paused to admire the way it clung to the ripe swell of her breasts, hugging the soft curves of her hips before plunging down to swirl about her ankles.

"I want to go downstairs," she said with just a trace of pout in her voice.

"Then downstairs you shall go, my love." Without warning, he moved to her side and lifted her into his arms.

"Ryan!"

"What?"

"Put me down this instant! I'm not an invalid."

He shifted his hold, gathering her more securely in his grasp. "I know that." He grinned down at her. "Hmm. It seems as though you have done more than languish in bed, my sweet. There is one pastime in which you have been indulging that I didn't hear mentioned."

"What's that?" she asked as she draped her arms around his neck.

"Eating." He chuckled. "Unless I'm mistaken, you're putting on a little weight."

Brianna gave Sudie a worried look. "I . . . I . . ." she stuttered.

"Don't worry, my sweet. I don't object. In fact, I think it might even become you." He glanced into her eyes. "You have a certain glow of late that I find more intriguing."

She worried her lip with even teeth, sheltering her face with a bowed head. It had been nearly two weeks since her injury and she still had not found the courage to tell him. In truth, Brianna did not even know if she should or would speak of the pending event.

"Now you be careful, Massa Ryan," Sudie cautioned, hovering behind them like a brood hen. "I don't want you droppin' my baby down no stairs. She's done had enough hurts."

"I'm not going to drop her. Why don't you go have Cook prepare a small repast. We'll be in the main parlor. You can bring it to us when it's ready."

Once she had seen them safely on the landing, Sudie hurried out to the cookhouse, allowing the couple some time alone.

"Really, Ryan. I can walk."

"Don't deny me this small pleasure."

Brianna held back further objection. In her heart, she wasn't sure if his words were as innocent as they sounded. She wasn't sure of much of anything. In silence, she reviewed the past twelve days.

Each morning he had joined her for breakfast in her room, sharing his plans for the day. After giving Sudie detailed instructions for her care, he would leave.

She could hear him ride out, and Brianna would wait anxiously until she heard the hoofbeats that signaled his return.

Her days developed a routine of boredom. The lengthy naps grew shorter, coming with less frequency as she gradually regained her strength.

When sleep eluded her, she turned her attention to embroidery. Half a dozen painstakingly monogrammed handkerchiefs were tucked away for Ryan's Christmas.

She felt only half alive in his absence, enduring the hours until he joined her for dinner.

After a leisurely meal, they would talk, mostly polite nonpersonal talk, but she never tired of listening. On occasion, he would read to her. Oh, how she enjoyed the sound of his voice, their lively discussions of the more controversial books.

It was the later times that bothered her, keeping her quiet about the secret that threatened to reveal itself any day now. He would sit in a chair, sipping his drink, watching until she fell asleep.

Not once did he share her bed or even indicate that he wanted to claim his rights as a husband. *He doesn't love me.*

The admission cut deep into the heart of her. It warned

her to hold back. Too well, she knew the pain of loving, of not having anything left to show for it but pain.

No, she decided. She wouldn't tell. She would wait, watch, and when he decided to leave, she would still have Lagniappe and—her hand rested on the slight swell of her stomach—her baby.

"What do you think of it?"

Blinking, she stared around the room. "It's a . . . a Christmas tree."

"Aunt Sudie said you mentioned decorating before the . . ." He inhaled deeply, then continued. "She said you wanted to decorate for the season. I don't know much about the celebrations here. I hope it's all right."

Brianna admired the tall fir with its handmade ornaments. "It's beautiful."

Chains of holly berries looped about the tree in an array of color. Cookies baked in different designs dangled from bright swirls of ribbon. Gaily colored bows, rock candies, and dozens of tiny candles completed the decorations.

"Do you not celebrate Christmas in Ireland?"

Ryan settled down beside her, pulling her into his arms, her back resting against his chest as they watched the last candle being lit. Then they were alone. "We do, but in Tyrone we have a special ceremony where we drag in a huge Yule log. It is lit from an unburned portion of the previous year's log."

"Why?"

He gave a hearty laugh. "According to superstition, it's supposed to keep the house safe from fire and lightning."

"And does it?" she persisted.

"We've never suffered either calamity," he teased.

"Do you believe in . . . superstition . . . magic?"

Ryan thought back to the day he had found her. It had been his intent to locate the drums, to put an end to the fear that that pagan sound instilled. Greshna had been the most logical choice.

Glancing at Brianna, he shuddered to think what would have happened if he had not heeded the old woman's urgent warning. It had been Greshna who had urged him to set his mount to galloping along that lonely stretch of road. Superstition? Magic? Or had it been witchcraft? "I don't know," he answered. "Do you?"

A slight frown furrowed her forehead. Her rosy mouth puckered into a pout of concentration. "Sometimes," she began, "I think I remember things."

"What kind of things, my sweet?"

Brianna shook her head, her eyes getting a misty quality as though she were drifting away from him. "I don't know. Strange smells come to me. I see tiny lights, like hundreds of fireflies all winking at once."

"Go on."

"There's not much else to tell. There's singing but it isn't really a song. It's more like words recited in a sing-song tempo."

"More like a chant," he suggested.

"Maybe. I'm . . . not certain." She reached out to him, her hand seeking his touch. "Oh, Ryan, I don't want to talk about it. Tell me more about Christmas in Ireland."

"As you wish." He settled her into the crook of his arm, trying to recall the traditions of his youth but silently vowing to learn more about the dreamlike happenings his wife revealed.

"There were always platters of bannock cakes."

"I've never heard of them."

His laughter lightened the mood. "No doubt. Our cook was from Scotland. She's the one who introduced me to them when I was but a young lad." Shifting his position, he shaped his hands into a large circle. They look like large flat disks and are made of oats and taste incredibly sweet. She insisted we couldn't have a proper Christmas without them."

Brianna chuckled in amusement. "I doubt that she heard any objection from you."

"None."

"Then I shall speak to Cook. She's very ingenious. Maybe she can make some of these bannock cakes."

With one finger, he traced the curves of her lips. "You would do that for me?"

In her eagerness to learn more about him, the offer had been given without thought. She stared into the warmth of his eyes. *Yes, my love. I would do all you ask . . . and more.*

Tiny flames licked at each sensitive nerve, heating her flesh. She held back her declaration. "Tell me more of your home," Brianna said, turning the conversation back to him.

With a sigh, he acquiesced, unwilling to challenge this fragile link that seemed to emerge like an answer to his prayers. "Our castle was festooned with lots of greenery. I fancied that it looked more like a forest than like the drafty pile of stone it is."

"You live in a castle?" Brianna found it strange that even though she knew he was the Earl of Tyrone, she still knew nothing about him.

"Lived, my sweet siren. Now I live here."

"For how long?" The question was out before she could catch her tongue. "I didn't mean . . ."

"It's all right." The words felt thick on his tongue, breaking free in gruff clumps of sound. He had vowed to take his time but he wondered if time was perhaps his greatest enemy.

"Ry . . . Ryan?"

"Yes?"

"Why did you do all this? The tree, I mean."

"Sudie said it would make you happy."

She twisted around so she could see his face. "And what of you? What would make you happy, Ryan?"

He reached out, catching a lock of hair, twining its silk around his fingers as he studied her question. "You are a complicated lady who has a penchant for asking difficult questions. Do you know where your happiness lies?"

She felt her face warm. *I know. But my happiness might well be in another world.* Brianna turned away, unable to hold his gaze. "I . . . I see what you mean," she stammered. "I guess happiness is different for everyone."

"Hmmm. Some people never find happiness and there are those who shun it when it calls to them."

"They are fools," she snapped.

Laughter shook his chest. "Fools? How quick you are to condemn." He bent his head, nuzzling the nape of her neck.

Tingles of anticipation flitted across her flesh like nervous butterflies. She held her breath, fearful the least move would end his tentative foray.

One hand slid around her rib cage, moving up until it pressed against the swollen globe of her breast.

Her tongue darted out to moisten her lips. For the first time, Brianna was happy she was clad in only her nightdress and wrapper. She could feel his thumb flick across the aroused nipple. Her eyes closed. She savored the touch of his experienced hand, silently crying out for more.

"I hope this will keeps you two happy until dinner is served. Cook's having a hard time and I don't wants to ruffle her feathers by takin' myself back there again."

Sudie's outspoken wish broke the spell. Ryan's hand moved discreetly out of sight as she placed the tray before them.

"Nothing serious I hope."

"Naw suh. I guess not. 'Pears something done got in de henhouse and catched two of de best layin' hens we got. She says we is right poor in eggs."

"I'll look into it," he promised.

"I'll be telling her." Wiping her hands on her apron, Sudie left the room.

As much as she craved his touch, Brianna forced herself to move away from him, using the pretext of pouring the hot tea. "It may not be an animal," she said.

"May not." He accepted a cup.

"Has . . . has there been any more news of runaways since . . ." She couldn't bring herself to continue. The memories were still too raw.

"No, and the drums have stopped."

Brianna frowned, trying to remember the last time she had heard them. "I hadn't noticed."

"Not a sound has been heard for a week now. Everything has been very quiet. I met with several landowners at Belle Terre four days ago. They all reported things are running smoothly at their places."

"I didn't know you were at Belle Terre. You've been going there frequently."

"It seems the most logical place as it's centrally located. Willowgreen and Lagniappe to the south, Briarwood to the west, The Pillars on the east, Glenbrook and Bayou Bleu to the north."

"I see. I didn't know the Maxwells and the Fontaines were having problems too."

"They aren't."

"Then why are they involved with these meetings?"

"The unrest seems to be coming primarily from Fargus and Arlington lands. But as you know, when a few of their slaves broke free, the bordering properties got drawn in because our lands were used as an escape route. Fontaine, like ourselves, experienced having a few of his slaves sneaking off when the drums called."

"And Henry? Did his people leave too?"

Ryan gave a full-throated laugh. "No. For them to heed the drums, they would have had to cross the entire width of Lagniappe. Too risky."

"It sounds as though they think we are waiting to set dogs on them."

"No, nothing like that. As strange as it sounds, the fact that some of our own slaves have attended these clandestine meetings appears to be unknown among the slave populace."

"Surely they don't worry our people will stop them."

"Maybe, or maybe they figure if our own people aren't involved, there is nothing to risk. I don't know."

"It is strange."

"Yes, but enough of this talk. I have some good news for you."

She flashed a bright smile. "What is it?"

"Henry mentioned that Mara has been worried about you and is anxious to see for herself that you are properly recovering. I invited them to spend the weekend with us."

"Oh, Ryan. How wonderful." Impulsively, Brianna

threw her arms about his neck, hugging him tightly. "Thank you."

"I thought you might enjoy a change of routine."

"Oh, yes. Yes."

He leaned back, tilting her head to study her face. "Are you sure you are up to entertaining? If not, I'll send a messenger to The Pillars and beg off until a later date."

"Don't you dare." Her eyes widened and her lips parted. "Mara is my dearest friend."

"I don't want you to get overly tired."

"I won't. I promise." She gave an exasperated sigh. "If I feel the least bit fatigued, I'll excuse myself and go rest. Mara would be the first to understand. But I won't get tired. You'll see. I'll be feeling perfect."

No longer could he contain his amusement. "Very well then. The invitation stands. They should be arriving around three. We thought it best not to chance being on the road any later."

Recalling her own experience, Brianna was quick to agree. Mentally, she began making plans, barely shaping an idea before she tried it out on Ryan.

The time flew as they shared suggestions of activities to fill the weekend. Sudie's arrival to announce dinner surprised them both.

In high spirits, they adjourned to the dining hall where they continued their animated conversation.

Only when it came time to retire did the atmosphere change, the polite reserve rising to extinguish their new-found relationship.

Like polite strangers, he bestowed a chaste kiss on her forehead, then left her at her door and made his way to the adjoining quarters.

* * *

Sitting in his favorite chair, feet propped up on the small footstool, Ryan nursed one last drink. He stared at the waning embers of the fire, brooding over her words. One by one, the secrets of Lagniappe were slowly revealing themselves.

Restless, he rose, abandoning the comfort provided by the fire. He needed to sharpen his senses if he would solve this mystery. The latch clicked with a small sound, yielding to allow him to step out on the small balcony.

The night air greeted him with brisk fingers of cold. He embraced it, his mind growing more alert with each breath he took.

He no longer harbored doubts. Her description tonight left no question in his mind. Brianna was under some kind of spell. "But what? Why?"

Ryan leaned against the rail, searching the darkness in hopes of learning the answer. Governed by logic, he found it difficult to accept, but there could be no other explanation.

Even Ivy, with her pretense of knowing everything, had professed ignorance as to the circumstances surrounding the death of Brianna's mother. All she knew was that the woman had died.

He scowled into the inky blackness of the night. From the bits and pieces of information he had gleaned, Ryan surmised that there were two witnesses . . . and one of them could only face death in the throes of terror.

Twice he had confronted the voodoo woman. Twice he had failed to learn what he sought. The thought chafed, but he accepted the inevitable. She would not surrender the secrets she guarded. Force was not the answer. He held no illusions on that point.

The witch would go to her grave before she told anything. It left only one recourse. He had to get his answers from Brianna.

"I'm sorry," he whispered. Abandoning his solitary post, he retreated into his room.

To fight a battle, he needed a plan. Strategy would shape itself, then shatter as he contemplated the risks involved. "Damn!"

The same problem kept presenting itself, denying him any safe solution . . . Brianna.

Before he could win her heart, he had to break the spell that kept her from him. But at what cost?

He had seen the horror that filled her eyes when she saw the bayou before her. Water of Death, she had called it. Would his probing send her into a world of terror from which she would not return?

The thought brought a painful churning to his stomach. And what if her memory takes flight? he questioned. He had looked deeply into the clearness of her eyes, had witnessed the innocence of her words that day.

There had been no knowledge that fear had sent her bolting from that place as though the devil himself pursued her. No trace of her experience remained upon her countenance.

He buried his head in his hands and groaned. "I could lose her forever."

Curses spilled from his lips as he vented his anger in the quiet of his room. He regretted the words he had spoken that had set the *Peregrine* sailing for Ireland.

Why hadn't he demanded she return to Ireland with him? Carry her bodily aboard ship if he must?

"Too late now," he muttered.

There was only one course he could chart.

"After the Maxwells leave," he promised. "Surely there can be no harm in knowing a little happiness first."

A gnawing sensation filled his stomach, undermining his determination and filling his soul with disquiet.

A little happiness. Then what? *Are we destined to pay for it with a lifetime in hell?*

The harsh beat of his heart accelerated, matched by the staccato of distant drums.

Chapter 20

"I can't tell you how relieved I am." Mara stood back, studying her friend with undisguised pleasure. "When Henry gave me the news, I was stunned. For something like that to happen on Lagniappe is unbelievable."

"I know what you mean." Brianna concentrated on filling the teacups before her. "I've always considered this to be a place of absolute safety."

"Mmmm. From what I've been hearing, I can't help but wonder if there is such a thing as a safe place, absolute or otherwise."

"Gracious, I never thought of you as one to listen to rumors."

Mara glanced around to make certain they were still alone, then leaned forward as she lowered her voice. "Not rumors, Bri. There has been more trouble, and unless Henry is wrong, there will be a great deal more to come."

"What kind of trouble?"

"Just yesterday, the body of a traveling man was found. His throat had been cut."

Brianna touched her own slender throat lightly, hearing again the harsh demands of one of her attackers. *Kill her. Kill her.* "Where did this happen?"

"His body was found near Bayou Bleu. Henry thinks it was one of the slaves from Arlington's place."

"How awful. Elyese must be terrified."

"Fortunately, she is in New Orleans visiting her mother. Her husband was planning on joining her for Christmas, but now he's hesitant to leave their plantation."

"I shall send an invitation at once for him to join us tomorrow. To spend Christmas alone is unthinkable."

"Splendid idea." Mara clapped her hands. "The more the merrier, as they say."

"You sound like Ivy," she chided.

"Ah, the open house. Of course, you would have received an invitation, if for no other reason than to lure that handsome husband of yours to Belle Terre."

"She doesn't need anything as grand as an open house to lure my husband. I don't know how many times he has been to Belle Terre about this situation with the slaves. Just last evening, he told me of another meeting."

"I declare, Brianna. If I didn't know better, I would swear you are jealous of Ivy."

"Me? Jealous? That's nonsense." Her tongue felt as if it were going to tangle on each word, but she refused to admit it. The truth was plain to see. Ryan didn't love her. He was only doing what any man in his position would do.

"Of course it's nonsense. You're much prettier than Ivy, and anyone can see that Ryan is captivated by you."

"They can?" She didn't miss the feeling of irony that swept through her at hearing the word *captivated.*

She had oh-so-cleverly talked him into marriage,

promising a business arrangement. And he had oh-so-willingly agreed, ensnaring her into a trap that found her wedded to Ryan Fleming . . . Earl of Tyrone.

"Of course," Mara answered. "He loves you."

The urge to cry prevented any reply. *He doesn't love me. He loves the sea . . . his freedom.* She bit into her lower lip, desperate to stop the trembling.

"Brianna. What's wrong?"

"Nothing." She looked at her friend through a watery blur. "I don't know. It seems lately, I have the most peculiar urges to cry . . . for no reason," she hastened to add. "It must be the slave trouble, maybe the sound of the drums."

"Hmmm. I agree those drums are difficult on one's nerves." She tilted her head to one side, studying Brianna carefully. "Then again, it could be something entirely different."

Brianna wiped her eyes, barely listening.

"Are you *enceinte?*"

"Wha . . ." She stopped. Never in her life had she lied to Mara. She couldn't start now. "Oh, please don't say anything."

"You haven't told Ryan." The hushed statement fell like a heavy anvil on her heart.

"No."

"When are you planning to?"

Brianna shook her head, misery adding itself to an already-heavy burden. "I don't . . . know."

"Well, you better decide soon. This isn't the sort of thing you can keep secret for long. Ryan doesn't strike me as the kind of man who would want to find out the wrong way."

Ryan. She knew Mara was right. There was no guessing how he would react, she realized. He already had control of Lagniappe. If he learned of the baby, she would lose it, too. "Just don't say anything . . . to anyone."

"If . . . if that's what you want, you have my word."

"Thank you."

Silence permeated the room like a heavily scented candle. She knew Mara wanted to ask questions, but good breeding held her quiet. For once, Brianna was grateful for the customs she had so often scorned.

The sound of men talking in the foyer signaled Ryan's return. Brianna pasted a bright smile on her face, forcing a light laugh as she initiated polite conversation.

"It's good to see you ladies enjoying yourself." Henry's appearance brought a real smile of welcome to her face.

"And you, Henry? I hope you enjoyed your visit with Ryan."

At the mention of his name, Ryan stepped into view. "We decided we preferred admiring your lovely faces more than looking at each other."

"Well spoken," Henry said as he ambled across the parlor to plant a kiss on his wife's forehead.

Ryan moved more slowly, selecting a chair across from Brianna with scarcely a look of acknowledgment.

Pain curled itself about her heart, squeezing it tightly. How she missed the soft touches, the caresses that excited her blood. And the passion, she thought. Would she ever be able to forget that wild passion?

Around her, the conversation was lighthearted, each in turn enjoying a moment of amusement. Only Brianna remained quiet, lost in dark thoughts that grew more bleak with the passage of time.

"Do you feel up to the ride, Brianna?"

The sound of her name jarred her from her reverie. "Ride?"

"Yes," Henry said. "Since they are your closest neighbors, we thought it a good idea if we all ride to Belle Terre tomorrow for the open house."

"Brianna may not feel up to it, dear. It may be a bit too soon, considering her harrowing experience on that road."

Ryan watched his wife, noting the sudden paleness that touched her face. He had enough ghosts to banish if they were to have a marriage. The thought that this latest tragedy could well encourage her to become a prisoner in her own home could not be tolerated. "There is a difference this time. I'll be with her."

Her lashes fluttered upward, making lacy arcs against her skin. Pink lips parted, then closed without a sound.

"You do trust me to protect you, don't you?"

Protect? Brianna felt an inane urge to laugh. Protect . . . as in an investment, she thought with a twinge of bitterness. That's what she was . . . an investment. "Of course."

Ryan frowned. How softly she had spoken, as though the thought of his protection was admission of a personal defeat. The possibility pricked his pride. "Then it's settled. Tomorrow, the four of us shall call on the Arlingtons."

"What of *M'sieur* Fontaine?" Mara asked, drawing a curious glance from the men. "When I mentioned to Brianna that he is alone at Bayou Bleu, she suggested he join us here for Christmas."

"Excellent suggestion." Henry's gruff baritone filled

the room. "Another armed gentleman in our party can do no harm."

"I agree." Ryan rose and started from the room. "I'll write him a note and send it over by Eli." He looked back at his wife. "No doubt it will afford Brianna a greater sense of security."

Leaning against the door of her bedroom, Brianna closed her eyes and felt the tension as it gradually released its tenacious hold on her muscles.

The evening had been fraught with anxiety. Each time he looked at her, every word he spoke, gave her the oddest sensation of being skewered on the point of a rapier. "He knows what is in my heart, and he seeks to flaunt his power over me."

It only proved she was right. Anger swelled, a malignant infection that surged through her to distribute its poison. The sound of a nearby door opening caught her attention.

"What do you want?" she snapped, glaring at Ryan as he stood at the doorway connecting their quarters.

"A few honest answers."

"How interesting. You speak of honest, yet you have little use in applying such a trait to yourself." She turned her back on him, walking toward her bed.

Determined not to be dismissed, he followed, his hand stretching out to stop her flight. Firmly, he turned her back toward him. "I have never been dishonest with you."

"Really? And when did you plan on telling me you are the Earl of Tyrone?"

A dark scowl hovered over the granite-hard contours

of his face. "Try again, Brianna. That issue has been settled. You accepted my explanation."

"Did I?" Her chin held a defiant look. Her eyes challenged him to tell her what had been settled . . . accepted.

Inhaling with a sharp hiss of sound, he spoke. "I see. Perhaps we should discuss it."

"I don't want to discuss it. I'm tired of the subject."

"Then let's talk of something else," he suggested.

"Such as?"

"Such as . . . the death of your mother."

Fear welled in the jade depths of her eyes as she stared at him. "My . . . mother? Her . . . death has nothing . . . to do with us."

"I think it does. I have reason to believe it has everything to do with us."

Taking her hand in his, he guided her toward the chaise lounge. Stunned by the abrupt turn of events, she meekly followed.

"One morning when we went riding, we ended up at Bayou de Mort," Ryan said.

"You're mistaken. I never ride there."

Pressing his hands to her shoulders, he gently eased her onto the lounge, then sat beside her. "You did that morning."

"No."

Ignoring her protest, he continued. "You became . . . disoriented when you realized where we were."

"No." She pushed at his chest as if to separate herself from him.

"You became frightened, just like now."

"Why shouldn't I be afraid? Ever since you arrived, there has been nothing but trouble. Lagniappe was peaceful."

Except for the twitching of a muscle along his jawline, Ryan's face remained passive. "Tell me what happened, Brianna."

"I . . . I don't know. I was told she drowned. Leave me alone."

"She drowned. How? Did Greshna kill her?"

You killed my wife! She's dead! The accusation thundered through her mind. She covered her ears, trying to shut out the shrieking indictment. "No. No. Leave me alone!"

Gathering her into his arms, Ryan held her, saying nothing as she sobbed in despair. The violent spasms eased, dissolving into gulping sobs, then tiny whimpers.

At last she was still, exhausted. Lifting her, he carried her to the bed. Lying beside her, his arms kept her in a protective embrace. He kissed the tearstains that streaked her cheeks, nibbled lightly at the fullness of her lips.

"Ryan." A sigh? A plea? She did not know. He did not ask.

His hands answered for him, stroking every inch of her flesh. His mouth sought the most sensitive parts of her, teasing, tempting, and at last, conquering.

As he took, she gave, the violent storm within her building until her very soul quaked. Her own hands tangled in his thick locks, then broke free to explore the hard sculpture of his lean face.

Onward they moved, crossing the breadth of his muscled chest, diving downward to the flat planes of his stomach. She did not stop . . . could not.

His tormented groan reached her ears like the sound of thunder in a distant sky. His hands tightened about her waist.

She felt herself being lifted, carried upward by unseen forces until she found herself atop his hard body.

Strong hands cupped her face in a gentle embrace. A slow smile touched the sensual contours of his mouth. "Tonight, my sweet siren, you shall captain this ship. To what exotic lands shall you guide us?"

For a brief instant she remained still, poised like a proud vessel that momentarily found itself suspended above the water.

Her breath caught, then the riotous waves rose to greet her, setting a tempestuous course. The winds of passion whipped about her, bowing her head until her mouth found his.

The thick silk of her flowing mane shielded them as she accepted the challenge. With an instinct as old as time, her tongue plundered his mouth, stirring instant response.

Denying him satisfaction, she pulled back, arching her back to display twin globes of cream for his pleasure until work-hardened hands captured them. Her head tilted back to expose the slender column of her throat. She drank deeply of the crisp air through slightly parted lips . . . lips swollen with desire.

Fingernails lightly raked through the inviting bed of coarse curls, following their ever-narrowing trail until she reached her ultimate destination.

As one, they rode the towering waves, climbing nearer the pinnacle with each thrust until their bodies were slick, their souls sated.

The fierce storm waned until nothing remained but the haunting memory of its undisputed mastery over the meager resources of man . . . and woman.

"How sweet the song that has lured me to your shores," he whispered.

The poignancy of his words plucked at the threads of memory that bound her to him from that first day, that single night spent locked in each other's arms in the deserted cabin.

Saying nothing, she pressed her face to his chest, breathing deeply of him. Her eyes closed, she imagined the sharp scent of the sea clinging to his flesh, untamed by the rain.

Would it always be this way? Brianna asked herself. Her wayward heart could only protect itself with distance. One touch, one softly spoken word, and her world became his, to do with as he chose.

The sound of voices raised in reverence filtered toward her from the slave quarters. *Midnight.* "It's Christmas," she whispered.

"Please don't tell me we must get up and greet the people," he said, his plea quivering with restrained laughter.

"You sound as though you prefer your Irish ways of just leaving a lighted candle in the window," she teased.

He bestowed a kiss on her temple, pulling her closer. "Mmmm. It's less distracting."

Tilting her face toward him, she returned the kiss, lingering over the full curves of his carnal mouth. "Candles can be dangerous."

"So are sea sirens," he muttered with a low moan.

Her arms looped around his neck, slowly tightening. "If it will make you rest easier, our presence isn't required. This is their special time."

"Ah, I'm beginning to like your customs more and more, though I doubt they will offer any rest."

A steady heat built within her, rising gradually to her face. *Just this one Christmas,* she prayed, then gave herself once more into his tender keeping.

"Merry Christmas." Brianna grinned at her guests as she greeted them in the upper hallway.

Moments later, Ryan stepped forth to add his own salutations. "Glorious morning, isn't it?"

"If you call one o'clock morning," Mara teased.

Brianna ducked her head, leaving Ryan to explain his way out of the faux pas. She was determined nothing would dim her spirits this day.

Amid laughter and jovial banter, the two couples wended their way downstairs. Contrary to her usual behavior, Brianna hung back, not accompanying the others into the dining hall.

As they continued to chat, she slipped away, making a short detour before entering the parlor that smelled of Christmas with its giant tree. Clutching a gaily wrapped box, she hurried forward to tuck it among the other gifts that lay under the tree's boughs.

"You're not seeking an early peek, are you?"

The resonant voice brought a smile to her lips. "I am not." She lifted her skirts as she turned, then presented her haughtiest manner. "I, sir, am a lady, and ladies would never resort to such devious tactics."

"Ah, my sweet, but you're wrong. Ladies are the most devious creatures I know."

"Have you known many ladies, Ryan?"

The bluntness of her question caught him off guard. "I . . . er . . ." he stammered.

"I'm waiting."

"Er . . . so you are, and my sense of self-preservation tells me I should continue to let you wait." Taking her arm, he began leading her toward the dining hall.

"You aren't going to answer me, are you?"

Stopping, he framed the soft oval of her face with his hands. "Suffice it to say, I have only known one very seductive sea siren, and beside her, all others pale in comparison."

"I think the Irish have rather glib tongues."

He kissed her. "A rather handy device in saving our rather valuable lives." His quip was followed by another kiss, this one lingering to savor the velvet texture of her mouth.

"Ryan." She peeked around his arm, nervously glancing toward the end of the hallway.

"Is there something wrong with sharing a simple Christmas kiss with my wife?"

"It's not the kiss, it's . . ." Her hand raised to her lips, cutting off the rest of her sentence.

Eyes like the morning dove darkened. His mouth slanted upward in amusement. "Is it possible your agile mind is already thinking beyond the kiss . . . to more rewarding pleasures?"

A flush heated her face, increasing her discomfort. "Behave yourself, *M'sieur* Fleming." Hurrying around him, she quickened her pace, but to no avail.

He matched his step to hers, whispering quietly. "You haven't answered."

"And I won't."

"All right. Maybe later, you might be willing to show me."

"You are an absolute rogue!"

"And you are absolutely enchanting."

Her heart felt as if it were melting within her breast. If only the Maxwells didn't have to be considered. If only . . . "Blast it all!"

"What is it?" The look of worry that marred the smoothness of her face brought instant concern.

"The Arlingtons. We have to go to Belle Terre."

"We can stay here, if you'd rather."

"I'd rather, but that's impossible. When you wrote Jean Fontaine, you also sent our acceptances to Belle Terre. We are committed."

He winced. "I guess I'm just naturally a proper sort of person. Where are you going?" he asked when she walked away.

"To eat."

"Fascinating. Do you always solve your problems with food?" The laughter in his question goaded her onward.

"No, but in this instance, it's likely the best choice."

"My curiosity is aroused. How have you come to such a conclusion?"

"It is either attack a plate of food or . . . attack your ever-so-proper person."

Her answer sparked the laughter that had hovered so near the surface from the beginning of their little verbal duel. It exploded in gay abandonment, making them the picture of happiness as they joined the Maxwells.

Brianna watched shyly as gifts were opened. Henry proudly modeled the neck scarf she had spent most of the summer making. "It's beautiful, Brianna."

The silken sachets filled with dried violets brought a

gleeful shriek of joy from Mara. "You haven't forgotten my favorite scent."

Brianna responded in kind to their own thoughtful offerings, but felt a special surge of joy as she watched Ryan tuck one of the carefully embroidered handkerchiefs in his shirt cuff.

"I believe you have another gift under the tree, Ryan." Not waiting, Brianna bounded from her chair and retrieved it for him. She dropped to the floor at his feet, waited nervously for him to open the package.

"Two gifts, my sweet? I'm honored."

"Open it." She held her breath, hoping it would meet his approval.

"What are they?" Mara asked, peeking into the box with open curiosity.

Ryan's gaze turned to his wife, the warmth of his look conveying more than words. "Bannock cakes." Lifting one out, he bit into it, chewing slowly to savor the full taste.

"Is . . . is it all right?"

"I've never tasted anything quite so good."

He offered a sampling to their guests, briefly explaining the story of his lifelong affection for the treat.

"You'll have to have your cook pass along the recipe," Mara said. "They are delicious."

"Cook didn't make them."

Three pairs of eyes stared at Brianna with such incredulous expressions, she couldn't help but feel defensive. "She didn't."

He reached out, tucking his hand under her chin to tilt her head where he could better watch her. "You made these?"

"Yes."

"Don't tease Ryan," Mara chided. "You know you don't know any more about cooking than I do. You have never even liked the domesticity of tatting or any type of sewing. I can't imagine you being willing to attempt anything as difficult as cooking."

"I can." His voice was a low caress of sound.

She didn't care that Mara doubted her. It was unimportant. All that mattered was that Ryan believed, which he did. She could read it in his eyes, could see it in the soft curve of his mouth.

"I can think of no better gift. Such generosity deserves a fitting reward."

Her eyes widened.

He carefully sat the box aside, reaching into his coat pocket as he turned back to her. "Your present, my darling."

She stared at the wide box. "You didn't have to . . ."

"I know," he interrupted. "I wanted to. Open it."

"Oh, Ryan. It's lovely." Nestled inside the box was the most exquisite necklace she had ever seen. Two strands of solid diamonds made up the chain. Held together at intervals by intricately carved bands of jade, the piece was highlighted by a jade pendant suspended from filigreed silver.

Carved into the medallion was a ship. *We will sail our ship toward the open seas.* He had remembered. Hope flickered. "When? How?"

"I ordered it shortly after our marriage," he confided.

"And Ryan arranged for a courier to deliver it to The Pillars when we accepted his invitation to spend Christmas with you," Henry added.

Lifting the jewelry from her hands, Ryan carefully

placed it around her neck, managing the delicate clasp with aplomb.

Dimly, Brianna was aware that Mara and Henry were quietly making their way from the room. She knew that as their hostess, she should protest. She didn't.

"Do you approve?"

"How could I not? It's breathtaking." Her fingers brushed the cool stone that rested at the swell of her breasts.

"Not nearly as breathtaking as the wearer, though." He lifted her up from the floor, gathering her onto his lap.

"Merry Christmas, Ryan."

"Merry Christmas."

His fingers burrowed into her hair, scattering the pins and destroying her carefully arranged chignon.

Brianna said not a word of rebuke. She hungered for the taste of his lips, the feel of his hands upon her body.

Her emotions gleamed from her eyes, radiated in the pink glow of her cheeks, the subtle parting of her lips. He had no intention of disappointing her.

"We should return around dawn." Ryan gave brief final instructions to Toby and mounted his horse. With a nod to the driver, the carriage made its start, Brianna and Mara the sole occupants.

On the left rode Henry Maxwell and Jean Fontaine, with Ryan remaining on the right of the conveyance. Each man wore a pistol, and rifles were secured in their saddle boots.

Should trouble arise, they were well equipped to defend themselves. Brianna hoped such need would not be required. Her hand touched the necklace, offering a small measure of comfort.

"I do hope Henry and Ryan become the very best of friends," Mara said.

"I'm sure they will. I know Ryan speaks highly of your husband."

An unladylike snort met her opinion. "I'm not concerned with how Ryan views Henry."

"I don't think I understand."

"I'd be far more pleased if Henry would avail himself of some of Ryan's ideas on gifts for certain ladies."

In the dim light of the carriage, Brianna grinned. "Why, Mara, I am surprised. I never thought of you as the mercenary type. That's more Ivy's area of expertise."

"Oh fiddle! You know perfectly well what I mean. The chapeau Henry selected is . . . well . . . you know."

"It's distinctive," Brianna supplied.

Both women burst into giggles, thinking of the item. Tears sprang to Brianna's eyes, streaming down her cheeks. "I'm sorry. I shouldn't make fun."

"Nor I," Mara added. "Dear Henry tried. That's what counts."

"And the fact he was so easily persuaded that your gown this evening is not suitable for so elegant a headpiece should count, too."

More fits of laughter ensued as Brianna and Mara delighted in the difference in taste between men and women.

"It's good we can amuse ourselves now," Mara said. "I doubt that you will be quite so cheerful once we reach Belle Terre."

"Why would my mood change then?"

"Wait until Ivy sees what Ryan gave you. She will be ready to scratch your eyes out."

She placed the palm of her hand over the medallion as though to protect it. "Even Ivy has better breeding than to be too obvious."

"Does she?"

Brianna pondered the question, thinking of her last visit. Ivy had all but stated she wanted to bed Ryan. And what Ivy wanted, she usually got.

Tilting her head to one side, Brianna glanced out her window. Ryan rode nearby, sitting straight and proud in the saddle. She couldn't deny he cut an impressive figure. Just the kind of man Ivy would set her sights on.

Would Ryan be receptive to her wiles? Would he succumb to those charms Ivy Arlington applied so well? The worrisome thoughts nagged at her, chipping away at her newfound confidence.

If only her own relationship with him were not so precarious. If only Ryan were not so handsome or Ivy so alluring.

Chapter 21

On reaching the portion of road that had nearly proven fatal, the tree-shrouded terrain plunged the interior of the carriage into darkness.

Brianna felt the tension settling in her muscles. She tried to cover her nervousness with bright conversation. It didn't work.

Glancing out the window, she stared at the silhouette of the man who had sworn to protect her. For an instant, she yearned to have him by her side, holding her, shielding her from the unknown that lurked within her fertile imagination.

"We'll be in the open soon."

Mara's voice touched her. She gave no answer, her own voice having abandoned her. She tried to swallow, acutely aware of the pain within her parched throat. Lips, once moist, felt dry and stiff. Helpless to speak, she could only nod in appreciation.

Closing her eyes, Brianna realized for the first time that she didn't know how Ryan had come to be there at her moment of need, or why he had chosen to travel the road.

Could he have been on his way to Belle Terre? Ivy? she wondered. Her private musings added to her discomfort. "I should have begged off making this trip," she said, her voice cracking with the strain.

"It would have been better," her friend agreed. "In your condition, you must learn to refrain from vigorous activity."

Staring at Mara, she let the words sink into her pores. She hadn't considered any potential danger when she drove herself to Belle Terre. Only when it appeared too late did she realize her mistake. "Yes, I will."

"I don't mean to pry, but I hoped when Henry and I left you two alone, you would give Ryan the news. I assume you didn't. At least, he hasn't mentioned anything."

"It's . . . complicated."

"At a time like this, a woman needs the comfort of her husband. How can he provide it if he is kept ignorant?"

In the darkness, Brianna smiled. *Ryan? Ignorant?* It was a concept she had never considered.

"I do realize it is a delicate issue. Some men are said to become almost incoherent at the prospect of becoming a father. Ryan may be among them. I suppose you can best judge that matter." Mara studied her words then promptly discarded them. "I doubt that though. He seems capable."

"That he is," Brianna avowed. Capable of rendering me a quivering slave to the mastery of his touch, her mind added. A frown sought the softness of her mouth.

Had his demonstration of the previous night brought harm to the baby? she wondered with a trace of fear. Knowing nothing of the mysterious state of childbearing, it was a circumstance she must consider. I'll simply resist his advances, she silently promised.

A plaintive sigh escaped. How easy to say. How difficult to do.

"At last," Mara exclaimed. "The sun appears, a bit dull and lackluster, but it affords light."

Checking for herself, Brianna was relieved to see they were past the heavily wooded area, rolling along across terrain now uncluttered by the thick stands of trees. "A fog's rolling in."

She breathed deeply, inhaling the slight tang of brine that filled the air. Next to Lagniappe, she cherished the heavy scent of the sea. It gave her an exhilarating sense of freedom.

Thoughts of Ryan intruded. How could she blame him for balking against the restraints of a proper marriage? Impending fatherhood would only tighten the bonds, severing his ties with the alluring call of the sea.

She loved him. No longer could she make excuses or try to deny her true feelings. She alone knew the words to chain him forever to her side. It mattered not that he craved the land, showed no sign of restlessness.

It was but a temporary respite. He had spoken often, lovingly, of his fascination with the sea. He talked of sailing uncharted waters, unfettered, free to exalt in the majesty of its infinite grandeur. Even his choice of names, siren of the sea, told of his desires.

No, she resolved. She could not take this from him. She must be strong. If he would not choose to reclaim his freedom now, then she would take the necessary action. She would leave.

A temporary measure, she told herself. Once she left, he would soon weary of the lonely restraints of plantation life. He would renew his quest. Then she could return, pick up the threads of her life. A pang of sorrow struck deep into the core of her. *What life?*

Quietly, she shaped her plans. Plotting the course she must follow. It would require help, she realized. *Jeffrey.* He had promised to assist her in casting off the shackles of this marriage.

With a hurried look out the window, Brianna determined their position.

Soon, she told herself. Anytime now, they would reach their destination.

Soon. She would appeal to him for assistance. Jeffrey would not fail her.

Soon. The word resounded once more. Ryan would be but a beautiful memory; her life would once more belong only to the land, only to Lagniappe and to the child that slowly grew within her.

"Judging from the array of carriages, it appears no one has allowed the recent events to dissuade them from pleasure," Mara commented as their carriage rolled to a stop.

"I don't blame them. There is so little joy, one must take it when they can if they are to endure the trials life presents."

"My, but we are in a bleak mood. Try as I will, I cannot blame Ivy for your dour outlook."

Bowing her head, Brianna felt a trace of embarrassment. "I shall endeavor to improve," she promised, taking Ryan's hand to alight from the carriage.

His lips brushed her fingertips. "I fail to see the possibility that one can improve on perfection, my sweet."

She blushed in the face of his compliment but made no comment.

Together, they joined the rest of their company, entering the stately antebellum home which reverberated with sounds of partying.

Ivy Arlington greeted them, profuse in her welcome. Brianna was quick to notice how swiftly she attached herself to Ryan. Jealousy whispered and hinted obscenely to her imagination.

"You don't mind if I borrow Ryan for a few minutes, do you? I must introduce him to someone."

"Of course not. Where's Jeffrey?" she asked, her query earning a stern look from her husband.

"Oh, I don't know." Ivy waved her hand around the crowded room. "He's here somewhere, no doubt sulking in some corner or another."

Ivy turned her attention to Ryan, continuing her conversation as she guided him away, ignoring Brianna's presence. "He spends most of his hours thinking up new forms of retribution against the slaves for this insurrection, as he calls it."

"You better keep close watch, Bri. Else she might easily forget Ryan is on loan. I think your action is one of extreme generosity, if you don't mind my opinion."

Brianna cast a bemused smile at Mara. "If I minded, you would give it anyway." She patted the woman's hand, quickly excusing herself.

Alone, she slowly circulated around the room, keeping a watchful eye out for the man she sought. Smiling, she would stop on occasion to offer season's greetings to distant neighbors, then move on, increasing her search pattern.

From a distance, Ryan quietly observed his wife's

movements, his own brooding thoughts returning to the last occasion he had seen her with Arlington. The picture of Arlington embracing and kissing her rose with vivid clarity. It rankled, sparking a slow deadly anger deep within the core of him. He was not a man to be duped. He vowed to remain vigilant. Too many secrets prevailed to suit his taste.

Now, there was a new one to consider. *Why does she not say something?* Could her latest secret be one rightfully meant for Jeffrey Arlington? he wondered.

Ivy's vapid voice floated upward, demanding his attention. He presented a polite smile. Barely had his gaze been diverted than Brianna slipped out an exit, her steps taking her toward the library.

"My dear, to what do I owe the pleasure of your company, though I have no complaints?"

Jeffrey held up one hand in an offering of peace. In the other, he clutched a glass of the always-present bourbon.

"I need to speak to you."

"I am flattered." He rose, offering her a chair.

The steadiness of his gait came as somewhat of a surprise. Brianna had no doubt he was a long way from indulging his first drink of the day. "I'm in hope you may be able to help me."

He returned to his own comfortable chair, settling himself, a smug look upon his face. "Ah. Dare I hope there is trouble in paradise?" he asked.

Brianna lowered her head. Wanting to refute his pessimism, she found she couldn't. There was trouble . . . big trouble. She broached the subject cautiously. "There was a time you offered me the hospitality of Belle Terre."

"I did."

"Is . . . is your offer still open?"

He leaned forward, his eyes agleam with interest. "Are you asking for my protection?"

Protection. How eager men were to offer protection, she mused. Glancing at her host, Brianna gave a small smile. In her heart, she knew that Jeffrey's protection would be nonexistent if Ryan made his objection known. The prospect seemed remote, she decided. "I would like to pay an extended visit to Belle Terre . . . if it isn't too much bother."

"Your presence is never a bother. But what of Fleming?"

"He won't be joining me."

His laughter was harsh, brutally cold to her ears. "I didn't think he would. What does he think of your residing at Belle Terre?"

"We . . . we haven't discussed it."

"Are you going to discuss it?"

She shook her head. "No."

"I see. Then I am correct in assuming you are leaving him."

It sounded so final. Brianna lowered her head, unable to face the glow of satisfaction that filled his face. "Yes."

"Does he beat you?"

The question shocked, then angered her. She had never considered such a thought possible. "No! He's very kind."

"Then he is miserly, unwilling to keep you in the manner you deserve."

Her fingers sought the medallion, its cool, hard texture soothing her. "He is most generous."

Her response emboldened him. His laughter grated on her nerves.

"Kind . . . Generous . . . How interesting. He sounds like an absolute paragon of virtue. There can be only one other reason to bring you to my doors. He is . . ."

"Don't say it, Jeffrey." Her mouth hardened into a firm line of determination. She would not permit him to cast further aspersions against Ryan.

"My apologies." He inclined his head.

"Accepted."

"Forgive me, Brianna, but I am confused. From your description, I assume he is an . . . adequate husband. Why, then, would you leave him?"

Brianna held back an angry retort. She couldn't afford to alienate him. Jeffrey was her only hope. "Let's just say you were right. Ryan and I are not mutually suited. My marriage was a mistake."

"Did you make that discovery before or after you learned he is the Earl of Tyrone?"

"How did . . ."

His hands raised, barring her question. "Westman told me. It seems your husband finally got around to properly introducing himself."

"No doubt, he found the revelation amusing."

"Unexpected," he said. "The poor man is still chafing at the dressing-down Fleming gave him."

"I didn't know."

"That's not important. You do realize this complicates matters."

"In what way?"

"He is your husband. By law, that gives him legal control of all you own . . . including your person. By your own admission, he has not been unduly harsh with you.

Even more importantly . . ." he paused for emphasis, "as the Earl of Tyrone, that control has been sanctioned by your own father."

"I suppose."

"Don't suppose, my dear. Take my word on it. It is a fact of law."

"What are you getting at, Jeffrey?"

"If Fleming objects to your presence at Belle Terre, the law is on his side."

"He won't."

"You seem pretty certain."

"I am." Shame engulfed her. "He doesn't care for me. His interests lie elsewhere."

"Do you think he will sell the plantation?"

The idea hadn't occurred to her. She was forced to think on it. "No," she answered. "He cares little for money or the land. He won't sell."

"How can you be sure?"

"He owns a great deal of property in Ireland, more than the small acreage of Lagniappe. He even has a castle. Lagniappe is a substitute for his real love." *The sea.* The admission cut deep.

"I fear your confidence is greater than mine. I've had occasion to share his company several times of late. He seems vastly interested in Lagniappe."

"A temporary infatuation," she responded.

"And you? Were you a temporary infatuation, too?"

With razor sharpness, his words sliced through her. She bit the inside of her mouth, concentrating on the pain to blot out the greater pain that pricked her heart. "I don't . . . think I was ever . . . of any importance."

"Against my better judgment, I'll accept your opinion."

"Then you'll let me come to Belle Terre?"

"Of course. I have never been able to deny you anything, Brianna. You know that."

"Thank you." She knew he meant it. She also knew he had never offered anything she wanted. Ryan was her only desire, and it must be denied. "Mara and Henry will be leaving tomorrow. They are planning to travel to New Orleans for the season."

"Then I shall expect your arrival late tomorrow."

She thought of the dense wooded area. "No. I shall wait until the following morning. I don't wish to travel alone so late in the day."

"I understand. Would you prefer I come for you?"

"No. You're doing enough just offering me shelter."

"I would offer you much more than shelter, if you'd allow me."

"Please, Jeffrey. Not now."

"Of course."

Brianna heard the door behind her open, saw the guarded look that appeared on Jeffrey's face. Instinctively, she stiffened.

"Good evening, Fleming. What brings you to my humble surroundings?"

"I am seeking my wife. Someone told me they thought she came in here."

"So she did." Jeffrey smiled. "She had been telling me how kind . . . how generous you are."

"Then my arrival must be more timely than I imagined." He gave a curt bow. "I would hate to think Brianna might bore you by extolling my many qualities."

She grew chilled at the sound of steel threading his casual comment. There was no choice but to remain silent. She couldn't risk a scene now. Belle Terre was filled with guests. Mutely, she prayed that Ryan would keep his temper tightly leashed.

"I would never suggest Brianna could be boring."

"Nor I." Ryan stood beside her, his hand outstretched. "In truth, I find I sorely miss her presence. Brianna."

Not meeting his gaze, she placed her hand in his. Rising, she dropped a curtsy to Jeffrey. "I appreciate your hospitality, Jeffrey."

"My pleasure." His smile of acknowledgment was met with a deep scowl from Ryan.

"We shall not detain you, Arlington. I'm sure you are anxious to attend your other guests."

Turning sharply, Ryan led her from the room, not speaking until they were safely away. "Do you care nothing for your reputation?"

"My reputation? What are you saying?"

"Simply put, a married woman does not closet herself in a room alone with a man not her husband."

"Ridiculous. I've known Jeffrey my entire life."

His hand tightened about her arm in a constricting band. "Then know this. In the future, you will not be alone with Arlington or any other man without my express permission."

"Your permission!" She seethed with growing ire. "I don't need permission—yours or anyone else's—to speak with my friends."

"Jeffrey Arlington is not the friend you think him."

"I beg your pardon, m'lord. I wasn't aware you had become such an expert."

He guided her through the crowded room, propelling her out into the solitude of the gardens. "I know a lot more than you give me credit for, my sweet."

The night air chilled her flesh, but his oblique warning threatened to freeze the marrow of her bones. "I don't . . . know what you mean."

"Don't you? Forgive me if I question your protest." He let go of her arm, holding his hands rigidly at his sides, as though loath to touch her.

"Why do you dislike Jeffrey so? He's never harmed you."

"That remains to be seen. In the meantime, I continue to abide his presence, odious as it may be, as a matter of courtesy."

"You're being unfair."

His brows shot up, assuming a lofty perch above eyes that had grown cold. "I consider it unfair that his cruelty has resulted in the injury, even the death of others who had no choice in their fate. His vicious management of his slaves has brought them to the edge of revolt."

"You can't know that."

"I have seen the signs, heard the rumors that continue to grow. Stay away from him, Brianna. Continued association can only pose serious risks. I will not have you in danger."

"As you once told me, life is a risk. I will not be disloyal to friends simply because their choices are not popular, not always right. I will decide with whom I associate."

"Then you must be prepared to pay the penalty for your decisions, my sweet. For both our sakes, let us hope the price is not too high."

Turning on his heel, he marched away, leaving her to ponder the wisdom of what she was about to do.

"You're too late, Ryan. The price of love has already proven too high to bear. Goodbye." Tears of remorse

olled down cold cheeks, spilling unheeded as she stared
fter him.

"Are you sure you two won't join us in New Orleans?"
Mara tried one last time as she offered her cheek to Ryan.

"Perhaps later," he told her. "With the state of things,
don't feel this is a good time to leave Lagniappe."

It's the only time, Brianna thought as she waited by his
side to offer farewell.

The return trip to Lagniappe had been without incident, increasing her confidence that Ryan's warnings
were made in haste. Still, they lingered in the back of her
mind.

Even the recent silence of the drums failed to reassure
her. She hugged Mara, barely holding back the tears as
her friend whispered words of encouragement that she
speak with Ryan.

Mara couldn't know that it was too late. She hadn't
heard his harsh ultimatum, hadn't witnessed the stony
silence in which they endured the long hours so recently
passed.

Their return to Lagniappe had found him once again
making use of the quarters next to hers. For hours she
had lain awake, watching the door that separated their
rooms.

Oh, how she had yearned for him to open that door,
come to her, profess his love. Even as she held tight to the
dream, a part of her knew, reluctantly accepting the
truth. He wouldn't come. "Travel with care," she told
her friend.

"Don't worry," Henry said, taking Mara's place to
offer Brianna an affectionate squeeze. "After we cross the

ferry, we intend to bear as far south as possible. I've no
wish to become embroiled in the trouble at Fargus's
place, either."

He shook his head, directing his remarks to Ryan.
"Considering the militancy of people like Arlington and
Fargus, I think those dissidents to the North would do
well to save their energy. Given enough time, we are apt
to destroy ourselves."

"I agree, but few are willing to allow destiny its due.
They are intent on making what they will of everything
and cannot resist the temptation to take matters into
their own hands."

Laughing, Henry agreed, climbing into his carriage
with a final request that Ryan keep an eye on the destiny
of The Pillars until his return.

"That I will, my friend."

Brianna studied his observation, sadness overwhelming her. To wait for destiny could only prolong the agony
of watching the destruction of all she held dear. She had
no choice. She must handle her own affairs, even if the
course she had chosen was not one to her liking.

Raising her skirts, she headed into the house. There
was much to be done. If only the Maxwells had left as
planned, she fumed. Instead, they had chosen to wait
until this morning. Brianna recognized the wisdom of
their decision but found it most inconvenient.

Her own start had been considerably delayed. There
was no choice but to make the best of it. She couldn't risk
Jeffrey becoming concerned if she did not arrive. He
might well ride to Lagniappe. It was a problem she did
not need.

Brianna knew Ryan would soon ride out to make his
rounds of the plantation. Then he would scout the situa-

on at the Maxwells. His duties would keep him out until late. By then, she told herself, she would be safely ensconced behind the walls of Belle Terre.

Unlike the recent scene with Mara and Henry, there would be no farewells when she left Lagniappe . . . left Ryan. She would say nothing to anyone.

Both doors had been carefully bolted when she returned to her quarters, though she had no reason to assume there would be any intrusion.

Quilts and linens, once stored in the large trunk at the end of her bed, lay in neat piles atop her mattress. In the trunk, she had packed clothes for the weeks ahead.

Her hand pressed to her stomach. There was little she had seen reason to choose. Soon she would be unable to wear the many gowns she owned. Her needs would be few and simple in the months to come.

As her condition became more pronounced, her presence would be excused from any public functions that might arise. The thought gave her comfort.

Confined to the rooms of Belle Terre, there was little chance she would be placed into circumstances of being in Ryan's presence. "No doubt, my being at Belle Terre shall deprive Ivy of a certain amount of his presence, also," she murmured as she tucked a nightdress into her small carpetbag.

Only the most necessary items went into the small carrier. She did not wish to encounter any problems that might arise should her decision become prematurely known.

Brianna made a final check. Satisfied everything had been properly attended, she settled herself by the window to wait. Later, she would have Jeffrey send someone to

fetch her trunk. Mentally, she reviewed the scenario sh
had envisioned.

Ryan would make a gesture to get her to return. I
would be expected. Then he would console himself witl
the running of Lagniappe. In time, that too would hav
little interest for him. The sea would beckon and h
would follow.

The precise timetable seemed hazy but Brianna wa
convinced it could not last overly long. Ryan was not ;
man given to enduring monotony. Of that much she wa
certain.

She continued listing the passing of each event. Onc
he left, she would return, resuming her former life a
Lagniappe. In time, the child would be born.

Hugging her arms about her still-slender frame, sh
wondered at the future of the baby. Would it be a boy o
a girl? "Boy," she whispered, convinced that a child o
Ryan's could be no other. A wave of sadness washe(
over her.

Would he be a miniature of his father? she wondered
Closing her eyes, she tried to picture the babe she had ye
to meet. Yes.

She could see him. Hair of midnight would frame th
strong lines of his boyishly handsome face. Eyes o
quicksilver would solemnly meet her gaze, asking al
kinds of questions. "And how will I tell you of you
father, my precious?"

Pained by her thoughts, Brianna sought diversion, he
eyes searching the winter-browned landscape of her be
loved Lagniappe.

In the distance, she saw him, riding away from th
house. His back was straight as he proudly sat his saddle

Her heart twisted within her breast, wanting desperately to call him back.

With slow deliberation, she rose, making her way to the small writing desk. Reading her note one last time, she took it to his room.

Without a welcoming fire, his quarters seemed cold, deserted. She shook off the tiny voice that urged her to retreat. At his bed, she stopped, carefully placing the note upon his pillow.

Atop it, Brianna laid the jade necklace, her fingers lingering on the fragile outline of the carved ship. Blinking back unbidden tears, she hastily retraced her steps, closing the door softly behind her.

Getting a firm grip on the handle of her small bag, she slipped out of her room, hurrying down the back stairs.

Her heart pounded against her ribs, her breath coming in shallow gasps as she made her way toward the stable. There would be no turning back now. She paused once, shifting the weight of the bag that felt unreasonably heavy. The palms of her hands tingled.

The muscles in her arm ached from the strain, but she kept going, her eyes riveted on the quiet stable that seemed so close yet so far away.

"You can do it. You have to," she mumbled. "Don't give up now."

There was no time to waste. Her mind kept nudging her with reminders of that ominous stretch that waited between Lagniappe and Belle Terre.

"No. Don't think about it," she ordered, her voice trembling in spite of her resolve to be brave.

Ducking into the empty stable, her arrival was marked by the soft, monotonous thud of drums. "Damnation."

Struggling against the urge to throw her heavy burden

to the ground and race back to the security of the main house, Brianna kept moving forward.

Unable to enlist help, she knew she must forgo the convenience of a saddle. No saddle meant no stallion. She sought a smaller, more manageable horse, one she could mount bareback.

The tempo of the drums increased. "Why now?" She couldn't help but feel the sudden renewal was a bad omen.

A shiver of apprehension raced along her spine.

Chapter 22

Staring at the calling card, a smile of immense satisfaction touched the corners of Jeffrey Arlington's thin mouth. His mustache twitched. "Send *M'sieur* Fleming in."

Moments later, Ryan strode inside the ornate parlor to face him. His face remained implacable, hiding all signs of the feeling that churned within him.

"Ah, Fleming. To what do I owe the pleasure of this unannounced visit?"

"I believe you know why I'm here, and whether it is a pleasure or not remains to be seen."

"Touché." Jeffrey indicated a nearby chair. "Make yourself comfortable. Care for a drink?"

"No." Ryan accepted the offer of a seat, forcing himself to remain calm.

Settling himself comfortably, his host evaded the purpose of the call to touch on other subjects. "It's risky business taking to the roads at this hour. I hope you encountered no difficulties in reaching Belle Terre."

"None." He continued staring at his host, his gaze unwavering.

"Good. Perhaps these heathens have decided their little rebellion is not the proper route after all. It's about time they recognized our superiority."

"I doubt the stranger traveling through Bayou Bleu feels quite so superior."

Jeffrey stared into the amber liquid that half filled his glass. "Yes. Nasty business, but I've no doubt his murderer will be found. I've bounty hunters scouring the area."

"I find their presence to be more a danger than that of a few frightened slaves who only seek freedom."

"Interesting comment." He leaned forward, offering a gracious smile. "Do bounty hunters frighten you?"

"No, but then I'm not a lone female, traveling without protection."

Jeffrey stiffened visibly, his smile disappearing. "I offered to provide escort, just as I have offered the protection of my home."

"Then Brianna is here."

"She is."

"I will see her."

"I'm sorry, Fleming, but as you can surmise, Brianna was somewhat fatigued by the journey. She is resting now."

"She can rest later. I didn't ride all this way to converse with you. I want to see my wife."

"Ryan. What a lovely surprise."

At the sound of the feminine voice, both men rose, turning to greet the woman who joined them.

"Ivy." He bowed, extending every courtesy despite his desire to conclude his business.

"Or perhaps I should address you as m'lord." She smiled up at him, fluttering her lashes coyly.

"Ryan will do just fine."

Jeffrey cleared his throat, resuming control of the conversation. "With this nasty slave situation, I have been absent from Belle Terre a great deal of the time. Oliver only recently was able to contact me with the news of your true identity."

A bemused half-smile fleetingly touched Ryan's mouth but he provided no comment, leaving Ivy to fill the awkward silence.

"I really should have guessed. You have a . . . regal bearing about you." Her arm securely linked with his, Ivy traced the muscular length of his forearm with a teasing finger, then skillfully guided him toward the settee as she continued to make idle conversation.

"Of course it must have been distressful to dear Brianna."

"She managed to cope."

"Ah, then it was not your chicanery that brought her to Belle Terre?" Jeffrey waited patiently for a answer.

The question startled him. Ryan's dark brows dipped into a deep vee. *She hasn't told him of her secret either.* The thought puzzled, then sent his spirits soaring.

Of course. Brianna had often demonstrated a boldness and daring, but in many ways he had found her delightfully shy. Such a secret would only be shared with one person. For the first time since his arrival, his smile was genuine. "As I said earlier, my being an earl is of no importance." *But . . . what is?* Try as he could, the answer to Brianna's action continued to elude him.

"Ryan's right, brother. Even Brianna would not be so foolish as to allow such a minor thing as a title to unduly upset her."

She moved closer, her shoulder brushing his. Her hand

casually came to rest on his thigh. "Whatever did you do, dear boy?"

"I'm not certain," he answered. "That's why I'm here. I intend to find out." His hand covered hers, politely but firmly removing it from his person.

A low, seductive chuckle sounded within her throat. "And if you don't like what you hear, what then? Brianna has a way of being . . . difficult." Ignoring his hint, she repeated her previous effort to secure bodily contact.

"I'll manage."

"As Ivy said, Brianna can be difficult," Jeffrey intoned. "You may find it isn't quite that simple."

"Or worth the effort," Ivy added.

Ryan rose, standing firm in his decision. "I think it is. If you will tell me where I might find my wife, I'll not impose upon your hospitality."

Standing, Jeffrey's own face reflected equal determination. "I cannot permit it. Brianna is under my protection."

"Permit? You cannot deny me, Arlington. She is my wife. Send for her or I will search the premises."

"How dare you suggest . . ."

"Now, Jeffrey, let's not overreact." Ivy's mouth shaped itself into a pout. "Two grown men arguing over Brianna . . . why, it's not sensible."

"Damn the sensibility." He stepped forward, his nose flaring in anger. "I have pledged to protect Brianna, and I will honor that duty . . . at any cost."

Ryan studied his opponent through narrowed slits. "I would advise you to exercise caution in carrying out that duty."

"Gentlemen! That's enough."

Her cry demanded attention. Both men waited, allowing Ivy to hold sway over the dangerous conversation. "I see no reason to forbid Ryan a moment of conversation with his wife."

Her suggestion offered compromise, a way to salvage his pride and avoid violence. "What if he wants more than conversation?"

"You have my word as a gentleman, Arlington." His oath was quiet, causing his host to strain to catch his pledge. "I shall limit myself to speaking with her."

"You won't force her to leave Belle Terre?"

The blunt question caused him to cringe in disgust. Never had he forced any woman to concede to his wishes. But, God help him, Brianna was not just any woman. "I will not."

"There. You see, Jeffrey." Ivy's voice stroked, soothing her brother's mistrust. "Surely you can grant so small a request."

The obvious strain melted from his face, replaced by a certain hint of satisfaction. "Very well."

Ryan held his turbulent emotions in check. He found no pleasure in the thought of challenging Arlington. In truth, he recoiled from taking such overt advantage of anyone. All he wanted was to speak with Brianna, to hear from her own lips why she felt compelled to leave Lagniappe.

"Splendid. Now if you gentlemen will resume your seats, I shall send for her." Not waiting for their reply, she whirled away to summon a servant to deliver her message.

* * *

"Is there nothing you would add?" His question held a hollow ring, striking a death knell within her heart. Brianna stared at her hands, unable to meet his probing gaze.

"We've both known from the beginning that our . . . arrangement was . . . temporary."

"Have we?"

Long lashes flew upward, her eyes widening as she sought his face. Hope rose, then plummeted when she viewed the hard set of his expression.

His query had not been spawned by love, she decided. It was only his masculine pride that spoke, an ego that refused to accept that she would spurn his occasional attentions to her.

Bitterness, anger and unrelenting pain wormed its way into her answer. "We have, but then, I did not know that you were the Earl of Tyrone. I did not expect you to seek permanent control of what is rightfully mine . . . Lagniappe."

"Lagniappe!" He stopped, suddenly mindful that the privacy of his conversation was subject to interruption at any moment. No doubt the Arlingtons lurked in close proximity to the closed door of the study, he thought with no small amount of chagrin. Ryan continued, lowering his voice. "Do you really think it is Lagniappe I crave?"

In abject misery, she nodded. "What else could it be?"

After all they had shared, he found it difficult to accept that she did not know how much he loved her . . . did not love him in return. "Indeed." The word spat forth in harsh rejoinder. "What else would keep me prisoner in this backwater place where values are so twisted, men hunt down human beings . . . think no more of them than chattel."

Inwardly, she winced, certain now her instincts had been correct. Hadn't he just compared himself to a prisoner? Blinking back tears, Brianna struggled to retain her composure.

Pacing the room, he continued his brutal tirade, never once looking at the woman who silently bore the brunt of his own tormented rage. "Obviously, madame, we have both been subjecting ourselves to needless discomfort."

The urge to laugh mingled with the need to weep. Discomfort. He saw their relationship as one of discomfort, she mused, her mind answering with a morbid sort of humor.

"I see no reason to continue this pitiful charade of a marriage, do you?" He whirled toward her, his face dark with anger.

Beneath his punishing glare, she meekly agreed. "No."

"Then it is settled. I shall send a proper carriage for you in the morning. Be ready to return to Lagniappe."

"I am perfectly content to remain at Belle Terre. Jeffrey has assured me of my welcome." Each word was issued with stiff decorum.

"I don't give a damn what Arlington assures."

Her nerves twitched convulsively as though she had been struck.

Guilt hammered at his conscience. It had not been his intent to frighten her. His hands balled into hard fists. The strain was threatening to overpower what little control remained. "You should be in your own home at a time like this."

"What do you mean . . . a time like this?"

In frustration, he cursed his slip. *It is her place to speak of it, not mine.* The confusion that filled her upturned face could not be denied. He silently resolved not to force the issue. "There is too much trouble here. Your presence can only put you in danger."

"I am not afraid."

The slight squaring of her small shoulders, the stubborn tilt of her chin, both served to remind him of her bravery. Born of sadness, regret, a brief smile appeared. "I know."

"Then I can remain?" she asked with a trace of hesitance.

"No, you cannot, but you have no call to fear. Once you are returned to your rightful home, I will leave."

How could she quarrel? The heart within her breast continued to beat, but life as she dreamed it died as his words resounded with finality. *He is leaving.*

"Where will you go?"

"I shall book passage on the first ship for Ireland. Once there, I will resume my duties as the Earl of Tyrone."

"I suppose you have missed the . . . excitement of your life before . . . before fate cast you upon our shores."

Expelling a sharp laugh, he gave a crisp bow in her direction, his eyes mocking her words. *"Tedium* is more accurate a term, but then how can you be expected to understand the burdens of the aristocracy?"

Resentment gained a hold within a tiny crevice of her mind, climbing upward. Clenching her hands to her sides, she rose. "I understand more of burdens than you can know, *m'sieur."* Dipping into a brief curtsy, she started for the door. No longer could she remain in the same room with him.

"Be ready by eleven o'clock. A carriage will call for you then."

"As you wish. Are there any other instructions, *m'sieur?*"

"Only one, madame. You may inform your friend Arlington that there will be no divorce."

Twirling about, she faced him, her lips parted in shock. "But you said . . ."

"I said I am leaving, and I am."

"Then I'm afraid I don't understand."

"It's quite simple really. Although the marriage hasn't worked out, there is still the matter of your father."

"My father?" she repeated.

"Yes. He wished that the Earl of Tyrone retain control of your assets until you are twenty-five or suitably married." His lips formed a tight, controlled smile. "We both know your penchant for finding ways around the wishes you do not like."

"You despicable scoundrel!" She started toward him, each word bringing her closer as she vented her own rage. "You insufferable cad! How dare you!" Tiny fists raised to pummel his chest, but he proved the more agile.

He caught her wrists, deflecting her attack as he easily turned her arms, holding them in a relaxed grip behind her back. He moved closer, not speaking until her body was pressed to his. "I dare because it is my right."

"And what other rights do you dare to claim that have yet to be spoken?"

The fire in her eyes was matched by the high flush of color that stained her cheeks. But it was the shimmer of moist lips that drew his attention. His head bent low, seeking the invitation of those smooth, satin petals.

His touch rippled through her, banishing her thoughts

as the tides erased scrawled words from the ever-shifting sands. A whimper of sound tore through her throat. Instinct led her closer until the small but firm swell of her stomach buried itself against the unyielding muscle of his flesh.

So small a gesture, yet it struck him forcefully, reminding him of the completeness of her rejection. He loosened his grip on her wrist, stepping back until there was no physical contact between them. "There are no other claims I will make."

Sudden, complete abandonment. It was the only reaction she could experience. Bewildered, she looked at him, searching for denial. There was none.

"You may manage Lagniappe as you will, but until you attain the age of twenty-five, there will be no change that does not have my approval."

"I see." Drawing the remnants of her battered pride about her, she sought to return the pain he had inflicted. "And what if I should wish to marry?"

"You have a husband, madame."

"A husband, yes. But what if I would have . . . love?"

Love. It burned like a flame-white coal in the pit of his stomach, cruelly searing his soul. Reaching into the deepest part of himself, he grasped the remaining vestiges of his strength. "You once said you would have no love but Lagniappe."

He looked deeply into her eyes as though to mortally wound her soul. "You have your wish."

Her gasp was soft, barely audible to his ears but there was no denying the pale face lifted toward his own. Heartrending pain stared at him from unseeing eyes. Without a word, she turned, running for the door. "Brianna!"

The cold metal of the latch moved, the door squeaked as she flung it open. Lifting the hem of her skirts, she never slowed as she continued her flight toward the stairs.

She didn't care where she went. She only knew she must remove herself from his presence while she could.

"Brianna, come back!"

Stepping from the parlor, Ivy barely missed being knocked down as Brianna raced past her. Only a few paces behind came Ryan, his face twisted with unspoken agony.

"Whatever happened, Ryan?" Ivy stepped in front of him, briefly impeding his progress.

"Out of my way." Firmly, he moved her aside, concentrating on the flurry of skirts that was ascending the stairway.

"Not so fast, Fleming."

One hand on the newel post, Ryan stopped, turning to confront the man who dared to give him orders.

Jeffrey stood at the edge of the foyer, facing him with self-assurance. In his hand he held a lethal-looking pistol. It was aimed squarely at his chest.

There was no doubt in Ryan's mind that the gun was primed, ready for firing. There was no doubt that Jeffrey would enjoy performing the task. He raised a brow in disdain. "Is this your quaint way of issuing a challenge, Arlington?"

"Not exactly. You might say this is my way of telling you that you have overextended your welcome." He gestured toward the front door. "I think you better leave."

"Very well. As soon as I get my wife, I will."

"Brianna stays here."

"Like hell she will!"

Having the advantage of a weapon, Jeffrey exuded a rare confidence. "You see, Ivy, how easily the aristocracy forgets. There is only honor when it is convenient."

In his frustration, he had forgotten his pledge. It rankled to know that one woman could so affect him that nothing else mattered. But it was true . . . he knew it. Looking upward, he caught a final glimpse of her figure.

It would wait, he told himself. He concentrated on Jeffrey, his scorn for the weapon obvious in his casual stance. "I can assure you, Arlington, I never forget . . . anything."

The smug confidence of his reluctant host wavered, providing a small measure of recompense. "Nor I. Now, I would appreciate it if you will leave the property of Belle Terre and not return."

Ryan sauntered toward the door, giving no indication of feeling anything beyond bemused disregard for the warning. "I'll leave." Pausing at the door, he bowed toward Ivy, then fixed a steely gaze on her brother. "Remind Brianna that my carriage will arrive at eleven tomorrow. Don't try to prevent her departure or I will be forced to pay you a visit in spite of your request. Good evening."

In an instant he was gone, leaving both brother and sister to stare at the closed door.

"He has nerve," Jeffrey exploded.

Ivy smiled. "Most brave men do, dear brother."

"Did you find her, Massa Ryan?"

Filling his glass, he didn't bother to look up. "Yes."

"Then I best go on up to her room and help her gets herself settled."

"She isn't upstairs, Sudie."

"Where is she, then?"

"Belle Terre." The words tasted like acid on his tongue, burning their way into his heart. He gulped down his drink, then poured another.

"What is you talkin' about? She ain't got no business bein' at that place. It's evil."

Memories of her face, the pain starkly written across the delicate features, rose to haunt him. "It's my fault."

"Has you done gone and hurt my baby?"

"I guess you could say it was a mutual happening."

"Uh-huh. And what kind of happenin' is that?"

He sat behind the massive desk, unable to defend his own behavior. "That's the kind where you start out intending to say all the right things, but"—he sipped his drink, swirling the liquid in his mouth before swallowing—"somehow they come out all wrong."

"You mean you done mistook yore own words?"

A wry grin tugged at one corner of his mouth. "Mistook? Hell, Sudie, I knew exactly what I was doing. I just didn't seem to have enough sense to know when to shut my mouth."

"Don't let it fret you none. Miss Bri is a right smart lady. I s'pect she'll come around to forgivin' you. Men can't rightly help being men."

He raised one brow, his droll response indicative of his fluctuating mood. "Don't get sassy, woman. Miss Bri was not the soul of discretion, a model of demure ladylike demeanor."

"Uh-oh. She done let loose that temper, I s'pect."

The observation was greeted with a howl of laughter as he replenished his empty glass. "Let loose is a mild description. She came flying at me with both fists swinging."

Sudie's eyes grew wide. "And what did you do, Massa?"

His thoughts turned inward. God, but she had been beautiful, he remembered. "I kissed her."

Scratching her head, Sudie's round face twisted in confusion. "Now that don't sound so bad."

"It was perfect." The questions rose, pricking his mind in search for answers that would not come. One more secret added itself to the growing pile that stood sentry like giant boulders to keep them apart. "But then, nothing is really perfect, is it, Sudie?"

Nervously, she moved forward. "Why don't I has Cook make you some dinner. You left here without nothin' to eat."

"I'm not hungry."

"You hasn't had a morsel since de Maxwells done left."

"I said I'm not hungry." He repeated himself with more determination.

"Being stubborn ain't goin' to help none."

He lifted his glass in salutation. "Then maybe being drunk—very, very drunk—will help." A generous portion of bourbon found its way into his empty glass.

"It'll help you feel like de devil is chewin' on yore head come mornin'. That's all de help you is goin' to find in that bottle." She scrutinized the rapid depletion of bourbon.

With a show of defiance, Ryan downed the contents of his glass. "And a fitting companion the devil will be. Now go away and leave me to the misery of my thoughts."

"Yes suh. I shore enough will do that. You ain't goin' to be fit company for much more than de devil if you keep on swiggin' that stuff like you is."

He gave no answer, allowing her to exit without rebuke. It didn't matter, he told himself. Nothing mattered. He lifted his glass. "Here's to you, my unpredictable siren of the sea. You have conquered so completely, true to your name. For surely, I have met my own destruction."

With single-minded concentration, he applied himself to emptying the decanter. Yet even as the contents dwindled, the memories grew larger and larger, denying him any peace.

"Massa Ryan, Massa Ryan." The steady pounding on his door provoked him, stirring him from the lethargy that hung like a damp pall about him.

"Stop that wailing and come in."

"Massa Ryan." Sudie came close, eyeing him with a certain degree of suspicion. "You has a visitor."

"Send them away. I want no company but my own."

"Naw suh. This here is important. You has got to see her . . . now."

He squinted at her through bleary eyes. "Who is it?"

"It's Greshna."

"I have no wish to listen to her mumbo jumbo. Send her away."

"I can't. She done come all de way from Freedman Acres. She says it's urgent she speak with you."

"I don't give a damn about what she says. It can't be that important."

"It's about Miss Bri."

He gave her a glazed look. "Brianna?"

She bobbed her head up and down. "Yes suh. You has got to hear her out."

Mention of his wife had a somewhat sobering effect on him. "Send her in, but give her warning. I won't listen to any more of her riddles. One time for her to fail to give a straight answer and she's out of here."

"I'll tell her."

"And bring me some coffee."

"I shore will do that."

Sudie shuffled from the room. Before he could gather his thoughts, Greshna was seating herself before him.

"Sudie says you have something to tell me about Brianna."

"You must get her away from Belle Terre."

He laughed. "You too?" He waved aside her protest. "I have taken care of the matter. I'm sending a carriage for her tomorrow."

"That is too late. *Mam'zelle* must be far from Belle Terre when the sun rises."

"Why?"

"If she is there at sunrise, she will die there."

The languorous stupor that hovered over him disappeared. His blood felt like the water in a fresh spring, icy cold as it ran through his veins. "What are you saying?"

"When the overseer's assistant comes to unlock the quarters at dawn, it will begin."

"What will begin, woman?" The roar of his voice did not shake her calm.

"The revolt of the people of Belle Terre. They will rise up and slay their oppressors. They will burn the symbols of their slavery to the ground. All who are there will die."

"How do you know this?"

"The drums. Have you not heard them speak?"

Ryan held his tongue, listening intently. She spoke the truth. He cursed himself for his weakness. Had he not been so intent on drinking himself into oblivion, he would have noticed . . . but he hadn't noticed. "Surely you have no interest in saving the Arlingtons or their property?"

"Non, m'sieur. But *ma petite* is there. Her I will save."

Forcing himself to exercise restraint, he probed deeper. "This is not the first time you have saved her." It wasn't a question. Deep inside, he knew it; had known it all along.

"Non. When she was but a small child, I pulled her through a serious illness. That is how the old master came to give me my freedom."

"I have heard about the fever." Ryan leaned forward, every nerve tense, every sense alert. "I want to know about her memories. How did you save her mind . . . and from what?"

A slow smile spread across her mouth, dissolving years from her face. *"Ma petite* has chosen well. You are a wise man."

"The truth, Greshna. Simple . . . and complete."

"As you wish." She bowed her head in acquiescence, then quietly revealed the past for the first time.

She told of Brianna as a young girl, dancing upon the bales of cotton. Shadows of pain flickered across her face as she relived the accident. The details of Brianna's fall that landed her in the murky water, the frantic dash by her devoted mother in an effort to save her; both were told in brief but vivid detail.

"She couldn't swim, but Madame would not be

stopped. She lost her footing. I saw her head strike the edge of the barge . . . hard."

"Go on," he gently encouraged.

"It was then that *ma petite* broke to the surface, her small face twisted in terror. She screamed for her maman."

Ryan frowned, recalling how Brianna had screamed out that day at the bayou.

Shaking her head sadly, Greshna continued. "It was too late. Madame was already dead. Her lifeless body toppled into the water, landing on the child. I thought they were both dead."

"But they weren't. Brianna is alive."

"This is true. *Le Bon Dieu* was with her. Madame's body sank where it fell, but moments later, *ma petite* popped up, near the dock pilings. I grabbed her. She fought like a cornered animal, screaming and kicking. She hit her foot against the wooden piling when I lifted her onto the dock."

Sympathy pulled at him but he ignored it, determined to hear the entire story. "She has dreams . . . nightmares, if you will. They have been more frequent with the passage of time."

"Ah, that is good. It has been too long it has been hidden."

"How can it be good?" he demanded. "She claims she killed someone."

An intensity filled the old woman's face. "You must believe me. I did not know until I was called when the fever threatened to claim her. The old master blamed me for Madame's death. When he vowed to kill me, I ran away. Only later did I learn the child's thoughts. I tried, but it was too late. I could not repair the damage, only cover it up so no one would learn the truth."

"Tell me the truth."

"There is not time. *Ma petite* is in danger now. You must save her."

"Why? So she can continue to be haunted by the past? That is no way to live. I will save her, but I will see her free from the ghosts that keep happiness away. Now tell me the truth."

"She was delirious, rambling on, giving voice to the pictures that filled her head. She had heard that her maman died of a blow to the head, heard her papa blame me for the death. But her memory whispered of her own little foot hitting something solid."

"She thought she kicked her mother in the head, caused her death?"

"Oui."

"My God! Why didn't you tell her then?"

"I tried, *m'sieur*. Over and over I told her. She would not hear, would not believe. She was a young child, and children often view life far different than adults."

"I see, but why does she still believe this? She is no longer a child."

"True, but she does not know what she believes. When I could not reason with her, I feared she would die of the terror of her ordeal. I called upon Dambella."

"Voodoo?"

Silently, she acknowledged him. "Dambella is good. I lit many candles, offered many prayers. He heard and took pity. He buried her thoughts deep within her soul, so she could not know them. Once the thoughts were gone, her body could fight the illness. She regained her health and I gained my freedom."

"Then why does she suffer bouts of memory loss now? For what reason does she cry out a confession that is not hers to make?"

"You are the reason, *m'sieur.*"

"Impossible!"

"Non, m'sieur. It is possible. It is true. These memories are not gone, only buried within the soul of her."

"I still don't know what this has to do with me," he admitted.

"Ma petite loves you. She would give you her greatest gifts . . . her heart and soul . . . but inside her soul is tainted by this secret, and she would not give you such a burden."

"You mean she must free herself from this unearned guilt before she can admit she loves me?"

The old woman gave a husky chuckle. "She has long ago admitted her love. But loving means a lifetime of commitment, and one cannot commit to something when it is chained to the past. It must be free. She is searching for that freedom."

"Then she will have her freedom, because I cannot have life without her love. You must help me, Greshna."

"What would you have me do?"

"Together, we will go to Belle Terre. Before the sun rises, Brianna will be free."

"It will be very dangerous, *m'sieur.*"

Laughter erupted from his mouth, deep and vibrant. "Life is worth the risk."

"Then, for life, we will tempt the Fates," she agreed.

"You will go with me?"

"I will go."

Chapter 23

"Eli. Saddle a mare." Ryan started for the tack, preferring to manage his own gear in hopes of saving time.

"Non, m'sieur. The big black."

Turning, he stared at the woman, uncomprehending.

"Ma petite will need a horse she knows and trusts. If she is to escape, it will take power and speed."

With a nod, he changed his instructions. "Put a sidesaddle on the stallion."

"We must have a plan, *m'sieur.* When we reach Belle Terre, what will you do?"

"I intend to warn them of the impending danger and get Brianna out of harm's way."

"You cannot."

Tightening the cinch, he grimaced. "I can and will. What those poor devils do to Arlington's property is of no importance, but I will not stand by and let anyone risk injury."

"It is not for you to say."

His jaw set at a stubborn slant, he challenged the old woman. "The hell it isn't."

"This day will have its hour. To interfere may cost *ma petite* her life."

"Don't talk riddles! Damn it, woman, what would you have me do?"

Eli reappeared, leading the anxious stallion.

She took the reins in her gnarled hands, mounting the huge animal with the agility of one much younger. "I will explain as we ride. We must hurry. There is not much time."

Setting a brisk pace, they headed north, formulating a plan as they rode. Frustration mounting, Ryan roared, his protests carried away as the air whipped past. Greshna remained firm, refusing to relent before his wrath.

At last they reached the plantation. "Perhaps an hour, no more, remains." She spoke with a serenity that denied the tension, the promise of mayhem to come.

"I don't like it," he said.

"I know, but it must be as I say. You can speak nothing of the matter, give no warning."

"The only reason I'm willing to go along with this is that Arlington is just arrogant enough to disbelieve the truth. I haven't time to convince him otherwise. Brianna is in danger."

"It is better this way, *m'sieur*. If you force her to leave, then she will blame you . . . and herself . . . for what must happen this day. She must follow the future if she is to bury the past."

Gray eyes slowly perused her, unable to fault her thinking. Brianna and the future they would share could not be lost now. It would be too great a sacrifice.

"Do not worry," she promised. "I will see that *ma petite* reaches Lagniappe safely. Trust me."

"I do." A simple declaration, but the constriction eased in his chest, a calm descending that brought everything into focus.

Together they walked toward the doors that protected the inhabitants of Belle Terre from the outside world . . . for the moment.

Disgust filled Ryan as he surveyed the slovenly appearance of his reluctant host. Wavering before him on unsteady feet, Jeffrey peered at him through whiskey-blurred eyes, mumbling weak protests for the intrusion.

Still dressed, Jeffrey's badly wrinkled suit bore stains of drink that had failed to reach the intended target. "I object," he mumbled.

"Too bad." Ryan continued advancing, forcing Jeffrey to move backward toward the parlor and away from the door. Once achieving his goal, he maneuvered the besotted man into a favorable position.

With relief, he saw Greshna slip into the foyer and start toward the stairway. Then he concentrated on his opponent, trying not to think of the old woman or her mission.

"You have no honor, sir!"

With a desultory glance, Ryan quietly responded. "How odd you speak of honor. I am not the one who covets another man's wife. I am not the one who claims to protect a lady while destroying her reputation."

"How dare you!" Jeffrey bristled with indignity, the insult digging through his alcoholic stupor to lend a hint of sobriety. "I offer sanctuary, nothing more."

A grim smile found his mouth. "A truth I will attribute

to the lady's refusal rather than to any virtuous behavior on your part."

Slumped shoulders straightened, pulling the lax muscles into a bulwark of self-righteousness. "You go too far, Fleming. My seconds shall call on you this evening."

The last signs of a night of overindulgence disappeared. Jeffrey glared back at him, his face filled with hatred.

"There is no need of seconds." Ryan's agile mind quickly shaped a new plan. If he could induce Jeffrey to leave the house, Greshna would have no problem getting Brianna and Ivy away. Then there would be no one remaining when the slaves descended upon Belle Terre. Greshna is wrong, he mused. *Destiny can be changed.*

"What are you suggesting?"

"We can dispense with seconds, forget the gentleman's code that governs such grievances. We can handle this like men . . . just the two of us."

Jeffrey gave a curt bow of acceptance. "When?"

With a shrug of indifference, Ryan made his proposal. "Now. We are both available. We can settle it quickly."

"Very well. Do you prefer rapiers or pistols?"

Calculating the time involved, Ryan chose the most expedient. "Pistols."

Following Jeffrey as he made his way to the study, Ryan concentrated on selecting a site, one close enough to save time yet distant enough to remove his rival from danger. The small grove he had visited with Brianna came to mind.

Nestled at the edge of the northern boundary, it was reasonably safe. He recalled Greshna's confidence that no harm would befall the land or people of Lagniappe. Safe, he decided, and less than half a mile away.

Clutching the box that held the dueling pistols, Jeffrey returned. He presented them for inspection. "Shall we step outside?"

"There is a small secluded grove nearby. I see no reason to disturb the ladies by subjecting them to our quarrel."

"Of course. I shall ready my horse and meet you there."

"No, I'll wait." He chafed at the delay, but it couldn't be helped. By remaining, he could hopefully hurry him along. Ryan glanced out the window.

The black veil was slowly lifting. A dark gray mantle hung across the land, distorting everything, creating peculiar sinister shapes of objects he knew would appear only average in the light of day.

In the silence, he listened for any noise that would reassure him Greshna was urging Brianna to flight. *Hurry. Hurry.*

Intent on his own part of the scheme, Ryan followed his adversary out the front door. Time was fleeting. Fighting the desire to return, to drag Brianna bodily away if necessary, he concentrated on putting one foot in front of the other, each step taking him farther from her.

Crouched behind the stairway, Greshna watched the proceedings. With infinite patience, she waited, holding her breath as the solitary figure standing on the upper landing of the stairway descended to stand within a few feet of her hiding place.

"Crazy fool." Wistfully, Ivy stared at the backs of the two men. "Oh, Jeffrey," she whispered, "you don't stand a chance. He'll kill you." A sob caught, then escaped in a strangled sound.

Greshna eased from her refuge, her foot touching the bottom step without a sound. Upward she started, determined to reach the woman she sought. Beneath her soft tread, a board creaked.

"Stop. Who are you? What do you think you're doing in my home?"

"I come to free *ma petite*. Take her from this evil place while there is still time."

"The witch-woman!" Ivy glared at her, anger twisting her face. "You're the only evil here."

Greshna turned away, ignoring the shrill accusation. She had one duty. She could not . . . would not stop.

"Don't you dare walk away from me." Ivy ran forward, her youth giving her the advantage. Long slender fingers grabbed at the shapeless garment Greshna wore.

"Leave me be."

"Get out of here." Ivy tugged more forcefully, succeeding in pulling the frail woman off balance. Greshna fell backward, her body twisting as she tumbled down the stairway to sprawl at the bottom landing. Blood, thick and dark, trickled from a nasty gash across one eye. "Evil! Evil!" Ivy taunted as her voice rose in hysteria.

Satisfied the old crone posed no further threat, she hurried up the stairs, eager to reach Brianna, who remained at the far end of the house, unaware of the drama unfolding.

Not bothering to knock, she threw open the door, shrieking at the top of her voice. "Get up! It's your fault. You have to stop it!"

Bolting upright in the bed, Brianna blinked in confusion. "Ivy, what . . ."

"Ryan challenged Jeffrey to a duel."

"Ryan." She shook her head in an attempt to clear the sluggish remains of sleep. "No. You're mistaken. He's sending a carriage. I am going back to Lagniappe."

"Apparently, you didn't make yourself clear to him. I tell you he has been here this very morning. They are on their way to God knows where." She threw herself at Brianna, clutching the sleeves of her nightdress. "You have to stop them. Ryan will kill him."

Weeping openly, Ivy continued. "He's not much of a man, but he is my brother. He's all I've got."

In sympathy, Brianna patted her trembling shoulder, still confused by the news. "Please. Ryan won't hurt him."

"Hurt?" Maniacal laughter punctuated the offered solace. "He's going to kill him if you don't stop them."

"Do you know where they are going?"

Ivy strained to remember the conversation, blurting out the briefly mentioned location in a relieved torrent of words.

"Get dressed, Ivy. It's not that far. We have to hurry."

Wasting no time with more questions, Brianna scrambled from the bed. With an economy of motion, she scorned the time-consuming rituals of proper dress.

Without the needed petticoats, her hemline dragged along the floor, slowing progress as yards of material twisted about her ankles. The chilled air wafted across bare breasts that were only slightly concealed by her half-hooked blouse.

Impatient to be on her way, Brianna had abandoned the search for footwear and hurried down the stairs on bare feet. A long, thick auburn braid bounced heavily across one small shoulder.

"Ryan." She cried out his name as she reached the bottom landing, her heart pounding harshly within her breast.

"Ma petite."

Hearing the familiar voice, she whirled around to find Greshna on her knees, clutching the side of the banister.

A blood-streaked face met her horrified gaze. *"Mon Dieu.* Dear God, what has happened?" she cried as she ran to the injured woman.

Using her skirt, she tried to blot away the blood. *"Non.* Do not worry over me." Greshna grabbed her upraised hand. "You must go. Your horse is tied in the copse of trees by the side of the house."

"You are hurt."

Ignoring her protest, the old woman continued in a steady voice. "No time. Go to him. I have promised."

In her heart there was no doubt as to the man of whom Greshna spoke. "Ryan."

"Hurry, *ma petite.* Do not look back. Do not stop until you are with him. Ride swiftly. It is your destiny."

"But what of you?"

A smile of indescribable sadness crossed the woman's lips. "I have my own destiny, *ma petite.* Do not concern yourself. Just go. Now!"

The urgency of her command sent Brianna racing for the door. There was no time to question; obedience was instantaneous as she hurried toward her waiting stallion.

Fear provided strength, allowing her to mount without the aid of a groom. Love gave an all-consuming purpose to each action as she spurred her horse into motion.

She rode toward the tranquil grove, the pounding of hooves drumming steadily against a backdrop of voices risen as one to proclaim victory.

Tears mingled with perspiration, streaking the dusty film that powdered her face. Ahead, she could make out the moss-laden oaks that sheltered the grassy area.

Deep pinks blushed the sky, pushing back the darkness. Yellow fingers of light wound themselves through the pastels, creating a bolder canvas that hinted of bloody wounds gouging deep into the pastoral setting. "Please be all right," Brianna pleaded as she rode into the clearing.

Sitting atop the winded stallion, she surveyed the scene. Empty space greeted her. Nothing appeared disturbed at first glance. She looked again, uncertain as to what she had expected to find. There was nothing, neither man nor beast, to testify to the claims Ivy had made.

But Greshna knew them to be true, she reminded herself. It was then she saw it. A tiny scrap of white lay alongside a large exposed tree root. "Easy, boy."

Patting the animal's neck, she dismounted, moving forward to investigate. Crouching to the ground, she retrieved the discarded material and examined it.

RF . . . The carefully embroidered initials met her gaze. "No. Not Ryan." Fresh blood soaked a large portion of the linen square.

"Why do you weep, *ma petite?*"

Startled to find she was not alone, Brianna looked up to see Greshna leaning against the tree. "I didn't hear . . . where did you come from?"

"It does not matter. I am here."

"Yes." Brianna stared back at the handkerchief, mesmerized by the sight of the blood. White . . . so pale, she mused. By contrast, the blood appeared so vivid. *His blood?* Her fingers drew near, absorbing the warmth, the damp stickiness that transferred itself to her flesh. "I have . . . blood on my hands."

Greshna stooped down, her withered hand squeezing her arm. "There is no blood on your hands. You have always been innocent, except in your own mind."

As though speaking to a small child, the old woman repeated the same words spoken so long ago, not stopping until the last word was said.

"I . . . was there? When Maman died?"

"Oui. Yes, *ma petite.* But she did not die by your action. You were innocent then." She gestured at the soiled handkerchief. "You are innocent now."

"Is Ryan . . . dead too?"

"Non. Return to Lagniappe. You will find him there."

Rising, Brianna ran toward her horse, allowing Greshna to offer support in mounting. She held out her hand. "Come. You will ride with me."

The old woman stepped back, shaking her head. "I will stay here. You have heard my words. Believe them."

"I do."

"Then it is good. There must be no secrets. Go to him, and never keep what is in your heart hidden. Seek your happiness in the sunlight, *ma petite.* Seek your happiness in the gifts of Lagniappe."

Nodding, Brianna gave her horse the signal to start. He is alive, her heart sang. Alive and waiting . . . at Lagniappe.

Though tears of sorrow welled within her eyes, she knew every inch of her plantation. On she rode, glancing neither left nor right as she raced across the fallow land.

Behind her, the tortured memories of the past had been lain to rest. To the north, the sky filled with soot as Belle Terre crumbled, consumed by fire. The southern boundary exuded a serenity that stretched lazily toward the wild, exotic temptations of the unpredictable Gulf.

None of these directions held her attention. She kept her eyes focused toward the east. To the east, the sun rose, shimmering in pale splendor like a magnificent jewel. To the east, Ryan waited. Together they would experience all the glory of Lagniappe. "I'm coming," she cried. "I'm coming."

"Please, Massa Ryan. You has got to calm yourself."

Like a caged animal, he paced the length of her room, his eyes dark, wild with unspoken fear. "Where is she?"

"I don't know, but she will be here. She's my baby. I'd know if she was dead." Sudie scowled at him. "You'd know too."

Stopping abruptly, he whirled on her, his every nerve stretched to the breaking point. "Then why isn't she here?"

He sank down onto the bed, running his fingers through his hair. Closing his eyes, he repeated the young slave girl's words. "She said Ivy killed the witch-woman, beat her with a candlestick until she bashed her head in. Is it possible there are others who are called witch-women?"

"Naw suh. Leastways not hereabout. Greshna came many years ago. It was said she was a high priestess."

"What else do you know about her?"

Sudie's dark eyes grew larger. "That's enough. Voodoo is powerful medicine. Ain't nobody would say they could match her power. If that gal said de witch-woman is dead, then she sure enough meant Greshna."

He buried his head in his hands. "Then what happened

to Brianna? The girl didn't see her. Claimed Brianna died in the fire."

Sudie gave a disgusted snort. "You done told me that gal was in a daze. You know she weren't thinkin' straight, else why would she have told a white man she stabbed Miss Arlington with a knife?"

"I suppose you're right."

"Now, where is you goin'?"

"Out to look for Brianna. If she didn't die in the fire, then she's roaming around by herself. I've got to find her."

"You has got to get some rest. You looks plumb pitiful."

Ryan didn't bother to refute her words. How else could she expect him to look? he wondered. Riding for over an hour to embroil himself in a duel that dissolved into a series of comedic errors hadn't been enough.

The overseer's arrival had sent him racing back to Belle Terre. His hand reached across to cover the ragged slash on his arm. He felt like a fool. Like an avenging angel he had ridden down on the crazed mob in search of the woman he loved. No odds . . . no risks were too great. Only luck kept him from death . . . luck and the drums that seemed to call the slaves to another place.

He hadn't even noticed them until he found himself alone with no one but a demented slave girl . . . and the burning timbers of Belle Terre.

"I must have been more than a little crazy myself," he muttered. "What else would have possessed me to ride among the frenzied slaves, armed with nothing but a dueling pistol . . . with one bullet?" The bittersweet thoughts continued to taunt him. Leaving Brianna wasn't an option. He knew that now. Without her, life had no meaning. "Oh, my sweet siren of the sea, I would gladly come to you if I but knew where you are."

Concerned by his strange mutterings, Sudie slipped quietly from the room in search of help.

Hurrying down the stairs, the worried woman gave a yelp when the front door unexpectedly swung open.

"Aunt Sudie." Brianna gasped out the words, stumbling toward her with outstretched arms.

"Lawdy, I knew you would be all right. I knew it." They collapsed into each other's arms, weeping quietly.

"I've got to find Ryan."

"That's de same thing he's been sayin'. I reckon now you can both rest easy. You is safe."

A relieved smile erased the tight lines around her mouth. She took a steadying breath. "Then he is safe?"

Sudie nodded with enthusiasm. "He is that."

"Where is he?"

A chubby black finger pointed toward the closed door of Brianna's room. "Up there. But you best be careful. With everything' what's happened, I ain't so sure he is in his right mind."

"I don't understand."

"He thinks you is dead." Sudie flashed a broad smile, showing gleaming teeth of ivory. "I done told him that was wrong."

Brianna stared at the closed door, gathering her courage. "A lot of other things have been wrong, too."

"What is you goin' to do, missy?"

"If I'm really lucky, I'm going to make them right again." Not waiting for an answer, she hurried to make good on her promise, easing silently into the room.

Ryan lay quietly on the bed, his hands covering his

face. Oh, how she ached to look on those strong features, Brianna thought as new yearnings crept through her.

Only briefly did she hesitate, then moved toward him as her heart thumped loudly within her breast.

"Ryan," she softly whispered when she stood before him.

His arm moved, revealing his face. A suspicious moisture glimmered in his eyes, but she said nothing, content to look upon him. Then she noticed the torn sleeve, the bandage that peeped through the ragged material. "You've been wounded." She sat beside him.

"It's nothing." Hard hands framed her face. "And you . . . are you all right?"

"I am now. Oh, Ryan, I have so much to tell you. I've been so afraid until now. I never knew exactly why." One word tumbled over another as she poured out her heart, revealing her terror when she had found the handkerchief. "I . . . I thought you were dead."

Gathering her into his arms, he sought to comfort her, his voice a low crooning sound. "No, it wasn't my blood."

"Jeffrey?" she asked.

He nodded.

"Did . . . did you kill him?"

"No, my sweet. I never intended him harm. I only wanted to get him away from Belle Terre so Greshna could get you out of there before the uprising. We were going through the motions of a duel when his overseer rode up screaming that the slaves had gone amok. They had killed his helper and torched the house."

"If you didn't . . ." She paused, frowning over the news. "How did he . . ."

A low rumble of laughter interrupted her. "Arlington

is somewhat of a nervous fellow, I guess. When his man rode up, he whipped about and his pistol accidentally went off." He shrugged. "He shot himself in the foot."

"Then what happened?"

"After seeing that the damage was minor, I told the overseer to take care of Arlington and rode for Belle Terre."

Her puzzled frown deepened. "But . . . then how did he die?"

Mystified, Ryan patiently explained. "He isn't dead, my sweet. No doubt he is safely at a neighbor's home telling of his ordeal."

Shaking her head in denial, Brianna quickly protested. "No. I am positive he is dead. So is his overseer."

"Why do you think this?"

"Greshna told me."

He stiffened, his eyes searching her face with renewed intensity. "When? Where?"

"In the small grove where you had gone. I . . . I followed you, but when I arrived you were gone. There was nothing there but this." She showed him the stained square.

Pulling her close, he wrapped his arms around her. "I went to Belle Terre in search of you." Gently, he began moving in a slow rocking motion. "There was a slave girl walking around, dazed. She said both Ivy and Greshna were in the house . . . dead."

"That isn't possible. I saw . . ."

"So did she, my sweet. Ivy had crushed Greshna's skull with a heavy candlestick. The girl stabbed Ivy to death, then the crowd torched the house. She is dead . . . her body burned."

"It isn't true." She wriggled free from his grasp, insistent upon being heard. "She was in the grove. She explained everything about Maman, told me why I couldn't remember."

He shook his head in denial, his action further distressing her.

Sitting up in the bed, she repeated her claim. "I know. I was there. I could feel her hand when she held my arm . . . here." She stuck out her arm, looking at the spot as she moved. A gasp punctuated her words.

His gaze followed her own, holding still as he studied the thin fabric of the white lawn shirtwaist. A smutlike stain crossed the width of her sleeve.

Slowly, he turned her arm until her hand faced him, palm up. On the underside of the sleeve the stain broke off into four long thin lines, with one shorter line set in the opposite direction.

"It looks like four fingers and a thumb," he said.

"Yes. Greshna's fingers . . . her thumb." Brianna looked up at him. "She said . . . she had her own destiny."

"It would seem she has gone beyond death to fulfill it with great honor," he mused.

"She said we have our own destiny. Our happiness is Lagniappe. But first, we must vow to have no secrets."

With infinite care, he freed the riband that held her heavy braid in place. His fingers tugged gently to loosen the twined ropes of auburn that hung over her shoulder. "No more secrets, my sweet. You are my Lagniappe . . . my 'something extra' that makes life worthwhile." He coaxed her to lie beside him.

"What of your freedom? Don't you want to sail the seas?"

"Only if you are by my side." Tilting her chin upward, his lips caught hers in a lingering kiss.

She did not realize she had ceased to breathe until he released her. Leaning her head against his chest, Brianna exhaled with a soft sigh of relief. "Oh, Ryan. I thought . . . I mean, I didn't want you to feel trapped. I couldn't tell . . ."

He laughed low, the sound reminding her of the distant thunder that rumbled across the vast waters of the Gulf to announce the coming of a wild storm. "Trap? Ah, my sweet siren of the sea, you have held me in the most tender of traps since that first morning when I awoke to find you by my side."

"You . . . you don't want to leave?"

"Leave? Why do you think I remained silent about my title? I refused to be rejected."

One corner of her mouth twitched, tilting upward as the truth unfurled. "You had your own trap, I see."

"Yes." He pulled her back into his embrace. "And if necessary, I shall continue building traps for the rest of my life, but never will I let you go."

A warmth stole through her body, stirring emotions so long denied. "May I make one request, m'lord trap-maker?"

"That depends. What is it?"

"Could you make your traps a little larger?"

"Is there a reason for such an odd request?" Each word came slowly, forced past a suddenly-dry mouth.

"I am with . . . that is to say, we are . . ." She eased back to watch his face, halting when she recognized the bright gleam in his eyes. "You already know?"

"How could I not? Not one change in your beautiful

body could ever occur that I would not see." His hand pressed the swell of her belly.

"You said nothing."

"Only a woman nurtures the seed of life to birth. It is her choice to speak or remain silent."

"Then I choose to speak, m'lord." Her hand touched the sharp contours of one cheek, reveling in the prickle of dark stubble that shadowed his bronzed skin. "As you have planted the seed, I charge you with building the most tender of traps to properly nurture your heir."

"No more traps, my love. We have greater gifts to offer."

Lips, colored like the blush of dawn, slowly parted. "We have?"

"Surely you do not forget," he teased, nipping lightly at her lower lip. "We have Lagniappe."

Her body arched toward him, eager for more intimate contact. "How true. I feel we shall enjoy many, many nights of 'something extra' for a great many years to come."

Her arms slid up, curling around his neck, pulling him closer. Her lips sought his, a soft sigh escaping when her quest was answered.

"Don't forget the days," he murmured, gently rising to hover over her. "There will be many days, my sweet, sweet siren of the sea."